LIBERTY OR DEATH

Forge Books by Kate Flora

LIBERTY OR DEATH

A Thea Kozak Mystery

Kate Flora

A TOM DOHERTY ASSOCIATES BOOK

NEW YORK

LIBERTY OR DEATH: A THEA KOZAK MYSTERY

Copyright © 2003 by Kate Clark Flora

This book is printed on acid-free paper.

A Forge Book
Published by Tom Doherty Associates, LLC
175 Fifth Avenue
New York, NY 10010

www.tor.com

Forge® is a registered trademark of Tom Doherty Associates, LLC.

Library of Congress Cataloging-in-Publication Data

Flora, Kate Clark
    Liberty or death : a Thea Kozak mystery / Kate Flora.—1st ed.
        p.   cm.
    "A Tom Doherty Associates book."
    ISBN 0-312-87791-9 (acid-free paper)
    1. Kozak, Thea (Fictitious character)—Fiction.   2. Women
detectives—Maine—Fiction.   3. Kidnapping victims—Fiction.
4. Conspiracies—Fiction.   5. Maine—Fiction.   I. Title.

PS3556.L5838 L43 2003
813'.54—dc21

                                                    2002032530

First Edition: January 2003

Printed in the United States of America

0 9 8 7 6 5 4 3 2 1

To my husband, Ken Cohen,
who always says, "Keep writing."

ACKNOWLEDGMENTS

Thanks to the people who patiently answered my questions and directed my research: Lieutenant Tom Le Min, Jim Moore (ATF, ret.), Lieutenant Joe Loughlin, who showed Thea how to hold a gun, Professor Frances Miller, and John Clark, librarian extraordinaire, with assistance from L. D. Welley, David Rosenberg, and Julia McCue. I have been well-advised. Any mistakes are my own. I am grateful, as always, to my readers: A. Carman Clark, Emily Cohen, Diane Woods Englund, Brad and Brenda Lovette, Jack Nevison, Nancy McJennett, John Clark, and Hilary Rubin. Finally, I need to thank all of Thea's fans, whose letters and e-mails of encouragement have sustained me through this long publishing gap. Please keep writing to authors. Your support makes a big difference. Map-savvy Maniacs may quarrel with my geographical liberties, to which I can only respond that this is a work of fiction.

Intreat me not to leave thee, or to return
from following after thee: for whither thou
goest, I will go; and where thou lodgest,
I will lodge. . . .
Ruth 2:16

I will rise now, and go about the city in the
streets, and in the broad ways I will seek
him whom my soul loveth. . . .
The Song of Solomon 3:2

LIBERTY OR DEATH

CHAPTER 1

JUST WEDDING-DAY jitters, I thought, that was why I couldn't catch my breath. I stood in the window, looking down at the lawn, watching Andre's three brothers, and my brother Michael, escorting people to their seats. Lots of people. Lots of seats. Women wobbling unsteadily as their heels sank into the grass. Men running fingers around their collars in anticipation of being too hot. All coming to watch the Thea and Andre show. After seven years in the consulting business, I'm pretty comfortable with public speaking, but being the main event at something like this made me weak in the knees. I've never been able to wrap my mind around the idea that such a personal and private thing as a declaration of enduring commitment should be a public spectacle.

Little bits of pre-wedding piano music floated in my open window. I checked my watch. Zero minus fifteen. Over by the transplanted piano, Andre's boss, Lt. Jack Leonard, stood talking to the minister. With three brothers to chose among, all of them sensitive and given to jealousy, Jack had been a diplomatic choice for best man. Like me, he was checking his watch. I looked in the mirror again. The bride was anxious. Her mother was waiting for her downstairs. The photographer was waiting. There were pictures to take. Soon we would be lining up and my bridesmaids would begin the slow march down the steps and out across the lawn. I would take my father's arm and go forth to marry Andre. There would be a moment when Dad would remember marrying my mother and I would remember marrying David. Perhaps Andre would remember his first wife. I hoped not. He never thought of her without bitterness. Then we would all pull ourselves forward into the business of this day.

I straightened my dress, arranged my veil, and cast one last look out the window. So many people I recognized, from every stage of my life. Witnesses to my commitment. Over the commotion of voices, I heard the phone ring. Saw a trooper cross the patio and set off across the grass, too purposeful for the occasion, straight for Jack Leonard. *Oh no*, I thought. Something to do with the Pelletier case? He was going to be our best man. Jack couldn't be called away now. There had to be someone else who could handle it. I watched as the trooper reached Jack, saw their heads come together. Saw Jack's eyes looking up at my window. Felt, across the distance, their cool blue chill.

I am not given to premonitions or moments of ESP, but it didn't take a psychic to figure this one out. Something was wrong. Something that involved Jack. He bent and spoke to the minister, then hurried back toward the house, the trooper coming swiftly behind him. The noise of conversation floated up to me, and then, with a flourish, the piano began to play some numbingly familiar bit of music. The voices didn't dim, and the whole blended together in a pleasingly distant cacophony I could barely hear over the pounding of my heart. I had to go downstairs and find out what was happening. I didn't want to leave the safety of my room.

I took another look in the mirror, took a breath as deep as the dress would allow, and turned resolutely toward the door. I had told my mother I'd be down in a minute five or six minutes ago. Maybe more. Most likely the pictures would have to wait until after the ceremony now, which was fine with me. I hated having my picture taken. Probably Andre was down there being driven crazy, too. Odd that my mother hadn't come pounding up to get me. She has little patience with those who defy her wishes. It was time to go down and rescue him. Almost time for that long walk down the aisle. Toward a future bright with promise, away from a past that had brought more than its share of pain. I hesitated while I moved the diamond from my left hand to my right, readying my finger for the gleaming inter-twined bands of gold Andre had chosen. Then I crossed the room and opened the door.

A man was coming up the stairs. Not Andre and not my dad. Not Jack Leonard, but someone moving slowly, as though in no hurry to reach me with his news. He raised his head and I saw that it was Dom Florio. My second favorite cop. One of my best friends. Behind him, moving more slowly, but that was because she had trouble walking and particular trouble with stairs, was his wife, Rosie.

"Rosie, you don't have to come up," I called. "I'm on my way down."

She looked up at me. Instead of the happiness I'd expected to find there, knowing how much she liked both me and Andre, I saw something like panic. And Rosie, warm-hearted, cool-headed Rosie, didn't panic. She was not hiking up these stairs to give me a good-luck hug.

Dom spoke first. "Thea, I think we should . . ."

But I was still looking at her pale and solemn face. "Rosie, what's wrong? Something's wrong, isn't it?"

They had reached me now, one on either side of me as we stood at the top of the staircase, Rosie with one hand on the banister I had slid down hours earlier in one last atavistic mo-ment here in my parents' house. As if in anticipation of their words, a cloud crossed the sun and suddenly the hall was dark and chilly. Dom put a hand under my elbow. "Thea . . . some-thing has happened . . ."

"Wait!" Rosie commanded. "Let's go back in your room, Thea. You should be sitting down when . . ." She didn't finish and I didn't ask. Numbly, I let them turn me around and steer me back into my room. Rosie sat down on the bed and pulled me down beside her.

I sat, feeling absurdly like a marshmallow as my dress billowed out around me, longing to put my hands over my ears, as a child might, to shut out what she was going to say. I wanted time to stop. If we never went forward from this moment, I would never have to hear what I was afraid I was going to hear. She tucked an arm around my waist, hugging me firmly against her. She smelled of roses. "Now, Dom," she said.

I had never seen Dominic Florio at a loss for words before. Florio is a detective with the Anson Police Department. I met him when my friend Eve Paris's mother was killed. I went to comfort Eve and Florio latched onto me as his liaison with the family. Much in the way that I began with Andre, Dom and I squabbled our way into a good relationship, with me being edgy, stubborn, and suspicious, and Dom being alternately pushy and surprisingly truthful and open for a cop. While I have a lot of trouble getting along with my own family, I seem to have no trouble attracting alternative families, and Dom and Rosie have become a pair of substitute parents. They can tell me that I'm off the wall without rousing a lifetime's worth of complicated feelings. And they don't hesitate to do so.

Dom looked out the window at the lawn filled with people, at the rose and ribbon-decked arbor my dad had built, and then around my room before finally looking at me. He was so miserable that I wanted to comfort him even though, as yet, I had no idea what the source of his misery was. Finally, fists knotted, he blurted out, "I don't know why the hell they sent me to do this when I haven't got a shred of finesse . . . I'm just no good at . . ." He shook his head, then dropped down on the bed beside me, making the springs groan, and put his arm around me, too, so that I was the filling in a Florio sandwich. I knew they were trying to cushion me with love from what was coming. I wanted to scream at them to stop hesitating and tell me, but I couldn't speak. "Thea . . . Andre's been . . . Andre's not . . . Oh, hell! Rosie?"

My heart stopped as the world fell silent. I forgot to breathe. He was dead, Andre was dead. That's what they couldn't tell me. What else could be so bad Dom couldn't say it? He was a cop. He delivered bad news all the time. A flat tire or a fender-bender wouldn't reduce him to stammering, not even on a wedding day. A comet had fallen out of the sky and crushed him. There had been another car crash like the one that killed David. Andre had stopped to help a fellow officer and been shot. It was always to be my fate. No man was allowed to love me. I would fall in love, let my heart go, and he would die.

It was Rosie, and not Dom the tough police officer, who told me. "Andre's been kidnapped," she said, ". . . by some militia group. They found his car on the side of the road with an American flag tied to the antenna, and a note on the driver's seat, saying that he was a political prisoner of the Katahdin Constitutional Militia. Oh, Thea, I am so sorry . . ."

"The Katahdin Constitutional Militia? Is this some kind of a joke?"

Dom shook his head. "This is no joke, Thea. It's domestic terrorism. They want to trade Andre for some guy who's in jail awaiting trial for assault."

"But why Andre? How did they even know he was a cop?"

"I think it was simply opportunity, that they grabbed someone at random," Dom said. "They say . . . they don't think . . . that he was specifically targeted."

"But how . . ." I began. Did they think I was born yesterday? It was no random act. This was all about Gary Pelletier. Pelletier had gone to check out a rumor about a militia group and ended up dead. Andre must have gotten too close to something. I'd been involved with cops too long to believe in coincidence. Why were they lying to me? But I wasn't ready to explore that right now. I was overwhelmed. I closed my eyes against the tears, clenched my teeth against the cries that rose in my throat. Gripped the delicate fabric of my dress in two tight fists.

It was so unfair! Nothing ever went right for me, did it? I was doomed to endure one sorry event after another. Life was a rotten, miserable thing and it really had it in for me. Here I'd let myself be talked into doing this ridiculous charade of a wedding, just to please my mother. I get all dressed up in this gaudily gorgeous dress, with the tent and the caterer, bridesmaids and a band, and look what happens. Other people got to have nice summer weddings and go off into the sunset with their beloveds. Other people got to have normal lives without death and catastrophe. Goddamn Andre! Why did he have to go and get himself kidnapped today of all days? And what was my mother going to say? She'd been waiting thirty-one years for this moment.

I realized that I was going to tear the dress. Relaxed my grip and took their hands. I tried to take a deep breath but my iron-maiden dress wouldn't let me. It was far too ladylike. It allowed little bits of air, little bits of food, little bits of emotion. My job today was to look beautiful and be happy. Only a lunatic, knowing her waistline was going to be expanding, would have chosen a fitted dress like this. But all the hoo-ha leading up to this day had made me a lunatic; this wedding, plus the surprise of impending motherhood, was something I was still struggling to get used to. My whole life felt out of control.

I checked out the lawn. It seemed like everyone was now staring up at my window and looking at their watches. The bride was late. What were we going to do with all these people? Send them home? Feed them lunch and cake and champagne and then send them home? Did I have to go downstairs and apologize to them all?

I looked at Rosie's face, at her beautiful, wise dark eyes. "Oh, Rosie," I said. "How could this happen to me?"

She shook her head, frowning. "Thea, it's happening to him."

On my dresser was a picture of Andre, in climbing gear, smiling and gorgeous, dangling off a rock face so steep it gave me vertigo just looking at it. I picked it up and stared at him, thought of the bonds that held us together, the invisible bungee cord that connected us, that would always bring us back together. Lord knows we'd tested it. Our courtship had been no picnic. In my head, memory repeated the solemn words from the Bible that would have been read over us today. "Love beareth all things, believeth all things, hopeth all things, endureth all things. Love never falleth." My thinking on this was all wrong. Rosie was right. This wasn't about me.

I dropped their hands and got up, pacing the room, my own

hands now clenched as Dom's had been. This was no time for a wave of self-pity. Self-pity never got anyone anywhere. I might be embarrassed but I was perfectly safe, while Andre was in terrible danger. In terrible danger and in a state even more emotionally wrenching than mine. If I closed my eyes, I could imagine his face. Not a benign face nor a frightened one, but the face of fury. Andre has a big temper. He doesn't lose it often but when he loses it, he's explosive. Right now, wherever he was, he was exploding with rage and frustration at whoever was keeping him from being here. If anything, he wanted this more than I did.

"Oh, God, Andre. Be careful."

I didn't know I'd said it aloud until Dom answered. "He will be. He may be mad as hell, Thea, but he's not stupid . . ."

"All men are a little bit stupid when they're mad." Rosie bit her lip and shook her head. "That's not what we ought to be thinking about right now. We have to—"

". . . figure out how to get him back," I said.

Dom stared meaningfully at my abdomen. "You are not going to get involved in this."

I crossed my hands protectively over little Claudine, unless it was Mason or Oliver. Our lucky accident. The catalyst which had stopped our dithering, changed the course of two fiercely independent people, and brought us to this day. What if Andre never—no! I shut my mind against the question. Love a cop and you learn to live with danger, learn to suppress it so you can go on breathing. "What are you talking about? I'm already involved in this."

"You know what I mean . . ."

"And you know what I mean."

"Thea, you know how much I love you. And how much respect I have for your abilities, but this is a job for the police . . ."

I sighed. "It always is, Dom. It always is." I'd had my moment to wallow in self-pity and I would probably have more, but I was a woman of action. I had to do something besides stand around being the pathetic, abandoned bride. I had to know what was going on. "Can you go downstairs and find Jack Leonard and tell him I'd like to see him?"

It was right there on the tip of Dom's tongue. I could almost hear the unspoken words about how Jack was busy and this was one of his men and there was a crisis going on, but to his credit, he didn't say them. Dom had some deliciously old-fashioned notions about what might be bad for a mother-to-be. Being sent into a state of uncontrollable rage was one of them. He knew my temper and he wasn't about to deny that I had a stake in this. When one of their own is threatened, the guys band together in an amazing way. They're already incredibly tight but this raises things to a higher level. You want to see male bonding, forget about sweat lodges and drumming, ropes courses and wilderness adventures. Go watch a bunch of cops. But they're very protective of families, too, because a strong family is a good thing for a cop to have behind him. I was part of Andre's family.

"I'll get him," Dom said, and went out.

Only then did I rest my head on Rosie's shoulder and cry, and when Jack Leonard came up the stairs, all his dread at having to face me evident on his narrow, strained face, I abandoned the comfort of Rosie's arms and stood up. "What do we do now, Jack?" I asked. "How do we get him back?"

CHAPTER 2

YOU EVER WAITRESS before?" the woman asked, narrowing her eyes and looking me up and down like she was buying a side of beef.

I shrugged. Everyone had waitressed some time. I'd done it one summer in college. Hated it, but there was no sense in telling her that. She might be desperate for help but she wasn't going to hire me if she thought I had an attitude. Besides, it didn't take a rocket scientist, and I wasn't looking to making it my life's work. "A couple summers," I said.

"Rosie said you were a nice girl. I hope so. I don't hold with girls who flirt with the customers or the other help. Slows things down. Makes people mad. Makes for bad feelings. You can't have people with bad feelings when you gotta run a business in a small town."

She sniffed loudly and gave me another skeptical look. "I'm not sure you ain't too pretty for the job, but that damned Mindy ran off and left me in the lurch, didn't give me notice or anything, she just ran off with that guy in the shiny new truck. Girl never did have the brains God gave a chicken. Sees the truck, thinks the guy's got money. Hell, they've all of 'em got trucks, long as they can make a couple payments."

Her narrow eyes studied me again, as if she could assess, by the intensity of her stare, whether I was a woman with a weakness for fancy trucks. "Guess I've gotta take a chance on you. It's the season, up here, such as we got. Have to make the money while we can, and them outta-staters haven't got the patience God gave a squirrel. Gotta have it right now or they're waving their arms around like one of those little spinning lawn ornaments or up at the register, complainin'. Some of 'em, you know, they'd like to just walk out . . ." Her smile was one of malicious delight. ". . . 'Cept they got no other place to go."

She squinted at me and said, ominously, "You'll see," which helped me realize that she didn't think she had to persuade me to take the job, she thought the choice was all hers. Well, I was supposed to be a desperate wife on the run, wasn't I? And the truth was, if I wanted to be up here in Merchantville, reputed militia capital of Maine, where I might hope to learn something to help Andre, I *didn't* have any choice. I nodded dumbly and tried to act as though I didn't find the idea of a roomful of arm-waving, complaining customers daunting.

Smiling bravely, I said, "I'm sure I'll be . . ." But my inquisitor wasn't listening.

"I don't know how she stands it down there in Massachusetts. Rosie, I mean. 'Course, with her being all crippled up and everything, I don't suppose it matters much where she lives."

I bit my lip, practicing self-control. It was good for me to practice self-control. Just ask my mother. Rosie Florio had fought her way back to her feet from a wheelchair after being hit by a drunk driver. Even lame and limping, Rosie got more from life than most people. Many days I would gladly have traded my youth and dexterity for a corner of Rosie's balance or joy. But her cousin Theresa didn't need to hear this. She struck me as one of those people who take comfort in others' problems.

She sighed loudly and picked up the coffeepot. "You want some?"

I shook my head. I'd given up coffee out of respect for the formation of little fingers and toes. I missed it terribly—even the smell was torture—but it was a small sacrifice.

"Well, I'd better make the rounds, then." She got up from

her chair and turned toward the door that led into the restaurant. "Come along and see . . ." It was one big room with booths
along the walls, a bunch of tables, and a long counter, with an
opening in one wall that led into the bar next door. She didn't
look much like Rosie, with her skinny body, her hunched shoulders, and her badly dyed dark hair. The only thing that was the
same was the eyes. On Rosie they were marvelous, glowing with
hope and expectation. On her cousin Theresa, they were sharp
and wary and spoke of a lifetime of disappointments.

She paused just inside the door and turned. "You can start
in the morning. Be here by six and I'll get you started. By six-
thirty, things are really hoppin', so wear some sensible shoes and
don't wear anything you mind getting' dirty, okay?"

"No uniform?"

She fingered her gray cardigan and gave me a look, like she
wondered if I was too stupid to hire. "This look like a uniform?
What Kalyn's wearing look like a uniform?" Kalyn must be the
small woman with the bright red hair skewered on top of her
head like a firecracker fuse, who seemed to be moving in and
out of the kitchen at the speed of light. "You get an apron.
Pockets, you know, for straws and your order pad and stuff. Just
dress decent, that's all I ask. I won't have a girl goes around with
her ass showing every time she bends over."

I didn't like her, or this place, or what I was getting myself
into. I didn't like being called a girl. I wanted to jump in the
car and drive back home, but then, I wasn't here for myself and
home was just another empty place without Andre. "Rosie said
you might know someplace I could stay?"

She pointed toward the ceiling. "There's a room upstairs you
can use. Got your own bath, if you don't mind just a shower.
And you can get your meals down here, of course. It ain't nothin'
fancy. Mindy took a gander and turned up her snooty little nose,
but then, there wasn't much about that girl to like, now I look
back at it. Give me a minute and I'll find you the keys." When
she came back, the pot was empty. She made a fresh one, then
opened a drawer and fished around until she found a ring with
two keys. "This'll open the back door, in case the place is closed,

and the shiny one's for the door upstairs. You can park out in the back there, by the Dumpster."

Parking next to a Dumpster and waiting tables in a place called "Mother Theresa's." It put me in mind of a line from *Tess of the D'Urbervilles*, "See how the mighty are fallen." My life was just one humbling experience after another, as if being left standing at the altar wasn't humbling enough. I felt perennially light-headed now. It seemed like I hadn't been able to get enough oxygen since Dom had told me about the kidnapping, even after I took off the Spanish inquisition dress. They might say that the idea of the heart as the seat of love is only a fiction, but my own heart had felt constricted ever since Saturday morning. The thought of Andre in danger had squeezed it like it lay in a giant's hand, and with every word of Jack Leonard's explanation, the giant had gripped tighter. I was getting a very good idea of what it was like to live with a chronic disability. Mine was fear.

I took the keys and put them in my pocket. "Thanks, Mrs. McGrath."

"Theresa," she corrected. "I hear Mrs. McGrath, I think you're talkin' to some old lady. You go along and get yourself settled. You look done in, you don't mind my saying so. I suppose, from what Rosie said, you haven't had an easy time of it. How'd you meet her, anyway?"

"Dom," I said. "He was kind of looking after me, when he could."

"Rosie's a lucky gal, got a good, handsome man like that to take care of her, stickin' with her after the accident and all. Lotta men, find themselves married to a cripple, they just walk out," she said. "She doesn't know how lucky."

She was wrong about that. Rosie Florio thought she was the luckiest woman in the world to have married Dom, and he thought he was the luckiest man. If anything, Rosie's accident had made them closer. If I hadn't liked them both so much, their happiness would have made me surly with jealousy. As it was, I hoped my own life would be a lot like theirs. Or at least, I had hoped that. I guess I still did.

From the other room, someone called, "Hey, Theresa, everyone die out there? Where the heck's that coffee?"

"See you in the morning," she said. "Six. And not any later or you can forget about the job. Got that?"

"I'll be here."

I trudged out to the car, got my stuff, and shuffled wearily up the stairs.

I put my bag on the narrow bed—the first single bed since college—sat down beside it, and looked around the room. The adjectives bleak and dreary came to mind, but they both did the room a kindness. Spare was good, though I had always associated spare with austere and austere with a kind of cold cleanliness. This room showed a marked absence of cleanliness. I could write my name in the dust on the dresser top and bedside stand, and the windowsills and the floor beneath them were thick with flakes of paint and the corpses of flies, spiders, and other insects who had died there, trying to escape. The wallpaper was beige on beige—toning, I believe is the current decorating term. The tufted bedspread had evidently once been white; now it was the yellow of old eyes, with occasional darker patches whose provenance I didn't want to know.

"Home sweet home," I said aloud. I needed to lie down. I hadn't slept Saturday night, except for a few nightmare-plagued hours. I ached with weariness and had the world's biggest head-ache, but I would not touch my body to the mattress until I'd gotten back in the car, driven down the road the twenty miles or so to Wal-Mart, and gotten some decent bedding. While I was there, I could get some dustcloths and a broom. I probably could have borrowed some from Mrs. McGrath—Theresa—but she was busy and I wasn't up for another complaining conver-sation nor further scrutiny from those disappointed eyes. I didn't want her to think I was fussy or ungrateful.

I picked up my purse, locked the door behind me, and went down the stairs to the battered, rust-blistered heap of sorry metal I was driving. As Dom had wisely noted, if I wanted to be inconspicuous, it didn't make sense to arrive in a backwater-Maine town claiming to be down and out, a battered wife on the run, and driving a nice shiny red Saab. The car Dom had given me was damned deceptive, though. Despite the hideous exterior, the seats were extremely comfortable, it had a hidden radio, and it went like a bat out of hell. He hadn't told me about that part. Heading north, I'd merged cautiously onto the highway, put my foot down expecting very little, and almost knocked myself into the backseat. For about five minutes, coming up from Boston on I-95, I'd felt like I was back at the racetrack in Connecticut, where I'd had a brief, high-speed adventure as part of an effort to rescue my mother's protégé, Julie Bass.

I didn't know how the other superheroes felt, but I was getting tired of rescuing people. It was beginning to seem a lot like washing dishes. You did the dishes, put them away, and damned if there wasn't another load needing to be done. When Andre was around, he did the dishes, just like he did a lot of rescuing people. But Andre wasn't around. Only heaven and the bad guys knew where he was, and I was in Merchantville, Maine, known to be a hotbed of militia activity, hoping to be a fly on the wall and learn something that might help save him.

I'd had to fight like a tiger to get here, and once Rosie had gotten Dom to agree—a grudging, nervous agree—my instructions had been quite clear. "You're just there to listen, Goddammit, and not to act!" Dom had said. "You don't want to do anything to put yourself in danger. Andre has enough to worry about . . . we all do . . . without worrying about you, too."

Jack Leonard had made Dom sound positively benign. Far from approving the plan, he had been icy with fury and resignation. Since I didn't work for him, he couldn't pull rank, he could only tell me in a dozen different ways what a fool I was being and how I risked putting Andre in greater danger. "You know what I think, Thea? I think you should stay home and take care of yourself and let us look for Andre. We've all got enough to worry about. But I could talk till I was blue in the face and not change your mind, and I've got a missing trooper to find . . ."

Here he had held up his hand to ward off the angry words I was about to shout in his face. ". . . I know that there is no way we can keep you out of this. You can go off on this wild-goose chase you and Florio have cooked up, so long as all you do is make like a fly on the wall and listen. But if I hear that you're sticking even your tiniest toe into my investigation . . . if you do the slightest Goddamned thing to put yourself or my trooper in danger, I'm going to snatch you out of there so fast your head will spin. If necessary, I will lock you up someplace where you can't do any harm. And I won't give a damn about your so-called civil rights. You got that?"

Life forces me to be schizophrenic. These days, I often think this is simply woman's lot. At work, I am the professional fix-it person. I'm the tough troubleshooter called in to help our client schools deal with hard problems, public relations nightmares, difficult admissions, or image problems. I was the fix-it person in my own family. I was used to taking charge and solving problems. At five eleven, I was used to being among the biggest and strongest. But I'm an attractive woman with a nice shape, and the world expects me to be a tough, no-nonsense professional in a womanly way.

So when Jack read me the riot act, I'd lowered my eyes and tried to look demure and submissive. I'd gotten it. Watch myself or it was Rapunzel's tower for me. I'd even kept my mouth shut and nodded. It had been, still was, a genuine crisis, mine as much as theirs, but there had been so much testosterone in the air I could almost feel hair sprouting on my upper lip.

I couldn't remember much about the rest of my wedding day. A blur of sympathetic faces, people murmuring in my ear, hugging me. My mother's declaration that as the food was al-ready paid for, we might as well invite the guests to eat. An awful luncheon in the tent, with me in my lovely dress, sur-rounded by my gleaming bridesmaids. Peach-colored linens. Soft peach roses. The scent of flowers, the clink of cutlery. Sub-dued voices. People that I loved. Aunt Rita and Uncle Henry. Suzanne. Dom and Rosie. Sarah, acting like the perfect secre-tary, pushing a steady succession of tissues into my hand and taking away the wet ones. And Jonetta Williamson, singing. I think she sang "We Shall Overcome." Suitably militant and hopeful. I sure hoped we would. I know she sang "Amazing Grace," which we would need plenty of. Jonetta was one of my heroes.

I remembered Jack Leonard grabbing my arm and shoving a uniformed trooper into my face. "You know Roland. He's going to stay here, to be your liaison. For the moment."

One look and I'd known that much as Roland Proffit wanted to stay and comfort me, he wanted that much more to be back in Maine, looking for Andre. I remembered shaking my head and saying, "No. He's one of Andre's friends. He needs to be on the job. With you. Looking for Andre." Seeing in Roland's eyes his gratitude. Seeing that Jack understood.

"Right," he said. "You're right." Looking around at his men. But all the ones here were Andre's closest friends. "I'll send you someone."

"Just don't send Amanda." Amanda, who had had her eye on Andre. Her presence would not be comforting.

The oddest thing of all, and the thing that I would probably remember longest about the day, long after the roses faded and Andre and I were heading into our comfortable old age, was Michael. I love my brother Michael because he is my brother. Because we share a past, a childhood, a family, a history. But Michael isn't very nice. He's an amazingly talented painter, but he wastes his talent and his time. He's mean-spirited and lazy and makes no effort to be nice to people. He has married a woman who is very similar, and between them, they fan the flames of each other's worst qualities, so that over time, they've gotten worse to be around, not better. So when Michael had approached me, as I was standing on the lawn staring at Dad's arbor, so gaudy and romantic and hopeful, I steeled myself for an unpleasant remark.

Instead, Michael had put his arms around me, given me a very tender hug, and said, "Thea, I'm so sorry. I'm hoping . . . no, I'm praying . . . that everything will be all right. That we're all back here soon watching you two get married. More than anyone, you deserve to be happy." Then he had hurried away, but I had seen his face. I had seen tears. And I was left astounded.

Wal-Mart is twentieth-century America in a nutshell. A modern, air-conditioned bazaar offering products from all over the world at irresistible prices. No one sits on a carpet and haggles with you only because the Grand Vizier has already read your mind and priced the things you want at the prices you want to pay. No human interaction is necessary. Just pile up your sterile metal shopping cart with all the things you need to keep you happy, pay with plastic, and carry them back to your mobile home in your pickup truck, where you can add them to the hordes of other products you bagged on earlier expeditions. We live in a culture where shopping has become a recreational activity and the passive, glassy-eyed stare of the shopper suggests we are all being controlled by some higher authority which has replaced our minds, our souls, our will with a single emotion: the desire to shop.

Today, I was as glassy-eyed and acquisitive as the rest of them. If I didn't keep my eyes wide, I'd fall asleep against a pile of beach towels, or sink down into a lounge chair, never to rise again. My heart leaped up only once, upon passing the guns. I wanted to buy the biggest, meanest, most powerful one of all and ride forth like an avenging angel, blasting into the kidnapper's lair and setting my loved one free. But I didn't know much about guns. They scared me. I'd resisted most of Andre's efforts to teach me, though he had put me through my paces a few times. Now, much as I longed for one, I couldn't have it. Even in a hunting state, like Maine, you needed a permit.

I settled for towels and sheets, a mattress pad, and a soft pink blanket. A new pillow. A mop and bucket, dustpan and brush, dustcloths and dusting products and Spic 'n Span. A reading lamp to go beside the bed and a tidy little rug for the floor. It was like fitting out a dorm room—and an incredible waste of money. I didn't intend to be here for long. I had a couple weeks—that was all. My honeymoon time. Then I had to go back to work.

I was the lucky winner of the black humor honeymoon contest. A honeymoon for one, in a small Maine town, accommodations to include a creaky single bed, cracked linoleum, and a rust-streaked shower stall with a limp, moldy curtain. I got a mirror that had lost half its silver, so the face that stared back at me looked at least as awful as I felt. A dingy room that smelled like mildew and old grease. Recreational activities to include a Wal-Mart shopping spree, mosquito swatting, and fly-corpse sweeping. If I really wanted to live it up, I could buy a six-pack and throw my empties out the window on the way home.

After an orgy of cleaning and bed-making, I submitted myself to the shower challenge, a spa technique featuring alternating streams of icy-cold and scalding-hot water to stimulate the system and get the blood flowing. Feeling thoroughly dejected, cynical, and furious with the world, I set my alarm for the crap of dawn, climbed into bed, and cried myself to sleep on a pillow stiff and scratchy with sizing. The only amenity missing was bedbugs.

CHAPTER 3

I AM NOT a morning person but for as long as I can remember, I've been dragging myself out of bed at horribly early hours to meet the demands of my life. So it was on Monday, when my new alarm clock, bleating like a sick cat, summoned me forth to greet a day as gray and lifeless as I felt. Without fully opening my eyes, I pulled on socks and underwear, a short black twill skirt and a white polo shirt. My own version of what a waitress should wear. I brushed my teeth, splashed cold water on my face, and pulled my hair back in a barrette. Then I locked the door, went downstairs, and put my purse in the trunk of my car—in my capacity as a spy, I couldn't be too careful about my true identity—and presented myself for duty.

A heavily built man in overalls and a sleeveless undershirt was standing by the stove, talking loudly to a skinny teenage boy with big dark eyes who was peeling a million pounds of potatoes. A couple of tons of chopped onions probably accounted for the fact that the boy's eyes were red. The man gestured from time to time with a spatula that dripped grease onto the floor. The boy nodded and murmured. Neither of them noticed me. Or so I thought until the boy said, "Shall I show you how to make the coffee?"

"Sure. I'm Dora." As in Theadora. When inventing, stick as close to the truth as possible.

"Natty," he said. I assumed it was his name and not a comment on my appearance. He jerked his chin toward the big man. "That's Clyde."

"You're the new girl," Clyde said. "Hungry?" I nodded. He looked me up and down, but it wasn't lecherous, it was the assessment of a food provider sizing up a customer. "Two eggs over easy, and some white toast. Natty, you show her how to do the toast and coffee, eh?"

Natty stood up. He was taller than I'd expected, one of those boys who's grown so fast they're nothing but skin and bones and giant feet. His eyes were dark jewels in his pale, pinched face. "Theresa's a real nut about always having fresh coffee," he said. "So you'd better learn to keep an eye on it." He showed me where everything was, and walked me through the first pot. "Orange is decaf. And don't mix 'em up. People complain. We got lots of customers can't have caffeine. But Theresa says you've got experience, so I guess you already know that."

"I haven't done it for a while."

He bobbed his head. "Well, you need to know anything, you just ask me or Clyde. We'll help you out." I nodded. I'd been in the kitchen for all of five minutes and I was already feeling overwhelmed. "Waitresses make the toast, bagels, English muffins. You use this." Again, he led me to a piece of machinery and showed me how to use it. He waved a hand at the loaves of bread on the counter. "You got white, wheat, and rye. You got English muffins. Bagels. Butter's here. They wanted toasted blueberry or bran, that's Clyde's department. Spare bread's through there." He pointed at a door. "You do the toast, put it on a plate, hand it to Clyde."

My own toast came out of the toaster. I picked it up and put it on a plate, handed the plate to Clyde. Got it back with two perfect eggs. Natty showed me where the silverware lived. I got a fork, sat down, and ate. First food I could remember since my wedding luncheon. Natty slid a menu across the table. "Better study this. Won't be long before all hell breaks loose. Everything has a number. You write down the number, kind of toast, how they want their eggs." His eyes danced. "Clyde'll tell you if you get it wrong."

I looked at the menu. It seemed pretty simple. "Where's the juice?" I asked. He showed me. "Cream or milk for coffee?"

"Already on the tables, but you gotta keep an eye on it."

"Ketchup?"

"Tables. Also sugar. Syrup's here." He touched big plastic bins. "Honey. Jam. Butter."

"You're good. How come you're not waiting on tables?"

"Don't like people," he said.

Clyde laughed. "Natty gets nervous. Pours coffee in people's laps." When he laughed, he shook all over.

Theresa came through the door carrying an empty coffeepot. She tore off three order sheets and stuck them on a rack beside the stove. She picked up the fresh pot I'd made and jerked her head toward the dining room. "Better make some more coffee and come on out here. Place is filling up." I tied on an apron, made the coffee, and went to work.

From 6:30 until 10:30, I scampered back and forth between the kitchen and the dining room, made enough toast to feed the Russian Army, and enough coffee to float the *Titanic*. I was so busy I didn't even have time to pee and pregnant women always have to pee. As hard as I worked, Theresa worked harder, while Clyde calmly and deftly served up endless plates of eggs and bacon, pancakes and waffles, homefries and hash, and Natty rinsed, stacked, and fed hundreds of dishes, cups, and glasses into the dishwasher. Just about at the point where I thought I would collapse, I felt a big, warm hand on my shoulder and Clyde said, "Better take a break now, while it's quiet. Won't be long before the early lunch crowd comes in."

Gratefully, I climbed upstairs on my rubber legs, used the bathroom, washed my sweaty face, and fell onto the bed. No wonder Mindy had quit to run away with the guy in the truck. A person would have to be insane to stay at a job like this. As I lay there with my eyes closed, I mentally reviewed the stack of militia materials Jack had made me read in preparation for this job, and considered whether I'd heard anything useful.

I'd heard that it was a good season for trout, and several theories why that was so. I'd heard that the Brannan boy had knocked up Stetson's daughter, and if the boy didn't come up with an engagement ring soon, Stetson would be out for blood. I'd heard that there had been a break-in over in Riley and that what the cops didn't know was that old man Fitch, whose house had been broken into, had had at least fifty guns, some of them illegal, in the storage space under the eaves, and that the thieves had gotten away with most of those. I'd heard that Perry Packer's wife was on a new cabbage-soup diet and he was so damned sick of cabbage soup he wished she'd just stay fat. And I'd heard that Mary Harding, whose son Jed was the one the Katahdin Constitutional Militia wanted released from jail, was having a hard time with her grandson, Lyle, who missed his daddy something fierce.

I knew how Lyle felt. I missed Andre something fierce, too. Just saying his name started up an ache in one of those internal organs that aren't involved in the emotions of love. Four hours on my feet. Even in Reeboks they ached. Even with sorbothane insoles. And not a soul had confessed to the crime. I didn't have much to report to my state police contact. Still, I'd come here hoping to contribute in some small measure to his rescue, and had no idea what might be important. Maybe the news that Lyle Harding was unhappy could be used to pressure his father to talk? Maybe the story of the stolen guns? It wasn't up to me. I was just a piece of human blotting paper, soaking stuff up. I hoped the afternoon would be more profitable.

My eyes wanted to close. My body wanted to stay horizontal. I was ready for sleep. It had only taken four and a half hours of hard physical work to put me back in touch with reality and remind me that all that thinking I usually did, all those reports I wrote, and all those meetings I went to, weren't as essential to the running of the world as feeding people. And all that insomnia I suffered? I could cure it in a day, just by getting a real job. If I was ever impatient with a waitress again, God should strike me dead.

I groaned and pushed myself back up. Twenty minutes. I'd been lying here for twenty minutes and it felt like two or three. And I had no idea how long I was entitled to. For that matter, I had no idea what my hours were or whether Theresa expected me to work three meals a day, or only two, and whether anyone else was coming in to help. Forget one day at a time. I was taking it one plate at a time.

When I got back down to the kitchen, Theresa was sitting at the table with a cigarette and a cup of coffee, her feet up on the other chair. Another boy had joined Natty with the food prep and another woman, wearing an apron, was making coffee. "Dora, meet Kalyn," she said. "Kalyn works lunch and helps out with dinner when we're real busy, which is most of the time, lately. She'll show you the ropes at lunch, and then help out with dinner tonight. I don't want you wearin' yourself out your first day here. This afternoon I'll make a schedule and then everyone'll know when they're working. Okay?"

I nodded a greeting at Kalyn and acquiescence at Theresa. "Guess I ought to study the lunch menu."

Kalyn handed me one. "Just like breakfast," she said. She was tiny, the biggest thing about her was her hair—hair red enough to glow in the dark—and a high, girlish voice. She had hot-pink lips and nails to match. "Everything's got numbers. Just with the sandwiches, remember to write down whether they want 'em toasted or not, and with the soup, what kind. We do the soups. Over here." There was a row of kettles along the counter. She pointed. "Clam chowder. Split pea. Chicken noodle. And bowls are here. Don't forget the crackers, either, 'cuz a lot of the guys complain. They're just like kids, aren't they, Theresa? Gotta have their crackers to play with."

"It's harmless," Theresa grunted, drawing on her cigarette.

"Theresa!" a voice boomed from the other room. "Can't we get no service in here?"

Theresa cast a weary glance at the door. "Don't get up," Kalyn said. "I'll take care of it."

As the door shut behind her, Theresa sighed. "Being in business means there's always some folks you wish would go away and leave you alone. He's one of 'em."

I sat down across from her, longing for one of her cigarettes and my own cup of coffee. And I don't even smoke. It was just that right now the process of raising and lowering it, and inhaling, seemed very relaxing and luxurious. "Is it always this busy?"

She shrugged. "This ain't so busy. Wait'll you see dinner. Folks get up here on vacation, comes late afternoon and the kids are whiny, and all they can think of is maybe it'll help if they eat out. Never occurs to 'em to play a game with their kids. Get out some cards, or read a book. Lotta these camps, people rent 'em without asking if there's cable, and then they get up here, haven't brought toys or books or puzzles and stuff, and then start bitchin' because we don't have all their city amenities out here in the backwoods."

She snorted and got up from her chair. "I got no patience with that sort of thing, even if it does pay the bills. You wanna have kids, you gotta raise 'em, not let the damned boob tube do it."

"You have kids?" I asked. I couldn't remember what Rosie had said.

"Four. Two turned out okay. One of 'em's still working on it. One's a useless sack of shit."

I put my hand under my chin and pushed my mouth shut before a fly flew in. Theresa's frankness went beyond blunt. I checked my apron pockets. Pencil. Pad. Straws. "Guess I'll go learn about lunch."

Theresa stubbed out her cigarette in the ashtray and grinned. "Shocked you, didn't I? I'm not *the* Mother Theresa, you know. Just one of 'em. You didn't have any kids?" I hesitated, then shook my head.

Kalyn rushed in, stuck up some orders for Clyde, and said, "I could use some help out here." I followed her back into the dining room.

Around 2:30, feeling like a candidate for a double amputation, I limped out of the kitchen with what I hoped was my last order for a while and found one of my tables filled with four big men. I grabbed four menus and was about to hand them out when the man sitting closest to me said, "Don't bother, honey. We know what we want. Four of them clam rolls with fries, four draft beers, and what you got for pies?"

I tried to remember, but all I knew was that we were pretty low and that Theresa had sent Natty to see someone named Josie to pick up some more. "We're low," I said. "I'll have to check. What kind did you want?"

"Blueberry."

"Cherry."

"Apple."

"Raspberry, if you got it; if not, lemon."

A little bit of individuality, anyway. "I'll go check." I scribbled their order on my pad on my way into the kitchen. "Honey," the first speaker called after me. "Send Theresa out, will you?"

Honey went into the kitchen, gave Clyde the order, and checked on the pies. Their order would wipe out the cherry and the blueberry. And the raspberry guy was getting lemon. We still had plenty of apple. Theresa wasn't around. "Some guy out there wants Theresa," I told Kalyn. "Any idea where she is?"

She jerked her chin toward the back door. "Over to Lemoines. Every Monday afternoon. They talk about money."

I went into the bar, got the beer, and carried it to the table. Didn't bother with glasses. No coasters and no little drink napkins. The surface of these tables must have been half an inch thick in polyurethane. Nothing was getting at the wood. The guy who seemed to be their spokesman had an olive T-shirt, faded camouflage pants, and a dingy bandana around his neck. Thick, hairy arms with indistinct tattoos ended in big, dirty hands with broken nails. He had a belly so big it barely fit in the booth. His greasy graying hair was pulled back in a ponytail. Except for the belly, he would have been sort of attractive if he was cleaned up. I couldn't tell, despite the hair, whether he was closer to forty or to fifty. The other three were variations on the same theme.

He grabbed his beer out of my hand and drank off about half the bottle. "You tell Theresa I wanted to see her?"

I shook my head. "She's gone out."

"That's bullshit," he bellowed, seizing my arm and hauling me closer. "Now lissen. You go back in that kitchen and you tell Theresa that Roy Belcher is out here and he's got a message for her. You got that, honey?"

I stared down at the fingers that held me captive. They were going to leave bruises. "Roy Belcher?" I repeated.

The beast actually smiled. "In the flesh."

"Kalyn?" I called. She was across the room, putting silverware in bins. "Can you send Clyde out here a sec? We got a problem." She took in what was happening and didn't hesitate.

"What the hell?" Roy Belcher said, puzzled. "I didn't ask for Clyde. Goddammit, I told you. I wanna see Theresa."

"*You* didn't ask for Clyde. I did," I said, as he came through the doorway. He was carrying something that looked like a cross between an ax and a sledgehammer. Swinging it low and easy at his side, though it must have been heavy. A Clyde transformed from the delicate, mountainous engineer of the perfect egg into something considerably more dangerous.

He sauntered up to the table and joined me in staring at the fingers that gripped my arm so roughly. "Roy Belcher," I said. "Mr. Belcher seems to be having some difficulty understanding the nature of my job."

Belcher released my arm and rested his hands on the table. I resisted the urge to rub the spot he'd been holding. His fingers had left deep red marks on my forearm, with little purplish white circles where his nails had dug into the skin. "Aw, hell, Clyde. I didn't mean nothin'. Just tryin' to explain to this new girl that I wanted to see Theresa."

I lowered my eyes to the floor, trying to hide my anger. Trying not to make a scene, to let Clyde handle this. "I told him she wasn't here. He didn't believe me."

Clyde's eyes made a slow circle of the four men before coming back to Belcher. "She tell you Theresa wasn't here?"

"Yeah," he said sullenly.

"You know this girl?"

"Hell, no. She's new, ain't she?"

"You don't know her but you decided she was a liar?"

Belcher shrugged. "I just wanted to see Theresa. You know. I'm supposed to give her a message."

Clyde grunted. "You're a damned fool, Belcher, you know that? Every Monday, long as I can remember, Theresa goes to see Lemoine." He shrugged. "Why should today be any different? We just got us this great new girl, works her tail off, nice as she can be, and what happens? Asshole like you comes in, her first day on the job, and you do something like this!" His fingers fluttered over my bruised forearm, gentle as butterfly wings. "You a moron or what? You know how Theresa feels about customers pickin' on her help . . ." The big shoulders rose and fell in a resigned gesture. "Theresa decides to shut you out and that's it. You don't eat here no more." His eyes circled the table again. "All four of you, not just Belcher."

He set the swinging mallet, or whatever it was, on the floor with a thump. "I gotta go see about those clams. You got a message for Theresa, you can give it to me and I'll tell her when she gets back."

I kept my eyes down, trying to remember that I wasn't tough-as-nails Thea Kozak, who didn't take stuff like this from anyone. I was Dora the waitress, a battered wife on the run from her husband. Timid and apologetic and used to being beaten on. Roy Belcher's attack was no more than I deserved. I raised my eyes. "I'll go get your food." Looked shyly at the raspberry-pie guy. "There's no raspberry left. You sure lemon's okay?" He nodded.

Clyde turned to leave. "Hold on," Belcher commanded. "You ain't heard my message yet. Tell Theresa that Jimmy's got some important business on Saturday and he needs the truck. Okay? He'll be out at the camp."

Clyde said, "Okay," and hurried out of the dining room.

I took another order and went to get the clam rolls. There was no one in the kitchen. Through the screen door, I could see Kalyn and Clyde out on the back porch, smoking. Four plates with clam rolls and fries were on the counter. I put the four of them on a tray, added little containers of tartar sauce, and carried them into the dining room. I handed them around and left before the men could ask for anything else or before anyone could grab me again.

I sat down at the table and put my head down on my arms, shaking all over from exhaustion and pent-up anger. Two days ago, a bride in a glorious dress. Now a waitress being mauled by Neanderthal customers. It was my own life and I could hardly keep up with the changes. I wanted to go upstairs and sob into my pillow. I wanted to climb in my car and run away but I had nothing to run to. The door slammed as they came back inside. I didn't look up. I was so tired. I wanted to snatch a little more rest before it was time to go risk my life delivering pie to those pigs in the other room.

"Hey," a voice boomed. Roy's voice. "Hey! Can we get a little service out here?"

Reluctantly, I raised my head. "You stay sitting down, Dora," Kalyn said. "I'll go see what those jerks want."

"They want their pie," I said, gesturing to the plates I'd prepared.

I lowered my head again. Felt a warm hand rest lightly on my shoulder. Clyde had a very light touch for such a big man. "You haven't eaten anything since breakfast," he said. "Can I fix you something?"

I considered. What were Mason or Oliver or Claudine in the mood for today? I was too tired to eat. Too tired to even think about eating. "Whatever you fix is fine," I said. "Surprise me." I laid my head down again and closed my eyes. My feet were throbbing and my legs ached from top to bottom. My arms trembled from the weight of all the trays I'd carried.

I'd come into this thinking I was in pretty good shape. Fresh from Coach Lemieux's training camp. Andre was a fitness nut. Well, Andre was a nut about all sorts of things physical. He loved running and swimming and skiing and in-line skating. Weight training. Dancing. Sex. And eating. Andre would have been in heaven here in Clyde's kitchen. And for six months, I'd been right along beside him, becoming just as buffed and tough as he was. I had the arms and shoulders not of a beauty queen, but of a fitness queen. They had looked gorgeous rising out of the lace and satin of my dress. Now they were good for carrying trays. At least I'd stay in shape until my coach came home. If my coach came home. I took a deep breath, ashamed of myself. There could be no "ifs" about it. He had to come home.

I heard the clink of ice and a thunk as something was set on the table near my ear. I turned my head to see. A tall, frosty glass of lemonade, followed by a fork and a napkin. Then a plate. I sat up. Lobster roll and fries. Chunks of juicy lobster meat, mayo and celery in a buttery, toasted roll. I smiled over at Clyde. "You are an angel," I said. "I love lobster rolls."

"I can only do it when Theresa's not around. She practically counts the pieces. But after what happened?" He shrugged. "We don't want you to quit on us . . ."

I took a deep drink of lemonade. It was just right. Icy cold, tangy, and refreshing. I could feel it chill my empty stomach. I smiled at Clyde. "Thanks. This is perfect." I watched him moving around, getting things ready for dinner, cleaning up the grill, hauling in a replacement tank for the soda machine. "Don't you ever rest?"

"Three months every winter. In Florida. Sitting on the beach. Going to baseball games. Catching fish. I don't even cook. Eat out every night."

Kalyn came in, deposited the dirty plates, picked up the four slices of pie, and went out again. Her energy made me feel guilty, but I wasn't ready to get up and start bustling about. Didn't yet feel like filling little paper cups with tartar sauce or applesauce. Natty and the other boy were gone. Despite the air-conditioning, the kitchen was warm. "Clyde, Theresa didn't tell me anything about my schedule. Do you think she'd mind if I went upstairs for a while?"

He shook his head. "That's a good idea. Get some rest before dinner." He reached down under the table and handed me a big enamel basin. "So you can soak your feet."

"It's that obvious?"

"Spent my life in restaurants since I left the army," he said. "You notice things."

Carrying my basin, I limped upstairs, took off my shoes and socks, filled it with water, and sat on the edge of the bed, soaking my feet. Then, unable to keep my eyes open, I dried my feet and lay down. I was asleep as soon as my head hit the pillow.

CHAPTER 4

AT ELEVEN P.M. I was parked in the garage of a small ranch-style house about ten miles south of Merchantville. As promised, the door had opened upon the command of the remote in my glovebox, and, as instructed, I had closed the door behind me and stayed in the car, waiting. Normally, I didn't wait well. I inherited impatience genes from both sides of the family, and in combination, they make me as restless as a Mexican jumping bean. But tonight, after working breakfast, lunch, and dinner at Mother Theresa's, the only thing that was holding me up was the steering wheel. Right now, I didn't care if the trooper I was supposed to be meeting never showed up. All I wanted to do was sleep, even if it meant sleeping sitting up.

I did sleep, head resting on the steering wheel, only wrested from Morpheus's gentle arms when the lights came on and the garage door began to lift with a series of creaks and moans so fearsome it sounded like a metallic monster rising from the depths. By the time the door had opened, I was a trembling wreck. These days, my nerves seemed too close to the surface. I was easily shaken and half the time I barely felt like myself. I was used to being driven and under stress; what I wasn't used to was this constant state of subhysteria, this sense that anything could knock me off balance and send me spinning out of control.

Under the circumstances, it wasn't an abnormal reaction. Two days ago, I had been laughing at my own bridal giddiness and reflecting on the chain of circumstances which had led me to be marrying Andre.

Couples always like to ask each other, "How did you meet?" Our answer is a bit of a conversation stopper. We met because he was the detective on the case when my sister Carrie was murdered. We'd started as enemies and look where we'd ended up. Or would have ended up. Suddenly, my whole life had been put on hold. All I could do was wait and hope, things I was terribly bad at. Waiting frayed my nerves and hoping made me crazy. On top of it all, trembling atop the whipped cream of my frenzied nerves like the cherry on a bad sundae, was fear. The fear that something would go wrong. Fear that I might never see him again. Fear that the baby I was carrying would be growing up without a father. I was so scared I felt like my insides had been through a Mixmaster. And I didn't do scared. I was a tough guy.

If I was this anxious, this consumed by fear, how must it be for him? It had been a revelation for me, his overwhelming joy at impending fatherhood. Such a contrast to my own ambivalence. I'd felt sulky, confused and trapped by this accidental pregnancy. His delight and unconditional acceptance had been like a life raft, sustaining me through my confusion. I could only hope that now it would do the same for him. That perhaps, however miserable his circumstances, the thought of me and the baby, waiting, might give him strength.

Oliver, Mason, or Claudine. Not names I would have picked. When he found out I might be pregnant, they had rolled off Andre's tongue with a fluency and readiness that stunned me. While I was still in a dither about being pregnant at all, about being the victim of such an unforeseen accident, he was happily naming our child. While I was still in a snit because I hadn't gotten to choose whether I would be a mother, he was dragging me into the children's book sections of bookstores and picking out "must have" books for the baby. While I was throwing up and feeling too miserable to live another day, he was pricing

polar-fleece baby bags and L.L. Bean baby backpacks. He had
already begun to make a tiger-maple cradle.

Though he was the constant centerpiece of my life, I skit-
tered over my thoughts of Andre the way I'd rush across slippery
ice, not pausing for fear I'd trip on a memory and fall, unable
to regain my footing. It had happened to me once today. Catching sight of a departing man's broad back and shoulders, his
bristling dark hair, I had seen Andre, my tough, burly state
trooper, kneeling in the breakdown lane beside the car, oblivious
to the passing traffic, asking me to be his wife. I'd temporarily
become deaf and blind to the clamoring of my hungry customers.

I shut my eyes against the wash of tears, biting my lip and
fighting for control as a nondescript brown car pulled in swiftly
beside me. As soon as the garage door was shut, a slim, handsome, red-haired woman got out and came around to knock on
my window. I opened my own door and got out to meet her.
Tired after a day of rushing around, my legs felt shaky and
undependable. I felt like a total scatterbrain next to her neat,
self-contained calm. Maybe it only made sense that I wouldn't
feel like myself, when I was pretending to be someone else.

"Norah Kavanaugh," she said, shaking my hand firmly. "You
look beat. Hard day?"

"I'm not as young as I used to be. If they had asked me to
carry one more teeny sandwich, I would have burst into tears
and quit."

"One day and you're ready to quit?" Maybe she didn't mean
it, but I read into her words an implicit criticism of someone
who was ready to quit after just one day. Another time, I might
have gotten my back up, but tonight I was too tired to take
offense. She didn't know me, and probably my tenacity wasn't
legendary in the state of Maine yet. It wasn't the kind of information Jack Leonard was likely to share. I shrugged. It must
have been a pitiful gesture, because she actually put a comforting
hand on my shoulder. "None of us do very well," she said, "when
stuff like this is going on." Leaning against the car, she pulled
out a notebook and flipped it open. "Got anything for me?"

I shifted my aching shoulders and searched my weary brain for information. "I don't know. Maybe." I told her about the break-in where the guns had allegedly been taken, pleased to note that she wrote that down, and then I told her about Jed Harding's mother, Mary, and the trouble she was having with his son, Lyle. She wrote that down, too.

"There are a lot of people, not just militia people, who think Jed Harding's a saint. They can't understand why we don't let him go."

I realized that in the craziness of the last two days I'd never learned about Jed Harding, other than his name and the fact that Andre's kidnappers had demanded that he be let out of jail in exchange for Andre's release. Five pounds of remedial reading about militias and the religious right, black helicopters and the New World Order, and one sentence about Harding. "They never told me anything about Jed Harding. What's his story, anyway?"

"Jack didn't tell you?"

"Jack wants me to stay home and crochet pink and blue baby blankets."

Kavanaugh's eyes dropped to my waist. "You're pregnant?"

It sounded a little too much like, "You're stupid." And being constitutionally inclined to get huffy about such things, I folded my arms over my chest and glared. "The failure rate of even the best birth control is eight to ten percent. I'm a statistic."

"Don't get your back up," she said calmly. "I'll bet Lemieux's happy as a clam digger at low tide. He loves kids. I just didn't know and I like to know the facts about my witnesses . . ." She stopped and stared down at the floor.

Funny. She thought I was her witness. I thought I was a spy and she was my contact. Probably we were both wrong and I was just an ineffectual fool, wasting both our time on this wild-goose chase when we should have been doing more useful things. I should have stayed home, unpacking my new office, while she went out hunting bad guys. There were always plenty of bad guys and there was always plenty of work to be done, especially with the whole office in chaos.

How odd, I thought. That was the first time I'd thought about work—my own work—in days. Normally, I'm an obsessive workaholic. And since we'd just moved the whole shebang from outside Boston up to Maine, there was plenty to obsess and be a workaholic about. Yet despite the boxed-up files and the waiting desks and cabinets, I'd thought about little beyond pie and coffee all day. But awash with hormones and steeped in fear, who knew what I was turning into?

"Jed Harding," I reminded her.

"Vietnam vet," she said. "Fifty-one years old. High-strung. Taciturn. Weird but decent. Partially disabled. Six years ago, he was knocked off his feet by a sweet young girl who came to town to work in a restaurant for the summer, name of Paulette. Mother Theresa's restaurant, same place you are. She got pregnant. They got married. But when the baby was born, it wasn't all right. The baby boy, Lyle, was born with spina bifida. Harding was convinced that the baby's problems were a result of his exposure to Agent Orange while he was in Vietnam, and he went to war against the VA, trying to make them responsible for the baby's care. The harder he pushed, the more they resisted."

She shrugged. "The mother stuck around for a while, trying to care for the boy, but she was young and interested in having fun. Eventually, seeing that her summer adventure had landed her in a lot more trouble than she was interested in handling, she moved out, started seeing other guys. I guess Harding and the child were both pretty upset about it . . ." She hesitated. "Recently, she . . . uh . . . disappeared into the sunset, leaving Harding and his elderly mother with this poor little boy."

"Sad," I said, "but how did he end up in jail?"

"Guess they pushed his buttons one time too many," Kavanaugh said. "The VA, I mean. Government decides they will cover Vietnam veterans' spina bifida children, some Agent Orange exposure thing, but some asshole down at Togus—that's the state VA hospital—decides he still won't take care of Harding's kid and won't approve Harding's paperwork. Kid needs a lot of stuff, special braces, physical therapy, things like that. So, after he tries working through the proper channels and running into a brick wall every time, Harding loads up his shotgun, gets in his pickup, and drives down to Chelsea to have a chat with this guy at the VA."

"And?"

"Ends up shooting out the guy's window and executing his desk, his bookcase, and his chair. I think the only reason the bureaucrat survived is that he jumped out the window while Harding was reloading."

"No bail?"

She shook her head. "Can't let him out. Harding swears that he'll go right back there and finish the job."

"So his mother is left holding the kid, so to speak?"

"So to speak. And she's none too healthy herself. Nor young. He's a sweet little boy, is what I hear. Smart as a whip. Got a great disposition. Only thing is that he can't walk very well, so he's stuck in a wheelchair. And maybe he could, if he'd gotten adequate medical care. Still might. I don't know. It's a lousy business. And I can't help thinking . . ." She stopped. Whatever it was, she wasn't ready to share it with me. Not surprising. Cops don't share their speculations with civilians. She tapped her notebook with the pencil. "Anything else?"

Even though I had no idea what it meant, I told her about Roy Belcher and his mysterious message about someone named Jimmy needing the truck. I told her that the pastor of the Salvation Baptist Church had expressed sympathy for Jed Harding over his bran muffin and coffee, and the chair of the Board of Selectmen, Germaine Janelle, had expressed a similar sympathy over a piece of apple pie. "I might hear more," I said, "but Theresa won't let me work in the bar."

She nodded. "I don't think you'd want to," she said. "You know you're right in the hotbed of militia sympathy. If they could, many of the good citizens of Merchantville would form their own state, the Democratic Republic of Merchantville. Not, given the way these guys think, that it would be very democratic. Unless you're a guy . . ." She smiled wryly. "Which we aren't. Since the papermill closed, there's been a lot of paranoia around here, which has gotten worse with this talk about a national park or a national forest. Lot of people aren't too keen on more government employees telling them when and where they can and can't do things they've done all their lives."

She cleared her throat. "Excuse me. Allergies. I'm afraid I tend to make speeches, but this is a serious subject and you need to know what you've gotten yourself into. Paranoia's what feeds into this militia frenzy. Poverty, paranoia, change, fear of outsiders, and fear of change. Bad things happen, people start looking for someone to blame. Enact some very basic, reasonable gun control, and suddenly people see a conspiracy to disarm them so the United Nations can take over the world." She paused. "You know about this stuff?" I nodded. "We've been trying to get some insiders . . . infiltrate the groups . . . but the people who are attracted to this stuff, they tend to be pretty paranoid. I wouldn't be surprised to find out the whole town's in on it. Lemieux could be in the town hall basement . . ."

She frowned and rubbed her neck. She looked good, but she looked tired. Everyone was working this thing 24/7. Cops don't like it when one of their own is at stake. "And that shooting in Jackman didn't help any, though any time you've got a crazy woman with a gun, the cops can't win. Sorry. Don't get me going on this stuff. I'm pretty much a law-and-order type myself. Guess that's kind of obvious, isn't it? Just because the system doesn't always work doesn't mean we have to tear it down, or that if we disagree, we get to opt out of following the rules. Better we should work to fix it." She smiled. "I ought to carry a soapbox, huh?"

She had a nice smile. It looked friendly, but Andre said some of her coworkers called her the Ice Maiden. I could understand that. I'd been called some names myself when men found out I wasn't a sweet and easygoing pushover. I'd been called "bitch" often enough I could have come to believe it was my name. It used to sting until I started regarding it as an acronym. BITCH. Babe In Total Charge of Herself. And Kavanaugh had it worse.

It was hard to be a successful woman in a man's world, and the cop's world, despite the progress women had made, was definitely a man's world. A woman as attractive as Norah Kava-

naugh walked a fine line. Act too tough, they call you a
ball-buster; act too feminine and no one feels safe working with
you. So you act like one of the guys, always weighing and ana-
lyzing as you try to strike the right balance. It's like trying to
juggle while you're keeping your balance on a rolling barrel. I
didn't envy her. But no one ever promised it was going to be
easy.

I was working on that balance myself, playing Dora the
timid. It was hard going. I'm used to being tough, forceful, and
in charge. I'm bad at holding my tongue. I leaned wearily against
my car, acutely aware of my body, of how physical everything
seemed compared with my ordinary life, where I lived so much
in my head. "Anything new on your end?"

She shook her head and I knew, from her face, that if she'd
had even a tidbit to give me, she would have. I'd never met
Norah Kavanaugh before, but I knew she was involved with a
state trooper herself, so she lived daily with the same fears I did.
She had her own gun and her own Smokey the Bear hat and
her own share of trooper attitude. She carried herself in a firm,
no-nonsense way, and I was willing to bet that she could lock
emotion off her face just like Andre, but we were both tough
gals with lovers' hearts and guys in dangerous jobs.

"It's hard to believe," she said. "He was snatched in broad
daylight, and no one saw a thing. No one who can be bothered
to come forward. We keep hoping." She broke off with a bob
of her head, a little embarrassed at giving me the party line.
"How are you holding up?"

"If I survive a week at this job, I'm going to need a month
to recover. I forgot how hard manual labor is."

"I know what you mean. I did an undercover in a Boothbay
Harbor restaurant a while back. Nothing in life has ever made
me so glad I'm a police officer. You ask me, they ought to take
every kid who's thinking about dropping out of high school, and
put them in a mandatory work program for a few months. It
would do more good than a year of lecturing at them. Same
thing with juvenile offenders. Skip jail, make 'em peel potatoes.
There's nothing like hands-on experience."

This time it was more like an impish grin than a smile, a surprise after her cautious reserve. She wasn't much like Amanda, another trooper Andre had worked with a lot last year. Amanda had a big smile, sparkling eyes, and taffy-colored hair. Amanda had been open about her interest in Andre. Too open for my taste—at a point where I was struggling to balance independence and interdependence. Back then, I was struggling over how to deal with Andre's need to protect me when those protective instincts got in the way of my work—at least as I perceived it—and he'd been struggling to give me the freedom I wanted. Amanda's openness and simplicity must have seemed very attractive, a mirror reflecting back what he wanted to see.

I didn't think Kavanaugh was open or simple. She was more like me—an ambitious and independent woman trying to find a man whose own complicated jigsaw edges fit together with her own. The gap in my life caused by the absence of my adjoining puzzle piece left me incomplete and vulnerable. It was as raw as a fresh cut. Like me, the guy in her life was a cop, and she'd had to deal with his protectiveness. I wished I could sit down and talk with her. She would understand. But we were both busy and tired, and tomorrow was rushing toward us. I didn't know about her day, but mine was starting at six again.

"They all call you 'honey'?" she asked.

"Until I want to throw up."

"I understand," she said, "and you can't talk back." She checked her watch. "How about Thursday, same time, same station?"

"Sure. If I don't show up, it's because I fell over."

"You have any trouble getting away?"

"Merchantville goes to sleep early."

She shook her head, her expression wary. "Don't count on it," she said. "It only looks that way. Keep your eyes open, you'll see a lot of movement. But you weren't followed?"

"I did everything Jack told me to do, and I didn't see anyone."

"All right." She snapped the notebook shut and tucked it away. "Just keep paying attention, okay? Try not to underestimate them. The people we're dealing with aren't stupid. And they're quite paranoid. Have you got a gun?"

"I don't know how to use one." That wasn't quite true. I was afraid of guns, had resisted owning one, despite Andre's lessons. But more than one innocent soda can had met a terrible fate at my hands, shot full of holes. Bottles were more fun but shooting bottles wasn't ecologically sound. Cans could be recycled, wounded or not, but not even a good doobie like me was going to pick up a million shards of shattered glass.

She opened her car door and leaned in, coming out with a shoebox in her hand. She held it out reluctantly. "Jack wants you to have this."

I took the box cautiously. "A gun?"

Kavanaugh nodded. "And a permit. And ammunition."

"A permit? How on earth . . ."

"We issue the permits, Thea."

"But I don't want . . ."

She shook her head vigorously. "None of us wants any of this, do we?" she said. "Humor him. Jack is in a very hard place, you know, trying to let you be a player when he wants to lock you up somewhere. You don't have to use it." She fell silent, wondering, I knew, where she was supposed to draw the line in her communications with me. Cops are an us vs. them group. I wasn't one of them, but I was one of theirs. There was a tendency to treat families like treasured mushrooms. Kept in the dark, but cherished. Her eyes fell to my waistline, a little embarrassed. "And there's Andre to consider. Above all, he wants you safe."

"He probably wants me to be crocheting blankets, too." It wasn't quite true. Andre had an instinctive protective side—how could he not, given what he did—yet he loved and respected me for what I was, fiercely independent and a risk taker.

"He knows you won't be, doesn't he?" she asked.

"Would you be sitting on your hands if it were Tommy Munro instead of Andre?"

"You know the answer to that."

I did. The cops would have done their best to keep her be-

hind the lines, so Tommy wouldn't worry. And Norah Kavanaugh would have moved heaven and earth to rescue her man.
Her man. God! It was so primitive. But then, love was primitive.
It was an incredibly powerful, deep-seated thing that wasn't subject to rational control.

I opened the box and took out the gun. A nice fit in my
hand. Small. Feminine. Almost pretty. "What's this? A Barbie
Smith & Wesson?"

Kavanaugh looked grimly from me to the gun and back
again. "It's enough firepower to stop someone in their tracks, if
necessary, and allow you to get away. It may look pretty but it's
plenty lethal." She sounded disapproving. "I don't know why
Jack had to go and get some girlie-looking gun, but people do
funny things sometimes. Maybe he thought you'd take it more
readily if it was attractive. You know how to use it?" Without
waiting for my answer, she quickly walked me through loading,
holding, and firing. Doing what she could to protect me.

Pistol-packin' momma? I tried it on. It was a bad fit. I put
the gun back in its box. Circumstances were forcing me to do a
lot of strange things. This was just one more. "Tell Jack thanks
a lot. And tell him that I've promised to be careful."

She nodded, a single, decisive bend of her head. She still
seemed angry but I didn't think the anger was directed at me.
She was angry that we were in this situation at all and she was
angry that I was being treated like a girl. And I thought that
part of her anger was that she, too, felt like she had to be protective, when what she wanted was to tell me to buck up and
go give 'em hell. When she wanted the two of us to go over the
hill together and bring back bad-guy scalps on our belts.

I wanted to stay. Just standing there with her, I felt closer to
him. But I was running out of steam. "Is there anything else I
should know? Anything special I should be looking for?"

She shook her head. "Just keep doing what you're doing.
Keep your head down and your ears open. Don't do anything
to get yourself noticed. Pay special attention to names . . . anyone who seems particularly militant, who might be a leader . . .
anyone whose name comes up in other people's conversations a

lot, that people seem to defer to . . ." She turned to go. Stopped, considering, and turned back. "I know you think you've got to do this," she said, "and I understand that. But I'm not sure you understand how dangerous your situation is. These are not nice people, Thea. They don't play by our rules. They do horrible things . . ." She shook her head, her lips tight as if she'd already said too much. "Just be careful, okay?"

I nodded and filed the information away for future processing, wondering if I could stay awake long enough to make the drive home. Right now, being careful meant keeping the car on the road. And home was a ridiculous term for where I was staying.

"I'll go first," she said. "You wait ten minutes before you leave. I'll be parked somewhere along the way, watching your back. But you won't see me."

The door creaked up for her, like a monster in chains, and ten minutes later it creaked down after me. Maybe next time I'd bring a can of WD-40. I watched carefully all the way home, but I didn't see Kavanaugh or anyone else. I parked beside the Dumpster, shoved Jack's gift into my bag, and got out, locking the car behind me.

Just as I was sticking my key into the lock, I saw the glowing red end of a cigarette on the porch beside me, and a voice from the darkness asked, "So, honey. Where you been?"

CHAPTER 5

SURE, KAVANAUGH HAD warned me, yet only a minute before, the night had seemed benign. "Driving around," I said, trying to force the key into the lock.

"Kalyn said you were so tired you couldn't hardly stand up." Belligerent and disbelieving. Now I recognized the voice. It was the guy from the restaurant. The one who'd grabbed me. Roy something. Belcher.

Dammit! How I felt and where I went were no one's business. I made up a lie but didn't have to fake the shake in my voice. "I was. I am. But sometimes I think about my husband . . . that he might find me . . . or I think I see him. Then the fear comes and I can't sit still or sleep or anything, so I go out driving. It calms me down."

I didn't know what Roy Belcher knew about me or if he'd heard my story, but obviously he'd taken the time to question Kalyn. I didn't know what he was doing on the back porch of the restaurant in the middle of the night, either, and I didn't intend to stay around and find out. The marks he'd left on my arm told me all I needed to know about Belcher. He was violent and he was mean. The schoolyard bully grown up. Still traveling with a knot of admiring hangers-on. Still picking on weaker people for the fun of it. If I lived a thousand years, I'd never understand how someone's manhood was enhanced by picking on weaker creatures.

Finally the key slid home. I turned it and pushed the door open. "Good night."

"Hey," he said, and took a few steps closer, heavy feet thudding on the warped fir planks. Not so close he was touching me but close enough so I felt a ripple of goose bumps along my arms, a catch in my chest. "You don't have to run away so quick. I just wanted to say I was sorry about what happened this afternoon. I didn't mean to hurt you."

And I was born yesterday. Had Clyde made him apologize? Did Clyde have that kind of power? "I'm kind of used to that," I said.

"So I heard."

Of course. This was a small town. My business was everyone's business. I couldn't see his face in the darkness, didn't need to to know this was a man I wouldn't trust as far as I could throw him. Which, even in my current buffed state, wouldn't be very far. With a beer-gut that big, he was an easy 240. Yet I wished him far, far away. The hair on the back of my neck prickled and I suddenly knew how it felt to be Dora, the runaway battered wife, always afraid of what might be coming out of the darkness, unable anymore to believe in the goodness of men. "I'm fine, really," I said in a conciliatory voice. "It didn't hurt much."

"It won't happen again. I promise. I just wish you wouldn't of sicked Clyde on me." The cigarette arched away through the darkness like a little red rocket. Then his heels clomped across the porch, and he was gone. A minute later, I heard an engine start.

I closed the door behind me and leaned against it, panting. I realized that I hadn't been breathing. My undependable legs were shaking. I sat on the gritty stairs with my head in my hands. The stairwell was hot and close and smelled so strongly of cooking I could almost have wrung the grease out of the air. Was what was going on here transparent to everyone but me? While I naively thought I was undercover, were they—whoever they were—all watching me like a mouse in a maze? Despite the heat, the thought made my skin dance with goose bumps again. Was I making a big mistake being here? No one wanted me to be in this dangerous, scary place, not even me. But what else could I do? This was the only way I could think of to help. I grabbed the banister, pulled myself up, and climbed the stairs.

I pulled down the cracked green-canvas shades and closed the flimsy curtains. The yellowed cloth was stiff with dirt and crumbled to dust between my fingers. The shades covered the windows but moved in and out with the breeze, making soft scraping sounds on the sills like the room was breathing. It was the rough, unsteady breathing of someone ancient and unwell. I stripped off my clothes and stepped into the shower, bracing myself for the irregularities of the water. Tonight it wasn't so bad. I pulled on a nightshirt and climbed into bed, too tired even to think. I expected that the second my head hit the pillow, I'd be off to dreamland but the rustling of the window shades kept me awake.

Finally I crossed the room and raised them, letting the night into my room, a warm, moist night with enough breeze to move the shades but not enough to cool things off. It was so quiet here. I was used to the ocean, which was never still, and the muffled comings and goings of my condo neighbors. Here there were no cars passing. No radio or TV noises. Far off, a dog barked and another answered. Some insects hummed. Andre was somewhere in this same night and I couldn't help but wonder. Was he hot and miserable like me? Hungry? Hurt? Was he frightened of what might happen? Was he worrying about me? Was I wrong to insist on doing this? Did I make things worse for him by taking some risks, instead of sitting safely at home? Could I have sat safely at home?

I knew the answer to the last question. No. They may also serve who only stand and wait, but that wouldn't work for me. I was a doer. I always had been. If Dom and Rosie hadn't helped me find this job, if Jack Leonard had locked me out of the operation completely, I would have found my own way in. It would have sounded mushy even to my own ears to say that this was about love, but it was. Besides, what comments about love and commitment didn't sound mushy? In our society, people might be allowed to complain, but they weren't encouraged to talk about the good things, the happy things, the solid, underlying relationships that make life work. We're allowed to be miserable, frustrated, complaining, and angry, but not to be happy. Andre and I were happy.

I hadn't wanted to let Andre into my life; after I lost my husband, David, I'd sworn never to fall in love again. But in he had come, forceful and persistent. Comforting and good to me. I hadn't thought so at first. From the moment Andre showed up on the doorstep, investigating Carrie's murder, I disliked him. If there's an opposite to "hit it off right away," then that's what we did. I thought he was pushy, insensitive, and rude. He thought I was being a prissy obstructionist who really didn't want to find out what had happened to my sister. He pushed me over the edge when he forced me to look at the pictures of my sister's body, showing in graphic detail how she had died. I stormed out of his office, sick with horror.

Later, he showed up at Carrie's apartment, which I had been cleaning out, bringing dinner as a peace offering. It was an uneasy truce. After what he'd done, I didn't entirely trust him, and because I'd tried to keep things from him, to protect Carrie's privacy, he didn't entirely trust me. But we've come a long way since then. He still can't help being too protective and I still can't help being a bit too assertive—we're both oldest children—but we're working on it. Not long ago, walking along the beach in Hawaii, where I'd gone for business, I realized that whatever our difficulties of personality, career, and geography, I wanted Andre in my life permanently, and was willing to make some sacrifices to make that happen. Was this my sacrifice?

I straightened my pillow and lay down again, closing my eyes. I had to get some sleep. It was after midnight. Day two in my life as Dora the waitress would be starting in less than six hours, but I'd reached that state where I was too exhausted to sleep. I'd just drift off and I'd find myself awake again. The sheets felt scratchy. My body ached and I couldn't gulp my usual

Advil or soak in a warm bath. A determined mosquito made repeated forays after blood. The stiff canvas shades rustled too loudly. I was hot and sweaty and disoriented. Tomorrow I'd have to get a fan.

The noise of the shades was driving me crazy. I threw off the covers and went to put them up. Got to the window and realized I already had. That rustling sound wasn't the shades at all. Cautiously, I peered out into the night. It was so dark all I could see was shadows on shadows. But one of the shadows was right beside my car. And it was moving. I watched the shadow circle the car, trying all the doors, trying the trunk, before picking up something and scraping at one of the windows. Someone was trying to break in.

My purse wasn't down there. Tonight it was up here with me. And I had no way of knowing whether this was any more sinister than someone trying to steal a car or whatever might be in it. Maybe that was how they greeted all newcomers in the town of Merchantville. A little welcoming vandalism. But with all the tourists about, they didn't need to pick on a poor waitress. I grabbed my shorts, tucked in my nightshirt, and went pounding down the stairs. Without even thinking, I threw open the door and yelled, "Hey you! Get away from my car!"

There was the clank of something being dropped, and the figure turned and ran away. I had an impression of someone tall and slender. Nothing more. Heart pounding, I flipped on the outside light and went out to inspect the damage. Other than a few ugly scrapes, the rustmobile was in pretty good shape. I knelt down and picked up the tool that he had dropped. Pry bar. Nice, handy, burglarious tool. Carrying it with me, I went back inside, locked the door, turned off the light, and went back to bed, the sturdy metal bar on the table beside me.

The surge of adrenaline must have put me right over the top, because this time, as it subsided, I fell into a deep sleep. I slept like a rock until I was dragged from sleep by my alarm clock. Feeling like I'd been beaten from head to toe with a cast-iron frying pan, I limped into the bathroom and tried to compose my face and hair into something vaguely human. Then I pulled on some clothes, whatever was on top of the suitcase, and headed for the stairs. This was a lot like summer camp. Roll out of bed too early, sleepy and sore from exercise, in steamy, rustic surroundings, pull on slightly damp clothes from an undifferentiated heap, and head out to start the day. Only this time, I wasn't having any fun.

Halfway down the stairs, a sudden thought snapped me back like a bungee cord into the room. My purse and my gun. The purse could go back in the car. It was probably safe enough in daylight, with all the comings and goings at the restaurant. But just in case, I didn't want to leave the gun there. On the other hand, I didn't want to leave it lying around my room, either. People were already showing themselves a bit too curious about me. I finally left it at the bottom of an ancient box of sanitary pads under the bathroom sink, protected by half a dozen of the ugliest spiders that ever crept across the planet. I expected it would be a guy who came searching, if anyone did, and no guy I've ever known will cross a barrier of spiders and a jumble of cleaning products to reach into a Kotex box. Even if it was a woman, my deterrents were pretty good.

Theresa, Clyde, and the boy who had come yesterday to help at lunch were already in the kitchen. No sign of Natty. I mumbled good mornings, poured myself a desperately needed cup of coffee, and remembered that I'd reformed. Just this once, I thought. Only half a cup. I put some wheat toast in the toaster, and started checking supplies. We needed more bread. More muffins. More butter and syrup and jam in the tubs. Mechanically, I performed my morning tasks. Without being asked, Clyde fixed me scrambled eggs. I made more coffee. Gulped my breakfast. Picked up my apron and was about to tie it on when Theresa said, "You might want to look in a mirror before you go into the dining room." I ducked into the bathroom and checked. Aside from a decorative cluster of cobwebs in my hair and the fact that my T-shirt was wrong-side out, I looked fine.

Restored to order, I went back to the kitchen. "Thanks," I said. "Too little sleep last night. Someone was trying to break into my car."

Theresa exchanged glances with Clyde, then shook her head. "It won't happen again," she promised.

I tied on my apron, checked the pockets, picked up the coffeepot and headed for the dining room. It was amazing how little sound carried through the kitchen door. The room was already half full, though it wasn't officially opening time yet. I recognized a few people from the day before, and lots of new faces. A couple people even made a point of saying good morning, and asking how my first day had gone, doing their best to make me feel welcome. The whole place was buzzing with talk about something in the news, but I was so busy I couldn't catch more than snatches of conversation. I didn't count the number of trips, but it felt like close to a thousand, back and forth, back and forth, until I was no more than a robot with aching feet.

Gradually, from the bits I heard, I understood that there had been some kind of shootout involving the police, but that was all I could learn. I didn't dare seem too interested, and I was so busy I didn't even have time to glance at the paper. It was an exquisitely cruel form of torture, especially for a knowledge junkie like me. I collect information and provide answers for a living. I have a compulsion to know and understand. But today I was Dora the waitress, running her feet off, too busy for even snatches of conversation. Once I caught, ". . . heard the cop's name was . . ." And another time I heard, ". . . expected to recover, but the . . ." I lingered to listen, but someone called for coffee. And that was all.

Finally, it was that magic time of the morning when people stopped eating breakfast and it was too early for lunch. Around 10:30, a silence suddenly fell over the place. Clyde scraped down his grill and went out onto back porch to smoke. Natty arrived and started, without a greeting to anyone, to work on preparations for lunch. He was followed shortly after by Kalyn, who dropped her pack on the table and said, "Hotter 'n hell out there. Gonna be a scorcher." She'd come on the back of her boyfriend's motorcycle and was all pink and windblown.

I got myself a glass of milk and sat down at the table, putting my feet up on a chair. They ached with a throbbing that was almost like a second pulse. I was too tired even to go to the bathroom.

"You see the paper yet?" Theresa asked.

"Been too busy running the Boston marathon," I said. "I didn't think there were that many people in the whole town."

"Aren't," she said. "They come from miles around." She shoved the paper at me. "Big story. Something about a state trooper and a shoot-out."

My heart jumped as a surge of anxiety, the anxiety I'd kept at bay for hours, shot through me like an electric shock. Time, other people, and the kitchen all slid away as I grabbed the paper and bent over it, frantically scanning the words. Anyone in the other room would have to wait. The headline got right to the point and restored my heartbeat. FEMALE TROOPER WOUNDED, MOTORIST DIES, WHEN TRAFFIC STOP TURNS DEADLY. It wasn't Andre, then. But was it Norah? I read on, rushing through the paragraphs. It was Norah, or, as the papers put it, Trooper Norah Kavanaugh, a five-year veteran of the force, twice-decorated daughter of a Connecticut police chief.

According to the story, Norah had been traveling south on Route 4 when she encountered a car being driven erratically. Although she was off-duty and driving an unmarked car, she had called for a trooper to back her up, then mounted a portable light on her car and pulled the driver over. As she approached the driver's window, a man had stepped out of the car with a gun in his hand. When she identified herself as a police officer, he had opened fire. Despite being wounded, Trooper Kavanaugh had managed to draw her own gun and return the fire, killing the shooter. Kavanaugh's injuries were not life-threatening and she was expected to make a full recovery.

I closed the paper and stood up, hoping that my feelings—a confusing mixture of guilt and relief—didn't show. It was my fault that Norah Kavanaugh had been in that place at that time. My fault, in a way, that she had gotten shot. If I already felt rotten, today's news didn't make me feel any better. There had been little in the story about the identity of the man who was shot, pending notification of his family. I looked around the busy room. "Anybody hear anything about the guy that trooper shot?"

Theresa rushed past me and picked up the coffeepot. "Local kid," she said. "Young guy. Hot-headed moron in love with guns. Came in here sometimes. Always rude. Always in too much of a hurry to bother to use his brain. Now see where it got him." But no name. No description. No comment about his family or connections. Or why he might have pulled a gun on a state trooper.

I nodded, not sure what I was agreeing to. Maybe Clyde would tell me more, if I asked him in a quiet moment. I moved on to the next item on my agenda. "Anyplace in town where I might find a fan?"

"Hardware store might have 'em, if they're not sold out," she said. "You'd better go now. A day like this, lotta people gonna have the same idea. Some of those camps get real hot and stuffy, especially to folks used to air-conditioning." She pointed toward the dining room. "Things are quiet right now. Out the door, turn right, and it's two blocks down on the corner."

Sidewalks in Merchantville were a hit-or-miss kind of thing. There was one in front of Mother Theresa's, but it petered out at the end of her building, then a cinder track meandered along past her parking lot and past a gas station, and then there was some sidewalk again. I limped down to the hardware store, got the last fan in the place, and started limping back. Almost back, passing the broad, weed-strewn gravel lot that served as parking for the restaurant, I heard something that sounded like a cat crying. I stopped and listened and decided that it sounded more human than animal. Maybe someone had left a baby in a car. I'd read about that. Terrible things happened when it was hot. Babies died.

Lugging my fan and limping along, I checked all the cars. I found nothing, but I could still hear the crying. It seemed to be coming from the back of the lot. Behind the lot, there was a steep hill, and between the lot and the hill, a weed-filled ditch to catch the water that flowed down the slope to keep it from flooding the parking lot. I walked slowly along the edge, peering down into the ditch, hoping I wasn't going to find some poor animal tied up in a sack and left to die, or an abandoned baby. At the far corner of the lot, where it ended and the ditch disappeared behind a shabby brick building, I found the source of the noise—a small towheaded boy in an overturned wheelchair.

He was sweaty and dirty and bleeding from a cut on his forehead, but otherwise seemed to be all right. I dropped my fan, climbed down the bank, picked up the boy and the chair, and carried them back to level ground. Then I set him back in the chair and knelt down in front of him, the million questions of a worried adult bubbling to my lips. Two escaped before I could stop them. "What were you doing there?" I asked. "Are you all right?"

He stared at me but didn't answer. His dirty face was smudged with tears. I pulled a napkin from my pocket and carefully wiped off the worst of the dirt. "I'm Dora, and you?"

"I was running away from home," he said.

"You chose a pretty odd way to do it."

"I didn't know about the ditch. You got anything to drink? I'm thirsty."

"I haven't, but I work over at the restaurant. Mother Theresa's. Bet we could find you something there. You like lemonade?"

"Don't got no money," he said.

"Well, I've got lots. I'll treat you. But first, we have to get you over there." Something of a problem. I had one boy, one wheelchair, and one fan to get across a rutted gravel lot. "Tell you what." I picked up my fan. "If you can hold this on your lap . . ."

He grinned up at me. Even red-faced and dirty, he was TV-camera perfect, right down to the missing front teeth. "You'll push the chair, right?"

"Right." I set the fan in his lap. "Hold on. It's going to be a bumpy ride . . ."

We clattered back across the lot and I lifted him, the chair, and the fan up onto the back porch of the restaurant. I wheeled him into the kitchen and up to the table. Took the fan off his lap and set it on the floor. Then I poured a glass of lemonade, stuck in a straw, and sat down beside him, steadying the glass with my hand.

"I can do it myself," he said impatiently. "I'm not a baby."

Theresa came in with her coffeepot, set it down, and stared at the two of us. "What in tarnation's going on here? Dora? We can't be having children in the kitchen."

I got to my feet, instinctively planting myself between Theresa and the child. "I found him in a ditch. I didn't know what else to do, so I brought him here . . ."

Theresa put her hands on her hips and stared at the boy in exasperation. "Lyle, your momma doesn't work here anymore, so there's no sense in trying to come down here to see her. I'll call your grandmother. She must be worried sick . . ."

"Wasn't looking for her," he said, "I know she's gone. I was to look for anyone, it would be Mindy. But I ain't. I'm running away from home."

Ignoring him, she picked up the phone and dialed a number. Waited, then said, "Mary, it's Theresa. Yes, he's here. Our new waitress just found him out in the parking lot. No, I don't see how I . . . we're awfully busy. Yes, well, I guess maybe the new girl can. If she comes right now. I'll ask her. All right. All right. I know. I'll send him home."

She rolled her eyes and hung up the phone. "That poor woman. As if she didn't have enough on her plate already, now her boy's been arrested for trying to make the damned government do what it's supposed to do. Person her age ought to be taking it easy." She shrugged. "As if anyone ever got to take things easy. Dora, I hate to ask you this . . . everyone working hard enough already . . . but we've got to get the boy home. How a kid in a wheelchair can still manage to be hell on wheels . . ." Here she stopped, as if aware of how ludicrous her remark had been.

"It's only a few blocks, then down that street past the church. Lyle can show you where . . ." She fanned herself with her hand, though it wasn't that hot in the kitchen. "Damned global warming. Mary Harding. She's his grandmother, bless her poor tired soul. I doubt she's got the energy to come and get him. Go on," she pointed at the door. "Get him out of here. We've got work to do."

I guess I really wasn't being asked, was I? But then, Theresa didn't know what she was doing, ordering me to help Jed Harding's child. Wearily, I turned back to the boy. He'd finished his lemonade and was eating a doughnut that Clyde must have given him, powdered sugar mingling with the dirt on his face. He gave me his gap-toothed grin again, seemingly unaware of Theresa's animosity. "Are you taking me home?"

"Yes!" Theresa snapped. "She's taking you back where you belong. And this time, do us all a favor and stay there. Your grandmother has enough on her mind without worrying about you." She picked up the coffeepot and disappeared through the doors.

"Don't pay her any mind," Clyde said. "She don't mean nothin' by it." He seized the chair handles in his big hands, piloted it out of the kitchen, and lifted it down the steps like it was a feather. He wheeled it around the front to the sidewalk and pointed down the street. "Just past the church, there. You see it. You go down that street, four, five houses. He'll show you."

"Thanks," I said, and Lyle and I set off down the sidewalk, the heat shimmering around us like a warm, wet cloud. It didn't take much effort but I was soaked with sweat by the time we reached the church. Lyle seemed unaffected, chattering away like a magpie as he gave me the fifty-cent tour of his town. Every house, signpost, rock, and tree had a story, and Lyle knew them all. Twice in our five-block journey, tourists stopped to ask directions. I was blank, but Lyle did his best, and both times I received compliments on how sweet my little boy was.

It reminded me of a girl I'd met in Hawaii, an A+ kid named Laura Mitchell, and how good it had felt to be mistaken for her mother. I'd never given much thought to motherhood. It had always been something I'd get around to someday. I'd been busy with other things. But like it or not, after thirty-one years, life had suddenly dubbed me a mother. Mother-to-be, anyway. It felt awkward, but sometimes it also felt good.

"My mom used to work at that place," Lyle said. "But she's gone away and I'm not never going to see her again."

"Oh, I bet you will," I said. "Mothers don't like to leave their children."

He shook his head solemnly. "I think she's dead," he said. "And dead mothers don't come back." It was an awful speech for a little child, but before I could think of anything to say, he started talking about something else.

We rolled on, Lyle's words washing over me, but I wasn't really listening. I was thinking about Andre's child, about how surprised I'd been when I told him I might be pregnant and discovered he'd already made a list of names. I might be ambivalent about motherhood but he had no reservations about fatherhood. He'd be delighted to be here with a great kid like Lyle. I'd be delighted to have him here. And there was still no news. The state wasn't likely to satisfy a bunch of terrorists by releasing a prisoner, even if it meant getting Andre back. And just how likely was it that the militia would give him back, no matter what the state did about Jed Harding? They'd shot Gary Pelletier, hadn't they? But I couldn't let myself start thinking like this. Hope was what I had. Just about all I had. I stumbled on through a blur of tears.

CHAPTER 6

SOME FITNESS QUEEN I was. By the time we reached his house, I could barely wheel boy and chair onto the porch, even with the help of a ramp. I was parboiled by the heat and had to catch my breath before I knocked. The woman who answered the door looked like she'd been dipped in bleach. Colorless hair, colorless skin, colorless clothes. Her lips were almost bloodless. Even her blue eyes were faded. Her hand dropped from the knob as soon as the door was wide enough to admit us and it stayed at her side even when I offered my name and my own hand. Not, I thought, because she was unfriendly, but simply because it was too much effort to raise it again. Even the few shuffling backward steps she took to let us pass seemed difficult. She so entirely embodied the word "weary" that I was surprised when she managed a smile for the boy.

"Look at you, child. You're dirty as a pig. Where were you this time?" she asked. Her voice was thin and weak. "Trying to visit Mindy again? I told you she doesn't work there anymore."

Lyle stared down at his lap, all his ebullience suddenly gone. "I'm sorry I'm so much trouble, Grandma," he said. "I wasn't going to the restaurant. I didn't mean to go there." He pointed a grubby hand at me. "She took me there. I was running away . . ." His voice faltered and there was a muffled sob as he covered his face with his hands. From between the fingers he said, "I was trying to go see Daddy."

"Oh, Lyle . . ." Mary Harding sighed and gave a little shrug of her shoulders, looking at me apologetically. "I'm sorry to be dragging you into this," she said, "when it's got nothing to do with you." She glanced down at the watch that flopped loosely on her skeletal wrist. "I'm sure you've got to be getting back to the restaurant. The lunch crowd will be coming in and I know how Theresa is. She's a fair woman but she works her people hard." She looked down at the boy. "Lyle, tell the lady that you're sorry and thank her for bringing you home."

He raised his tear-stained face. "Thanks for bringing me home," he said. "Sorry if I was any trouble."

She was right. I did have to get back to work. "It wasn't any trouble," I said. "He's a nice boy." I turned to go, hating to leave her. She looked like someone needed to be caring for her, and there she was with a sobbing child to clean up, comfort, and care for. According to Suzanne, Andre, and my mother, it is one of the flaws in my character that I always think I have to help people smaller and weaker than myself. It's the result of spending my childhood as "Thea the fixer," the role that my family assigned me because they couldn't get along with each other. Unless it's because I am, quite literally, a "big girl" at five eleven, and big girls have to look after the others.

As Thea the human tow truck, I keep finding people broken down on the road of life, and stopping to see if I can help. I often have cause to regret it, but, in this department, I'm a slow learner. Not this time, I told myself resolutely. In my current circumstances, I had absolutely no time or energy left over for other people. Particularly when those other people were related to the cause of all my problems. If it hadn't been for Jed Harding and his damned shotgun, Andre wouldn't have been kidnapped and I wouldn't be here. I'd be on my honeymoon. Smiling the smile I don't use enough. Sleeping—actually sleeping, not just lying in a horizontal position waiting for dawn to come—in Andre's arms. These were the last people I wanted to help. I should want to kick them, hit them, or scream at them instead.

And yet. There was poor exhausted Mary Harding, fragile as an old dry leaf, and poor sad Lyle, as much a victim of this as I was, missing his daddy. It hurt to walk away, but I did.

I'd gone all of three steps when Lyle called, "Dora, do you have a car?"

And his grandmother said, "Hush, Lyle, hush."

"Because if you have a car, you could drive me to see my daddy, couldn't you?"

"No, she can't, Lyle," his grandmother said. "It's a very long way, the woman has a job, and she's a complete stranger. We don't ask favors from strangers." She moved quickly to shut the door, to drown out Lyle's pleading voice, and to keep me from seeing any more of the chaos of her life. It was the New England way—keep things to yourself, don't let people know your troubles, and don't ask for help. Chin up. Shoulders back. Pride intact. The door closed behind me with a distinct click, but all the way down the street, until I turned the corner by the church, his cries followed and made me feel wretched.

Someone in the church was playing the organ. Someone new to the job, from the sound of it, just getting a feel for how the instrument worked. For as long as I was in hearing distance, the child's cries were replaced by that stirring war song, "A Mighty Fortress is Our God." The first stanza, over and over and over.

Back at the restaurant, things were getting wild, even with three of us. In addition to our regular crowd, which was plenty, we had a group of Canadian tourists whose bus had broken down, crabby and voluble, with time on their hands and a free lunch courtesy of the tour company. It was a nightmare. Freebies, far from making people happy or grateful, seem to enhance their greed. I ran until I was sure my feet were going to start bleeding right through my shoes. I half-expected to look down and see bloody footprints on the floor. The only good thing was that it kept me from thinking about sad little Lyle Harding. The only good thing.

Kalyn, hangdog and apologetic, left early for a doctor's appointment, and then we were two. I hated to see her go. She was wonderfully good-natured and observant. She'd pulled my ass out of the fire several times already. The fire of Theresa's wrath. If I'd had a dollar for every time she grabbed my shoulder and pointed angrily at something, I could have doubled my tips. I wasn't the only one running. Kalyn ran twice as fast as I did. And she could juggle. I mean, really juggle, not just balance stacks of plates. At one point, I heard laughter and turned around to find she had a whole table in stitches as she kept an apple, a hot dog, and a small stuffed lobster in the air. Even Clyde, who was one of the sweetest-tempered men I'd ever met, was getting snappish.

Just about at the point where I thought I was going to collapse, the kitchen door opened and a woman who looked like a younger, prettier version of Theresa hurried in, tied on an apron, and said, without preliminaries, "The sitter was late. What tables shall I take?"

"Take the row of booths along the wall," Theresa said.

"Righty-O," she said, and hurried into the dining room.

No one bothered to introduce me, but no one really needed to, and anyway, this was a business, not a social occasion. Clearly, this was Theresa's daughter, and equally clearly, from the way his eyes had followed her as the burgers burned, Clyde had a soft spot for her.

"The burgers, Clyde," I reminded him, as I tore open a packet of coffee, dumped it in, and stuck a batch of buns in the toaster. He cursed and flipped them. I hurried into the storeroom to get more buns, more bread, another tub of coleslaw, and a jar of tartar sauce. This all would have been easier if only I had three arms. There was no sign of Natty today, nor of his sidekick, and the mountain of dishes that awaited them loomed ominously. We were dangerously low on plates and glasses but there was no way I was adding dishwashing to my other tasks.

Things didn't quiet down until after three, when I was left with only one table, four old-timers telling fishing stories. They'd been there so long I was thinking of charging them rent, and they'd drunk so much coffee I wondered that their bladders didn't burst. As I leaned in with my pot one more time, one of 'em, the biggest, baldest one, said to the others, "Betcha I know where they're keeping that guy."

"Who's keeping what guy?"

"The militia's keeping that cop they took," Baldy said.

"Seth Muller's silo," my favorite one said. He was the one the others called "Bump." He had lively blue eyes and a kind smile and reminded me of my grandfather.

"Beliveau's potato house." This was the one called "Squint," who seemed to have only one eye. He was also the youngest and most foul-mouthed of the quartet.

"You ask me, they ain't keepin' him anywhere," the fourth one, the one with "Guy" embroidered over his pocket, said. "All that talk about tradin' him is bullshit. He's been dead and buried since the first day." The cold, decisive words made my throat tight and brought tears to my eyes. I looked down, hoping they wouldn't notice, and began clearing their dishes.

"Nope. Betcha not." Baldy again. "These guys are honorable, right? And they're serious about getting Harding out. I'm betting one of those survivalists has got him down in one of their bunkers. Great place to hide someone and they've already got 'em fitted out with food and toilets and things, right?"

Squint nodded sagely. "Wouldn't be a bad place to keep somebody, would it? Better'n a potato house. You ever smell one of them things, come spring?"

"Dumb idea," Bump said. "Those places are cold and damp, and crawling with mice and bugs."

"Don't expect they're thinking much about some cop's comfort," Guy said. "Not after what they done to Jed. And not after the way they've been since that statie got shot. All but peering up our asses, the cops were."

The first speaker, Baldy, the one the others called "Beau," said speculatively, "I wonder who around here's got 'em. Shelters, I mean. There was a real fad for building those shelters, ten, fifteen years ago. Fella I know, over to the civil defense, used to keep a list of 'em, just in case of, you know, war or somethin'. You do the civil defense, right, Bump, over to the library? They still got that list?"

Bump shrugged, looking bored with the conversation. "Doubt it. I've never seen it. Dang fool idea anyway."

"Hell, there's dozens of 'em around, them shelters," Squint said. "I wonder if the cops have thought of it?"

"Probably not. What do the cops know about us, anyway? They don't seem to give a damn that Jed Harding was in the right, do they? Push us around, stick their official noses into our business, try to keep us from exercising our constitutional right to protect ourselves, but they don't know nothin' about who we are. Fuckin' LURC's the worst, but it's the same for all of 'em." It was Guy, the one who thought Andre was dead and buried. Not a good Guy, I thought angrily. I had no idea what LURC was, but I'd sure heard it mentioned a lot. Guess I'd have to ask someone.

Bump was the only one bored with talking about shelters. The others seemed fascinated. Beau said, "Heck, out our road, there's three or four people I can think of who built shelters. Woman next door lets her teenager use it as a clubhouse. Him and his girlfriend, they're down there half the time these days, and I don't think they're playing cribbage, either." There was a general burst of laughter. But Beau wasn't finished. "You all know Elmer Hemphill, right?" A chorus of nods. "Well, his wife Joyce, she was entertaining the oil man down in his shelter while Elmer was sitting in the living room watching the baseball game."

"How do you know?" Squint demanded.

Beau grinned. "Oil man's my brother-in-law. Says they had it fitted out real nice, too."

"Hey, girlie, Theresa got any pie left?" Squint asked.

Girlie. Doll. Babe. Sweetie. Honey. I'd been called them so much in my two days at Theresa's that I was already getting calluses. For years, I've been something of a knee-jerk feminist, taking nothing from anyone that suggested I wasn't being taken seriously. The problem here was that I didn't want to do anything that might interfere with my job of collecting information. I also didn't care much whether I was taken seriously as a waitress. But that latter was just me being classist. If I thought about it, I'd realize that these were the real working women, the ones who needed protection from sexism, particularly wage-based sexism, most of all. But this wasn't the time or the place to take a stand. I wasn't here to change the world. I was here to try and make one small world—my world—right and normal again. So I bit my lip and didn't correct him, focusing instead on what the male diminutive might be. Boy? Sonny? Laddie? Beefycakes?

"I'll check," I said. I didn't want to leave, just in case they said something else about Andre and survival shelters, or speculated on where else he might be, but I had no more reasons to linger. "I doubt it. It's been like a plague of locusts in here today." I gathered up the rest of the plates and lugged the heavy tray into the kitchen. Natty was at the sink and the mountain of dishes was gradually turning into something more like a big hill. I checked the pies—only apple and lemon meringue left—and went to make my report.

They were still arguing about good places where a captive cop might be held, and I had to wait for a break in the conversation to report my findings. They ordered two apple and two lemon, asked for more coffee and more little packets of cream, and went back to arguing.

When I delivered the pie, the mean one, Guy, said, "So, girlie, where do you think they're keeping him?" For a second, my heart skipped, and I wondered how they knew to ask me, until I realized that it was something everyone in town was talking about, and I was just being included in the general conversation.

They really seemed to expect an answer, so I named the first place I thought of. "The basement of the church," I said, turning toward the kitchen, "that one down on the corner."

"Hey, hold on there . . ." a voice said loudly.

I turned back to find Beau halfway out of his seat, his face flushed with anger and his fists half-clenched, being tugged back into place by Bump. "Girl," he said angrily, "you got no call to be accusing . . ."

"Oh, Beauregard, sit down and shut up!" Bump said firmly. "She didn't mean anything by it. Girl's not from around here.

It was just a guess, wasn't it, honey?" He reached out and patted my hand, giving me a curious look. "How'd you happen to pick that place?"

I managed a smile even though, inexplicably, I felt like weeping, and nodded. "It was just a joke. You know. Pick the most unlikely place. I was going to say town hall, but I don't even know if Merchantville has one. And I was just walking past the church a while ago, taking the little Harding boy home . . ." I was ashamed of the tremor in my voice. Beau was still glaring and my tears were too close to the surface, so I didn't wait around to set things straight or to see how they'd work it out. I was too tired to get into an argument with a cranky and belligerent old man. I didn't have the energy to be placating. "Excuse me," I said. I limped into the kitchen, sat down at the table, and wrote up their check. Then I handed it to Theresa's daughter. "Would you mind giving this to those guys out there?"

She took it with a smile. "Not at all. Those old geezers giving you a hard time?" I nodded. "Sorry about that. They've got nothing better to do, now that they're all retired. Ma calls 'em the 'fish butts,' on account of the fact that they sit around on their butts all the time and talk about fishing, but can't get off their butts to go catch any fish." She stuffed it in her pocket and held out her hand. "I'm Cathy. Mary Catharine McGrath."

"Dora," I said, taking it without getting up. "God, my feet are killing me."

"New to this, huh? Better go upstairs and soak 'em. It's just the three of us again tonight and there's an event at the library, so everyone's gonna be coming in here for supper first. Ma says she thinks she'll have a schedule worked out, starting tomorrow, so you can get some time off. She'd never tell you, but I think she feels bad about working you so much, with you just being new and not used to it and all. She strikes people as hard, but she's really not. She don't . . . doesn't ask anything from other people she doesn't ask of herself. But I suppose you've noticed that."

She waved the check. "Guess I'll go deliver this. See if I can get them movin'. Ma wants to close up for a few hours, give us all a break. I mean, you know it's a bad day when Clyde gets cranky."

I put my head down on my arms and closed my eyes, too tired even for the walk upstairs. My feet throbbed and my head ached. I was starving but lacked the energy to get up and fix myself something. There was a thump as something was set down beside my head and I smelled the delicious scent of fried onions and bacon. Clyde's big hand rested briefly between my shoulders. "You gotta eat something, Dora," he muttered.

I murmured "thanks" without looking up, and a minute later I heard the back door slam and knew he'd gone out for a cigarette.

Brisk footsteps signaled Cathy's return. "Bump Peters asked me to apologize to you. He says they were a bunch of skunks today and they're ashamed of themselves."

"Maybe he is. I doubt if the rest of them are."

She nodded. "You got that right. I don't know why he hangs around with the rest of them. He's a decent man, while Guy LeBeau is mean as a junkyard dog, Squint Sturges hasn't got the brains God gave a goat, and Beau Nichols's got such a short fuse he gets mad at his own shoes 'cuz they can't tie themselves. Trouble with Bump is, since his wife died, he's got nothing better to do. She really kept him in line. Now he just sits around with the rest of those grousers, pissing and moaning about how the system's failing. They don't like it?" She shrugged. ". . . Maybe they ought to run for the legislature. They couldn't be worse than the rest of those jerks down to Augusta."

She took off her apron and hung it on a hook. "I've put out the CLOSED sign. Says we'll reopen at five. No sense in staying open for the few stragglers we'll see in the next few hours. Me and Clyde are going down to the beach for a swim. Want to come?"

A minute ago I'd thought I was too tired to even get out of the chair, but the idea of a swim was really appealing. I liked the image of plunging my hot, aching body into cool, refreshing water. I sat up and grabbed the burger Clyde had left me. It was pink and perfect and smothered with mushrooms and peppers and onions. Juice ran between my fingers and up my arm as I ate and I didn't give a damn. My mother wasn't watching. I try to eat healthy food but I believe in the restorative powers of meat, not so far evolved from the carnivores as I'd like to think. "I'd love a swim," I said. "But I don't want to be a third wheel, if you and Clyde . . ." I left it hanging, not wanting to impose, not wanting to pressure.

She shrugged with a not entirely convincing indifference. "Great. I'll tell Clyde. I've got a suit in my car. Soon as you've changed, we can go."

She hurried out, letting the screen door slam shut behind her. I finished the burger, delivered the dishes to Natty, and climbed the stairs, hoping that in my hasty packing, I had remembered to put in a bathing suit. I hadn't been thinking of this as a vacation, but Rosie had told me to, since the town was on a lake.

Five minutes later, I was changed and back downstairs, a T-shirt and shorts thrown over my suit, carrying a towel. Cathy and Clyde were waiting in his truck with the motor running. I hopped in and we took off in a shower of dust and gravel. For a moment, driving down the main street with hot wind blowing in the open window, music on the radio and the sounds of passing cars coming at me, it felt like summer again. The old, carefree summers of my youth. Work at a hard, menial job, get tired and grumpy and sweaty, then hop in a car with a bunch of friends and head out to the pool or the beach or someone's backyard, and have some fun. The feeling only lasted a moment. I wasn't here to have fun.

Something must have shown in my face, because Cathy dug an elbow in my ribs and said, "Lighten up, Dora. It's okay to enjoy yourself once in a while." I got the feeling, once again, that the whole town knew my story. A small-town gossip mill was as good as a story in the local paper. Battered wife seeks refuge in Merchantville.

There was a cop at the lake, turning cars away from the crowded lot, but he moved the barrier and waved us in, pointing to a choice spot way at the front. Clyde paused as we passed and said, "Thanks, Billy." They exchanged big grins and we drove on.

"Clyde's cousin," Cathy explained. "The Davis boys always look after each other."

Memory is a funny thing. Different people store things in different ways. For me, summer is stored in smells and sounds and feelings. The smells of green and damp, chlorine and coconut oil, fried food and dust. You could have brought me here blindfolded and I would have known I was at a beach. There were children screaming and splashing, lifeguards' whistles blowing, radios competing, and the lap of waves on the beach. I pulled off my T-shirt and let the sun fall on my shoulders. Cathy's eyes lit on a small purple scar on my arm.

"I got stabbed with a pair of scissors," I explained. She waited a minute, her eyes curious, but I didn't tell the rest of the story. It was unpleasant to remember and I didn't want to be dragged back to that parking lot in Hawaii, to the jarring ugliness of that tropical night, a swarm of emergency vehicles, and some people who saw violence as the answer to their problems. I didn't want to admit the terrible vision of that pair of scissors stabbing deep into my arm.

Cathy nodded as if she understood. Probably she thought my husband had done it. My imaginary, abusive one. Dora's husband. While we were all relaxed and easy, I wanted to ask her about Paulette Harding, and what Lyle had said, and about Mindy, the waitress who'd abruptly disappeared. But before I could speak, she dropped her towel on the beach. "Last one in is a rotten egg," she said. She grabbed Clyde's hand and headed for the water.

I watched them go, trying not to stare too openly. Clyde in a bathing suit was a sight to behold. He was not so much fat as simply massive. His arms were as big around as most people's legs. His legs were like furry tree trunks ending in huge feet, so wide for their length they looked almost square. He was decorated with tattoos. Instead of a bathing suit, he wore a pair of cut-off jeans. Next to his bulk, Cathy, who was slight, looked like Fay Wray next to King Kong.

I dropped my own stuff and followed more slowly. I was too tired to race, too old to care about being a rotten egg. I walked slowly among the clusters of people, trying not to step on pails or shovels or toy cars or giggling toddlers, stopping once to remove a hard, sticky peach pit from the sole of my foot. People will leave anything in the sand. Out of sight, out of mind.

The first bite of the water was icy but I kept on going, striding forward as it climbed past my knees, up my thighs, and finally, just as it was about to freeze some tender spots, I dove in, immersing myself in a breathless rush. The cool touch of it was so delicious, so exhilarating that I felt somehow cleansed. I surfaced gasping, awash with pure physical joy, and took my bearings. The swimming area was separated from the rest of the lake and protected from the busy boat traffic by a line of buoys. Out by the farthest line, beyond the lifeguard's raft crowded with noisy swimmers, there were no people.

I struck out for that emptiness and began swimming laps. I was working my body but it felt different, good instead of exhausting. It was as if the water somehow flowed right through me, washing away the poisons of worry and fear and weariness, leaving me renewed and refreshed. Alive again. Back and forth from one side-line to the other. Back and forth. Occasionally doing a lap on my back, staring up at the high green hills that rose around the lake, at the hot blue dome of the sky. Out here, away from the crowd on the beach, I felt alone in the world and at peace. I closed my eyes and floated.

Suddenly, someone grabbed my legs and pulled me down under the water, holding me there, dragging me deeper and deeper. Shocked, I gasped, took a mouthful of water, panicked, and began to fight. This was a place I had been before. A terrible place. I was not going there again.

CHAPTER 7

FURIOUS AND FRIGHTENED, I lashed out with my arms and legs, kicking at my assailant, flailing, slashing with my nails at the hands that held me. I was determined to draw blood, to inflict injury, to give as good as I got. If I was going down, so was he. My anger at him for bringing me back to this place I'd tried so hard to leave behind was like an explosion inside me. Just as suddenly as I'd been seized, I was released. I popped to the surface and struck out for shore, moving as fast as my arms and legs would let me, fueled by the surge of adrenaline that poured through me. I was moving so fast I practically walked on water.

My assailant swam after me, calling something, but I didn't care. I was heading for the safety of the beach. As I got to my feet and hurried out of the water, he came after me, yelling, "Hey, wait up. Wait up," like some pesky kid on the playground.

I sure as hell didn't wait up. I made a bee-line for my towel, picked it up, wrapped it around me, and turned to confront him, here where I was safely surrounded by a mob of people.

He came up to me with a grin on his face, saying, "Jeez, take it easy. I didn't mean to scare you. I was just having a little fun . . ." Shameful as it was, I took pleasure in the fact that both of his hands were bleeding and there were cuts on his arms and his cheek.

With his wet hair plastered down, it took me a minute to recognize him. Roy Belcher, the asshole from the restaurant. The man who had been watching on the porch last night. What the hell was he doing here? Here, there, and everywhere. What was going on? Was he following me or had he just come to the beach for a swim?

"Hey, honey," he said. "Come on. Lighten up. It's not like I was trying to drown you or anything . . ."

When she'd just been scared to death, Honey found it hard to lighten up. "That's exactly what I thought you were trying to do . . ."

Amazingly enough, he was still smiling. Either he was phenomenally stupid or his experiences with women had taught him that loutish behavior was attractive. "Jeez, Dora, you're a real tiger, you know that?" He looked down at his oozing cuts like he was proud of himself, then adjusted the waistband of his trunks, shifting his legs and hips with a little wriggle to settle himself back into place. His jutting belly jiggled. He slicked back his hair, running his hands through it as a woman might and carefully pushing the ends into place, then took a step closer, obviously unaware of my reaction to his little tease, still thinking this was all a game for both of us. Part of the mating game, I guessed, from the expression on his face.

I took a step backward and said, in a firm, loud voice, "Don't come any closer." I hoped he couldn't see how badly I was shaking. I try to be brave about water but it hasn't been very long since I nearly drowned, since I was pulled down into a black void and woke up, sick and miserable, on a stretcher being carried to the emergency room. I lead a pretty exciting life for a consultant. In the past few years, I've spent enough time in ERs to consider them my second home. But I don't want a second home, and I've reformed. I don't take chances anymore. I'm not alone on the planet; I share body space with another person, as yet unknown, for whose welfare I'm responsible. I'm on the cusp of a formal commitment that binds my life to someone else's. I wasn't letting this asshole or any other possessive jerk come along and put me at risk.

He came closer. I stepped back. "I mean it," I said. "It's not funny, you know, what you just did. It was mean and it scared me. Now please, go away and leave me alone." Adrenaline surges make me high and wired. When they ebb, they leave me shaken and depleted. I wanted nothing more than to hurry back to my hot, ugly room where I could curl up and cry. If we left now, I'd have just enough time for a good cry before it was time to comb my hair and start serving dinner. But I didn't know where Clyde and Cathy were.

He reached out and grabbed my wrist. "Jeez," he said, "you really are sore at me, aren't you?" I wondered who wrote his dialogue. He sounded like he'd been scripted back in the fifties and was just getting performed now. When I tried to pull away, his hand tightened and he jerked me forward so that I was knocked off balance and stumbled up against him. He put an arm around my shoulders and pulled me tighter, smiling down into my cleavage. His smile was predatory, like a fox trying to charm a bunny. "There. Now that's more like it," he said.

More like nothing I wanted any part of. I tried to step away but he locked his hands together and held me there. "Let me go, Roy," I said.

"Not until you give me a kiss." His grin was loose and stupid and didn't quite square with the vicious meanness of yesterday.

I was in some weird, crazy nightmare, thrown back into a world where the guys still talked and acted like Neanderthals. Back to the era where no didn't mean no. It meant yes, or at least, try harder and maybe you can wear her down and then she'll say yes. I knew I needed to settle down and handle this in a calm and reasonable way, but his joking attempt to drown me had thrown me way off balance. My pulse was still racing. I was badly shaken, my mind so filled with unwanted images from that other time I couldn't seem to pull myself together.

I struggled to get away. "I don't want to kiss you. Just let me go. Please let me go!"

"No." In that one word, yesterday's bully was back.

I was looking down at my feet, at my tightly curled toes digging into the sand, trying to avoid his face, which seemed to be seeking mine, so I didn't see Clyde arrive until he said, "You heard what she said, Roy. Let her go."

"Oh, hell, Clyde," he muttered, "what are you, her fairy godfather? What is this shit, anyway? Every time I make a move, the broad yells for help and you come running. If Cathy weren't standing right there, I'd think you had the hots for her yourself."

Clyde just folded his arms and stood there, dwarfing all of us. "I already told you the other night, Roy. She's used to her husband knockin' her around so maybe she's a little gun-shy and right now, she don't want to be touched. You want her to like you, you can't be acting this way. A woman says no, she means no. What's hard to understand about that?"

Roy dropped his arms and let me go, his breath hissing out like the steam of escaping anger. I stepped back and turned away, trying to hide my face so they wouldn't see my fear and embarrassment. I wasn't used to being bailed out by other people. I liked to stand on my own two feet and take care of myself. Although Clyde was being very kind to me, I hated the whole situation. It was confusing and humiliating. I felt alien and awkward and not myself. When I worked out, I had a wonderfully quick recovery heart rate. Normally, I was just as quick at recovering my emotional balance. In threatening situations, my mind stayed clear and calm and I didn't get scared, I got mad. But today I was shaken. I couldn't seem to recover my balance.

For the second time that day, I felt Clyde's warm hand on my back. Just a slight and gentle touch as he bent down and asked, in a low voice, "Are you all right?"

I was tough as nails. I could wrestle barrels full of bears and vanquish boatloads of fierce pirates. I could handle bad guys and bad gals and bad stuff. I turned around to say that I was all right and promptly dissolved in tears. Some heroine I was turning out to be. American's wimpiest spy. Marshmallow gal goes undercover.

"Jeez, Clyde," Roy whined. "Don't look at me like that. I didn't do anything to her. I barely touched her and look what she did to me." He held out his hands and arms for inspection.

"Serves you right," Cathy said tartly. "You're old enough to know better. You ought to have learned by now that women don't like men who maul them and paw at them and shove them around. You woulda learned long before this, if your momma and daddy hadn't spoiled you so bad. Right, Clyde?" She linked her arm through Clyde's and smiled up at him. Roy made a snorting sound and muttered something rude about women's libbers.

Despite my fragmented state, I was aware enough to notice that Clyde's tender attitude toward me had piqued Cathy's interest in him. Sexual politics were such a drag, all that flirting and jealousy and crap. Give me Andre Lemieux any day. Most of the time, he just says what's on his mind, no subterfuge, no game playing, no teasing and making me work for information. Give me Andre Lemieux. Please. God. Give me back Andre Lemieux. The man who is proud of me and loves me for being who I am, but doesn't hesitate to tell me to put a sock in it.

Two whole days pouring pie down hundreds of greedy gullets and I hadn't learned a damned thing. No wonder I felt like crying.

"You ready to go?" Clyde asked.

I nodded. "Unless you want to stay longer . . . I don't want to spoil your afternoon . . . I could walk back. It's not that far."

"Oh, we've got to be getting back anyway," Cathy said, looked pointedly at her watch. "Getting close to opening time again. We were lucky to get away at all. Summertime." She rolled her eyes. "Folks who live here are too busy to enjoy it."

I bent down and picked up my shorts, uncomfortably aware that Clyde and Roy Belcher were both watching my breasts as I bent. I pulled the shorts on, fastened them quickly, and pulled the T-shirt over my head. Depressed. Disappointed. Most of the restorative work of the swim had been undone again, though why I should expect to feel good about anything when the whole world sucked, I couldn't explain. In the truck on the way back, I wasn't thinking of the summers of my youth. I was thinking about dark, musty underground bunkers. I was thinking about fear and worry and imprisonment. The only way to get through the days was to keep believing he was alive.

I watched Clyde's hands on the wheel and thought about Andre. Andre had strong, capable hands with long, blunt-tipped fingers. Hands that could be so gentle, so erotic, so soothing. If I closed my eyes, I could see his hands a dozen different ways. Carefully, lovingly sanding the cradle he was making. Wrapped around weights. Curling in anger and frustration. Smoothing back the hair that's always straggling into my face. Straightening my arm and putting it through the motions so I'd stop throwing like a girl. I could see him doing that with his daughter. Pain at remembering spread through me. Sorrow closed my throat. I stared out the window so they couldn't see my face.

As I was getting out of the truck, Cathy put a hand on my arm. "Hold on a sec," she said. I held on, wondering what was coming. "About Roy Belcher. You don't seem interested, but just in case you're one of those girls who find outlaws attractive— don't. Roy's bad news. Most people think he's just a dumb-acting good-old-boy. He's not. He can act nice when he wants, but cross him and you'll see. He's got a mean streak goes right straight through him."

I barely had time to change and stuff my hair into a hasty braid, and I was swept back into the evening rush. Natty and the other boy were both there, working on great bowls of tossed salad and arranging fruit plates and plates of cold shrimp and avocado. Huge sagging plastic bags of frozen fried clams and french fries and breaded shrimp and breaded fish sat on the counter beside the stove, while a cauldron of spaghetti sauce bubbled and a vat of boiling water spat hissing streams of water over the side as the spaghetti rolled around inside. A man who looked like he could be Clyde's brother was already dropping hamburger patties onto the grill. Big chunks of swordfish waited on a plate.

On the table were a couple dozen lemons, a knife, and a cutting board. As I came in, Theresa waved a thin hand toward them. "Could you make wedges, for iced tea?" I sat down and grabbed the knife, pretending each lemon was Roy Belcher. The work went fast.

The evening was a big blur. We were insanely busy and I rushed back and forth from the kitchen to the dining room like a little wind-up robot. All over the dining room, there were conversations I wanted to eavesdrop on but there wasn't a chance. The whole place was buzzing with talk about the confrontation between Norah Kavanaugh and the boy who had been shot. That was normal. It was a small town, after all, and he was a local boy. It was the tone of the conversation that was surprising. Even in snatches, it made me shiver with fear for Andre and the other troopers I knew.

I heard it first from a motherly, gray-haired woman in a powder-blue cardigan. As I was setting down her dinner, she said to the man sitting across from her, "It's like I told you, Ben. The time of reckoning has come. When our authorities begin shooting us down, like that woman cop did to poor Danny Parker, just like that shooting over to Jackman, it has begun. Time for us to take up our weapons just like our forefathers did and stand up for ourselves." She patted her permed gray curls, asked for extra butter, and said, "There's nothing illegal about a citizen shooting a government official when that government has begun to operate illegally." I almost dropped her dinner in her lap.

I might have dismissed her as a crazy—motherly looking older ladies can be crazy, after all—but that was just the first of many. It's one thing to read about the militia movement—it's scary enough on paper—but to hear it, sense it, feel it seething all around me? There have been times in my life when I felt like an alien who had landed in a strange place where everyone looked familiar but sounded incredibly wrong. This was worse than the worst of those. I knew from my reading how plausible some of the ideas could sound to people who felt disenfranchised and helpless, and how that could lead to paranoia. Intellectually, I understood how those twisted second-amendment arguments could appeal to independent, rural, gun-owning folks, especially in a place like this where a bad economy, mill closings, and the threat of converting paper-company land into a national forest had affected people's lifestyles and livelihoods. But as I learn

over and over, there is a giant difference between book understanding and the real world.

The real world was right here in this room. A cheerful, noisy,
knotty-pine-paneled dining room in a small Maine town along
the shores of Rangeley Lake. A décor of mounted fish, deer, and
moose heads, with a few mediocre paintings by a local artist. A
full spectrum of the population, from fragile senior citizens with
walkers to tiny blanket-swathed newcomers to the planet. The
clink of silverware. Smells of delicious food. And lively conversation about hanging all the deputies from the county sheriff's
department from bridges or shooting them all like Gary Pelletier and dumping their bodies downstate.

That would send a message to those fools down in Augusta
who didn't understand a damned thing about how it was to be
an ordinary working man up here. State bureaucrats sent their
fish-and-game inspectors, their forest wardens, their park rang-
ers up here to tell people where and when they could hunt and
fish and hike and cut some firewood and snowmobile. These
were all things they'd done perfectly well their whole lives without no government busybody telling 'em when, where, and how.

"Goddamn government wants to tell us what color we can
paint our houses."

"They want us to register our guns. You know why? So they
know who has 'em. Then when the New World Order comes,
they can take our guns away. Gun control is just the first step."

"I heard they've got a big stockade up to the Limerock Air-
force Base. That's the first place they'll take people."

If I heard it once, I heard it a dozen times. "Well, I've got
my gun. Let 'em come up here and try to tell me what to do. I
know my rights. My constitutional rights. When the government begins to betray the Constitution, it's up to all of us—the
constitutional militia—to take matters into our own hands." It
all scraped on my nerves like sandpaper until I felt raw.

All right. Jack Leonard had tried to tell me, coldly and pe-
dantically, but he'd tried. "Believe me, Thea. You have no idea
what you're getting into."

And he was right. I hadn't. I've always hated to admit it when someone else is right. I've grown up and matured and gotten better at it. I'm striving for wisdom and balance. I can listen openly and fairly to the other side of an argument. Even though Andre still accuses me of being pigheaded and stubborn and too sure I'm right, I'm much better. Seasoned. More balanced. Able to consider the other guy's point of view. But these other guys' points of view, considered or not, scared me to death.

Any second I was going to drop a hot plate of food onto some poor, hungry, gun-toting customer. I had to get away for a minute and get a grip on myself. As I hurried through the kitchen, I called to Clyde. "I'll be right back. I've got to get some air."

Even the back porch was too bright. I needed the darkness. Someplace that wouldn't assault my senses. Someplace where I could feel alone and away from all the noise and commotion. They were only words but it seemed to me that the dining room was full of bright swords, slashing through the air, pricking me a million times. I did not bleed. What flowed out was my energy and hope. My head was bursting with the things I'd heard; my heart pounding with fear for Andre, for myself, for all of us. For where this thing was heading. I was the last person who should have been surprised to discover that the world was going to hell. I'd seen man's inhumanity to man up close and personal. But I suffered from persistent naiveté, stuck in the throes of an irrational optimism. I had come here believing I could help. I was a fool. That's all.

I leaned against my car. The metal, still faintly warm from the sun, seemed to be trying to comfort me. I closed my eyes and fought against fear and despair. For the third time, I felt that butterfly touch between my shoulder blades. Clyde.

"Dora, you okay?" he asked. In the cool air, his body gave off waves of heat. I wanted to hurl myself against his broad chest and wail. But I didn't win all those Miss Independence awards for nothing. Needing people is a step down the slippery slope. I needed one person. The one I couldn't have.

"I'm fine." F.I.N.E. *F*ucked up. *I*nsecure. *N*eurotic. *E*motional. I *was* fine.

"Here." He pressed an icy glass into my hand. I took a sip. Ginger ale. The universal tonic for the ailing. "Take your time. World won't end if people have to wait a minute for their dinners." And he was gone. It was eerie. He moved so quietly for such a big man.

I leaned against the car, sipped ginger ale, and stared up at the stars. As a child, I must have read too many novels. I still had a highly fictional view of the world. At work I was a cold-hearted realist, but in my own life, I was still something of a romantic. I hoped for happy endings and riding off into the sunset. Out here, with the soft darkness and the twinkling stars, the backdrop of murmuring voices, the clinking sounds of people enjoying their food, it still seemed possible. When I walked back though that door, though, I would be surrounded by the kind of thinking that had led to the bombing of the Alfred P. Murrah federal building in Oklahoma City. Thinking that justified blowing babies and small children to bits to make a point. Why would they release a state trooper, the very embodiment of the enemy? They shoot troopers, don't they?

The ache I felt as I walked up the steps and back into the busy kitchen wasn't from hours on my feet or lugging heavy trays. It was from the weight on my soul.

CHAPTER 8

AT THE END of the evening, I climbed the stairs to my room with Theresa's words echoing in my head like a benediction. "Day after tomorrow you can sleep late if you want. Cathy's going to give me more hours, so I won't need you till dinner." Get through one more day and I could sleep late! I wouldn't have to roll out of bed before six and stumble downstairs to the toaster and the coffeepot. A few more blissful hours when no one would call me "honey," try to grab my arm, or wave at me like a demented traffic cop. In just two days I had grown to loathe all those little plastic packets of slippery substances—jam, syrup, butter, and cream—that were the staples of breakfast. It was going to be hard to eat out for a while after this.

Even though my room was like an oven, I was so exhausted I wanted to throw myself down on the bed and sleep. Fully dressed. Unwashed, unbrushed, and unkempt. Instead, I opened the box, took out my fan, set it in front of the window, and began sucking in some cool night air. I lay down on the bed and let it blow over me, not daring to close my eyes. I knew, after the violent emotional climate of the dining room, that the evil director of my dreams would have it in for me. If I slept, I'd have nightmares. It was a kind of Promethean torture. Chained forever on the cusp of sleep, desperately longing for it and desperately fearing it.

My feet pulsed with a steady, throbbing ache. Every muscle in my legs begged for mercy. My arms and shoulders felt like I'd been holding up the world too long. Where was Atlas when I needed him? Or my good friend Morpheus. Sometimes, when he took me in, I slept without dreams. The clock loomed large ahead of me. If I had a restless night, I wouldn't get enough sleep. Not until the next day. My morning off. Then I could sleep as late as I wanted.

The truth was, I already knew how I was spending my morning off, and it wasn't sleeping. I was going to play fairy godmother to a sad little boy. If this town was the lion's den, then I was going deeper. I was going to stick my head in the lion's mouth. I was going to take advantage of my position as marshmallow gal undercover. If his cautious grandmother was willing to let him go off with a stranger, I was going to drive Lyle Harding to see his daddy. And in my truth-telling heart of hearts, it wasn't an entirely altruistic move. I had to see if I could make something happen, or learn something, before this fearful atmosphere drove me back to the safety of the Boston suburbs. Compared to what was going on around here, road rage, blind self-involvement, the incivility of people walking, driving, and dining while talking on their cell phones, the company of spoiled brats with too much money and too few manners seemed positively benign.

Eventually, the room cooled down, my eyes closed, and I drifted off to sleep. The dictionary defines sleep as: "the natural periodic suspension of consciousness during which the powers of the body are restored." Torture is defined as: "physical or mental anguish." Somewhere along the line, my brain had gotten the two mixed up. After a period of deep, restful sleep which might have begun restoring the powers of my body, I segued into nightmares. Usually my nightmares are coherent—surreal and yet lucid enough so that I can see what's coming, even if I'm powerless to prevent it. Tonight it was more like a film-clip montage assembled by a sadist.

Scenes from all the awful things I've experienced—my sister's body, tumbling cars crashing and burning, blood flowing from slashed wrists, car trunks popping open to reveal bodies, a handsome bully with a hard fist, a dead woman in suggestive lingerie. Helene Streeter, fatally stabbed, crawling toward her front door. Waking on my kitchen floor to the smell of smoke and an earth-shattering headache. Action scenes. Beaning an assailant with an IV pole. Leading a troupe of camouflaged commandos to raid a home for unwed mothers. Whacking a lunatic writer with a stick beside a mist-shrouded winter pond. Andre, rigid with anger, walking out of my hospital room without looking back. Fighting with my mother in her kitchen. Dreams colored red with anger, blue with sorrow, gray with confusion, black with despair.

I woke hot, sweaty, and disoriented, feeling like my skin was filled with worms. A cold shower didn't help. My body longed for sleep; my mind was too afraid. The only thing for it was to go out and walk. Keep moving and hope that I could tire myself out enough to fall into a sleep without dreams. And if I couldn't sleep, I might as well do a bit of detecting.

I pulled on shorts and a tank top, shoved my key and a tiny flashlight into my pocket, and set out down the street, feeling like the only person left on earth. In the damp air, the street lights glowed like giant, ephemeral balloons and all the green vegetation shone an eerie silver. My footsteps echoed loudly in the dense quiet and I stepped off the sidewalk and onto the adjoining grass to silence them. My feet seemed to have more purpose than my brain as they took me down the main street to the church and carried me across the rolling lawn. That old man Beau's reaction when I mentioned the church had been too violent not to mean something.

There was a faint path, probably unofficial, that led along the side of the building toward the parking lot. As I passed through a gap in a lilac hedge, I stopped and stared. I wasn't alone on the planet after all. The parking lot was filled with cars and trucks, even though it was well after midnight, and lights were on in the basement of the church. The grass muffled my steps as I slipped quietly along the blank white clapboards until I came to a basement window. I knelt down and peered in.

A man garbed more like a commando than a minister was walking back and forth before rows of men seated on folding chairs, gesticulating wildly. All men, I noticed. In one hand, he held a Bible, which he thumped periodically with his fist. I couldn't hear what he was saying and didn't dare get closer to the glass. To do so, I would have had to crawl down into the window well, about a five-foot drop, down into the leaves and the damp and who knew what else, and I'd be trapped there if anyone came along. Instead, I scanned as much of the audience as I could see for familiar faces. There were several I recognized from the restaurant. Baldy, or Beauregard, the man who had reacted so strongly when I suggested that Andre was in the church basement. Guy, the mean one. And Squint. The only one I didn't see was Bump.

I wasn't surprised find see Roy Belcher and his pals. He'd struck me as exactly the kind of guy who would be wherever the action was, dying to be in on it, whether he understood it or not. I was more than a little surprised to see both Clyde and Natty. But why should I have been? The militia appealed to those who felt disenfranchised, left behind, who felt that life wasn't giving them a fair shake and found comfort in blaming the government. Those ideas might have great appeal to men, and boys, who worked for low wages in restaurant kitchens. Once again I felt guiltily mainstream, middle class, and privileged. Out of touch with ordinary lives.

For the first time since I'd come here, I also felt a small thrill of excitement. This might mean something or it might mean nothing, but at least I was getting to be active instead of passive. It was what I'd agreed to do, but being confined to Theresa's, restricted to what I could overhear, was enormously frustrating. I also felt profoundly scared. I hadn't meant to be detecting. I'd come out on this walk to try and feel better, trying to calm down after the fevered atmosphere in the restaurant but what I saw made me feel anything but calm.

There were a lot of men in that room. From their faces, it

looked like a lot of angry men. Jack Leonard and the Maine state government had a serious problem on their hands. This was just one small town. One of many. Who knew how many similar meetings were taking place in other towns? And I had my own serious problem. How were we going to get these angry men to let Andre go even if Jed Harding were released? I had already heard Jack say, very seriously, "We do not bargain with terrorists." If they wouldn't bargain, what did that leave? Unless Andre managed to escape on his own, either a commando raid or an act of charity on their part.

I looked through the window at the rows of faces and saw nothing charitable. They looked, to a man, hard and angry and brimming with passionate zeal. Jack thought they were terrorists. They considered themselves patriots. It didn't make any difference to me. I didn't care what they were. I just wanted Andre back. Being this close and not being able to hear what was being said was too frustrating. There was only one useful thing I could think of to do. I went back to the parking lot, pulled out some paper and a pen, and staying low and using my flashlight, I started writing down license numbers.

I'd done about three-quarters of the plates when I heard the crunch of approaching footsteps. I slipped into the shelter of a low-hanging evergreen and crouched there, holding my breath. Silly me. I hadn't considered the possibility of guards. A man walked slowly past, coming within four feet of me. He stopped between my tree and a black truck, shook out a cigarette, and lit it. Then he put his lighter back in his pocket. More footsteps. Another man, coming from the opposite direction, stopped by the tree and said to the first man, "Quiet tonight. You got a cigarette?"

I crouched there, my thighs protesting the position, while they shifted their weapons and performed the lighting ceremony. The crackle of cellophane, the flick of a Bic. One of them said, "How's Patty?"

"Overdue. She's so Goddamned uncomfortable she's a bitch to live with."

The other man laughed. "Take her for a ride on a bumpy road."

"Tried that."

"You tried screwing?"

"She won't let me."

The other man gave a dirty little laugh. "Tell her it'll make the baby come."

"I told her it would make me come. She damned near took my head off. Don't know how I'd do it anyway. She's bigger'n a house."

"Take her from the back."

The first man made a humming sound. "She'd never let me. She thinks it's dirty, any way but the regular."

"Yeah, I know. Cherry's the same way. Women'll do anything for you till you marry 'em and then it's not tonight dear, and don't do that, I don't like it. It's uncomfortable. It's nasty. How can you ask me? Cripes. Then they wonder why you're lookin' at other women."

"I heard Paulette would do anything . . ."

"Yeah. Too bad about Paulette, huh."

"She deserved it."

"I heard they . . ."

I leaned forward eagerly to hear what he was going to say, the sudden weight shift digging my foot noisily into the ground. A stick snapped and they both fell silent. Then the first man said, "What was that?"

"Probably nothing. Cat or something in the bushes."

I'd been holding my breath so long I was turning blue, so I was grateful when they started talking so I could start breathing. Now if they'd only say something more about Paulette.

He must have read my mind, because he said, "Well, she practically blew the whole operation, didn't she? How's the job?"

"I get a paycheck. That's about all I can say for it. God-damned tourists. So. You doin' the armory thing this weekend?"

"Dunno yet. Still waitin' to hear. We'd better get movin'. Don't want the colonel mad at us. Thanks for the cigarette." Then they both walked off.

Just a bit of chitchat about wives, sex, and prospective jobs, but they were carrying guns! I hadn't finished, but clearly it was time to leave. I was surprised they hadn't heard my heart pounding. It thudded in my ears like a jackhammer. I waited until I couldn't hear footsteps anymore, and started back toward the street. The paper in my pocket crackled, crying out as if it wanted to be found. Cursing silently, I rolled it into a cylinder and stuffed it into my bra.

At the front of the church I paused, staring up at the tall steeple, gleaming white against the blue-black sky, backed by a sprinkling of stars. This ought to have been a place of comfort and sanctuary. A place a troubled person could come and feel safe. Instead, it harbored men with violence on their minds. Harbored, and, if that minister had been doing what I thought he was doing, encouraged them to take up their guns and go do harm. Harm to Andre and other good men like him. Men like Gary Pelletier, shot nine times at close range. The thought gave me sharp, stabbing pains in my chest and suddenly I couldn't breathe. I sank down on the steps with my head in my hands, waiting for the spell to pass.

"Hey!" A gruff voice exploded close to my ear. "What do you think you're doing here?"

Startled, I jumped up and turned toward the voice. It was brighter out here near the street and I could see that my inquisitor was a thin, gray-haired man wearing a baseball cap, dressed in dark clothes, carrying a rifle in the crook of his arm. A rifle that was rather casually pointed at me. No wonder I was having trouble breathing. Around here the night spewed out startling encounters like popcorn from a popper.

Oh man. Think quick, Theadora. First I guess the church as a militia site, claim it's a joke, and now I'm found lurking outside in the middle of the night? Like R2D2's little projector, my mind flashed not on Princess Lela, but on Jack Leonard, saying a grim "I told you so."

"This is a church," I said.

"So?"

"So I was worried. And scared. And I couldn't sleep. So I came here."

He didn't know what to make of that. "In the middle of the night?"

"That's when people who are worried and scared can't sleep." I hoped I sounded matter-of-fact and not impertinent. Over the roar of my heart, I couldn't really tell. I could only hear that my voice was shaky.

"What're you so worried about?" He sounded skeptical.

Wondering what you murderous renegades are going to do next, I thought, as I pulled the mantle of Dora the waitress around me and began my familiar lie. I hated to lie. It hurt every time I did it. My nose didn't grow, but it felt as if my soul shrank. I wasn't good at being a situation ethicist. I liked the comfort and reliability of fixed rules—like tell the truth and thou shalt not kill. "My husband. My ex-husband. Finding me. He said if I ever left, he'd track me down and kill me. I thought I saw his car today." Was I telling him too much? Would I really say this to a stranger? Would Dora, confronted by a rifle-wielding menace, crumple like a wind-struck umbrella?

"Where?"

"Here. On Main Street. I was walking this little boy home. A boy in a wheelchair. I found him stuck in a ditch, down near the restaurant where I work. And this truck went by . . ."

I took a deep breath. God, I hated being scared all the time. My insides were all tied up in knots. My neck and shoulders felt like a vicious puppeteer was tightening the strings. But this was how Dora really would feel. Never safe, always looking over her shoulder. "Sorry. I don't mean to be telling a stranger my troubles. I was going to walk some more . . ." Trying not to look at his gun, I got up and took a few tentative steps toward the street.

"Hold on there . . ." he ordered, gesturing with his arm and attached gun, in a chilling combination of the lethal and banal. "I ain't done . . ."

Now that he was bossing me around, I looked openly at the gun. Obviously this guy's mother hadn't told him never to point a gun at anyone, not even a toy one. I didn't have to fake the fear in my voice. "Could you not point that thing at me, please?" He actually looked surprised, like it had never occurred to him that he might be scaring me. I pressed on with my timid-Dora act. "Am I doing something wrong here? I mean, is there a problem with sitting on the church steps? Because I didn't mean any harm by it . . . I was just . . . just . . . upset."

But he was too befuddled, too much a creature of reaction, not action. Instead of dropping the rifle, as I'd hoped, he reinforced his grip, aiming more or less directly at my pounding heart, and gestured with his head. "I think you'd better come along with me . . ."

Quiet as the street was, I wasn't too keen on leaving this public spot for someplace more secluded, not with a bunch like this. In a slow-motion pantomime of panic—slow so he wouldn't panic and shoot me—I raised my hands to my chest and said, "Oh, God! You're not . . . he didn't . . ." I took another deep breath. "Did he send you? My husband? He hired you to kill me, didn't he? That's what he said. That he'd never let me go. If he couldn't have me, no one could, and if he couldn't kill me, he'd find someone who would . . ."

I was backing away from him now, arms outstretched, toward the street. "I can't believe it. That you'd . . . Right here in front of a church . . ." I took a step backward. He took a step forward, his hands tightening on the weapon, bringing it right up against my chest. Now I was the one reacting. I screamed, the longest, loudest, shrillest, most terrified scream I could muster, gasped, "Don't," and collapsed on the lawn, folding my arms defensively over my head. Fat lot of good that would do against a gun.

They milled around me like a herd of restless animals, confused, noisy men trying to figure out what was happening. The man who'd challenged me answered with his own confused and defensive monosyllables. "I dunno." "She said she was out for a walk." "Asked me wasn't this a church?" "Then she says I'm trying to kill her, right, she thinks her husband's hired me." "Then she goes nuts and starts screaming." "Jesus, I dunno." "I didn't lay a hand on her." He summed it all up, "I dunno. Maybe she's crazy?"

Someone knelt beside me and put a hand on my shoulder. Not a gentle touch, like Clyde's, but firm, with fingers that dug in and held on and said, "Don't even think about trying to get away." It hurt. He smelled of a confusing combination of after-shave, bug repellent, and fabric softener. "It's all right. It's all right. No one is going to hurt you." The reassuring words were distinctly at odds with the message of his hand and the tone of his voice.

I cowered there, refusing to look up. "He's got a gun. He put it right up against me. I could feel it . . . "

"He only wanted to know why you were here."

Yeah, right. Like neither one of us spoke the same language. "But I told him," I said. "This is a church." I was huddled with my knees to my chest, one arm over my head to ward off blows. "He's got a gun . . ."

"And it's the middle of the night." Like the asshole had never heard of the concept of sanctuary? Like his parishioners knew enough to be troubled only between nine and five? Maybe his female parishioners knew enough to keep their places and never be troubled at all. But my questioner relaxed his grip, patted my shoulder, and turned to the crowd. "Anybody know this girl?"

I'd expected Clyde, but it was Natty's voice that answered, high and young and proud to be the supplier of information. "I do, Reverend Hannon. She's Theresa's new girl. Stays upstairs, over the restaurant. She's kinda skittish. Theresa says she's running away from a husband who beats her up." My life history in a nutshell. Former property of abusive husband; current property of Theresa. Kind of skittish. Like some small pet or beast of burden.

I lifted my head and looked around. Several of them were shining flashlights at me, blinding me, so that I felt like a trapped animal. I raised a hand and shielded my eyes. "May I go home now? Please?"

"Of course. Of course. We're sorry to have frightened you. Clyde can walk you back. Clyde?" He called but no one answered. "Where's Clyde?"

"He's gone home. Left early." The man shrugged. "He's got to be at work, crack of dawn . . ."

"All right. Nathaniel, can you walk this girl back?"

"Yes, sir."

The Reverend Hannon held out a hand and pulled me to my feet. He seemed surprised to find me at eye level. Surprised and not, I thought, entirely pleased. One of those men who want to be bigger than life, who resent the fact that I am. To appease him, I hunched my shoulders dejectedly and bent my knees, so that I was shorter. Then I looked up at him. Ah, the tricks that tall girls learn. "Whatever it is that I did, I'm sorry. I never thought there'd be something wrong with going to a church. I just thought maybe it would feel comforting . . ."

Hannon gave me a pitying look. "You're welcome to come and talk to me during the day, if you need to. This time of night, you should be home . . ."

Boy, was he right about that. I should be home. But without Andre, it was just a house. A dark, empty house. "I'm sorry I bothered you," I said. Not Thea Kozak's sarcastic "excuse me for living" but poor downtrodden Dora's genuine apology. It had seemed easy planning this with Dom and Rosie but I was finding Dora McKusick increasingly hard to be. She was so pitiful I wanted to shake her. Hannon seemed to like it, though. Dora was his kind of woman.

I turned and headed for the street, Natty trailing proudly after me as my bodyguard, walking "Theresa's girl" back home. We didn't exchange any words on the short walk back. He stayed behind me, as if he were herding me and he had to make sure I went back to the barn. When I said "thanks" and "good night" at my door, he mumbled something noncommittal and sat down on the steps. I went upstairs and went to bed. Sleep was still slow in coming. I had to wait for the adrenaline to subside. When I looked out the window an hour later, Natty was still there.

CHAPTER 9

BY DAWN, MY fear had subsided just enough to allow my curiosity and sense of mission to overrule my common sense. It's a failing of mine. Ask anyone who knows me. I have a fatal attraction to danger, unless danger that's attracted to me. In any case, it meant that I went into the kitchen, still sore and limping, intent on finding out what I could about the man they'd called Reverend Hannon. I knew better than to ask Theresa, she'd tell me to keep my head down and mind my own business. Clyde was scared of women, and besides, he was one of them. So was Natty. That left Kalyn.

I had to wait a long time with the question uppermost in my mind, while I fed a blurring succession of hungry faces, made and poured an ocean of coffee, and toasted a mound of muffins, bagels, and bread easily the size of a brontosaurus. Unless it was an apatosaurus. Those damned scientists. You learned something and then they went and changed it. There ought to be rules.

At least the bar wasn't open for breakfast. It didn't open until 11:30. Lunch and dinner I had to thread my way among the tables, trying not to breathe in the smoke, keeping my eyes down to avoid the stares and the leers. Too bad I couldn't close my ears, too. Commenting on my anatomy seemed to already have become a favored pastime. I was torn about the bar. It was pretty disgusting. I've never had much respect for people who start drinking at lunch. I've never even understood how they do it. I drink at lunch and I'm asleep by two. But I thought I might hear things there, alcohol being a great loosener of tongues. But in keeping with her theory about the danger of combining attractive waitresses and customers, Theresa had herself a barmaid in her fifties, about as wide as she was tall. And a bartender who was both a bastard and an extortionist. If we didn't share our tips, he'd drag his feet on drinks until our customers were furious.

It was 10:30 when Theresa told us to take a break, that she'd cover the dining room. Clyde dished up two plates brimming with steak and eggs and home fries and made me and Kalyn sit down and eat. It was really too hot for meat and potatoes, but it seemed just right. Clyde had that instinct. He knew what we needed to eat. Then he went out on the back porch for a smoke.

Kalyn grinned down at her brimming plate and said, as if she'd read my mind, "That Clyde. I'm absolutely starving today. How does he know?" She picked up her fork and knife and set to work.

I couldn't see where she put it. She was so tiny. I waited until she'd eaten a few mouthfuls, then said, "You been around here long enough to know who's who?"

She shrugged. "Sometimes. Why?"

"Something really scary happened to me last night. I was just wondering how badly I'd put my foot in it . . ."

She set down her fork and leaned forward, eyes wide. "What happened?"

"You know how hot it was?" She nodded. "Well. I couldn't sleep. I was thinking about my ex-husband, and how I'd seen a truck like his in town . . . probably my imagination . . . but when a guy keeps showing up, you can get paranoid. Anyway, I went for a walk. I mean, it seemed okay to me, this looks like a nice safe town and all, and I was over by the church. You know that one down on the corner?"

She said "yeah," but now she looked a little wary, like there was something about that church so obvious any sensible person would know enough to steer clear of it.

"There's something funny about the church, isn't there?"

Now she was definitely wary. "I don't know what you mean." She picked up her fork and started eating again.

"Oh, yeah. I guess you can't, can you, if I don't finish my story? It's like my mom always said, 'Dora, you've got to spit it out. People can't read your mind.' She's one tough woman, my mother. She told me not to marry him, but I was so sure I knew what I was doing . . ." Good. She was looking interested again. As long as it was about me and my husband, and not the church. Now to see if I could slip the question in.

"So I'm out walking and I passed the church on the corner and I stopped, because I was feeling scared and nervous . . ." I made wiggly motions in the air with my hands ". . . in my stomach. I get like that . . . with my husband I used to see him building up and I knew he was going to hit me and there was nothing I could do to stop it and I'd get those funny feelings. Well, anyway, these days, just thinking about him does it, and it was a church, you know. A place that was supposed to make me feel safer and more comfortable."

I stopped and gave her an apologetic grin. "I know. I know. I sure do take my time getting to the point, don't I? So there I am, standing on the church lawn, and all of sudden there's this man standing there pointing a gun at me . . ." Looking down, I saw that my hand was shaking. So much for acting. Even in my craziest or bravest moments, this place was so unnerving I didn't have to fake it.

Now I had her. She might not want to talk about it, but the idea of me standing there at gunpoint was too riveting. "God," she said. "You must have been so scared . . ."

I held out my shaking hand. "Look at me. Hours later, I still am. Anyway, this guy with the gun takes me to this other man, someone they all called Reverend Hannon, and he told them to leave me alone and sent me home. But Kalyn . . ." I had to get it out quickly. Just mentioning his name made her nervous. ". . . who is this guy? He's not like any minister I ever met. Why is he surrounded by men carrying guns? At a church?"

She shook her head vehemently, then reached out and grabbed my arm, pulling me in closer. "Oh, Lord, honey, you've got to be more careful. You came here to get away from trouble, didn't you?" I nodded. "Well, the last thing you want to do is draw their attention to you." Funny how I didn't mind it when she called me "honey." Maybe because she was so seriously concerned for me. "Those guys are trouble with a big T."

I put down my fork. I'd only eaten about half of my breakfast, while she'd cleaned her plate, but I'd lost my appetite. "I don't understand, Kalyn. Why do they care if I'm out taking a walk at night . . ."

"They probably thought you were spying on them. They're . . . what's that word? Para something."

"Paranoid?"

"That's it. They think everyone who isn't one of them is against them. That we're . . . that people are undercover cops or government informers . . . things like that." She shrugged. "My way of dealing with it, I just don't have anything to do with those people and hope they don't know I exist. With people like that, it's best not to ask too many questions. No. Don't ask any questions . . ."

She lowered her voice and leaned in again. "Terrible things happen to people who cross him. He's . . ." She lowered it to a whisper. ". . . one of them."

"One of them?" I asked aloud.

"Shsssh. Are you an idiot? The militia." She glanced around quickly to see if we'd been overheard, then added, "I forgot you're from away. Look, things are really crazy around here. They're everywhere. Nobody knows who is and who isn't, so you can't trust anyone. Just take however you feel about your ex and multiply by a hundred. That's how bad it is." Then, with a trace of a smile, she said, "Except they don't take women, so with women, it's more a question of who's likely to be talking to one of them and who isn't. Us they like barefoot and pregnant." She tossed her head defiantly. "And I don't intend to be either of those . . ."

It wasn't fair to drag her into this when she was so obviously frightened of these people, but I wasn't here to play fair. I thought, despite her professed practice of keeping her head down and her nose clean, that she probably knew a lot about what was going on. While I had her talking, I had two more things I wanted to test. "You worked here long?" I asked.

"Coupla . . . two years, maybe? Seems like a lifetime."

"Did you know Paulette Harding?"

She pushed her plate away and pulled cigarettes out of her pocket. "She was one of the dumbest women I ever met. Thought the whole universe revolved around her, what she did, what she wanted to do. She had no sense . . ." The ponytail swiveled around decisively. "I mean no sense . . . not of what she was getting herself into, nor of what she might be getting other people into. We're all better off now that she's gone . . ."

"Everyone says she's gone, but no one seems to know where she went . . ."

"That's right." She shoved back her chair and stood up. "Something you need to understand, Dora, for your own good. Nobody around here talks about Paulette Harding. You go around asking questions about her and you'll have worse than your ex-husband to worry about. A lot worse."

With that, she walked out the door, letting it slam shut behind her, leaving me to read the bold words between the lines. What little Lyle had told me yesterday was true. If Paulette Harding had left town, it hadn't been of her own volition, and wherever she'd gone, she wasn't coming back. It was one more ugly thought to file away in a mind that was already dripping blood and crawling with spiders. The sharp pain in my stomach wasn't about Paulette Harding, though. It was about people who kill with impunity, and the pathetic hope that Andre was worth more to them alive.

I gave her a minute to light up and inhale that soothing

nicotine, then followed her outside, checking to be sure Clyde had gone back to his stove. "Thanks for the warning." She shrugged. "How do you live with it?"

She shrugged again. "It's like anything else. You put it out of your mind as best you can, and get on with things. What else can we do? If it weren't for them, this would be a really great place." She pointed at her boyfriend's motorcycle, parked next door behind the garage where he worked. "Sometimes, when it really gets to me and I feel all seized up inside, I get Andy to take me for a ride. Someplace really curvy and bumpy and we go real fast. God. It's better than a carnival ride. And then . . . don't know why . . . it settles me right down and I'm okay again."

She gave me an "I dare you" smile. "You want, things get real bad for you, I'll ask Andy to take you for a ride. But I gotta warn you. He's crazy." She said it with pride. Being a crazy man's girlfriend was too cool.

There wasn't time for more questions, even if she'd been inclined to answer them. Theresa appeared in the doorway, wearing one of her more poisonous faces. "Anytime you ladies are inclined to come back to work, we've got a dining room full of hungry people waiting . . ."

With a sigh, Kalyn pitched her butt over the railing and headed back inside. I followed her with a sigh of my own, wondering. Was there a connection between what had happened to Gary Pelletier and Paulette Harding's disappearance? Between her disappearance and Andre? Was there any real possibility that the fish butts had been right and Andre was in a survival shelter? And was there a list of those somewhere in the library? Why would civil-defense records be in the library anyway? Even if they were, were they filed in a way that would make sense to me?

It was hard to have so many questions and no one to ask. But Kalyn had been pretty clear. Go around asking questions and bad things could happen to you. For the time being, though, I had more pressing things to worry about. I put my questions on a mental shelf until after lunch. For now, I was going to be too busy to wonder about anything, except vital stuff, like what kind of bread, did they want it toasted, and would we run out of pie?

CHAPTER *10*

THE MERCHANTVILLE LIBRARY was so diminutive it looked like it had been taken out of Richardson's pocket and snuggled into the little patch of ground between the town hall and the fire station. It was a pretty thing, with its soft brown stone and the curving arch over the door, but didn't look big enough to hold any books, never mind also house a civil-defense office. On the other hand, Merchantville itself wasn't very big, so maybe it didn't need much defense. At least until recently. Now it seemed to me it needed all the help it could get.

A skinny girl with a skimpy ponytail was coming down the steps with a squirming baby in her arms and a toddler pulling on her arm, chanting, "Read, Mommy, read." It made me feel old as the hills. The mother didn't look old enough to be riding her bike off the sidewalk. As I watched, she smiled, dropped down on the steps, and pulled a book out of her bag. Without hesitation, she began reading aloud. As I passed, she was saying, "I do not like them, Sam I Am . . ." I wanted to sit down, too, snuggle up beside her, and listen. Anything to avoid what I was doing. It seemed such a lovely contrast to the raw ugliness of my day.

Inside, the room was dark and cool and had the pleasant, musty, old-book smell of all libraries. A small, round woman with graying dark hair skewered on top of her head peered at me through half-glasses and smiled, pushing back one of the strands that had escaped. "You're the new girl over at Theresa's, aren't you?" she said. "Welcome to the library."

So much for anonymity. I nodded. "I've always loved libraries and this one is especially beautiful."

"Too small," she said. "We're hoping to build an addition. Basement's not accessible for our older patrons and it's too damp anyway. Imagine it. A children's room where we could do story hour. A place where authors could talk, if any were to come and visit us. Enough space for computers and videos and audio books. Not that that's likely to happen anytime soon. The addition, I mean." She smiled. "Was there anything in particular you were interested in?"

"Junk," I said. "I mean, fiction. Light fiction. I'm so tired when I'm done work that my brain's not up to anything else."

"Theresa's a hard woman," she said. I noticed that she didn't add the usual qualification about Theresa's fairness. "I'm Mrs. Wilkerson. Mary Lou Wilkerson." She got up from her chair. "Shall I give you the ten-cent tour?" She didn't wait for an answer but began walking around the room, pointing at various alcoves and shelves. "New books, fiction and nonfiction, are here. They circulate for only two weeks. Other books go out for four. Paperbacks. They don't hold up well, but the patrons like them. Here are our audio books. Quite a good selection, really. We have a summer resident who buys a stack of them before she comes up every year and then donates them when she leaves . . ."

Behind us the door opened and shut, and heavy footsteps crossed the floor. "Going down to the office for a few minutes, Mary Lou," a man said.

"Be my guest, Bump," she said. "You have the key?"

He patted his pocket and there was a jingle. "Right in here," he said cheerfully.

" 'Cuz if you didn't, I've got half a dozen of them in my desk drawer."

"Save 'em for the forgetful old f . . . old duffers. Who's that with you?" He thumped across the floor toward us. Bump Peters, my favorite member of the group Theresa called "the fish butts." Not a very big man but his feet sounded like they were made of lead. "Oh, hello, honey. Glad to see you found our library. Oh, heck . . ." He smote himself in the forehead with the palm of his hand. "Sorry. My daughter Edith says I'm not supposed to call women honey anymore." He squinted at me, as if assessing whether I was offended. "Guess I don't know what else to call you, come to think of it. Theresa's new girl doesn't sound much better than honey, now, does it?"

"Dora," I said, holding out my hand. "Dora McKusick."

"Bump Peters," he said, grabbing it and working it like a pump handle. "Well, good to see you. Got to get to work." He dropped my hand, saluted Mary Lou with the edge of his hand, and thumped away toward the stairs.

We stood together and watched him go. "Man's got feet like an elephant," she said. "Guess he never could sneak up on anybody, could he? Which brings us to the mystery section. I used to shelve them with all the rest of the fiction but we've got so many mystery readers I finally decided to make life easy for them. Our patrons read more mystery than any other type of fiction. You read mysteries?"

I nodded. Actually, I didn't read much of anything, though I loved books. By the time my work days were over, I'd curl up with a book and fall asleep almost immediately. You don't get through many books in a year that way. I'd done a little better since I'd found audio books. Here in Merchantville, I hadn't even bothered with a book. But I wasn't about to tell Mary Lou Wilkerson that. I could tell but the way her fingers lingered over the bindings as she straightened errant books that she was a dedicated bookwoman and this place was her pride and joy. "What do you recommend?"

She hummed a little under her breath as her fingers skimmed along the shelf, touching, rejecting, touching another. She turned and looked at me thoughtfully. "It's hard to guess someone else's taste, so I'm going to give you three of the best. Laura Lippman. S. J. Rozan. Michael Connelly." She pulled out the books and handed them to me.

"I don't have a library card," I said.

"Not a problem. I know where you live and where you work. And you have an honest face."

Everyone in town seemed to know where I lived and worked. Too bad more of them didn't think I had an honest face. I took the books with a murmur of thanks and followed her over to the desk, where we went through the ceremony of obtaining a library card and checking out the books. It impressed me almost as much it had when I was a kid. A small rectangle of cardboard, now plastic, that was the key to this whole kingdom. But I still needed to get into the basement and had no idea how to do it.

"Is there a ladies' room here?"

"It's unisex, I'm afraid, the library being so small. Downstairs in the basement." She opened her desk drawer, fished though a pile of keys, and handed me one with a big wooden clothespin attached. "Keeps people from accidentally putting it in their pocket." She pointed toward the stairs. "Just go down there and it's at the end of the hall on the right. I'm going to run across the street and grab a soda. This heat's too much for me. If I'm not back, stick it in the drawer when you're done." She picked up her purse and walked out. Totally trusting, leaving me behind with a grateful, pounding heart, an honest face, and a larcenous mind.

As soon as the heavy door had shut behind her, I went behind the desk, opened the drawer, and looked in at the mess of keys. There were five that looked identical with little red DODGE dealer key tags on them. I helped myself to one of them, slipped it into my pocket, and headed for the stairs, leaving my books behind on the desk. At the bottom of the stairs, I hesitated, wondering how long Bump Peters planned to be in the office. He answered my question by coming out at that moment and shutting the door behind him. He checked it to see that it was locked, patted his pocket to be sure he had the key, and headed toward me, whistling.

As we passed, he grinned ruefully and jerked his head toward the door he'd just closed. "Couple of us check the office regularly and sign the log book. For years there wasn't a lot of civil-defense business, but now with this terrorist stuff, we're paying attention. Come hell or high water, we'll be ready for it, and high water's always a possibility. Hell, too, I suppose." He paused, pleased with his own wit. "Still, be a damned . . . darn . . . sight better if they'd concentrate on these Arabs and leave good people alone. See you over to Theresa's." He sketched a salute like he'd given Mary Lou, and thumped away up the stairs, dapper and cheerful from his retired navy cap that had U.S.S. something on it in gold letters to his neatly trimmed white mustache and his thundering white topsider-clad feet.

I waited until I heard the door shut, then tried my key. It went into the lock smoothly enough but then it didn't want to turn. I had to grab the handle and pull the door toward me before the tumblers reluctantly exerted themselves and allowed the door to be opened. I closed the door carefully behind me and looked around. It was a surprisingly large room with a lot of mysterious equipment, desks, many telephones, a computer, copy machine, fax machine, shelves with rows of thick notebooks, and a bank of sturdy file cabinets. An open notebook I took to be the log book lay open on one of the desks. I had no idea where to begin and I didn't have much time.

I checked the log book first. It appeared that the same two or three people were in and out of here on a regular basis. Bump Peters. Someone named Kendall Barker. And Col. Stuart Hannon. Colonel. Why was I not surprised? And why did my untrusting soul suspect he hadn't earned that title in the military? A shiver ran down my spine. They were everywhere, weren't they?

I grabbed the first notebook off the shelves and opened it. Nothing that looked useful. An evacuation plan. I checked another. A hazardous-materials response plan under Public Law 99-499. Another was a log of operational tests on an automatic-starting diesel generator. Checked a few more, trying to skim through the books while looking over my shoulder and listening for footsteps. Maybe I should check the filing cabinets. I opened the first drawer, running my eyes over the file tabs. Nothing. Second drawer. Nothing. Third drawer. Nothing.

Footsteps rumbled overhead but I didn't hear anyone on the stairs. Maybe it was Mary Lou coming back. I was going to have to think up some plausible excuse for such a long visit to the restroom. I pulled out the fourth drawer. Pulled too hard. It came flying at me, halting with a metallic thunk when it reached the end of its runners. Hastily, I studied the labels. Nothing. Nothing. Nothing. Nothing! Dammit. Didn't it have to be here somewhere? I was approaching cardiac arrest.

Outside I heard footsteps on the stairs and then coming down the hall, and a voice—Mary Lou's voice—calling "Dora?" Past my door and down to where the bathroom would be. Knocking on the door and calling, "Dora?" again. Then they came back down the hall and went back up the stairs.

I reminded myself to breathe and pulled out the drawer again, more quietly this time. And finally found it. A file labeled "Shelter Census." About thirty pages, in no particular order, giving locations, sizes, basic equipment, and food and water stocks for shelters in the area. I didn't have the time or the information to do an inventory. And I didn't dare simply steal the file. Cautiously, I rose to my feet and went and turned on the copying machine. It was one of those old, portable models that take a few minutes to warm up. I cursed myself for not thinking of this sooner.

I checked the paper supply and began making copies. It moved as slowly as molasses. In a real emergency, it would have been a useless piece of equipment. A good citizen would have left a note, telling them to replace it. But I was not that good a citizen. Or that big a fool. "Come on, you idiotic machine," I whispered. "Hurry it up. We're almost out of time." The machine continued its clickety-clacking back and forth motion, complete with flashing lights, as it slowly spat out the precious pages. I was about three pages from the end when, in a lull, I heard footsteps come down the hall and stop outside the door.

Quick as a wink, I snatched the copies out of the machine,

hit the off button, and replaced the file. Then I shoved the drawer shut and looked for someplace to hide. A more experienced spy would have thought of the hiding place first, but I was new at this. If I had my way, this would be my first, and last, break-in into a government office. My last summer by a peaceful Maine lake. My last stint as a waitress. And hopefully not because I was going to meet a bad end.

There was a small space between two filing cabinets that held a coatrack upon which rested several voluminous black raincoats. I slid the coatrack forward, squeezed in behind it, and crouched there, wedged halfway between standing and sitting, trying to keep from gasping from stirred-up dust and fear. I had strong thigh muscles but profoundly hoped that whoever it was didn't plan on a long visit. They were already trembling and I was getting a cramp under the arch of one foot. I gritted my teeth, stifled a groan, and willed the muscles to relax. Felt the papers in my hands beginning to slip and clamped my fingers more tightly together.

Keys jingled as the door opened. I sensed him standing for a moment in the doorway, surveying the room the way I had, and then footsteps came toward me. Everything seemed amplified—the crunch of gravel from his shoes, the slight whistling sound his breath made, the jangle of keys as he set them on the desk. I smelled fabric softener, bug spray, and aftershave. There was a sound that I thought was a notebook being pulled off the shelf, the slap of the cardboard cover against the desk, and then footsteps walking across the room. A door came open with the slight reverberation of a hollow-core door when it sticks, and then the click of a light switch.

I heard a grunt of satisfaction, returning footsteps, and the click of a pen. Some scratching noises as information was entered in a notebook. The cover snapped shut. The book shoved back on a shelf, and the jangle of keys being picked up. Footsteps heading for the door, hesitating, returning. He had to be able to hear my heart. Everyone in Merchantville must be able to hear my heart. He shoved the coatrack back into its space between the filing cabinets, knocking me suddenly into the wall.

A protruding peg caught me squarely in the nose. A coat button on a swinging sleeve hit me in the eye, causing intense pain and tears. Blood began to pour from my nose. My hands were full of papers. I had to let it bleed.

"There," he said. "Everything as it should be." He left, closing the door firmly behind him.

I dropped the papers, fumbled a tissue from my pocket, and pressed it against my aching nose. Goddamned prissy Stuart Hannon. I was going to shoot him. I was. I hated getting hit in the nose. It was worse than anything. It hurt so much!

As quietly as I could, working with one hand, I moved the rack, crept out of my hiding place, and started cleaning up. I stuck the papers I'd copied into my purse, including the last three, which I hadn't had a chance to copy and hadn't returned to the files. What were the chances anyone would ever notice? I wiped the scattered drops of blood off the floor. Anything else? Just to be sure, I checked the copy machine, and it was a good thing I had. I'd left the last page I copied inside. They say God looks after fools, drunkards, and the United States. I hoped it was true.

As I left the room, closing the door behind me, I realized that this nosebleed was actually a boon and not a bane. That my cloud had a silver lining. Now I had an explanation to give Mary Lou Wilkerson about my marathon stint in the bathroom. And why I hadn't answered. I hurried down the hall, let myself in, determined that yes, indeed, there was a chair in there, in which I could claim to have been sitting. I checked the mirror. Not just blood, but streaks of black grime. These guys might be able to prepare for and manage an emergency, but none of them could dust. I washed the blood off my hands and face—there was nothing I could do about my clothes—and went upstairs, a paper towel pressed against my nose.

With my free hand, I dropped the key back on Mary Lou's desk and scooped up my books. "Sorry I was so long," I said. "My nose started bleeding all of a sudden and I couldn't get it to stop. When you knocked on the door, it was gushing so much I was afraid I'd choke if I tried to speak."

She pulled open the drawer, deposited the key, and from another drawer got out a fistful of tissues. "Here. These are better than that paper towel." I dropped the towel in the trash and replaced it with the tissues. Much nicer on my poor wounded nose. "My son used to have nosebleeds," she said. "I used to think it was allergies. You have allergies?"

I started to shake my head, thought better of it, and used words instead. "Not that I know of. These just happen sometimes. Not often. I hope it stops soon, though. I've got to get back to work."

"And Theresa's *so* understanding. Well, you go back and lie down for a while, and I'm sure you'll be fine." She came out from behind the desk. "I'll just get the door for you, shall I?" She followed me across the room and held the door as I exited into the blinding sunshine. "Hope you like those books."

I climbed into the car, set the books on the seat, and just sat there, my head tipped back, waiting for the bleeding to stop. It must have been over a hundred in there but I was shaking like a leaf. I was getting too old for this nonsense. As soon as I got Andre back, I was going to do what everyone wanted—retire from dangerous pursuits and take up knitting baby blankets. At least I'd have something to show for that besides ulcers and lines in my face, and it wouldn't take years off my life.

I was dying to look at the papers I'd copied. But not here, and not back in my room. I drove slowly down the main street, past Theresa's, and parked in the lot of the little market. Then I pulled them out and began to read through them. It was no use. I had lots and lots of information, including names and addresses, but I didn't know my way around, so what good was it? I needed a local map. And I needed a good place to hide these damned papers. I didn't dare leave them in my room, and they didn't seem much safer here in the car, not with a thousand eyes watching me all the time.

Then I remembered. When he gave me the car, Dom had showed me some of its little tricks, like the hidden radio. And like the secret compartment built under the passenger seat. Press a button that was hidden under the edge of the carpet, and a drawer folded down. Press the button again, and the drawer disappeared. Nifty. At the time I had thought it was silly and wondered what on earth it was for. Now I knew. It was for these papers, and other papers I might acquire. And for my gun. My sweet little pearl-handled Barbie special.

I fumbled around until I found the button, checking to see if it worked. The store had a big sign in the window that said COPIES 5 CENTS. I was planning to stow the papers away as soon as I'd made copies. Time was short. I'd only had an hour to start with. I grabbed my purse, hurried inside, and asked the girl behind the counter where the copy machine was. She pointed toward the back corner. "By the ice cream," she said, "if it's workin'." At the back of the store I found it, another one of the slowest machines in creation, but at least it did make copies. It reminded me of the one at work, the one my secretary, Sarah, finally threatened to push out the second-story window if I didn't replace it. This one was about ready to go for a swim.

Stately and ponderous, it rolled back and forth, making faint black slimy copies. I kept looking over my shoulder, afraid that at any second Stuart Hannon or one of his brutish entourage would appear and my goose would, as they say, be cooked. Just as the machine spat out the last copy and I'd shoved it in my purse, my fearful prophecy was fulfilled in the form of Roy Belcher, swaggering down the aisle with a basket loaded with beer and junk food.

"Hey, Dora. I didn't know they ever let you out of that place." He leaned back from the waist, parking the basket on one cocked hip, his free thumb stuck casually through one of his belt loops. It looked like something he'd practiced in front of a mirror. Too bad the effect was spoiled by that jutting expanse of gut. He gave me his usual rude inspection, his eyes coming to rest on the blood on my shirt, then rising to my nose. "What happened to you? Get in a fight?"

Yeah, I killed Stuart Hannon, I thought. Aloud, I said, "Nosebleed. I get them sometimes."

He nodded. "You workin' tonight?"

"My third meal today. And my feet are already killing me."

"Yeah," he said, "that Theresa's something, ain't she?"

Everyone is something, I thought. And then, *hey, that would make a good title for a children's book. Maybe that could be my new career. It had to be better than this.* "I should get going," I said. "She'll kill me if I'm late." People around here were like that, killing at the slightest provocation. I picked up the basket I'd set beside the machine and did a little rapid shopping. A bottle of cold lemonade. A box of tissues, the extra-soft variety with lotion. A small container of detergent to wash the blood out of my shirt. And a copy of the Maine Guide and Atlas, with maps showing every little highway and byway. A large envelope to mail the shelter census sheets to Jack Leonard.

Roy was still in line as I left but he called after me, "Hey, maybe I'll see you later." I smiled and waved and left. Smiling hurt my face. My nose felt swollen and ugly. He came out of the door just as I was leaving the lot, and got into a battered old van. I was surprised that it wasn't a pickup truck. That's what guys drove, and Roy was a real "guy."

I stopped at the post office and mailed the copies to Jack. Probably a careless move. No doubt the postmaster and all the clerks, despite their good, secure government jobs, were rabid antigovernment militia members as well. Unfortunately, I didn't think of that until I'd handed the envelope to the clerk, too late to get it back without calling attention to it. What else could I do? I didn't know when I'd get another contact person, or how Jack would let me know. Maybe tomorrow, on my morning off, I'd call, let him know this was coming and see how he wanted me to pass future information. Sighing, I turned and trudged out on tired feet. It was time to go to work.

CHAPTER 11

I SLEPT BADLY and woke with the birds, cranky, aching, and ready to strangle every chirping one of them. I was starving, unable to remember whether I'd ever gotten dinner last night, and unsure whether I could go downstairs and get breakfast when I wasn't working. Discretion seemed the better part of valor—if I appeared in the kitchen, they might put me to work—so I ate a half-melted Slim-Fast bar, not so nasty and chemical as some, and walked to a convenience store where I got some orange juice. Then, fortified, I drove to Mary Harding's house and knocked boldly on the front door.

If it was possible, she looked even worse than the last time. Probably worn down from the heat as well as all her other troubles. She stood in the doorway, staring at me with dull eyes, and I wasn't sure whether she was holding the door open or the door was holding her up. After a minute, she shook herself and managed a faint smile. "Yes?"

"Mrs. Harding? I don't know if you remember me . . ."

"The girl from Theresa's. You brought Lyle home."

"Yes. And when I did, he asked me if I had a car, and when I said yes, he asked if I could take him to see his father . . ."

"He never should have done that."

"He's just a child, Mrs. Harding. He misses his father. I know this is probably very presumptuous of me. You don't know me from Adam, but I've heard from the people at the restaurant about Lyle and his dad. How close they are. And I thought, since I don't have to work until dinner today . . . that maybe I could take him to see his father? If you'd let him go with me, I mean."

Mary Harding gave a decisive shake of her head. "No. I'm afraid not. It's kind of you to offer but we don't take favors from strangers." She began to close the door in my face.

Behind her, I heard a wail, and then Lyle's voice. "Grandma! She wants to take me to see Daddy. Why won't you let her? Nobody else will take me. He must be very sad so far away from us. And lonely. Daddy gets lonely. Sometimes he cries. I've seen him cry, Grandma . . ." The boy's voice was insistent and im-passioned, the way kids were when they sighted on something and wouldn't let go. "He cried when Mom left and when I walked a little and when those men came. I bet he's down there now, crying because we don't come see him. Grandma. Please! Please! Let me go. It's all my fault he's in jail anyways."

"It's not your fault." Mary Harding sighed. "Lyle, you stop nagging at me. The Harding family isn't so bad off we need to take charity from strangers, you hear me? I'll get you down there to see your daddy just as soon as I can."

"But you can get me down there today, Grandma. She said so. That woman. Dora. She's a waitress just like Mindy. And she's nice like her, too."

I felt like a voyeur, standing there on the porch, but I lin-gered, just in case she changed her mind.

"She's a stranger, Lyle."

"You let me go with that man named Roy because he said he was a friend of Daddy's, and we didn't know him."

"That's different. He's a neighbor. He lives right here in town . . ."

"So does Dora. She lives upstairs over the restaurant."

"You make me tired with all that arguing," she said.

"If you let me go with Dora, you can go back to bed and sleep all morning."

"Since when did I ever sleep all morning? I've got chores to do. Laundry, cleaning, grocery shopping . . ."

"Then you'll let me go?"

"I never said . . ."

"But you'll get so much done without me around being a nuisance."

"You're never much of a nuisance . . ." There was a lot of love in her voice. ". . . except when you keep nagging at me like this."

"She's still waiting out there on the porch, Grandma. Open the door and tell her it's okay."

Mary Harding pulled the door open again, staring dubiously up at me. "I don't know about this," she said, hesitantly.

"I don't blame you a bit, Mrs. Harding. You don't know me. But you can set any conditions you want, and give me any instructions. You can even come with us, if it would ease your mind. I kind of thought you might like the break . . ."

She sighed and pulled the door wider. "Come on in," she said. "You want some coffee?"

Lyle chattered at me merrily for the first twenty minutes, stared out the window for the next ten, giving me a running commentary on everything we passed. When he went quiet, I looked in the rearview mirror. He'd fallen asleep in that sudden, boneless way small children have, his bright head bobbing gently on the worn upholstery. I took advantage of the moment to call Roland Proffit and ask if he could meet me. He suggested a small shopping center up the road from the jail, and we agreed on a time. He didn't tell me he disapproved of what I was doing, and I didn't ask. Tone of voice was enough.

After twenty minutes with Lyle and his father, I was ready to join the "Free Jed Harding movement." It wasn't because of anything he'd said. Harding was a man of few words, at least to me. It was because of the way he was with his son. The way his face lit up when he first saw Lyle, the gentle way he gathered the boy out of the wheelchair and onto his lap. It was the way he listened and heard and responded to Lyle's eager babbling. It was the way he looked at his son with tears in his eyes. He ignored me, after a first polite nod, not because I mattered so little, but because his son mattered so much.

I knew this was a man who had threatened a veteran's hospital worker with a loaded gun. If I'd read an account of it in the paper, I would have wanted him arrested and taken off the street, but watching Jed Harding with his son, I was sure the threatened man had deserved it. Life had driven Jed Harding to his limit. What he had done was wrong. I'd been at the barrel end of a gun and knew how terrifying it could be. Maybe he needed some counseling, but he didn't belong in jail.

Then again, perhaps I was being influenced by my own incipient parenthood. Two years ago, I hadn't had more than a passing interest in children. Then my partner, Suzanne, had had a baby, and taken to dropping him into my lap at odd moments. "Feeding your baby lust," she'd said. "Those of us with stretch marks and sleepless nights can't bear it that the rest of the world isn't with us." At first, it had just been rather pleasant, holding her baby. Then one day, I found myself nuzzling his head and wondering what it might be like to have one of my own.

About that same time, Andre had started showing an increased interest in children himself. He'd begun talking about our wild brown girls and willful boys. That had scared me to death. I preferred the Andre who fretted over his sister Aimee's seeming inability to control her reproduction to the one who talked with shining eyes about making me pregnant. But there is something immensely sexy and profoundly moving when a man who loves you wants you to have his child. At least for me. And then fate, or chance, had intervened and planned it for us.

Right now, I could see I was a third wheel. I stood and picked up my purse. "Why don't I leave you two alone for a while and go run some errands."

Harding gave me a quick smile over his son's head, and nodded. "Sure. If you don't mind. Take your time."

On my way out, I asked the guard if there was a limit on how long the visit could be. "Usually," he said. "But with this guy . . . if we can't let him go . . . the least we can do is give him some time with his kid."

"Right. If they ask for me, I'll be back soon." I rushed to my car, and drove up the street to a little shopping mall, where I bought myself some shorts with elastic waists, a voluminous sundress, and a couple of loose tops. All my clothes were getting too tight. It seemed too soon, but Suzanne said every pregnancy was different. Mine looked to be the elephantine variety. At this rate, by the time I delivered I'd be as big around as I was tall. And that would be substantial.

Thinking about the long drive home, I popped into a grocery store and got a pack of juice boxes, a bottle of water, two apples, and some oatmeal cookies. I passed up the beckoning candy bars and bags of chips. This baby of mine was going to be made with good ingredients. I also got a coloring book, a drawing pad, and a package of markers for Lyle. I wanted some time to talk to his dad.

When I came out, Roland was leaning against my car, arms folded. In the wilting heat, he looked freshly pressed and formidable. I don't know what it is about uniforms. They make some guys look so great. Roland was one of them, his cop attitude unaffected by the fact that he was holding a gaudy pink-and-gold Victoria's Secret shopping bag.

"How's Kavanaugh?" I asked.

He smiled. "Why did I know that would be your first question?"

His crisp affect made me feel more dowdy and disheveled than ever. Fat, unlovely, and ineffectual. Maybe it was the heat. "Because I feel responsible." I sagged against the car beside him, even though the sunbaked metal burned right through my clothes.

"Uh huh. You're not. That could have happened any time, any place." I didn't argue, because it was true. The potential for sudden, unexpected danger is one of the dark undercurrents in a cop's life. I still felt guilty. "She's fine. We've made out that it's worse than it is. Doesn't look too good for a cop who shot to kill to walk away with not much more than a scratch . . ."

Macho guys. Macho gals. I didn't believe him. "A scratch, Roland?"

"She was wearing a vest. Well, yeah, it's more than a scratch. It's a gouge and a cracked rib. It's not pretty and it will leave a scar . . ." He adjusted the tilt of his hat and looked away. Tough guy that he was, that they all were, and schooled though they might be in nonsexist attitudes, it was hard to have a sister trooper get shot. And it was hard to have a pretty woman left with a scar. "Bullet caught the edge of the vest, which slowed it down, but didn't quite stop it. The angle was a problem. Trouble with vests is that they don't fit women so well. Still . . ."

He held out the shopping bag. "Jack wants you to wear this."

I took the bag, peered in, and fingered the heavy navy-blue vest. I looked down at my sleeveless blouse. "It's ninety degrees, Roland."

He thumped his chest. "I'm wearing one."

I thumped his chest, too. "Man of steel," I said. He swung a fist toward my chest, stopping well short of the mark. A modest guy. "When am I supposed to wear it?"

"Use your judgment."

A bulletproof vest. My own handgun. A dingy room in a town so full of menace the air almost shimmered with it. Nothing in my life held even a shred of normalcy anymore. I gripped the bag with both hands and stared at Roland. "I feel like I have less of that every day."

"I don't like to hear things like that." There was a protective growl in his voice.

I was afraid he'd report my lapse to Jack Leonard as evidence that I was losing my nerve, so I changed the subject. "Heard any good moose stories lately?" Roland collects moose stories.

"Haven't heard *anything* good lately," he said grimly.

"Kavanaugh's not dead." I pulled out the list of license numbers. "I don't know if this is worth anything, but these are some of the plate numbers from the guys who were at a militia meeting two nights ago. After midnight. In the church basement."

He took it gingerly between two fingers and did not show the appreciation I'd hoped for. "Jack's gonna be pissed."

My disappointment was tempered by reality. Had I really

expected him to be proud of me, when I wasn't even sure I was proud of me? Getting this stuff had been an accident, and even then, it had scared the pants off me. Besides, Jack wanted me to stay home and dust the ferns and Roland was Jack's man. There wasn't anything I could do, short of leaving, that would please Jack. "So don't tell him. Or tell him you got it from a high whitehorse souse. Or from the Bard of Bored Overseers. I don't care. But when you get the list, I'd like a copy."

"Jack's gonna . . ."

I grabbed his wrist. "Roland. Goddammit! This is my life . . ." He gave me a look, pure cop attitude, and I dropped my hand, shaken. He didn't usually do that. Usually he was my friend. But a threat to one cop intensified the "us vs. them" in the rest, and I, alas, was them. Sort of. Enough to have forgotten you don't grab a cop. Maybe I was too judgment impaired for this job.

"What church?" he asked.

I shrugged. "I don't know the name. It's the one on the opposite corner, down the street from the restaurant. Corner of the street Harding's house is on."

He shoved the list into a pocket and raised a hand to his hat, cool, crisp, and inscrutable. "Yes, ma'am. Catch you later."

"Roland, wait . . ." He paused, a wary expression on his face. "Norah Kavanaugh was my contact. What am I supposed to do now?"

What he wanted to say was on his face and in his eyes—get the hell out of there—but he didn't say it. All he said was, "We'll be in touch."

"How the heck . . ." But he just shrugged and turned away. The trouble was, I reminded him too graphically of their failure to find Andre. And seeing him reminded me that I wasn't doing much better.

"You really wanna help?" he said.

Here it comes, I thought. He's finally going to say it—stay home and stay safe. But he didn't. Instead, he said, "See if you can get Harding to tell you why he doesn't want to be let outta there. Or . . ." He hesitated before he said it, so this was the real inside stuff. "See if he knows what happened to his wife, Paulette . . ."

"She left town," I said.

His eyebrows arched. "Oh, really? In a box, a barrel, or a bag?"

Shoot, I thought. There wasn't any aspect of this that wasn't a can of worms, was there? Because I knew Roland wasn't just trying to scare me. He was observant enough to know I was already scared silly. "What do you know?" I demanded.

"Know?" he said bitterly. "Next to nothing. But what we suspect is that the woman who called Pelletier was Paulette Harding. And both Paulette and her roommate, Mindy Parsons, have disappeared."

It was hot enough to fry eggs on the sidewalk, yet I felt chilled to the bone. *Never let 'em see you cry,* I thought. *Never let 'em see you're shaken. Not even your friends.* I'd gone into this thing knowing it was ugly, but I was just a citizen. I could still be shocked at how it kept getting uglier. I swallowed. Tried for levity. "Yeah. Okay. I'll see what I can find out without asking any questions. Tell Jack to let me know when he wants to meet again. He can leave a message in the hollow oak or something." He nodded but I could see he didn't get the lit ref. He didn't grow up reading Nancy Drew.

I put my shopping, including Jack's latest gift, in the trunk. A bulletproof vest in a lingerie bag. Looked like Jack hadn't completely lost his sense of humor, either. Or his sense of the absurd. That was more like it. There is little in the world less sexy than a bulletproof vest. More like a straitjacket and about as comfortable. At least it wasn't pink.

Back at the jail, I got into the visitor's room so easily it was scary. The place wasn't heavily guarded. Didn't they know there was a rampaging militia out there threatening to storm the joint? Maybe not. Everyone was going around like it was just another peaceful summer day. But it's like so many things, until you hear about it, it doesn't exist, and then, suddenly, it's everywhere. Less than a week in Merchantville, and I'd become totally paranoid.

I saw danger lurking behind every rock, a potential threat behind the wheel of every pickup truck.

As long as he could be in the same room, Lyle was happy to settle down and draw, expressing delight over the variety of colors and the marker's paintbrush tips. I pulled up a chair and tried to make conversation with his father. It wasn't easy. Jed Harding had no small talk.

He was a slight, wiry man with graying blond hair pulled back in a ponytail. His face was deeply lined. I knew he'd suffered a lot from his Agent Orange exposure, and the story of it was right there, etched in deeply around his eyes and mouth and in the gaunt hollows beneath his prominent cheekbones. He wore the defeated look of a man who was trying not to let life get him down but who'd been punched one too many times to have much faith left anymore. He still had an outdoorsman's leathery tan, but there were smudges under his eyes, and, like his mother, he looked utterly worn out. I was torn between competing desires: to feed him hearty soup, and to tuck him under my arm and run out of there.

"I hope you don't mind my bringing Lyle down. It was a bit forward, with you not knowing me, but he asked and I had the time . . ." I didn't know what else to say. In the silence, there was nothing but the squeak of markers. "Lyle's kind of . . . I don't know . . . hard to resist."

"You're the new girl over to Theresa's?" he asked. I nodded. "He likes going over there. Drives Theresa nuts. He took a shine to one of the other waitresses. Girl named Mindy. Paulette's roommate. She used to baby-sit for him sometimes." He hesitated, then added, "His momma used to work there."

"Your wife," I said.

Jed Harding stared out the window, not nonchalant but tense, the muscles in his neck taut. He hesitated, his eyes shifting briefly to the boy, and then back to the window, where they stayed, before he nodded. "She run off. Town was too small for her." He swallowed and ducked his head. A bad liar.

"Won't she come back now, with what's happened? You in jail and Lyle needing someone to care for him?" I asked.

He shook his head and I waited, eager for what he'd say, but all he said was a flat, "That ain't gonna happen." I couldn't ask why not without being too pushy.

"Good of you to bring the boy down. I miss him something fierce." He reached out and tousled Lyle's hair. "He's a good boy. How'd you meet him? He come around bothering you at the restaurant? I wouldn't of thought my momma would let him do that."

I shook my head. "She didn't. I found him in a ditch at the back of the parking lot. He'd run away from home, trying to come see you."

His hands were clasped on the table in front on him and when I said this, the knuckles went white. "Rough on him. Boy loves his daddy," he said simply. "Hard to figure, with me being such a hotheaded jerk and all."

"Everyone is trying to get you out, you know," I said.

He nodded. "I heard."

"And you know about the cop they've taken?"

Another nod. "Yup. Got a state cop in here 'bout once an hour, wanting to know am I a part of that. Who's in the militia? Who's behind this? Asking where are they keeping this fella they took. Telling me things'll go easier on me if I cooperate." He shrugged. "I told 'em. I'm no part of it. The kidnapping. I don't hold with that sort of thing. And, the way militia's organized, I don't know who's in charge. I don't think they believe me, though. Can't tell 'em who did it if I don't know, can I?" He said it to the table, not to me.

I was sure what he said was part of the truth. I'd done my reading about militias. Knew about the philosophy of organizing in small cells for protection. It was also part untruth. I'd seen that meeting at the church. Maybe they didn't know the command structure, but the players knew each other. Still, he had his reasons for not helping the police. Jed Harding had been part of the militia. He could disapprove of what they'd done in this case and still not want to rat out his buddies. Maybe it went deeper than that. He couldn't rat out his buddies and expect to survive once he got out of here, and he had a child to take care of. A child who was still out there and vulnerable.

"Cops don't believe me when I tell 'em this, but the militia, they didn't entirely trust me, know what I mean?" He tapped his temple. "Got somethin' wrong in my head."

"There's a lot of support for you in Merchantville. Talk about maybe taking some more steps . . ."

"Oh, Jesus, no!" he burst out. "I lost my head, that's all. I never meant for it to come to this . . ." Lyle looked up in surprise, noted that his father was okay, and went back to coloring.

I was supposed to be subtle. Just a casual visitor conveying his son, chatting for a few minutes before heading back north. I'd already talked too much; asked too many questions. But I couldn't hold it in. I asked the one question I needed answered. "You know these men. Do you think, even if they let you go, that the militia will release that cop?"

He shook his head. "How could they?" he said.

"They're not going to trade you without seeing him."

"Don't want to be traded," he said, abruptly. "Never asked to be."

"What?"

"I don't want 'em to let me out of here. I keep telling 'em that. Nobody seems to listen."

This was what Roland wanted to know. "But why?"

"They keep asking me that, too. I can't answer them, though."

I knew I should shut up, but I didn't. "They'd probably give you bail if you promised not to go after that man at the VA." He shrugged. "And then they've got no reason to hold that cop . . ."

He shrugged again. "I'm in, I'm out, it makes no difference about that cop, once they took him . . ."

He was pulling away from me, drawing in. I took a chance and asked one more question. "Mr. Harding . . . I don't understand. Your mother is elderly and in poor health and she really needs your help. If you can get out, why won't you?"

He shook his head, a stubborn set to his jaw, and cast a fearful look at the boy. "No more questions," he said. "Hell, honey, you're starting to be as bad as them."

Honey bit her lip and choked back her words. There were a hundred follow-up questions I wanted to ask but I could tell from the look on his face that he wouldn't answer any of them. If I persisted, I'd blow any chance remaining that he thought I was just a nice girl who was a bit too curious. I looked at my watch. We had to get going if I was going to be back in time for dinner. It didn't seem like I'd accomplished much, other than learning how adamant he was that he didn't want to be let out. And that the vanished Mindy had been Paulette's roommate. Maybe another time he'd talk to me. Not too likely, though. Jed Harding meant to keep things to himself. I'd been lucky to have as much conversation as I'd had.

It wasn't very satisfying to drive an hour and a half each way to hear his laconic opinion that Andre was unlikely to survive this. Only a masochist like me will drive for hours to be punched in the stomach. I stood up. "I'm sorry. We've got to be getting back. I have to work tonight. Maybe I can bring him down again, if I ever get another morning off."

"That Theresa sure does work 'em hard. Fair woman, though. Her girls make good money."

"That's what everyone says. Lyle, give your daddy a hug good-bye."

"Wait," Harding said. "How's my momma doing?"

He wanted me to say something reassuring, I knew. And I could have. But I was feeling a little mean. Discouraged by what he'd said about Andre. About the whole visit. "Not very well," I said. "She's pretty worn out."

He sighed without speaking, then turned and took Lyle in his arms. It was a long hug that made me feel like weeping. My tears were close to the surface these days anyhow. I packed up the markers and the coloring book and drawing pad. On the top was a picture Lyle had drawn of himself in his wheelchair, with Lyle crudely printed, sporting a backward E. "Don't you think your daddy would like to have this?" He nodded. I tore out the picture and handed it to Harding. "Some artwork for your cell. Until next time."

He stood up, slow and unsteady as a much older man, and took a step toward me. For the first time, I noticed his limp. I held out my hand to say good-bye. He captured it between both of his and held it there, looking at me from serious gray eyes. "Anyone asks, you say I'm doing fine. You say I had a great visit with Lyle and I'm fine. You're a real good person, Dora, for doin' this," he said. "You take care of yourself." He bent to settle his son in the chair.

Sometimes, when my lesser nature doesn't get the upper hand, I try, I thought, as I turned swiftly away so he wouldn't see my tears. I gripped the handles of the wheelchair. "Okay, Lyle. Here we go. I've got some apples and cookies in the car."

"Anything to drink?"

"Juice boxes."

"What kind?"

"You have a choice. Apple or fruit punch."

"Okay."

"You're supposed to say 'thank you,' " his father reminded him.

Lyle gave me one of his endearing smiles. "Thank you, Dora."

He ate three cookies and an apple, drank a box of juice, and fell asleep clutching the pillow his grandmother had insisted he take. I wished I could nap, too. I was so tired. Tired and discouraged and wondering why I was doing all this. Worried for Andre, a worry that keyed up a notch as I noticed how many places people had spray-painted "Free Jed Harding" on billboards, barns, rocks, and road signs. Lyle woke up cheerful when we got to his house, gave me a hug and a cookie-crumb kiss, and immediately started drawing again, with the "great new drawing things Dora got me."

I must have looked as tired as I felt, as tired as we all felt, because Mary Harding studied my face when I tried to say good-bye and then put a thin, dry hand on my arm. "Excuse me, I keep forgetting my manners. I've got some iced tea and sandwiches. Before you rush off to work again, come on in the kitchen and tell me about my son."

CHAPTER *12*

MARY HARDING'S KITCHEN was clean and spare, a bare-bones, worn-out place that matched its occupant. The windows were open but no breeze came through. It was that kind of day. Stagnant and stultifying. The kind where I almost wished I didn't have too much pride to lie down in a shady patch and pant like a dog. Pregnancy seemed to have raised my body temperature or diminished my ability to cope. Something was different. I felt flattened by the summer heat in a way I never had before. The air felt like I could clasp it in my hands and wring it out and the damp had made my always difficult hair impossible. I looked like Medusa.

Despite my offer to help, she motioned for me to sit, then got out a pitcher of tea and a plate of sandwiches, set places for the two of us, and lowered herself wearily into her chair. She rested her hands in her lap for a moment, shoulders hunched, eyes shut, summoning the energy to continue. "Lyle can eat something later," she said. "I was hoping we could talk alone." She gestured toward the plate. "Go on. Don't be shy. I'm sure you must be hungry . . ."

I took a couple halves and put them on my plate but I wasn't really hungry. I'd thought, eating for two, that I'd be ravenous, but fear worked far better than Phen-fen or amphetamines at killing my appetite. She took one, took a tiny nibble, and set it down. "Tell me about my boy," she said, leaning forward eagerly.

I didn't know what to say. I didn't know her well enough to gauge whether she wanted comfort or the truth. I wasn't even sure I knew what the truth was. "What did you want to know?" I asked.

"Everything. How he looks. Is he eating? Do they treat him well? Is he getting his medicine?" Suddenly this stiff, taciturn old woman was as eager as a girl.

"I don't know about his medicine. He didn't mention it. He looked worn-down and tired . . . but it's bound to be a strain, being locked up like that." I decided I might as well be frank. "He looked like a man who has suffered a lot, but he didn't look sick. He was rational. I got the impression that he's not very talkative, but he made polite conversation. He had a nice visit with Lyle. It was obvious that he loves his son and Lyle loves him." I wished I had more to tell her.

She reached out as if she was going to touch my arm, then pulled her hand back and put it in her lap. "Is he . . ." She searched for the word she wanted, and then said, "Did he seem scared?"

I shook my head. "Not to me. Of course, I don't know him, but he seemed to be at ease. The guards are all very sympathetic, Mrs. Harding. When I asked if there was a time limit on visitors, they said that if they couldn't let him go, at least they could let him visit with his son as long as he wanted."

"Eat your lunch," she urged, staring down at her own barely touched food. "It was good of you to take the boy. He wants so badly for his daddy to come home . . . and of course, Jed can't . . . not after what . . ."

I pounced. "After what?"

She shook her head but didn't answer.

"I don't understand, Mrs. Harding. All he has to do is say he won't go shoot that VA guy, and they'll let him go. It doesn't make any sense. Lyle needs him. You need the help. Why doesn't your son want to be let out?"

She went on staring at the plate. "Did he say anything about his wife?"

Her voice was so soft I had to lean forward to hear. Did she know something about what had happened to Paulette? Was the whole town in on this big secret? More important, did she believe her son had had something to do with it? "Just that she used to work at the restaurant. And that she was gone."

She nodded and seemed relieved, but I had no idea why. She had the kind of face that wasn't easy to read—a blank, severe façade. I picked up a sandwich and took a bite. Egg salad. And very good. I ate both halves, drank my tea, and stood up. "I wish I had more to tell you, Mrs. Harding."

"Don't apologize, dear. You did your best. More than most people have done for us, and I've lived here all my life. So's Jed, of course. And Lyle. It's something to know he's not sick and they're treating him decent. He didn't seem . . . nervous?"

"Nervous?" I didn't understand.

She stared down at her hands, not answering. Maybe it was unfair of me to take advantage of her weakness, but I had a stake here, too. My life was just as wrapped up in her son's situation as hers was. "Mrs. Harding, I'm sorry if I seem confused, but I just don't understand. Your son could get out. I know he could. All he has to do is promise to stay away from the VA. It's obvious that you need him here, that Lyle needs him. Yet he won't do it, and you act like that's perfectly acceptable. Why?"

The gnarled old hands knitted together in her lap, twisting around each other and clutching at folds of fabric. She stared down at the tabletop. "Jed's afraid to get out," she said. "You have to know him, I think, to understand. He's a kind boy, really. A kind man, I mean. Too kind. Gentle and giving and an easy mark for anybody's got a sad story and an open hand. When he was a boy, he was always bringing home strays—cats, dogs, mice, squirrels. Brought a baby skunk home, once. I didn't let him bring that into the house. He cried and carried on, but I was firm about that one. Well. He grew up and darned if he wasn't the same."

"Still bringing home animals?"

She shook her head, smiling faintly at my misunderstanding. "By then it was people. Lost souls. Down and outs. Crazy folks. He understood, see. After Viet Nam . . ." She said it like it was two words. Pronounced it crossly, as if the words had a bitter taste. "He got messed up real bad over there. Not just the chemical stuff that gave him the cancer and the pain, so's he was never healthy again. It messed up his mind." She sighed faintly, looking toward the window, but she wasn't seeing anything. She was remembering. After a moment, she sighed again and shook her head.

"You'd never believe it, to see him now, but he was the spit image of Lyle. He was so beautiful. My boy. I sent a handsome, high-spirited young man off to that damned war and got back a sickly, haunted man who jumped every time you slammed a door. Come hunting season, it was like he was in some torture chamber. Sometimes . . . not always . . . a gun goes off and he's down on the floor, eyes rolling, looking like maybe his heart's gonna stop." Her hands folded like she was praying. "And the dreams! Sometimes I wonder if he'd of been better off if they'd just killed him, once and for all, instead of this long slow killing of him that's been going on ever since. But then . . ." Her eyes shifted toward the doorway. "Then we wouldn't have the little one, would we?"

Her head moved from side to side, slowly, sadly, a faded ghost of a woman in a hot, shabby kitchen. Too much heartache had really taken a toll on this family. "I guess it's an awful thing, a mother wondering if her own child would be better off dead. I don't mean it. I only wish he could have some peace. But things just go from bad to worse."

I was almost out of time and though I'd heard a lot, I still didn't have the answer to my question. My heart wanted to comfort her, to take over and see if I could make her life better, but I resisted the impulse. Like everyone always tells me, I'm not responsible for the whole world. "But why is he afraid to get out? Why won't he come back here and help you?"

She looked at me then, tears welling up in her faded eyes.

"He wants to, you know. It's no easier on him being separated than it is on the child." She held out her hand, two arthritic fingers crossed, middle over index. "They're this close. Always have been. Boy's mother wasn't much. Oh, she tried, within her own limits, but she wasn't much more than a child herself. Didn't have the backbone. She thought having a baby would be like playing with a doll. Not that Lyle was easy . . . but she shouldn't have taken up with another man. Not around here. Not with Jed being in the . . ." She shook her head sadly. "It wasn't right . . . girl never had no common sense."

"About your son, Jed," I reminded her. "Why won't he . . ." Pressing her, torn between my need to know and my reluctance to be aggressive with such a fragile person.

Her silence hung like a curtain between us in the hot, heavy air. At last, reluctantly, she said, "He's afraid. Says he's worried about what might happen. Won't tell me what he means." Her eyes slid away to the window again, but this time, I thought it was evasion and not reverie. Something she didn't want to tell me. "Jed gets these flashbacks sometimes. Thinks he's still over there. Wants to fight back. Lash out. Used to drive his wife crazy. She didn't try too hard, tryin' hard wasn't something Paulette understood, but living with him wasn't easy. Once or twice, he jumped on her in his sleep, grabbed her by the throat. Thought she was the enemy . . ."

We were getting closer. I thought she might eventually answer my question, but I was out of time to listen. Impatiently, I said, "You're not making sense. He's afraid to come back here because of the flashbacks?"

She went on without looking at me. I wasn't sure she was answering my question. She seemed to be in a place of her own. Remembering again. "A while back. Something terrible happened. Jed doesn't know . . . doesn't think . . . that he was there . . . but he isn't sure. He's afraid about that. He's afraid of what he'll remember if he thinks about that." She slapped her palms down on the tabletop, as if to signal that the conversation was over.

But it wasn't over. It was only beginning. "What kind of terrible thing?"

She wouldn't meet my eyes. I ran the conversation though my mind to see if there was something I'd missed. "Does this have something to do with his wife?"

"Paulette," she said. "Never did anything but harm to everyone around her. Still . . ."

"What about Paulette? Are you saying she didn't leave? That something happened to her?"

The pale blue eyes locked onto my face anxiously. "Paulette's gone. Jed's in jail. And we've just got to sit tight and see things through. Hadn't you better be getting back to work?"

It was as clear as mud, but she was a hard person to question, and I was out of time. "You're right. I'd better be getting back to the restaurant," I said. "Thanks for the sandwiches." I was exploding with frustration. I wanted to pick the woman up and shake her until she told me all she knew. But she was old and frail. She had a child to care for. And a core of Yankee stubbornness like her son's that would prevent her from saying any more. She'd said enough already.

Her listlessness had returned and she shuffled to the door as though it was an awful effort.

"I can let myself out," I said.

She shook her head. "I'm not so worn out I can't do the right thing and see my guest to the door. Had a nice nap this morning, while you and the boy were out."

It seemed to me that she needed about a month of nice naps but I didn't say anything. Just thanked her again and left, wondering, on my short drive back to the restaurant, whether she'd answered any of my questions.

I only thought about quitting a thousand times during dinner, mostly when people grabbed my arm or waved their arms in the air like they were greeting long-lost friends or yelled, "Miss, Miss, Miss" like this was a ball game and I was the batter for the visiting team. My sister Carrie worked as a waitress, her last summer, and it was the thing she'd complained about most. People seemed to think that their need to have their desires met

instantly superseded any requirement of manners or considera-
tion for the needs of others. I'd lived with Andre Lemieux for
the past two years, and with David before that. I knew how
irrational hungry men could get. That didn't make me any more
patient with a whole damned room full of them. I wasn't being
sexist. It seemed like the place was full of men who, in lieu of
going out and snaring a wild animal to feed their families, were
determined to snare a waitress instead. If I hadn't had to stay in
this trap, I would have chewed off my foot and crawled away.

At long last, the tide of hungry mouths seemed to be on the
ebb, with more flowing out the door than were flowing in. Clyde
went out on the back porch for a smoke. The other boy, whose
name I still hadn't learned, began to make some headway with
the dishes. Theresa poured herself a cup of coffee and sat down
at the table. Only Kalyn and I were still on our feet and, despite
her good disposition, she didn't look any happier than I was. I
was making coffee and thinking about some dinner for myself
when the kitchen door swung open and a man I didn't know
came into the room.

I didn't need to know who he was to know what he was. He
had a grimy REMEMBER WACO T-shirt. One of them. He ran his
eyes over all of us and beckoned toward me. "Come on outside
a minute, honey," he said. "Man needs to talk with you."

In your dreams, buddy, I thought. I put my hands on my hips
and eyeballed him right back, a bit testy after being ordered
around all evening. "Excuse me?" I said. "I'm working right now.
And I don't know you from Adam."

"Who I am don't matter," he said. "The Reverend Hannon
sent me. Wants you to come over to the church. He's got some
questions he wants to ask you."

I wasn't about to step outside with him and let him march
me off to a meeting with Hannon. Minister or not, he was a
bad guy. That whole church was a hotbed of bad guys. I checked
my watch and shook my head. "I'm not finished working. Can
you tell him that, please, and ask if he can come back later?"

"Reverend Hannon doesn't like women who don't know
their place. He says come, you come." The man reached out

and grabbed my arm. A no-no in my book, even if I wasn't wearing my NO GRABBING T-shirt.

"My place is here until dinner is over." I jerked my arm away and stared down at him, wondering what I was going to do if he insisted. Dora the waitress, after all, was something of a timid soul. Unhappy about being manhandled, but would she resist like this?

I didn't have to wait to find out. Theresa shoved her chair back with a clatter and crossed the room to join us. "Kendall Barker, what in tarnation do you think you're trying to do? I've got a business to run here. You can't come in here and haul my waitress away in the middle of dinner. I've got people out there in the other room waiting for their food. And this poor girl's been working so hard she hasn't even had time for her own dinner yet. You start pickin' on her and she'll quit on me. And then where will I be, with help almost impossible to get? Can you tell me that?"

He looked down at his shoes and then back up, defiantly. "Gotta take her, Theresa. The Reverend says . . ."

Theresa jerked her chin toward the dining room. "Better check on the other room . . ."

I didn't hesitate. I picked up the coffeepot and disappeared through the door. When I came back with a couple new orders, my would-be abductor was gone and Clyde was back at the stove. Theresa gave me a curious look. "Kendall says you took Lyle Harding down to the jail today to visit his father?"

I shrugged. "Yeah."

"Well . . ." She seemed to be searching for something to say. "Well, that was nice of you. How'd it go?" I could sense everyone else in the kitchen was listening.

I said what Jed Harding had asked me to say. "Jed Harding's doing fine and they had a very nice visit." They went on staring, but I had no idea what they were waiting for. "Clyde, are there any trout left?" He nodded. "Would you fix me one? I'm starving."

"He talk to you?" Theresa asked.

I shook my head. "I don't know him like the rest of you do," I said, "but he didn't strike me as much of a talker. I dropped the boy off and went and ran some errands. When I came back, it was time to leave. He said 'thank you,' but that's about all. I've had longer conversations with people at toll booths. But he really loves that boy."

Theresa nodded vigorously. "Too much, if you ask me. Spoils him with all that attention. Still . . . boy hasn't got much . . ." She looked around the room for confirmation. ". . . With his mother running off like that and his daddy being sick so much. Well. You've got some orders up, Dora." She went back and sat down. It seemed to me that she was relieved but I didn't know why. I grabbed the plates Clyde had fixed and carried them into the dining room.

When I came back, my trout was waiting on the table. I grabbed some silverware and sat down. "Theresa," I asked, "who was that man who wanted to take me away?"

"Kendall Barker? He works over at the Texaco station. He's cousin to Danny Parker, the kid got shot by that state cop."

"I meant, why is he after me? It seems like every time I turn around, someone is trying to grab me. I go swimming and someone grabs me and tries to drown me. Two nights ago I couldn't sleep. Ended up at the church and I thought they were going to tear me apart. The only time I've been more scared was when my husband dragged me into his truck and held a gun to my head. I don't understand it. It's like there's something going on around here that everyone understands but me."

"You're too damned curious, that's all. Folks around here mostly keep to themselves. Gotta keep your head down, girl. You just do your job and mind your own business and everything will be fine," Theresa said, "and stop tryin' to do for people you don't even know. They were doing fine long before you came along." Like I was seven years old, she was my mom, and I'd been pestering her. Or like I was seven and I'd shown a precocious interest in sex that had to be squelched.

"But that's what I've been doing . . ."

She sighed and picked up the coffeepot. "If that's keeping to yourself, girl, I'd hate to see you curious. Now eat your dinner before it gets cold. And I hate to do this to you, but can you work all three meals tomorrow?"

I sighed for my poor feet and nodded. "Long as I can get a couple-hour break in the afternoon." My, I was getting tough, wasn't I? It was better to work anyway. When I wasn't working, all I did was brood and worry. At least aching feet kept my mind off other things. Pain concentrates the mind nicely.

"Shouldn't be a problem," she said. "I'm hoping by tomorrow, I can get that schedule put together, and then things will begin to make some sense. For all of us. Believe me, it isn't usually like this. Cathy's more regular and Kalyn's not running off to the doctor all the time. I don't like this confusion any more than you do. How's the trout?"

"Good."

"Have some pie. You don't eat enough to keep body and soul together." This admonition delivered, she bustled away.

Seemed like I ate enough for my body, as much as I had an appetite for. I laid my head down on my arm and closed my eyes, wondering how pie was going to heal my soul. "You done?" Clyde asked. "You didn't eat much. Theresa's right."

"Sorry, Clyde. It's not your cooking. I never can eat when I'm tired. I wish they'd all go home." I wanted to go upstairs, lie down, and consider the events of the day. Like a hungry peasant, I needed to glean through my experiences, looking for some morsels I could use. It was hard to sit back and watch, to play Dora, to keep my eyes on the ground and my ears open, when I wanted to rush out the door, stand in the middle of the street and scream Andre's name until he answered. I felt like a string that was wound too tight.

"Me, too. You want some pie? I saved you a piece of blueberry."

"How did you know?"

"I notice things. You want ice cream with that?"

"You work too hard already. You don't have to wait on me."

"Something about you . . ." He shrugged. ". . . Makes me want to."

Don't come to like me, Clyde, I thought. *I'm just a great big fake. Here to pick your brains, steal your secrets. Here for one thing only. Here to rescue Andre, no matter what. No matter who gets hurt.* People around here didn't give a damn about me and I didn't give a damn about them. Except, of course, that I kept getting sidetracked. Like with Lyle.

"Here are those burgers," he said. "Want me to deliver 'em?"

"You do enough," I said. "I'll do it. Just don't let anyone touch my pie." I loaded them onto a tray and went to make a delivery. The dining room was finally quiet. Only a few couples at tables talking in low voices over coffee and dessert. I delivered the burgers to two guys who looked like truck drivers. Asked if they wanted anything else, knowing they'd order pie, and wasn't disappointed. I was learning my job. Give me another week and there would be no more surprises.

Back in the kitchen, Kalyn was hanging up her apron. "I'm out of here," she said. Through the screen door, I could hear the impatient revving of a motorcycle engine. She gestured toward the back door and motioned for me to follow. Outside, she stuck a folded piece of paper into my hand. "My number," she said, "in case you need me later. About Kendall Barker and them . . . they're just a bunch of stupid bullies, except Hannon. He's evil. Keep your head down, act as simple and humble as you can, and they probably won't hurt you much."

My arms folded around my body, involuntary and protective. "I don't even know what I did . . ."

"You went to see Jed Harding," she said. "I wish you'd asked me . . ." Down below, her boyfriend revved the engine and I wanted to rush down, jump on, and ride off into the night, away from this crazy place.

"But why is that bad?"

"Believe me, the less you know, the better. Look . . ." She hesitated, and the solemn tone hung eerily in the following silence. "There's not much I can do to help you. I'm not that brave . . . but I don't agree with what they're doing here. You should be okay . . ." She sounded dubious. "But if you need me, you've got my number . . ."

"Looks like you'll have a cool ride home," I said, raising my voice to normal.

"You bet. Except for the bugs in my teeth, it's a great way to travel." She gave my arm a comforting squeeze. "See you in the morning." She slung her bag over her shoulder and clattered down the steps. I watched her go, wanting to holler "Don't go." Wanting to run after her. When the bike had disappeared into the shadows, I turned and went inside.

I totaled the check for the truckers, fixed them oversized pieces of pie, and delivered it all to their table. Then I finished my own pie, hung up my apron, and headed for the stairs.

I never made it. The screen door clattered open, and there was Kendall Barker, standing in the doorway like the Grim Reaper, come to take me away. "Hey!" he barked. "Where do you think you're going?"

"To the bathroom."

"Well, hurry it up," he ordered. "The man's waiting."

Hurry it up? Every time I turned around, someone was yelling at me. I was like a bottle of Coke being rolled down a cactus-covered slope. Shaken up until I felt like I was going to explode, abraded by every encounter. Instead of climbing the stairs, I shut myself in the little pink bathroom and wondered if I could crawl out the window and escape. There was only one problem. The room didn't have a window.

But poor, timid, innocent Dora didn't have anything to hide, except herself. I thought of throwing myself on Clyde's mercy and asking him to help me. But I didn't want to drag him into this. And I didn't want him appointing himself my protector. Getting too close to anyone threatened my mobility and my independence, getting too close to me might do the same to them. I had a serious case of bad karma.

Well, I couldn't hide in here all night. I cast a quick glance at the mirror. Circles under my eyes dark enough to look like bruises. My impossible hair looked like the president should declare a disaster area and call in FEMA. And I looked even more scared than I felt. How come Nancy Drew never got scared or looked like hell? What was I doing wrong? Feeling reassured and empowered, I marched forth to meet my fate.

CHAPTER *13*

BARKER WASN'T ALONE this time. There were two men with him. I recognized them from the meeting at the church. I'd never seen them in the restaurant. "Let's go," he said, holding the door open. I walked through it, wondering if this was what it felt like to be marched to the gallows. The other two men followed behind us. I decided not to make conversation. I wasn't sure I could trust my voice anyway. Our footsteps echoed in the nearly empty street as we marched down the sidewalk, across the church lawn, and up to a side door. All the way, though I'm as brave as a barrel full of bears, I kept wishing Kalyn and Andy would sweep past and rescue me.

Barker paused at the door and knocked. It swung open but the room beyond was dark. When I hesitated, he grabbed my arm and shoved me, propelling me through the room and up to a second door. Here he didn't knock, just pushed it open. "Go on!" he muttered. "I told you. The man's waiting."

The air had a damp, musty smell, as if the room we were in was rarely opened or aired. There was a shuffling of feet around me, another none-too-gentle push, and then, suddenly, I was alone in the darkness. The door shut and I heard the sound of a key being turned. I closed my eyes—I've found darkness is less scary if I close my eyes—and walked forward with slow, shuffling steps until I hit a wall. Keeping my left hand on the wall, I began to slowly circle the room. Three steps to a corner. Turn. Five steps to the next corner. Turn. Two steps to the door. Three more steps to another corner. Turn. Five steps to the corner. And turn. I was in a room not much bigger than a closet. Given the lack of a window, it probably was a closet. And there was nothing in here except me.

I didn't know what brand of religion this church espoused but it was sorely lacking in Christian charity. Locking the poor, friendless servant girl in a closet was positively Dickensian. Too tired and shaken to stand any longer, I slowly let myself slip down until I was sitting on the floor with my back against the wall, my legs sticking out in front of me like a doll on a child's bed. I was alone in the darkness, my nostrils filled with the scent of Theresa's kitchen and my own scared sweat. I had to keep busy. Not think. Stave off the fear and claustrophobia. Remember that I wasn't here for me.

Cautiously, I explored the floor around me. Rough. Wooden. I thought, from the grit between my fingers, that it hadn't been swept in a long time. With nothing else to do except be scared, I concentrated on exploring, on knowing everything I could about this space. Shifting from place to place, I traveled around the room, always in my sitting position, letting my fingers roam. I was almost around to the door when I felt something wedged into the crack between the wall and the floor.

It was stuck but I persisted, wiggling it until it came free. I couldn't see, of course, but it felt like a tiny cuff link, smooth and rounded on one end, with a little anchor or tail on the other. But a tiny cuff link was an odd thing to find in a closet in a church basement. And then, with a suddenness that took my breath away, I realized what it was. A shirt stud from a dress shirt. And Andre had been wearing a dress shirt when he was taken, because he was on his way to a wedding.

At some point, like me, Andre had been here in this closet. Oh, sure. This was a church. Probably it had seen lots of weddings, some of them with guys who wore shirt studs. But I knew, with an electrifying certainty that might have been pure delusion, that it was Andre's. It was ridiculous but I felt an overwhelming sense of elation, as though I had reached through some forbidden dimension and touched him, while we were temporarily connected through our imprisonment. There were footsteps outside the door, and the sound of a key turning. Quickly, I shoved the stud into my bra, where it was less likely to be found. The way I kept storing things there, I ought to get some bras made with pockets. I held my breath, wondering what was coming.

When the door opened, someone shone a very bright flashlight right into my eyes. I put my arm over my face and waited. I didn't plead or whimper or ask any questions. I didn't even get up, or look at them. I simply waited.

"Okay, get up and come with me." A new voice. These people were so pitiful. A whole army against one poor waitress. Lord knew how many of them it took to walk a dog. But I didn't share this insight. I would have bet money these guys were humorless. I just clambered to my feet, stiffly, now that I'd let myself stretch out, and followed, slowly, shuffling, keeping my eyes downcast. We went through a couple of rooms and into some kind of an office.

"Sit down." I sat, staring down at the twined fingers in my lap. "Look at me when I'm talking to you."

Power corrupts, I thought, raising my eyes to his face. It was no more appealing or attractive than it had been last night. No more kind or generous or understanding, either, but almost savage and angry, but whether it was simply a professional angry pose, or whether he was mad at me, I didn't know. I did know that a reasonable person would be scared of this man. I didn't have to fake the tremble in my voice as I asked, "What do you want? Why am I here?"

"I ask the questions," he said.

I'd heard that before. From a big, scary Hawaiian cop. From an angry bully just before he broke my nose. My eyes began to water in anticipation, my already tender nose began to tingle. I felt a surge of righteous anger. But I wasn't Thea Kozak. I wasn't going to get right up in their faces and dare them to do their worst. Thea had PTSD, she did crazy things when people pushed her around. Dora was just a beaten-down woman trying to get over her belief that she deserved to be treated badly. As Dora, I wasn't throwing down challenges of my own. I wasn't sticking to my guns, come hell or high water. At one time or another, hell and high water had both come, and left me hot, sore, and wet. Nearly drowned. Nearly burned alive. I'd been a sole agent then. Today things were different. I had responsibilities to others besides myself. I nodded and waited for his questions.

"You drove Lyle Harding down to the jail to visit his father today. Why?"

"He's a sweet little boy. He misses his father."

"He's a complete stranger. You drove for three hours so he could visit. Why?"

"I felt sorry for him. He asked me if I would take him. I had the time off, so I did."

Hannon's fist banged down on the desktop, loud in the quiet room. "Don't lie to me! I asked you why?"

"He was hurting, and I know something about that. But I don't understand," I said, in the slow, puzzled way of someone who truly didn't. "He's just a helpless little kid. I like kids. Is it wrong to feel sorry for a sad little boy? You're a minister. I don't know what kind of a church this is, but do you think there's something wrong with doing for people less fortunate than ourselves?"

"Please, Mrs. McKusick . . ." He waved a hand at the other three men in the room. "Do you think we're idiots? People don't do what you did without a reason. Shall I tell you what I think?"

I didn't know what kind of a response he wanted, but I figured he was going to tell me what he thought no matter what, so I just sat there, hoping he wasn't one of those bullies who like to hit women for emphasis. Those people always make me lose my composure.

"I think you're a cop," he said.

I almost laughed out loud. Here I was being so Goddamned

passive I made myself sick, and he thought I was a cop? "You're kidding, right?"

He shook his head. "I think you're a cop they've sent here to see what you can find out. They think we're so dumb that we won't suspect you because you're a woman."

I stared at him stupidly. "You're kidding, right?" I repeated. "I mean, it's almost funny that someone would think I was a cop. A cop whose husband regularly beat the crap out of her and she couldn't do anything about it? Look, if you don't believe me, you could call Dom Florio. He's the guy who sent me here. He really is a cop. A cop married to Theresa's cousin Rosie. Call Florio or call the Anson Police Department and ask them if Michael McKusick used to get hauled in regularly for beating me up. For beating up his wife, Dora. I'd give you the number, but I always just called 911. Or you could call the hospital."

It was a bit of a gamble. If he called my bluff and did contact the Anson PD, I could only hope that Dom had alerted people to the situation so they could back up my story. And as for the hospital, I doubted if they'd give out any information to a stranger. But it didn't matter, because the Reverend Stuart Hannon wasn't buying my story anyway. He sat behind his desk with a piece of pipe clenched in his fists, playing with it and watching me with a smirk on his face.

"Oh, I have no doubt that any misinformation needed to back up your story has been cleverly planted."

I shook my head sadly. "Looks like you're even crazier than my husband," I said. "You guys must have your own reality. One that doesn't have anything to do with the real world."

"What do you mean, 'you guys'?" He made a sudden angry gesture with the pipe in his hand and I was off my chair and cowering in the corner so fast it surprised him. He stared at me, a puzzled look on his face that made him look ridiculous. I didn't answer. I stayed in my corner with my arms protectively over my head and waited, making little whimpering sounds, to see if I could shame him into behaving better.

"Get up," he said. I stayed there and kept whimpering.

"Look," he said finally, "I'm not going to hurt you. I just want to know about your visit with Jed Harding."

I didn't move.

"This is ridiculous," he said. "Get back on your chair."

I still didn't move.

"Kendall? Timmy? Would you help the lady up, please?"

I didn't make it easy for them. Crouched down like that, wedged into the corner with my arms folded over my head, it was hard for them to get a grip on me without grabbing, and they didn't quite want to grab, especially since he'd promised they wouldn't hurt me. "Come on. Hurry it up," he barked. "We haven't got all night."

Awkwardly, they grabbed my arms and dragged me back to the chair. I took my arms away from my head and folded them protectively across my body. "I'm pregnant," I declared. "That's why I had to leave him, finally. Because he killed my last baby, kicking me in the stomach, and he would have killed this one, too. Even if you don't care about pushing women around, you aren't a baby killer like him, are you?"

It was a risky question. After Oklahoma City, we all knew that the militia did kill babies, when it was deemed necessary to make a point. But there was a big difference between parking a truck and walking away, and actual, face-to-face confrontation. I didn't think Reverend Hannon wanted to start beating on a pregnant woman in front of his men.

"You want to know about my visit with Jed Harding? I went to the jail, I dropped the boy off. I did some errands. I picked the boy up and came home. Jed Harding asked me how I met the boy. I told him about how I'd found Lyle in the ditch back there behind Theresa's parking lot, when he'd tried to run away from home. I told him I worked at Theresa's and he said she was hard but fair. He thanked me for coming and said I was a good person for doing it. I put the boy in the car and came home. It was my sense that that was about all the talking he ever did."

"How did he look?"

"You mean, like were they beating on him or anything?" He

nodded. "I didn't see any bruises. He didn't look healthy, though."

"Did he say anything else?" I shrugged. "Did he talk about being released? What they were saying? Whether they were discussing it?"

"No."

"What about his wife? Did he talk about her?"

"He said she used to work at Theresa's before she left town. That the town was too small for her."

"Did he talk about us?"

"This church?" I said. "No."

"The militia," he said impatiently.

"He said the cops came all the time and asked him questions about that trooper they . . . you . . . took, like where he might be and who's in charge, and he tells them he doesn't know anything."

Hannon smiled and picked up the pipe again, shifting it from hand to hand like a lethal toy. "That's all?"

"I told you. He didn't talk much."

I wrapped my arms more tightly around my body. "I never expected to meet a minister who kidnapped people in the middle of the night, locked them in dark rooms, and gave them the third degree because they made the mistake of doing something nice for somebody. But hey, what do I know? Given my history, why should I be surprised? It seems more likely to me that I really am a battered woman working as a waitress and you aren't a minister. You sure don't act like any minister I ever saw. Even though I've read that God works in mysterious ways." That last escaped before I could stop it.

Hannon glared at me in irritation. I got the impression that he did his best work through intimidation and I was causing major-league frustration. It was hard to bully and intimidate a person who was already beaten down and expected to be mistreated. It was hard to interrogate someone whose responses alternated between lucid and ridiculous. It was hard to use force against a woman who'd just declared that she was pregnant and had lost her last child as a result of abuse.

"Stand up," he barked, setting down the pipe and coming around the desk. I stood up, head lowered. If he was going to hit me, I didn't want to see it coming. Not when I couldn't fight back. I waited, passive and trembling, as he came up to me. "Hold still." He ran his hand across my body from one pelvic bone to the other, then from my waist down, violating my privacy and that of Mason or Oliver or Claudine, his palm lingering over the growing bulge the way Andre's did. He managed, in the process, to let his hands wander well beyond the reasonable search area. I kept my head down and bit back fierce words of objection and the choking bile that rose in my throat at his violation.

Finally he dropped his hand and stepped back, his face, for a second, hesitant and uncertain, struggling to square his belief in women's incompetence with his notion that I was a cop, his theory that I was acting with the evidence that I was pregnant. Was it improbable or the ultimate trick to send a pregnant cop? "All right. Get out of here," he ordered, walking back behind the security of his desk. "Don't let me see you coming around here again. And believe me, young lady, don't think I've bought a word of your ridiculous story. We'll be keeping a close eye on you." He gestured toward the door with the piece of pipe, and suddenly I had a vision of him using that pipe, swinging it savagely against the body of someone helpless or defiant. Inwardly, I cringed and felt bleak and cold. And somewhere, in the back of my head, a more ambitious idiot wanted to get that pipe and take it to the crime lab.

"Kendall. Timmy. Take her home and get right back here. Understand?" They nodded. I got up stiffly and walked slowly out between them, limping on my sore feet, hoping their understanding didn't include some secret instructions that involved me. Me and violence.

CHAPTER *14*

I WOKE THE next morning feeling more like myself than I had since Andre disappeared. That is, instead of waking in my normal, pathetic, Dora-the-waitress slump, I woke up mad. My body still ached and my feet still hurt. My head still felt like an ogre had come in the night and sucked out half my brain, but the part that remained was working, and what it was working on was a good old-fashioned snit. I couldn't understand why the people around here put up with the crap that the Reverend Hannon and his ilk were dishing out. Yes, I knew that a lot of people supported them, but what about basic rights—basic constitutional rights, not the rights of the Constitutional Militia—like the right to travel? Freedom of speech? Freedom of association? Freedom from harassment by assholes and their goons?

There had been other times in my life when I felt my liberties were being compromised. I'd been in situations where, when the cop asked if he could search my car, I knew the choices weren't between saying yes, having him search, and running the risk he'd find something I didn't want him to find, and saying no, and having the search not take place. I'd known that if I said no, my car would be searched anyway, and probably so would I, and probably I'd also have spent the night in jail. Plus the search would have been much more intrusive. The guy would have torn my car apart and left me to put it back together. But this was ongoing, this was pervasive, and this was much more menacing.

I ought to have woken up in a cold sweat, wondering what hassles and unpleasant encounters the day would throw at me, but I didn't. They had stolen my husband and they had stolen my life. Last night they'd compounded the matter by stealing my person and threatening me and my baby. It was finally enough, somehow, to break through the paralytic fear and tap into my impulse disorder. Why not? Half the population these days seems to suffer from some sort of impulse disorder. My impulse is to react with anger and a "come back at you" instinct when I'm cornered and threatened.

I woke up ready to break Jack's rule about staying a fly on the wall. As I dressed and combed my hair and brushed my teeth, I was wondering when, during the course of the day, I could get away to a pay phone to call Jack and tell him about the shirt stud. I wasn't supposed to use my cell phone except for emergencies. And I wouldn't use a cell phone around here for anything else. Too much risk of the conversation being overheard. Of course, I wasn't supposed to call at all except for emergencies. That broke the "don't call us, we'll call you" rule.

But I was thinking about worse things than calling Jack. I woke up wondering whether I'd gotten anything from my break into the civil-defense office, and when I might get a chance to look at those papers I'd stolen. Then, once I'd looked at the papers, I might want to start driving some back roads and have a look-see. These activities broke every other rule Jack had articulated and many that he hadn't. They even broke the rules of common sense. But I couldn't help myself. There was the missing brain problem. There was the missing Andre problem. And there was my long-standing other problem—that I was headstrong and rebellious and needed desperately to do something. The better part of a week had gone by and I had squat to show for it.

There was another reason I wanted to call Jack. Paulette Harding. I'd been assuming all along that Andre had been working on Gary Pelletier's murder. Had taken it as true when Kavanaugh told me Paulette Harding had left town. But now I was sure that wasn't true. Everyone around here, even if they wouldn't talk about it, knew that something had happened. I was pretty sure that the same was true for the state police. Roland Proffit had told me that. They thought she was dead. And perhaps her roommate, too. Dead because she'd tried to get in touch with the police. To tell them what?

I wanted to know what Jack knew. What Andre had known. What and where the connections were. I wanted to know who the players were and what roles they played. This was no time, and I was in no place, to be treated like a mushroom. I now knew that Jack had been right. I shouldn't have come here. It was a far more dangerous place than I ever could have imagined. But then I'd seen that I had no choice, and nothing since had changed that. I just wanted to know everything I could. For now, of course, that would have to wait. I had to go feed the masses.

News seems to spread through small towns by some form of osmosis. Half the customers in the restaurant had heard about me taking Lyle to visit his father, and every time I poured a cup of coffee, I also had to answer questions about Jed Harding. How he looked and how they were treating him. Whether he was being fed properly and did he appear to have been physically harmed. How the visit had gone. And whether there had been any talk about him being released. I stuck to the script Jed Harding had given me, and reported to each questioner that he hadn't been very talkative, but that he was fine and he'd had a good visit with his son. No one seemed satisfied but I had no more to give them except what was on the menu.

Around 10:30, just as I was about to sit down with a plate of bacon and eggs and wheat toast and jam, Theresa came through the door, looking angry, and jerked her chin toward the dining room. "Couple of guys out there saying no one can wait on 'em but you." She shook her head and hurried into the pantry, but not before she exchanged looks with Clyde that I didn't understand.

I half-expected to find a couple cops in the dining room, but

instead I found my strolling companions from the previous evening, Kendall Barker and the man called Timmy. Didn't these
guys have jobs? When I approached their table, Barker stood
up. "Got something to say to you. Outside." Across the room,
I saw Kalyn hesitate, then pick up a tray and hurry into the
kitchen.

Wrong girl. Wrong move. Maybe I was out of character, but
I'd had enough of being bossed around by these guys. I stood
my ground, lowered my eyes, and said in a soft voice designed
to be heard by many, "I'm working now, Mr. Barker. Anything
you've got to say to me, you can say right here."

He looked at his companion, as though Timmy might have
a suggestion, but Timmy only shrugged—I'd never yet heard
him say a word—so Barker grabbed my arm and shoved me
toward the door. Evidently, these guys didn't know about alternative conflict resolution.

I hunched my shoulders forward and dropped my head but
I stood my ground. "Please, Mr. Barker, don't push me around
like this in front of all my customers. It's embarrassing. Besides,
you know I can't leave. Theresa's gonna think I'm in some kind
of trouble and then I'll lose my job." I looked around at the
staring faces, noting how they looked away to avoid meeting my
eyes. Theater in the round, except this was more like a Roman
amphitheater and I was the one being thrown to the lions. Customers were aware that something was happening but no one
seemed like they were going to intervene.

Most of the time, when you talk to people, even angry people, and you handle things right, you can make some kind of
human connection. That wasn't happening here. These guys
were like robots. Except as the object of their mission, they
didn't seem to recognize that I existed. The tables closest to the
door were empty. "How about over here," I said, walking toward
the empty area, "where no one can hear us?"

Barker grunted but seemed willing to accept the compromise. He and Timmy closed in around me, backing me up
against the wall, standing close enough so our bodies were
touching. I hated having my personal space invaded. I wanted

to reach out and push them away. I concentrated on my breathing. On controlling my temper. On not noticing how their bodies were touching me. They smelled of cigarettes and coffee and something flinty and metallic. Their hands weren't clean. Timmy needed a shave. Kendall Barker moved his T-shirt up so I could see the gun in his waistband. I was having trouble breathing, couldn't seem to remember how.

At least Barker didn't seem to be enjoying the encounter any more than I was. Physically we might be up close and personal but the agenda was professional. "Reverend Hannon asked us to stop by this morning and remind you that he meant what he said last night. You may think you've got us fooled but we're not a bunch of dumb yokels. Keep away from Jed Harding and his kid. Stay away from the church. Just stay in your place and mind your own business or you'll find that things will get very unpleasant."

Shielded by Timmy's body, he raised his hand, grabbed my breast, and squeezed, hard and then harder. Hard enough to leave a bruise. Hard enough to make me want to gasp with pain. It wasn't lust. It was menace and humiliation. A gross personal invasion. Filthy, rotten bastards. I stared at the pine knots on the wall as I blinked away tears. I wasn't going to let them make me cry or give them the satisfaction of a moan or a plea. I bit my lip and waited for him to stop. Maybe that's what Dora would have done. She was used to this. But men who abuse their wives want a response. Kendall Barker just wanted my attention.

"People will be watching you. All the time. And you won't even know who they are. So watch yourself, bitch. Understand?" He dropped his hand and they both stepped back, away from me, then turned together, a clumsy attempt at a military maneuver, and left the restaurant. I stared after them, hurt, scared, and furious, wondering what aberrant god had made these men.

The room was still crowded, but during the entire encounter, neither Kalyn nor Theresa had ever appeared. I assumed that meant they knew what was happening and had decided to stay out of it. I looked around at the sea of curious faces, choking rage rising in my throat. Cowards. Lily-livered chicken hearts.

Didn't they know they weren't special? That they weren't exempt? Sit on your hands and let one person be abused, and next time, it may be your turn and no one will help you, either. Let people begin to control how you can think and act, and you've begun to abdicate your freedom. I wanted to cradle my poor aching breast as I crossed the room, but I'd been humiliated enough.

I picked up the coffeepot, which I'd left sitting on Barker's table, walked through the kitchen, out the back door, and down the steps. Then, with a violent heave, I smashed it against the Dumpster, muttering every curse word I'd ever learned. If he ever came near me again, I'd take my cute little Barbie gun and blow his head off.

I must have been as close to hysteria as I was to tears because my next thought, and one that nearly made me laugh aloud, was that maybe this was why Jack had wanted me to wear that bulletproof vest. It would have protected me. And blown any chance I had of sticking to my story. And it was the absurdity of it, and my own confused helplessness, that finally brought the tears. I stood next to my ratty car, next to the smelly Dumpster, and sobbed, and Theresa stood on the porch and yelled, "Dora, step on it. You've got people waiting."

I'll step on you, you dye-haired old witch, I thought. *May you rot in hell for eternity.* I finished my shift with gritted teeth and lowered eyes, wincing every time I accidentally bumped myself with a tray. As soon as I could, I took off my apron and went upstairs. I hated them all. Clyde and Kalyn and Theresa for not helping me. The customers for being a bunch of selfish cowards. And the Reverend Stuart Hannon and his minions for believing that people don't matter. Jack wanted me out of here; Hannon wanted me out of here. How ironic that the idea of my departure should be so pleasing to both sides.

I hated Kalyn especially, since last night she'd acted like we were on the same side. Had that just been a trick? A trap to see what I'd do or say? Kavanaugh had told me not to trust anyone. It looked like she was right.

I'd added a backache to my list of complaining body parts.

A backache and a headache. I lay on my bed, letting the fan blow over me, staring up at the ceiling and counting the cracks, feeling light-years away from the brave woman I'd woken up as this morning. I was so full of helplessness and frustration and humiliation and rage that my empty stomach was tied up in knots. I wanted to pack up and leave, even if it meant admitting that Jack was right. If I couldn't do any good here, I might as well go home and knit baby blankets. If only it hadn't meant letting Hannon win.

As I lay there, wallowing in a veritable cornucopia of bad feelings, I realized that this was what Andre was going through, too. The same people. The same didactic idealism which allowed them to behave toward fellow humans with such indifference and cruelty. He would be experiencing the same fears and the same constraints. He couldn't be foolishly heroic, couldn't take chances, because he had to think of me and the baby. I groaned and pulled the pillow over my head. I could run away, back to someplace where I would be safe and protected, and let someone else do it. I could stop trying to help out here, because it was hard and it was scary. But Andre couldn't.

Someone knocked on the door. I ignored it. They knocked again. If it was the bad guys, they'd break down the door if it was important to them. And there weren't any good guys. I went back to staring at the ceiling. Counting the cracks. It was a demanding job, so many cracks it was hard to keep track. The knock came again. I ignored it again. But I'd lost count and had to start over.

"Come on, Dora, I know you're in there," Kalyn called. "Open the door. I've got my hands full."

We all had out hands full. Why should she be different? "Go away."

"Clyde said you didn't eat. He sent you up some breakfast."

"Go away," I said. "I'm not hungry."

"Look, Clyde's worried about you . . ." To this I had no printable reply. "He is," she said, "really . . ." She banged on the door again. "If you don't let me in, I'll have to go get him," she said.

"Is that supposed to be a threat?" I yelled. "And then what? He breaks down the door to make me eat breakfast? Where was all that door-bashing courage when I needed it?" This was too ridiculous for words. "Just take the Goddamned breakfast away and leave me alone!"

"Dora, please . . ." She sounded close to tears. "Just open the door and let me in. I really need to talk to you."

My head hurt. The pounding made it worse and she didn't seem to be giving up. It seemed the lesser evil to just let her bring the tray in and have her say. Then maybe she'd go away and leave me and my aching head alone. I crossed the room, unlocked the door, and jerked it open. In her surprise, she practically tumbled into the room. Good thing she was an experienced waitress. The tea in the cup didn't spill. She looked around for a place to put it and chose the bedside stand. Then she stood back, her hands on her hips, and met my eyes defensively.

"Look, this is probably hard for you to understand . . . but . . ." She stopped, tried again. "What did they do to you, anyway?" Of course I wasn't going to answer that. "Look, it can't be as bad as . . ." But suddenly, she changed her mind about whatever she was going to say. What she did say surprised me. "This isn't any easier on the rest of us, you know, living in a world that's gone all topsy-turvy. This used to be a nice place . . . Dora, I'm so sorry about all this. You don't know . . . can't know . . . what you've walked into the middle of . . . and it's . . . well, we're just a big bunch of cowards, that's all. We're letting them pick on you and doing nothing about it 'cause they're a bunch of paranoid assholes and we've let them scare the pants off us."

I sat down on the bed and stared up at her. Kalyn was spunky and refreshingly honest and she'd been nice to me. I had no reason to expect a young woman who worked in a restaurant to have the courage, or reason, to stand up to these guys. I just didn't have much use for cowards. Part of my own pathology. "Look," I said, "it doesn't matter. It's just . . . thought I was coming here to get away from stuff like this . . . the violence, the bullying . . ." I stopped. I was tired of the lie. If anything, I'd come here to get *to* stuff like this—the violence and the bullying. My choice, so why was I complaining?

"Don't mind me," I said. "I'm just so sick of being scared all the time. It was nice of Clyde to send up breakfast but honestly, I'm not hungry." That, at least, was the truth.

She stood her ground, the whole, taut, five-foot-three of her. Not a wasted ounce anywhere. The biggest thing about her was her hair. "Clyde doesn't know about the baby," she said. ". . . He just worries about you . . . about people. He's sweet that way. But you do have to eat."

I closed my eyes, shutting the world out for a moment, wondering what else she knew. What Theresa and Cathy knew. If they knew all my secrets or just this one. I felt even more vulnerable and intruded on than I had from my encounter with Kendall Barker. I couldn't believe I was so transparent but maybe that was because I could barely admit the pregnancy to myself.

"Are you okay?"

I shrugged. "Just trying to make it through life without the whole Goddamned world sticking its nose in my business. The part of the world that's not putting its Goddamned hands all over me."

"Pregnancy's kind of a hard thing to hide."

I thought I'd done a pretty good job. "Does everyone know?"

I couldn't stand it that she was being nice to me. Kindness made me homesick for Dom and Rosie, homesick and vulnerable, things I had no time for. Feelings that wouldn't work in this place, that made me less safe. Here I needed to be like that cop Hannon thought I was. Always with my antennae up. Cautious and wary.

She shook her head. "Theresa's too busy running around tryin' to keep the business going to notice, Cathy's got her head up her ass, trying to see in the dark, and Clyde doesn't notice things like that. Most men don't. But once you've been there . . ."

Against my will, I was drawn into the conversation. "You have kids?"

She shook her head again. "Lost it. Miscarried. Nearly broke my heart," she said. "I told you the story, you'd understand." End of conversation. As neatly as if she'd drawn a veil, that subject was dropped. "You'd better eat before it gets cold."

I turned toward the tray, picked up my toast, and took a bite. *Don't do this to me, Kalyn,* I thought. *Don't be nice. Don't tell me your stories. We can't get close. Real relationships are based on truth; Dora McKusick is a lie. And once I get what I want, I'm outta here.*

"Who are you, anyway?"

My hand froze in midair. I stopped chewing. "What do you mean?"

"It's just . . . you know . . . like I know you're running away from your husband . . . and I sure can relate to that, but sometimes I see this attitude, kind of like 'to hell with all of you' peeking through and I know you won't stay here. You'll get it together and go away and do something with your life."

"I'd like to," I said. "Before all the bad, confusing things happened, I was ambitious. I used to think I was going to save the world. Then I got into a relationship where there was a lot of stress and danger. Now I'd just like things to be normal and peaceful again." I could hear the longing in my voice.

She nodded. 'Yeah. I knew you weren't always a waitress. Not that you aren't good at it."

"I'll never be as good as you," I said. "You've got eyes in the back of your head. So what about you? What do you want to do with your life?"

"Ride off into the sunset with Andy," she said. But she didn't mean it. Andy and the motorcycle were the business she put between herself and what she didn't want to deal with. I knew about that. After David died, I started working seven days a week. Keeping busy was the only way I could cope.

She shrugged, resigned. "Theresa's about the hardest-working person I've ever seen, but she can't do it alone." A quick grin came and went. "Sure, she thinks she can, but she's not so young and running a restaurant's hard work. Cathy could help out more, but she's so stuck on herself, and so damned selfish. And Theresa's been good to me . . ." She caught my look. "I know what you're thinking . . . what you've seen . . . but it isn't always like this. You're catching us at a real bad time. Ever since . . ."

"Ever since what?"

"That cop got shot . . ." She looked down at her strong, thin arms, her rough, red hands. "I don't mind the work, I'd just . . . I don't know . . . like to do something more."

"Like what?" I asked.

"Work in an office maybe? Wear a dress and use my head? I can type . . ." She stopped. "What did they do to you, anyway, Hannon's goons?"

"I don't want to talk about it."

She shook her head sadly. "Hard to believe Clyde's one of them, isn't it? He's such a good man."

I shrugged, still angry. "He didn't help, did he?"

"Usually he's kind. But he's . . ." She hesitated. "He's one of them—militia, I mean—and that kind of thinking scares me. Not that they haven't got a point . . . got a lot of points . . . government's not always right in the way it treats people, but guys like Hannon. I don't know. There's something evil there, like it's not about making the government rethink some of the stuff it's doing. With him, it's about power and control and not caring who gets hurt in the process. His guys, they'll do anything . . . even deliberately . . . uh . . . hurting people to make a point . . ."

She shot me a quick look, swallowed hard, and stared down at her feet. "I should go. Let you eat in peace." But instead of leaving, she sighed and sat down in the only chair, her face suddenly serious. "Look," she said, "can I trust you?" She spread her hand over her stomach like a fan. " 'Cuz I've got this thing eating me up and I need to tell someone."

"Trust me?"

"Yeah. To keep your mouth shut?"

She couldn't, of course, if she was going to tell me something relevant to Andre or the militia. I felt a matching twinge in my own stomach—the part of me that hates lying. In an instant, it felt like the air in the room had changed. "I think so," I said. "I'm pretty good at keeping secrets. Besides, I don't know anyone around here to tell."

"That's right," she said, "except Theresa and Clyde. And you wouldn't." She swallowed hard and took a deep breath. "Look. I'm serious. This is heavy stuff. It's about . . ."

"Kalyn. Kalyn, can you come down here and help out, please?" Theresa's voice had an angry whine that brought Kalyn to her feet. "Guess I gotta go." She was gone in a flash, her feet thudding down the stairs, leaving me alone with my cold breakfast, cursing Theresa.

I forced down some toast and eggs and drank my lukewarm tea, staring toward the window and the rooftops beyond. "What?" I said aloud. "What the hell's going on here? What terrible thing has happened that has you all so scared?"

CHAPTER 15

Lunch was a whole lot like breakfast, with all the curiosity and questions about Jed Harding. At least none of Hannon's men paid me a visit. Except for the usual wear and tear on my feet and back, I escaped unscathed. Still, the backache and headache didn't seem to be getting any better. I was ready for horse liniment and a rubdown. I spent my meager two-hour break going through the shelter census and then driving around on some nearby back roads, but I didn't learn anything except that collecting junked cars and broken farm equipment seemed to be a common hobby. Apart from Kendall Barker, whose place I couldn't find, an Adeline Peters who might be related to Bump, and a Terrence McGrath who might be related to Theresa, none of the names were familiar.

Half a lifetime later, the dinner shift was in full swing. My back was aching, my feet were killing me, and I was making my millionth trip into the dining room with a tray that weighed a ton when I spotted Roland Proffit and another trooper I didn't know sitting at one of my tables. *Good timing*, I thought. I never had gotten a chance to call Jack. There wasn't a pay phone in town that wasn't dangerously public. I delivered the fish and steak and spaghetti I was carrying to a hateful family with three whining children, two demanding adults, and a sulky German au pair, pulled out my pad, and approached their table.

"Evening, troopers," I said. "Know what you'd like or do you need a little more time?"

"Got any trout left?" Proffit asked. He was a great actor. It was clear we'd never seen each other before.

"I think so."

"Good, I'll have the broiled trout, then, with rice and salad."

"Dressing on your salad?"

"Honey mustard." I wished I could ask him what he was doing here.

"I'll have the swordfish," the other trooper said. "Baked potato and salad. Blue-cheese dressing. Sour cream. Lots of sour cream. And lots of butter." He was short and sturdy, with crew-cut sandy hair and an intelligent face.

"Anything to drink?"

"Iced tea."

"Coffee. Black."

Across the room, three scruffy middle-aged guys in faded camouflage pants and T-shirts were standing in the door of the bar, staring at the troopers rudely, and murmuring among themselves. As I opened the kitchen door, one of them said, "Hey, why don't you guys just let Jed Harding go, huh?" His T-shirt read: REMEMBER RANDY WEAVER!

Proffit raised his hands in a helpless gesture. "Take it easy, buddy," he said. "It's not up to us, you know. It's in the DA's hands, now."

"You want to get your boy back, you'd better let him go."

"Buddy," the other trooper said, "give it a rest. We just came here to eat."

"Better keep an eye on the dining room," I told Theresa. "You've got two state troopers out there and a bunch of guys in the bar who want to make trouble." I leaned against the wall and rubbed the small of my back. It had been a long day. The thought of lifting another heavy tray made me want to cry.

"Thanks for telling me," she said, scooping up an armload of plates. "I'll take care of it." Theresa was small and rather frail looking, but though my experience was extremely limited, I'd already concluded that she could handle most anything that came along. There were enough people at any given time who were regulars so that an unspoken code of conduct seemed to apply in the restaurant. People knew how she ran things. Knew her rules about causing trouble.

I gave the troopers' orders and paused by the stove to talk to Clyde. "Do we have any special policy about feeding cops? I mean . . . I don't want to do anything stupid . . . but do we charge them for meals like everyone else?" I honestly didn't know. I knew cops weren't supposed to take freebies, but what people were supposed to do and what the practice was were often quite different. Some business people got genuinely offended if the cops didn't take their offerings.

"When they're done, Theresa will take them their check." And that's all he said, so I knew no more than before I'd asked. I also realized that it was going to be hard for Roland to slip me a note, in case that was what he was planning to do. I'd just have to find a way to communicate while I delivered their food.

"Things go okay last night?" he asked. "Stuart's usually more bluster than bite, but I know you've had it rough . . ."

What about this morning, I thought. *Are you blind?* But I didn't say anything about that. Maybe Clyde didn't know. He hadn't been in the dining room like Theresa and Kalyn. Maybe he thought I ran through kitchens and smashed coffeepots against Dumpsters all the time. Or maybe he thought it was a hormonal thing and that was territory he didn't want to explore. Besides, after working breakfast, lunch, and now dinner, I didn't have the energy to finesse, so I just answered his question. "He scares me witless, Clyde. First he locked me in a dark closet and then he kept swinging this hunk of pipe in my direction. If that's bluster, I'd hate to see his bite."

I thought I had seen his bite—in his eyes, in his intrusive hands, and in the vicious little degrading assault today by one of his goons. "I don't believe that man is a minister," I said. "He doesn't act like any Christian I've ever seen." Leaving Clyde to ponder on that, I ladled up two bowls of clam chowder, dished up four slices of fresh raspberry pie, scooped ice cream onto three of them, and headed back into the dining room.

In the brief time I was in the kitchen, things had gone from bad to worse. My table full of whiny brats was quiet, which might otherwise have been a blessing, but their silence was the result of all three staring, mesmerized, at my nemesis, the Reverend Stuart Hannon, pastor of the New Life Church, the camouflage-clad leader of the late-night meeting I'd observed. My charming host of the previous evening. *Colonel* Hannon, who had whacked me in the nose, albeit unwittingly. He was standing on a chair, staring down at the troopers, ranting about a jealous God who will smite his enemies. He must have arrived already wound up, because he hadn't had much time to get started and the words were pouring from his mouth like soda from a shaken bottle.

". . . and it is the right, nay, it is the duty, of every Christian man to take up arms, when necessary, against the depredations of a wrongful government!" he thundered, "to strike down the instruments of oppression and seize back the power and authority which reside in each and every free man as the basis of his citizenship. To protect our organic constitutional rights against an unconstitutional government."

It was comfortably cool in the restaurant but he'd worked up quite a sweat. Already, there were visible beads on his high, domed forehead, and dark half-moons beneath his arms. He paused for a chorus of amens, pulled out a handkerchief, and mopped his face. It was clear that the instruments of oppression he was referring to were the two troopers. A grim-faced Theresa stood before him, trying to get his attention, but he was steadfastly ignoring her.

"At this very moment," he continued, "our brother Jed Harding is languishing in a jail cell, twice a victim of the very government which he nearly lost his life serving . . . the very government whose use of poisonous chemicals without any thought for the risks has already condemned our brother Jed to a lifetime of anguished pain and suffering . . . a government . . ." here he paused for effect ". . . that has condemned not just Jed himself, but his innocent only son, Lyle, a poor little wretch crippled as a result of his father's chemical exposure, condemned both father and son to lifetimes of suffering . . ."

He stomped his foot down angrily on the chair. Theresa winced, gave up trying to get his attention, and headed for the kitchen. "Tonight, as he has been for many nights, Jed Harding is shut up in a jail cell, far from home and family. Why? Because he had the temerity to demand from his government . . . from our government, though it is clearly no longer a government of the people, by the people, and for the people . . . because Jed Harding had the nerve to demand medical coverage for his poor little child, medical coverage which the government has already agreed that it will provide in cases like this . . . medical coverage which the government, our government, in all its power and wisdom and goodness and mercy, refused to Jed Harding and his pitiful little son."

He paused again. "Jed Harding is in jail tonight because when the government, which hurt him so badly already, refused one last irrational time to give him the help he sought, he decided not to take 'no' for an answer."

Man, but the guy could speechify, though I didn't believe a word of it. I knew just how kind he could be, how concerned for others. He slammed his fist into the palm of his other hand and then spread them wide, as though giving the room his benediction. The whole restaurant had fallen silent. No one was eating. Most people were staring curiously, but a few tables, obviously of summer people, were beginning to shift restlessly and looked irritated. One was trying to signal for a check. Hannon was oblivious.

"Brothers and sisters, Jed Harding is in jail tonight because he decided to take matters into his own hands. Because he decided he'd had enough of the runaround, enough of the bureaucracy, enough of having his basic rights denied. Jed Harding was doing nothing more than you or I would do. He was fighting for the rights of his child. He was fighting to give his son a fair chance at life. A fair share of the pie. A decent shake for once instead of bureaucratic runaround."

Again he paused, his sharp, quick eyes circling the room to

be sure that people were with him, quelling the few people who were trying to ignore him and enjoy their dinners, glaring at the man who was again signaling for his check. Hannon had a sharp nose, bushy black eyebrows, and a narrow, almost lipless mouth. His eyes were deep-set and dark. His head narrow and his face long and bony. A mean-looking, unattractive man. The whole damned town was full of 'em. This one looked like he would have taken great pleasure in prosecuting the Salem witches. And he would have been unwavering in his certainty that he was right.

He cleared his throat loudly and resumed his oratory, clearly in love with the sound of his own voice. "When Jed Harding had finally had enough and couldn't take it anymore, he pointed his gun at the lazy, lying, corrupt bureaucrat who was refusing medical treatment for his son, and demanded what was rightfully his. Oh, he had asked and he had begged. He had filled out their endless forms and stood in their endless lines and shown that he had almost endless patience. To no avail. In the end, that patience ran out because he couldn't bear to see his boy suffer any longer."

He held his arms out to the crowd, palms up, as if in sup-plication. "Now I ask you. I ask you to ponder upon what I have said, and tell me: Which of those men belongs in jail—the hum-ble father, trying to care for his handicapped son, or the corrupt representative of an arrogant, too-powerful government? Who has lost their way? Jed Harding, an honored veteran and a hard-working citizen or the corrupt bureaucrats who put their time, not into serving the people, but into consolidating their power into an ever more centralized and indifferent government? A government whose various arms are so bent on amassing power they can't be bothered to work for the safety of all the people, never mind protecting the interests of one small child."

He shook his head as if in disbelief. "No. If we want a coun-try that's safe for our women and children and fair to the little guy, we're gonna have to take care of it ourselves . . ."

There was a scattering of applause. One of the men who had

been muttering earlier, a stocky redhead with a trim beard, a big, round head, and an expansive gut, stood up and said, "Well, hell, we got us two representatives of that government right here. Why don't we take them hostage, too? Keep on taking hostages until they let Jed go?"

But Jed Harding doesn't want to be let go, I thought. I almost said it aloud.

"Hostages, hell!" It was the guy with the Randy Weaver T-shirt. He and his two buddies had moved to a table in the dining room. "Let's hang 'em from the nearest bridge."

I was so scared for Roland and the other trooper, I felt like I was going to be sick. I had stomach cramps anyway, probably from something I'd eaten. Or hadn't eaten. I'd only nibbled on the breakfast Clyde had sent up and skipped lunch to save time.

Theresa had returned with Clyde and they both carried base-ball bats. She slammed hers down against the floor beside the redheaded man's foot. "There will be none of your damned rabble-rousing in here, Joe Parker," she said. "You can sit down and eat your dinner quietly or you can leave right now. You can start your wars on your own time. I'm not having this kind of disturbance in my place."

Joe Parker looked around for support, but found few people to meet his eyes. There might be a ton of support for Jed Harding in the room, but not many people seemed interested in showing that support by attacking two armed, uniformed state troopers in their favorite local restaurant. It was impossible to tell whether it was fear of authority, or fear of Theresa and of being banned from the dining room, or whether they were just hungry, but something was keeping them in line.

"Hell, Theresa," he bellowed, "whose side are you on, any-way?"

Theresa planted her hands on her hips and looked up at him solemnly, her face all points and angles, her voice hard and harsh. "I'm on the side of trying to make a livin' and trying to let people relax and enjoy their meals, Joe. I'm on the side of running a nice, peaceful restaurant where people will want to come and eat. I'm on the side of you taking this ruckus outside where it belongs and letting these poor hungry folks eat. And that's all. This ain't about politics."

Joe Parker spat, "Fucking government bastards," and a few other worn epithets at the troopers, and took his seat.

Theresa turned to the Reverend, who was still standing on the chair. Even though I was mad at Theresa, I liked what she was doing. I was silently rooting for her to whack him one with the baseball bat, but she didn't. "Come on down off that chair now, Stuart, and cut out this disturbance. I'm trying to run a business, here, and these people are trying to eat their dinners. You want to preach, you've got yourself a pulpit, which this place isn't. You want to start a war, you find someplace else to do it. There's hundreds of miles to chose from out there." She smiled wryly and made the first joke I'd ever heard her make. "This is a demilitarized zone."

The Reverend Hannon climbed down off his chair and stood glowering at her. "Sister McGrath, sometimes I fear for your soul . . ."

In response, she only thumped her bat on the floor again. "Then maybe you'd better go home and pray for me, Stuart, because I'm busy serving mammon here. We all of us have to do a bit of that, or you wouldn't have a church or a house or a pot to pee in." Hannon, his nose in the air, turned on his heel and stalked toward the door. I didn't believe it. I kept expecting him to whip out his menacing piece of pipe or summon his goons, but he didn't.

"Stuart," she said loudly, "this isn't a soup kitchen. You have to pay for your dinner just like the rest of these folks. No one eats here for free."

It was a lie, I knew. Kalyn had told me that in the off-season, Theresa often gave people credit when they needed a night out and a good meal. But she liked to chose her charities, not have them decide for themselves. He pulled out his wallet, gingerly tugged out a five, and dropped it on his table. Then he turned and left. Theresa picked up the bill, looked down at his check, and shook her head. "Two dollars short," she said, "and that's before the tip. I wonder what his god thinks of that."

I delivered the chowder and the pies, gave the check to the anxious man in the back, took a few orders, cleared off two tables, and staggered back into the kitchen under a load of dishes that would have given Samson pause on a good day. Theresa was standing in the center of the room, her eyes snapping, obviously at the end of a tirade. ". . . Ever since that Hannon boy found himself a jealous god and a bunch of morons who'll listen to him, he's been insufferable! Another outburst like that and he can find a new place to eat. They all can. This ain't exactly a thriving metropolis. Those boys ought to understand that. Politics are fine in their place, I don't blame some of 'em for being mad at the government, even if I don't agree with how they're going about it, but around here, we've got economic reality to deal with."

She shot a challenging glance around the room, as if we'd dare to disagree with her. "I've got a few months to make most of a year's living. A couple outbursts like that will drive the tourists away and then where will I be? They can . . . you all can . . . do what you want on your own time, but I don't need any damned militia types giving speeches in my restaurant and I sure as heck don't need no state cops showing up like they didn't know they were walking right into a hornet's nest."

She set her baseball bat down with unnecessary vigor. "Dumb bastards, all of 'em. I wish both sides of this damned thing would just stay home. If they used the sense God gave a gnat, they'd see no one's gonna win this thing."

"Amen," Kalyn said, as she shouldered a pile of meals and headed for the door.

I reached for my next meals, but Clyde put a hand on my arm. "Hold on," he said. "Are you okay? You're looking awfully pale."

"I don't feel great," I admitted, "but I think I'm just tired. Still getting used to this, I guess." I picked up the troopers' meals and followed Kalyn. Things in the dining room seemed to have settled down. If anything, it was noisier than ever. As I bent down to deliver their food, Roland said, very quietly, "Can you meet us at midnight? The usual place." I nodded.

His companion, who hadn't said anything, except to give his order, now added, "And bring your stuff with you. The lieutenant wants you out of here."

There was nothing I wanted more, especially after last night, but it was too soon. With all the seething passions around me, sooner or later someone was going to say or do something important, and I wanted to be here when it happened. I wanted to again go over those papers I'd taken. I wanted to learn Kalyn's secret. I wanted to sneak into the church and grab Hannon's piece of pipe. On the other hand, this afternoon I'd noticed a couple carloads of guys in camouflage with out-of-state license plates arriving and parking at the church, and that scared the pants off me. But I didn't say anything to Roland. Too many ears and eyes in the dining room. All I said was, "Can I get you anything else?"

"Pie," they both said, "blueberry."

I wrote it down.

"Hey, honey," a voice said from the other side of the room. "How about waiting on some real people for a change?"

What did he think these troopers were, baboons? If his car overturned on the highway, or his neighbor went bonkers and started shooting everything in sight, or someone was poisoning the public water supply, did he really want to have to sort it out alone? "I'll go get that pie," I said. "Enjoy your dinners." I bit my lip, picked up my tray, and went to see what the man wanted. What he wanted was blueberry pie, too, warm, not hot, with a generous scoop of chocolate ice cream. I got his pie and pie for the troopers, then scooted into the kitchen to put in some more orders. We were out of everything again, and I had to rush to the storeroom, refill the tubs, get another vat of coleslaw, and make another pot of coffee.

By the time I got back to the dining room, Proffit and the other trooper were gone. So were the three men who'd been antagonizing them. It gave me an uneasy feeling in my stomach, wondering what might be going on outside, but there wasn't anything I could do. I was just a waitress named Dora, rich as

Croesus with my pocket full of dollar bills and about fifty pounds of change, wondering how I'd get through the next hour until closing. Wondering how I'd stay awake long enough to keep my rendezvous. Wondering what would happen when I got there. When Jack said leave and I said no.

By 10:30, things were pretty well buttonedup and I was entertaining visions of lying down for a while before I had to go meet Jack. Just as I was hanging up my apron, the phone rang. Theresa answered it and handed it to Kalyn. "Your boyfriend," she said.

Kalyn took the phone, listened intently, and her shoulders slumped. "You're what?" she said. "But you promised you'd . . ." And then, "I really can't ask . . . not this late . . . it's not fair . . ." She listened again, then said, with resignation, "Well, okay, see you when I see you." She hung up the receiver and turned to me. "Dora . . . I hate to ask you this, but do you suppose you could give me a ride home?" She looked very unhappy. "Andy says his bike's broken down. It hasn't, it's just he's too drunk to drive, but that's what he says. Either way, I'm stuck without a ride."

She looked over at Clyde and said in a teasing voice, "I'd ask Clyde, but he can't do it. Cathy'd have a fit if he was to be alone with me . . ." She waited, hopefully. I was stunned, brainless, and dead on my feet. My back was killing me, my innards were uncertain, and I would gladly have consented to a double amputation if it meant my feet would stop hurting. Both were yelling, "No. Come on, girl, give us a break." But if I got her alone, she might talk to me.

"How far is it?"

"Five miles?"

"Okay. I'll get my purse and the keys. Meet you out by the Dumpster."

"Story of my life," she said with a flick of her russet ponytail. "Back doors, back streets, back alleys, except we don't really have alleys up here. Out back by the Dumpster." She shrugged. "Guess I should be used to it by now."

Climbing the stairs, my feet felt big as a Clydesdale's, and as heavy. The room was a sauna. I turned on the fan and pointed it at the bed, fighting my body's powerful need to sleep and my brain's desperate yearning for oblivion. I wished my system would hurry up and settle down. Before I went downstairs, I limped into the bathroom and splashed about a gallon of cold water on my face.

Partway down the stairs, I remembered the gun. Jack Leonard wanted me to have it, so I supposed that meant Jack Leonard wanted me to carry it. It improved my chances of shooting myself in the foot significantly. Good old Jack. Always looking out for my welfare. I reached carefully past the guardian spiders, into the box, and under the ancient pads. For a second, I couldn't feel anything. It seemed like the air stood still and my heart suddenly skipped before my fingers found the metal and I pulled it out. I stuffed it in my purse, checked my pocket for keys, and went out.

Then I thundered down on my gigantic feet to where Kalyn was waiting, leaning against the car.

I fired up the engine and we rolled down the windows. Air-conditioning was one of the amenities it lacked. "Where to?"

She rattled off a set of complicated directions. I waved them off. "I'm too tired to process all that. Let's take it one street at a time."

"Fine with me. You're good to do this," she said. "I could have asked Clyde. He's too nice to say no. Thing is, though, even if Cathy wouldn't have a bird, which she would, he's one of them. And after tonight, I've had enough of them for a while. They say they're doing this for everyone, but the truth is, they don't give a damn about anyone but themselves. Like I know they don't care that that damned Stuart Hannon's raving got a couple of my tables so spooked they left without a tip. Like it was my fault or something because I'm a local. Can you believe it?"

"There's little about human nature that surprises me anymore."

"Sheesh. It all surprises me. I think I've got people figured out and they go and do something strange. This thing got a radio?"

I reached out and snapped it on. "Not too many stations up here."

"Back ass of beyond," she said cheerfully, fiddling with the dial until she found a country station.

I was trying to think of an innocent way to lead her into talking about Paulette. My brain was too tired for much finesse, though. "That girl I replaced, Mindy. Did she really run off with a guy in a big truck?"

I'd expected one of her flip replies, but instead I got silence. The radio was playing something about a woman who didn't know she was beautiful, even though the whole room fell silent whenever she walked in. I guess we were supposed to think she was modest, but I thought she must be pretty dumb. Then again, after the past week, the ability to be oblivious was looking better and better. A life where I didn't notice much that went on around me might be rather blissful after a constant stiff neck from looking back over my shoulder all the time. After bruised and battered shins from keeping my head down the rest of the time, avoiding any offensive eye contact. Dammit. I was tired of this.

"Something wrong?" I asked.

Kalyn sighed. "You turn right just up there."

I turned right and drove a while in silence. "You as tired as I am?"

"I don't guess I know," she said. "I always think no one could be tireder than I am, but you sure did look tired tonight."

"Theresa never looks tired."

"Theresa is a witch," she said. "There's no other explanation."

"I was surprised at the way she stood up to Stuart Hannon tonight . . ."

"Oh, that," she said. "Maybe not as impressive as it seems. Not when her boy Jimmy's . . ."

I wondered if Jimmy was the one Theresa had meant when

she said one of them was useless. "Jimmy is what, Kalyn? One of them?"

"You bet your ass," she said. "A very important one of them, is my guess . . . luckily, we don't see much of him. He's the kind of bully makes Hannon look nice. Jimmy was around this afternoon, while you were off, talking to Theresa. She didn't look too pleased."

I thought about what I'd read, and about what Jed Harding had said. That the way things were organized, not even the militia members themselves knew who the top men were. "Do most people around here know who the leaders are?" I asked.

"They're pretty secretive. But we've got our opinions."

"And in your opinion, Jimmy is a pretty important guy, right? Why do you think so?"

Her only answer was to say, "Up ahead, just past that mailbox, you take a right."

"What about Roy Belcher?"

"Him? He's a bad-guy wannabe. Except that's wrong. He is bad. I wish that stinking bastard would rot in hell."

"Why?"

"Why do you keep asking me why, Dora? What do you care? I already told you. You don't want to know stuff. It's better that way."

"I want to know because I live here. I work here. Because these people have threatened me. I want to know what the hell is going on around here. I want to know how to protect myself. Who to watch out for . . ."

"Just leave," she said. "That's the only way to protect yourself."

"I thought I was protecting myself by coming here."

"Out of the frying pan, into the fire," she said.

I slammed on the brakes and came to a stop in the middle of the road. "It's not funny," I said. "None of this is funny. You can be as flippant as you want, but I know it bothers you. You don't like living in a constant state of fear any more than I do. The difference is, I believe in doing something about it. You and everybody else around here, you go around with your eyes on the ground like you were looking for pennies, while those militia guys run the town like it's a communist country and they're the only ones who are members of the party. Pushing everyone around, beating people up, killing people. And all the rest of you act like it's all right."

When she didn't say anything, I reached past her, grabbed the handle, and opened the door. "It can't be far," I said. "You can walk home from here."

In the sudden illumination, I could see tears on her cheeks. "Sheesh, you really think you're tough, don't you? You want to know why we're all so scared?" she said in a small voice.

"Yes, I do."

She reached out, grabbed the handle, and slammed the door shut again. "Okay," she said. "I'll show you. I hope you've got a strong stomach."

CHAPTER *16*

SOMETHING IN HER voice chilled me like a plunge into icy water. "What is it?" I demanded. "What are you going to show me?"

"Wait and see," she said. "It's the answer to your question. Why we all go around with our heads down and our eyes on the ground. Why we're such a bunch of scaredy-cats."

That's all she would say, except for giving me directions. Directions I tried to file in my tired brain, in case I needed them again, to come back here, or make a quick escape. Always, lurking at the back of my mind because of Kavanaugh's warning, and because of the craziness of this place, was the fear that this was a trap. A convenient phone call, a friendly request, and then what? Knowing these people, an ugly death. But this felt like a part of the answer. Like what I'd come here to find, so it was a chance I had to take. This whole business was a chance I had to take.

We drove several more miles down the same road, then a left and then a right, and onto a dirt road, hardly more than a rutted track, that climbed steeply uphill before coming to an end in a clearing. At the edge of the clearing was a mobile home, not quite level, looking forlorn and derelict in the light from my high beams. Kalyn pointed at it. "We're going in there. Hope you got a flashlight."

I hadn't put one in the car, but I was sure Dom had. He was too paternal to have let me drive off into the wilds of rural Maine without a flashlight. I was sure he'd never let either of his teenagers out of sight without a flashlight, a full tank of gas, and a first-aid kit. He was a belt-and-suspenders kind of guy. Sitting here now in the darkness, with mosquitoes whining in the windows, I wished he were here to back me up. This new life was too scary for me.

"Well," she said. "Are you coming?"

True, I'd been pushy before and she was right to be annoyed with me, but now I felt like dragging my feet, or rather, I didn't feel like getting out of the car. Stalling for time, I asked, "Whose place is this?"

"Nobody's, now, I guess."

"Then whose was it?"

"Paulette Harding's. This is where she and Mindy lived."

"I suppose you can't just tell me about it?"

"Look," she said, and her usually cheerful voice was grim, "you've been dumping on me tonight because I'm such a wimp. And I know you were thinking the same thing earlier, after those guys in the dining room did . . . did whatever they did. Well, before you go around accusing people of being cowards, you ought to know what you're talking about. You can't know unless you see this . . ."

Okay, I thought. *I asked for it, I had to face the music.* Except I already knew I wasn't going to like the tune they were playing. But it was my duty to go and see what she wanted to show me, and I was a slave of duty. Ask my poor aching feet, or my aching back, or even my tender nose. I reached for the handle and opened the door, ignoring the protests from my feet as they hit the ground. "Just tell me this," I said, not knowing why I thought it might help to know. "Is it bad?"

"It'll be the worst thing you've ever seen."

Oh, God. My stomach lurched like I was on a roller-coaster. I had seen some pretty awful things. I longed for some nice cool air—cool air makes me feel better when I'm queasy—but the night was like a steambath. A steambath with air still as death and void of any sounds except the wild wail of passionate insects, a shrill, high-pitched sound like mourners keening. I snapped on the flashlight and illuminated the rough path across the weedy lot to the trailer, following Kalyn up the steps to the door.

As she reached for the handle, I said, "Wait. Someday the police are going to be coming here. You don't want to leave your fingerprints."

"You watch too much TV," she said. "I already left 'em when I came here looking for Mindy . . ."

"She lived with Paulette? They were friends?"

"Roommates," she corrected. "Mindy needed a place to stay, Paulette had a spare room, and needed the money."

"Mindy could have lived at the restaurant . . ."

"Like you? And have Theresa watching her comings and goings? Theresa and everybody else in town? Never able to get away from the job? Mindy was too smart for that . . ." Kalyn sighed. "Sorry. You didn't know what you were getting into. Didn't know anybody. But Mindy did . . ."

She grabbed the handle and opened the door, and a wave of hot, stale, foul-smelling air rushed past us and escaped into the night. I gagged and put my hand over my mouth, stalled in my tracks, unwilling to go any farther.

"Come on," she said. "You've come this far. It's no worse inside . . . the smell, I mean."

She stepped into the room, reached over to the wall beside the door, and flicked a switch. A bare overhead bulb came on. We were standing in what must once have been a living room. At least, the chunks of demolished furniture looked like pieces of a sofa and chairs, cut into chunks with fluffy bits of stuffing protruding. The squashed lampshade was still recognizable as a lampshade. There were deep gashes in the walls. The curtains were shredded. There wasn't a thing in the room, other than the lightbulb, that hadn't been destroyed.

Kalyn looked around as if surprised to see it again, and said in an unsteady voice, "Chain saw, I think. That's . . ." Her voice failed. She swallowed, cleared her throat, and tried again. "That's what I think . . ." She pointed a shaky hand toward the kitchen, "Come this way."

There are days when I regret having inherited my mother's powerful will and self-discipline. Any sensible person would have turned at that point and fled. So far, all I'd had to face was the destruction of things. I knew I was heading for worse. But I pushed myself forward, up two steps, past a flattened table and smashed chair, into the kitchen. The room looked like it had been savaged by a madman.

Cupboard doors were shattered, hanging in splinters from their hinges. Glass jars and cans and cereal boxes were smashed, their contents a Jackson Pollock smear that spilled down the shelves, onto the counters, and onto the floor. Cheerios mingled with soup and spaghetti sauce and jam. Countertops had been gouged with what must have been an ax. The stovetop had deep dents, the glass in the oven door was smashed, the refrigerator stood open, hanging by one hinge, the shelves inside collapsed. Everywhere there wasn't food, there were streaks and splashes of reddish brown and blackish red. Clear handprints. Smudged handprints. Handprints vanishing in streaks down the wall. Large pools of dried blood on the floor.

Signs that something terrible had happened here. My eyes, like a camera recording this for posterity, swiveled around the room, taking it in. I tried breathing through my mouth, but that made me feel sicker. There was so much blood. Blood everywhere. Splatters of blood on the ceiling and at the tops of the walls, flung there as the blade rose and fell. Rose and fell. Deep cut-marks in the floor. Huge patches and smears of blood on the walls, floor, and counter as the victim staggered and fell, staggered and fell. And fell and was hacked to pieces.

"Paulette?" I gasped, my voice strangled. I turned and headed for the door, knowing I was going to be sick. Hoping I could make it. Kalyn started after me, ended up ahead of me, dashing out the door, down the steps, and stopping there, retching, not one whit less ill for having seen it before. I pushed past her, found my own clear spot, and bent, sick until nothing more could come up.

I staggered back to the car, the taste nasty in my mouth, and fumbled around until I found a water bottle. The contents were hot but I didn't care. I rinsed my mouth, drank deeply, and handed it to Kalyn. When she finally handed it back, her eyes still tearing and her face ghastly white, I repeated my question, "Paulette?" She nodded.

"How do you know?"

"Mindy . . ." She gulped and reached for the bottle in my hand. "Mindy heard them coming, so she ran out the back door and hid under the trailer. They didn't even bother to look for her. They just did what they'd come for. Took care of Paulette and left. The whole time, Mindy was hiding under the trailer, scared out of her mind, listening to the whole thing."

"A lot of people know about this?"

She nodded. "Now you understand why we're scared?"

I did and I didn't. Yes, it was terrifying. It was hard to think of an uglier death than someone coming after you with an ax and a chain saw. But if people put their heads down the first time it happened, instead of calling in the police, then the bullies knew it was working. Knew intimidation and violence worked. Knew they could get away with it. The horror of it threatened to overwhelm me. I had to keep talking, keep doing. Not let my mind skip to what people like this might do to Andre.

"When I saw it before . . ." Her voice had a strangled quality, ". . . last time, when I came looking for Mindy, she was . . . Paulette was . . . that is, what was left of her was still there . . ."

I couldn't imagine it. When I spoke again, my own voice was almost as shaky as hers. "You know where Mindy is now?" She nodded. "Does she know who did it?"

"Some of them."

"Where is she?"

She shook her head vehemently. "That's something I'm not telling you. You or anyone else. And don't you dare say anything about it, either. Nobody knows I know and I plan to keep it that way."

"Why Paulette?"

"I told you. Because she was the dumbest person in the history of the world."

"Yeah. You said. But what did she do to deserve this?" It was a dumb question, putting me right in the Paulette category. No one could ever do anything bad enough to deserve what had happened in there. Never.

Her voice was almost a whisper. "She called the cops."

"The cops? You mean, that trooper who was shot?" My mind reviewed what I knew about that. Not much. Gary Pelletier had gotten an anonymous call from a woman who said she had some information about a planned militia raid on a national guard facility. He'd responded, leaving no phone number, address, or other information behind other than that he was going up to Merchantville to check out a tip. Maybe he'd had no other information. Pelletier had turned up a few days later, way across the state, in a blueberry field in Washington County. He'd been shot nine times at close range.

"I don't know," she said. "I don't know anything about that."

That wasn't true. What was true was that her bravado was wearing off. The enormity of what she knew was getting to her. And she was realizing that, in an effort to make a point, maybe she'd just told a stranger way too much. I could have made an effort to bring her back, regain her confidence, coax more information out of her, but it would have taken a lot of work and a lot of time. And it was late. Incredibly late. I'd be lucky to drop her off and still be on time for my meeting with Jack. If I didn't show, who knew what he'd do? Comb the place, looking for me? Blowing my cover, just when I had my nose under the tent? I couldn't risk it. Besides, I had a lot to tell him.

"We'd better get going," I said. "Seems like morning comes earlier every day. You working tomorrow?"

"Not me," she said. "I told Theresa I needed a day off. Cathy's coming in."

"What's up with Cathy, anyway? What does she do when she's not working?"

"Beats me," Kalyn said. "She's got the two kids, but half the time, they're with sitters. I've never been able to get anywhere with her. We been working together the better part of two years, and she still acts like I'm the help and she's the boss's daughter. Kind of burns my ass, if you know what I mean. Theresa's not like that. But Cathy's always been stuck-up. Thinks she's too good for Clyde when he's obviously eating his heart out."

I got in the car, slammed the door, and started the engine. "I don't get Clyde, either. He's too nice to be one of them."

"I know," she said. "But he is. And much as I like him, I don't guess you can trust any of them, no matter how nice they act. You know? Look . . ." Now that she'd shown me this, she was having second thoughts. I didn't blame her. Who knew whom you could trust? "Look, you can't tell anyone about this. About anything that's happened tonight. I lied about people knowing. They know something's happened, but they don't know all this. Most people don't . . . didn't know where Paulette lived. You promise?"

I promised, hating to lie to her, knowing that I would have to tell Jack. I dropped her at her house, exercising amazing self-control, stomping down firmly on my almost uncontrollable desire to grab her and shake her until she told me everything she knew. Who had killed Paulette, if Mindy had told her that, plus where it was that Mindy herself could be found. Because whoever killed Paulette had almost certainly killed Pelletier. And probably knew where Andre was. But I did control it. Because lack of impulse control, and yielding to the urge to bully smaller, weaker creatures, was what made them what they were. And that was what I didn't want to become, no matter how desperate I was. If I was patient, she'd tell me more. She obviously hated living with it and was dying to tell. It was only a matter of time.

The second she was out the door, I gunned the engine and backed out of her yard, using speed and impatience as surrogates for curiosity and frustration. I drove like the proverbial bat out of hell until I reached the outskirts of town, then I slowed way down. The last thing I wanted to do was attract attention to myself. Especially given the kind of attention that was dished out around here. I drove down the main street with all the alacrity of a doddering grandmother. Once I reached the end of the settled area, I checked my rearview mirror. I was all alone. I put my foot down and blasted off into the night.

CHAPTER *17*

WHAT KALYN HAD shown me had broken down the barrier
I kept between my day-to-day existence and all the awful what-
ifs. What if Andre never came home? What if I had to raise our
child alone? How would I even know what to call it, when he'd
picked out the names? I'd survive, just as I had when my husband David died. But it would be a hollow, workaholic existence
and I never wanted to go there again. A wave of despair washed
over me, tears blurring my eyes until I couldn't see the road. I
felt that giant hand clenching my heart. But what could I do
except soldier on, as I imagined he was doing? I had to believe,
despite all the evidence to the contrary, that this would end well
and Andre would come home. I dashed away my tears and focused on the now—what I would say and do when I met Jack.

Because living in Merchantville was enough to make anyone
paranoid and because I'd been trained in the Andre Lemieux
school of preparation, before my first meeting with Norah Kavanaugh, I had checked out alternative routes. Andre loved to
make me read maps. He actually found it amusing and delightful
to be involved with a woman who was both decorative and competent, though it seemed to me he spent a lot of his time making
me more competent. Sometimes I worried that he'd get bored
with me when there wasn't anything left to teach. But maybe by

then he'd be busy teaching the kids to read maps and navigate overland.

I was driving down the road with the window down and the night air blowing in my face. At this speed, it actually felt cool. I had the radio on. No tape player, but at least this thing had a radio. Music was blaring in my ears. Bob Seeger was singing "Roll Me Away." Driving music. Songs for summer nights. I stomped down on the accelerator and felt, for a brief time, like any other young woman in a powerful car who liked to drive too fast on warm nights. The good feeling lasted only as long as the song and as long as it took me to realize that there was a car behind me. A car following awfully closely, considering how fast I was going.

Maybe I was being paranoid. Maybe it was just another driver like me, feeling the pleasure of the road and a big engine and no one else around. Except that there was someone else around. Me. I decided to test my theory on the next straightaway. I remembered one just over the crest of the next hill. Sure enough, there it was. Instead of putting the pedal to the metal and taking advantage of it, I slowed down. If the car behind me was out to have some fun, he'd go flying past and sayonara, buddy. If not, then I could start to get nervous. He didn't pass but stayed on my tail like an insecure friend or a baby duck. Tonight I wasn't in the mood for either one.

If he wasn't going to take advantage of the moment, I would. UB40 was playing "Red Red Wine." I stepped on it and felt the amazing power under the hood respond. This car was like a plain girl with a great personality. Or maybe it was a plain guy. No sense in being sexist here. Indeed, it being Dom Florio's car, I had come to think of it as a guy. I thought its name was probably something like Fred. We neared the end of the straight stretch going about ninety, and Fred slewed slightly as I braked and shifted down, accelerated through the curve, and took off again. My baby duck didn't do quite as well, but then, he might not have had the advantage of a racing short-course like I had.

Fred was more troublesome on the next curve but he seemed to like it, and by now I'd opened myself up a rather nice lead.

If I could keep it up, I knew that about half a mile ahead there was a road going off to the right that would also take me where I was going. I needed to put enough distance between us to make the turn without being seen. But the road was now a series of curves and, having had only the short-course, I was driving at the limit of my ability. I peered anxiously ahead for the turn. There it was.

I braked, shifted down, took my foot off the brake, and spun the wheel. I almost did a 180, but managed to hold Fred to the course. As soon as I had slowed enough, I cut the lights and pulled over to the side, watching my mirror nervously. Seconds later, I saw a pair of headlights flash by. I'd almost begun to breathe again when I saw taillights backing up, and the car turned down the road I'd taken.

Cursing, I edged the gun out of my purse and waited. Maybe it was just a cop, coming back to give me a ticket for driving like a maniac. Not bloody likely, but a gal can hope. Nope. Not too many cops I know drive battered, red pickup trucks. The state cops have got some nifty trucks. But they aren't red and they aren't battered. Two men got out. They were illuminated briefly by the cab light but I only had an impression of bearded and capped heads before the doors shut and they began moving toward me.

Their truck was about a hundred feet behind me. I waited until they were right beside my car, a dangerous gamble, given that they might be carrying guns, but then, this whole situation was a gamble. My being in town was a gamble. My whole life right now was a gamble. But I was willing to gamble a lot for Andre. Always have been, poor besotted woman that I am. Besides, if they had guns, they might shoot me anyway. I was better off as a moving target. As soon as they were beside me, I turned the engine on and gunned it, roaring out of there, throwing up gravel, my tires spinning on the pavement, driving like a teenager in heat.

This time I had a better head start. They had to run all the way back to their truck. I drove way too fast for an unfamiliar road, an unfamiliar car, too fast for common sense. Several heart-stopping, stomach-churning seconds later, I found the turn I wanted, took it, and shut off my lights, proceeding along the rough dirt road in the darkness, amazed at how complete it seemed. Not far along, I came to a big barn looming beside the road, a darker shadow in the darkness, sitting next to the cellar-hole of a burned-down house. I eased off the road onto a bumpy, unused driveway, hoping I didn't meet an enormous pothole or something worse.

I parked Fred behind the barn, switched off the interior lights, and got out. I was winded and my legs were shaky but it didn't feel bad. It felt vaguely intoxicating. Or I felt slightly intoxicated. Sometimes I worry about my reckless side and having all of this go to my head. People can become adventure junkies, developing a need for bigger challenges and greater dangers. I'm trying to go in the other direction. People close to me have suggested that I'm suffering from PTSD and ought to get treatment. I'm a big believer in self-help but sometimes I wonder if they're right. Sometimes I do get a charge when I succeed in doing something people don't want me to do, when I keep the bad guys from winning. It's not something girls—or women, for that matter—are supposed to enjoy.

I waited near the edge of the barn where I could see the road but duck back if necessary. Waited for an eternity, scarcely breathing, feeding about a pint of my blood to the whining mosquitoes. Waited with itching welts rising on my bare arms and legs, with a savage ache in my back. Longing to lie down and rest. Waited and watched. Finally something came rattling down the road, moving slowly. As it passed, I could see that it was a truck. I watched the red taillights bounce away and disappear into the night. I waited again to see if they came back. The road wasn't very long. If they didn't find me—which they wouldn't—I wondered if they'd come back or give up and go home. About the time I was getting faint from blood loss and my legs were trembling almost uncontrollably, they came rattling back up the road, passed the barn without stopping, and were gone.

I waited until I couldn't hear them any longer, then climbed back into Fred and headed off in the other direction. I drove with a constant eye on the rearview mirror but I reached the main road and turned right without seeing another car. Four miles down, I turned off onto the side road that took me to the dilapidated ranch. There was a police car already parked in the garage, and three men standing around looking anxious.

Jack Leonard looked at his watch as I climbed out of the car, gave me a quick cop up and down, and looked back at his watch. He didn't look pleased with what he saw. "You're late."

I gave him my own up and down back. He looked like hell, too. Haggard and exhausted and jittery. A lean, handsome man who right now looked extremely hard used. "Sorry. I was followed."

"What?" The word exploded in the crowded space. "Thea, I told you to be careful."

"I was. I lost them."

"Them?"

"Two men in a battered red pickup truck. You want the license number?" I rattled it off and the new guy went to run a check.

But Jack was on a protective tear. "Lost them how?"

"By driving like a bat out of hell." I patted the side of the rustmobile. "This baby may not look like much, but it can move . . ."

"Thea . . ." Jack sighed, and I was instantly ashamed of myself. He had enough to worry about without me being a deliberate pain in the ass just because my adrenaline was up and I'd had a crazy twenty-four hours. More than enough. This situation was a cop's worst nightmare. "I want you out of there."

"I want me out of there, too," I agreed. "Just not yet. I'm in the right place, Jack. I'm beginning to find things out. People are starting to talk to me. I'm sure that if I stay a little longer, I can find out something useful . . ."

"Thea . . ." He sighed again, and looked at Roland and the other guy. "You've got people following you. Why do you suppose that is? You stay a little longer and you may become another person we're looking for. This isn't some kind of a game, you know."

No. If this were a game, we could call it off and go home. If this were a game, fanatic militia ministers wouldn't be sending their lackeys to compel my presence, or to commit brutal assaults to make a point. No one would have gone after Paulette Harding with a chainsaw. I wouldn't be standing in this dirty garage all strung-out with shock and horror, breathless and gut-sick and aching.

"Jack, I'm the one who was left standing at the altar, remember? I'm the one in the beautiful white dress with two hundred puzzled guests, a swarm of dainty bridesmaids, and my mother having a major fit. I'm the one who hasn't taken an easy breath in days. I'm the one who thinks about Andre night and day, wondering if he's hurt or hungry or cold or hot, feeling my own frustrated desperation and knowing his is so much greater. I'm the one who wonders if his child is ever going to get to see him. Of course I know this isn't a game. I couldn't be more serious."

But Jack Leonard wasn't listening. He was staring at my waistline, a kind of stunned expression on his face. "You're pregnant?" I nodded. "Now we really do have to get you out of here."

"I was almost as pregnant several days ago, Jack, when we got me in here." I leaned back from the waist, trying to ease the ache, and wondered if this dizziness I felt was just from the adrenaline rush. I felt odd—intensely here and somehow not quite here at all. My mind kept flashing back to what I'd just seen.

"Oh, Jesus, Thea, use some common sense, will you? It's bad enough worrying about Andre and then worrying about you. But risking his child? You can't ask me to do that."

"I'm not asking you to do anything except find him, Jack. That's all any of us want. Now, do you want to hear what I have to say, or have I driven down here at breakneck speed with two maniacs on my tail just to listen to a lecture on how I ought to be more careful? I'm being as careful as I can. Nothing matters, don't you see, if . . ." Oh me. Tough-as-nails Kozak. I couldn't say it. I tried again. "If . . ." My throat closed. I massaged my neck as though that might make a difference. Squeezed out, "We're all on the same side here, Jack. We've got one goal.

Don't . . ." I took a breath. Why was this so hard? "Don't shut me out." The cramps were worse now; I really needed a bathroom. The house didn't look like much, but it probably had one.

"I'm just trying to keep you safe," he said. "He'll expect me . . . us . . . all of us . . . to look after you."

"He knows who I am. He knows what I'm like. He won't be expecting me to sit by the phone . . ."

"He says you're never there to take his calls anyway," Proffit said. Trying to defuse the situation, to get me and Jack out of each other's faces. Futile effort.

I took a step back and so did Jack. I didn't mean to be so difficult. Jack and I have always had this odd chemistry—like baking soda and vinegar. Put us together and things start fizzling. "And he's never there to take mine. But we've stopped keeping score. Okay, here's the Kozak report. Make of it what you will. At lunch the other day, some old guys were talking about Andre, and one of them suggested that the ideal place to hide him would be in someone's survival shelter. It sounds like there are a lot of those around here. Big survivalist movement. I'm trying to find out where they are . . .

"Then later . . . and I don't expect this means anything . . . but I've decided not to dismiss anything . . . one of these guys asked me where I thought they were keeping him . . ." Jack stiffened. "Not because they suspected me, Jack, just because everybody's talking about it. So I said, 'In the basement of that church down on the corner' and he nearly went ballistic. Why would he do that?"

"Because you insulted his church?"

I shook my head. "Because they hold their militia meetings in the church basement. There was one there two nights ago, sometime after midnight."

"How do you know?"

"Because I was watching through the window . . ."

Jack balled up his hands into fists, took a deep breath, and uncurled them again. "Jesus, Thea, you what?" He was inches away from snatching me bodily and taking me somewhere he could lock me in Rapunzel's tower until this was over.

"Not on purpose, Jack. I'm being careful . . . I was out walking. I noticed the lights . . ."

"You were out walking in the middle of the night?"

"I thought it was a peaceful small town. I couldn't sleep. I kept having nightmares." I gave up trying to explain. I was trying to be cooperative but I hated baring my soul like this. I like to keep my dark secrets to myself. "I'm a big girl, Jack . . ."

"You're a crazy woman, Thea. I just hope nobody saw you . . ."

"Well, abandon hope, Jack . . ." I turned to Roland Proffit. "That guy who gave the speech tonight? The one up on the chair? He's the minister of that church. The Reverend Stuart Hannon. After he heard I'd taken Lyle Harding down to the jail to visit his father, he sent a couple of lackeys to bring me in for a chat."

Jack looked like he was about to go ballistic. Maybe this wasn't the moment to mention the list of license plates? The third trooper cleared his throat. "I've got the owner of that truck," he said. He stuck out a hand, seized mine, and gave me a firm handshake. "Patrick Dunne," he said. "I'm a great admirer of your husband . . . uh . . . fiancé."

My throat closed again. I forced words through it. "Thanks. So who was chasing me?"

"Truck's registered to a James McGrath."

Jimmy. Theresa's son. The one who sent her messages through Roy Belcher. The one who wanted her truck. But why on earth would he be following me?

"Anyone you know?"

I shrugged. "Theresa McGrath has a son. They call him Jimmy. But I've never met him. I think maybe they don't get along. He sends her messages through other people. I didn't recognize either of the two guys who were in the truck. Neither of them looked anything like Theresa, but that doesn't mean anything. I think they were probably more of Hannon's goons."

Jack shook his head. He looked like a man in terrible pain. "You think. You think. You crash a militia meeting. One of the head militia guys sends for you to have a little talk about why you're cozying up to Jed Harding. Guys are chasing you around in the middle of the night in trucks and you aren't worried? These are guys who collect weapons, read manuals on how to blow up government buildings, and believe that a woman's place is in the home without the right to vote. Get real, Thea. Paranoid gun nuts willing to get involved in high-speed chases isn't something to take lightly." He was working one balled-up fist into the palm of the other hand and all but foaming at the mouth.

"You're right. They said they'd be watching me and I guess this means they were."

"You guess? Of course it means . . . Thea, use your common sense . . ."

But I wasn't done with the Kozak report, which I wanted to finish before I fell over. After all, I still had to drive back. Hopefully, a less stressful ride than the one getting here. "When I took Lyle Harding down to visit his father . . ." I swallowed. The air in here was so charged it didn't feel like I was getting any oxygen. I couldn't let him get me thinking about how crazy these people were, or how dangerous, or I'd stop breathing. Stop functioning. Become totally useless. If I wasn't already. Didn't he know I *wanted* to run away?

"That's the craziest thing I've ever heard," Jack exploded.

"Why is it crazy? Isn't Harding the key to this thing?" I exploded right back.

"What on earth did you expect to accomplish? You thought that if you brought his kid to visit, he'd go all soft and spill his guts?"

"No. I'm a realist, Jack. But I thought that making a connection might be helpful."

"And did it?"

"I wanted to let him out of jail."

"You and everyone else in the state of Maine," he growled. Again I was ashamed for pushing him, even though I couldn't help it. I respected Jack. I knew he was a good cop. But he wanted me to be something I wasn't. Compliant. The good little woman. Staying home and biting my nails while I paced the floor and waited for him to bring Andre back to me. But the suit didn't fit.

"He says he doesn't want to go, doesn't want to be let out."

"I know that . . ."

This, I thought, was part of what he wasn't telling me. "But why, Jack? Why? It doesn't make any sense. He adores his kid. The kid's so upset he tried to run away from home. It's obviously killing him being away from the boy, and Harding's mother is on the verge of collapse with all that care . . . I should think he'd be moving heaven and earth, trying to get home. Funny thing is that his mother agrees with him. She says he can't come home. But why?"

Jack exchanged glances with the other two troopers. "He didn't tell you?"

"No, he didn't tell me. He wouldn't tell me. But you know, don't you?"

But Jack wasn't listening. "If you think you've got trouble now, being followed around by guys in trucks, just wait until they hear you've been visiting Harding . . ."

"They've heard. I told you. That's why I was summoned to meet with Reverend Hannon, though he claims it's because he thinks I'm an undercover cop. But why should anyone care that I went to visit Harding?" Jack looked like he was having apoplexy. And when I strung it all together, it did sound like I'd been wildly careless and drawn the gaze of the enemy. But when I was there, in place, it didn't feel like that. The way they treated me seemed like just more of their general paranoia.

Jack didn't answer. Instead, he said, "If you're going to stay in Merchantville, you've got to start being more careful. Keep your head down. Stay away from the church. Stay away from Jimmy McGrath . . ." It was a repeat of Theresa's advice, and useless, especially after tonight.

"Then how am I going to learn anything? I can't do it just with pieces of overheard conversation—two guys in a restaurant talking about a gun theft or a couple of Hannon's goons talking about whether one of them's got a weekend job at an armory. It's like trying to do one of those jigsaw puzzles where everything is the same color. And I've never even met Jimmy Mc-Grath. Is there something special about him? Something I should know?" I wasn't the only one who wouldn't tell the whole story, was I?

All three of them were staring at me. "What is it?" I demanded. "What did I say?"

"Armory," Jack said.

"Stealing weapons," Roland added. "What else have you overheard that you haven't told us?"

"Nothing," I said sullenly. "I told Kavanaugh about the weapons theft, and what's so special about a job at an armory?"

But Jack was boring in. "Where did you hear about an armory job?"

"In the church parking lot."

"Know who was talking?"

I shrugged. "Two guys who were acting as guards during the militia meeting. I don't know their names but I could describe them." I looked at Roland. "And I gave him the license plates . . ." Suddenly I was too tired to stay on my feet any longer. "Can we sit down somewhere, Jack? In the house, maybe?"

"Go home," he said. "Get some rest. You look like hell."

"Thanks," I said. "I'd love to. But I've saved the best for last . . ." It was a stupid, ugly way of putting it, especially given what was coming. I wanted to deliver it in a sensible fashion, but I was so tired and overwrought I was almost incoherent, something that rarely happens to me.

He winced. He actually winced, like he didn't want to hear anything more from me. Did he really want me to go away? No. He just didn't want any of this, and didn't know how to deal with me.

"We can sit in the car. As long as the garage is open, we can have the air-conditioning on." He opened the door, and, as I bent to get into the backseat, automatically put a hand out to keep me from banging my head.

When we were settled and had started to cool off, he shoved a package at me. "Here. You need this. It's from Florio." I took the packet and opened it. Bless Dom. He had thought of everything. In the packet were a driver's license, social security card, and a couple credit cards, all belonging to Dora McKusick.

"Now you can give me your real stuff," Jack said. "It will be a whole lot safer."

For once, I didn't argue. I just handed over my own ID stuff and substituted the fakes. It was only then that I remembered the shirt stud. Duh. I didn't know whether it was pregnancy or overwork or emotional overload, not to mention a blood-splattered trailer and being chased by gun-toting men in a pickup truck. I don't normally forget things. But tonight had been unusual. I reached in my pocket and pulled it out. "Hold out your hand," I ordered. He opened his hand and I carefully laid the little thing on his palm.

"What's this?"

"Shirt stud. From a tuxedo shirt."

His eyes seemed to glitter as he stared from the stud to me and back down at his hand. "Where?"

"Stuck between the wall and the floor. In a closet. At Reverend Hannon's church."

"You don't know that it's his."

"Factually, no. Instinctively, yes. He was there. It's just what he would do. Try to leave us something . . ."

Jack nodded solemnly. "What were you doing in a church closet . . ." he began. Then stopped. "I don't think I want to know, do I?"

"I don't mind. Waiting for my chat with the Reverend Hannon." Jack's eyes rolled heavenward. He started to speak and thought better of it. "You probably know already. It looks like out-of-town militia are arriving."

He shrugged wearily. "And there's nothing we can do to stop them." He studied my face with his knowing cop's eyes. "There's something you aren't telling me."

This was what I was marrying into—a brotherhood attuned to deception, a family where they knew when people lied. I closed my eyes, feeling close to tears. Wanting to cooperate and afraid to. Angry at him for not sharing with me. Frustrated by my lack of success, my pervading weariness, the ugly despair that gnawed at the edges of my hope. "I broke into the civil-defense office and copied their file on survival shelters . . ." His eyes and mouth narrowed. "I just thought . . . maybe . . . because of that conversation I had, that it was a place to look."

"You did what!"

"Well, I didn't break in exactly. I mean I used a key . . . so they wouldn't know I'd been there . . . I had to do something . . ."

He shook his head. "You are one Goddamned amazing piece of work." He got out of the car and slammed the door. Then he opened the door again. "You are an idiot, you know that? I don't suppose you thought to bring it with you?"

"I didn't know when we'd be meeting. I mailed you copies." I assumed he'd gotten the papers I'd sent. But I hadn't included a note, told him why they were important. They had the manpower to check things out, but I believed that a general sweep wouldn't work, that the militia was sufficiently well organized so that we needed a—what did they call it on the TV news?—surgical strike. Otherwise, they'd go after shelters one and two, and the word would spread, and by the time they got to three and four, Andre would be dead or gone. I'd sent them to him, but I thought only I would know if what I'd found meant anything. Maybe. And then again, given Jack's forthcoming nature and the cops' penchant for playing close to the vest, they might know stuff which would make my data useful. If only I had time to think.

"You got that shelter stuff, right?"

He looked at Roland. "Did we?" Roland nodded.

"Jesus, Jack. I risk my life and you don't even know if you got the stuff?" I sounded sullen and bitchy. I felt like weeping. None of us had the energy to prolong this conversation and I hadn't gotten to the most important part. We were all hot and sweaty and tired and I wasn't feeling well. I was poisoned once, by someone who thought I was getting too close to the truth, and I was having some of the same unpleasant crampy sensations now. Not desperate and violent, as things had been then, but definitely like something I'd eaten hadn't agreed with me. Even if the house was a mess, I was going to use the bathroom before I got back on the road. It sure beat a roadside ditch, especially in a world filled with mosquitoes.

"What was Andre working on just before he was taken?" I asked.

Jack didn't answer. He had the right to remain silent, I thought. I didn't. I was supposed to spill my guts, even though anything I said could and would be used against me. Just as I had gathered myself to tell him about Paulette Harding, he started to talk, another lecture about how I had to be more careful. I've never done well, being lectured at. It brings out the worst, most pigheaded side of my nature. Then he started in with a slew of questions about my visit to Jed Harding, but I held up my hand to ward him off. I'd pretty much exhausted what I wanted to say about that, and had something I had to talk about. I'd put it off long enough.

"Paulette Harding." Just saying the name sent my adrenaline racing again. "I know what happened to her. I know where she was killed. And I know why . . ."

If he hadn't been sitting in the backseat of a car, he would have jumped to his feet. "Holy shit!" he said. And Jack never swears around me. "What do you know? Tell me everything . . ."

It felt, suddenly, as though there was no oxygen in the car. Being around him made me as jittery as he was. I felt weird and spacey and wired, all at the same time. "Have you got a map? I can show you where she lived . . . where she was killed." Jack was still staring at me like I had two heads. "She was the one who called Gary Pelletier. The one he was going to meet. They killed her because she did that . . . it's horrible, Jack. It's horrible, what they did. . . . "

I turned to Jack, unable to articulate the slaughterhouse horror of it. Grabbed him by the shirt and screamed in his face, "Why don't you find Andre? Why, Jack, why? Tell me what's going on, Jack. Tell me!"

Jack Leonard was pale, barely able to speak. "You think we're not doing everything we can?" he said.

"They killed her with a chainsaw, Jack. And an ax. Bit by bit. Suppose they've done . . . suppose they do that to him. . . . " I let go of his shirt. Got out of the car, and stood there, one hand against the wall. I closed my eyes but it didn't make any difference. I could still see the room giving silent testimony to what had happened there. Pain shot through me as if I were being stabbed. First one sharp pain and then another. Awful, tearing pains that made me gasp. Pains that had nothing to do with food poisoning, nor with what I'd just seen. I sat down on the floor, pressing my hands against my abdomen, trying to hold back the pain. The pain and what I knew was coming with it.

"Thea . . ." Roland Proffit's voice barely penetrated my fog. "Thea . . . Jesus, Jack. Tell her. Andre's alive. We've had a picture. Taken with yesterday's paper, so we could see the date."

When I didn't respond, he spoke more loudly. "Andre's alive, Thea. Now tell us about Jed Harding's wife, Paulette."

But I couldn't talk about that. I was somewhere else now. Traveling into a place where only women can go. Now I understood why I had felt slightly out of kilter all day. Askew. Unbalanced. It hadn't been lack of sleep, my backache hadn't come from carrying all those heavy trays, and all those vague pains hadn't been food poisoning. They had been separation. They had been the beginning of a small death. They had been signs that just as unexpectedly as he or she had come, attaching to me and filling me with unanticipated joy, Claudine or Mason or Oliver was leaving now. Tearing loose from the moorings and going away. Following Andre into the void. Leaving me completely alone.

CHAPTER *18*

I WRAPPED MY arms more tightly around myself and hung on, needing to do it, even though I knew it wouldn't make any difference.

"Thea? Thea? What's wrong?" Roland Proffit's voice intruded, dragging me back into human contact. Back into the garage, the night, the horror of what I'd seen, the reality of what was happening to me. He was kneeling down now, so his head was level with mine, and staring at me anxiously, so close I could see the flecks of gold in the irises of his eyes. Roland was a nice guy, and he'd been there for me during some pretty scary moments. I knew he was good and steady and that I could throw myself into his arms and blurt out my troubles and he'd be as tender and caring as I needed him to be. He'd take me where I needed to go, no questions asked. Hold my hand for as long as I wanted.

Trouble was, right now, I didn't know what I needed, whether I needed hospitals and doctors and drugs and procedures or whether I could just crawl into my cave and do this by myself. I only knew what I wanted. If I couldn't do this with Andre to hold my hand and rub my stomach, if I couldn't brace myself against his warm bulk and listen to the rumble of his voice, I wanted to be alone. I wanted to be home, too, but that was hours from here.

"Go away," I said.

He didn't. He sat down beside me and put an arm around my shoulders. I forget and remember, forget and remember, what these guys' lives are like. There's a lot of tension and a lot of boredom, and a whole lot of seeing people who aren't at their best. Like me, right now. As a culture, we tend to be resentful of cops. I know I am, even though I love one. But when the chips are down, when things get bad and stress or tension or shock or injury cause us to have trouble thinking for ourselves, cops are great to have around. It's one of their specialties— thinking for us when we're not at our best. I was not at my best; I was cruising, full speed ahead, toward my worst.

After a while, I began to relax against him. Only then did he ask more questions. "Why are you holding your abdomen like that? Are you sick? Does something hurt?"

My throat felt tight and I didn't want to cry. If I spoke, I knew I *would* cry. I tried for a minimalist answer. "It's all going to hell." Like I hadn't known that until now.

Jack was a few feet away, watching us closely, arms folded across his chest. He looked sick, like someone had just forced him to eat something awful. Like he understood what was happening and was as devastated as I was that there was nothing that could be done about it. And like he thought it was all his fault. That made two of us. I knew it was all my fault. That though I had tried to be careful, I must have brought this on myself though something I'd done. That all this stress which felt like too much for me really had been too much for the baby.

Roland hugged me tighter—a hug that said he wasn't going anywhere, that he'd be there as long as I needed him. He smoothed back my hair and studied my face intently. My Andre surrogate. "What's going to hell?" he asked.

There was another intense, cramping pain, the kind that makes you wonder whether to throw up or just die. Women never die from cramps, though. We just long to sometimes. I bit my lip. Soon I would need to curl up and writhe, which was hard with an audience. So was moaning. Men are great at moaning and groaning, but they don't watch it with equanimity.

"Roland . . ." I strove to keep my voice normal. "I just need to be by myself for a while. That's all. It was a shock . . . that room where Paulette died . . . thinking about Andre . . . about the things they do . . ." Something occurred to me then. What Jack hadn't wanted to tell me. What too many people in town knew or suspected. What all those strange looks had been about.

"This isn't just about setting Jed Harding free, is it? For both sides. It's about what happened to Pelletier and Paulette. The militia stuff is half bullshit. And Andre wasn't just a convenient victim . . ." It seemed like I had dozens of questions all at once. "Do you think Harding did this?" It was impossible for me to see the man I'd met doing what I imagined had happened in that house. Roland shrugged. That was a cop thing, too. Take all the information you can get; give as little as possible. So I answered my own question. Sometimes even if you can't get a phrase or a sentence, you can get a nod or a shake of the head. "You think Harding knows something about it?" I got a nod.

"But he won't talk about it?" Another nod.

"But you don't think he did it?" But this again got no response. "Was Andre working on it? On the murder?" All I got was a flicker of his eyes. I thought it meant yes. Some kind of yes. Yes for Pelletier, but had they even known about Paulette? They knew now. They must have known then. With rumors all over town, someone must have talked. And they'd been all over, looking for clues about what happened to Pelletier. Had Andre learned something? Was that why they'd taken him, because of what he knew, or was close to knowing, and not to trade for Harding? But they seemed so set on getting Harding out. What was that all about?

I hated being treated like a mushroom. Maybe they'd thought I'd be safer this way, but ignorance sure wasn't bliss. Neither, in this case, would knowledge be. This felt like a no-win situation. And I liked to win. So did the rest of them.

It was a warm night but I was shivering. Physically wretched. Emotionally wretched. Mentally wretched. I couldn't think about what was happening in Merchantville anymore. I could only think about what was happening to me.

He touched my hand and repeated his own question. "Thea, what's the matter? Something is wrong. Your face is pale and your skin is clammy."

I looked down at my hands, one pressed tightly against my body, the other curled up in my lap in a fist so tight my knuckles were white. "I think I'm losing the baby."

Roland put his other arm around me and pulled me gently against his chest, one hand making slow, comforting circles on my back while he murmured "I'm so sorry" into my hair. I rested my head on his shoulder, feeling unbearably sad.

Suddenly, Jack jumped into manic action. He got a blanket from the trunk, opened the car door, and gestured toward me wildly. "Come on!" he said. "Come on. Hurry. We've got to get you to a hospital. Maybe it's not too late . . ."

I was in no shape to argue although I knew it was too late. I was in awful pain now—steady, vicious cramps and bleeding. The worst pain, though, was psychic. This wasn't some fetus, some distant creature who would be developing into a child. This baby was real. It even had a name, or names. Andre had already begun talking to it, crooning silly little French lullabies into an imaginary microphone just below my navel. We already loved this child, this little surprise. Our accident. We'd heard the heart beat, holding our breaths as the doctor held a monitor against me and the steady little beat filled the room.

We hurtled through the night—I had no idea where we were—at speeds that made my earlier driving seem tame. I guess Jack had had the long course. Patrick Dunne sat in front with Jack. Roland came behind with my car. I sat in the back, bracing myself against the rocking, turning, and shifting, tossed around like a piece of flotsam on the sea of life. A shipwrecked castaway in some comfortless country where nothing was safe or familiar. We arrived at the hospital, stopped outside the emergency entrance with a wrenching jerk, and then Jack threw the door open and grabbed my arm. "Come on," he urged. "We're here."

We were nowhere. At least, I was nowhere. A nobody in

nowhere land. A woman coming apart. I wanted to crawl into a dark corner and pull the blanket over my head. If I had to do this in company, I wanted to do it with a tribe of wailing women, with mourning and ceremony and rituals. What I got was a skinny, bored orderly in soiled scrubs offering me a wheelchair ride. I got Jack bellowing for help at the top of his lungs. I got Patrick Dunne trailing along in our wake looking like he wished he were anywhere else on earth. I knew just how he felt.

Anyone would think, from the amount of time I spent there, that I liked hospitals. That they didn't connect to all my worst nightmares and send me into a state of almost paralytic fear. This was crazy. Utterly crazy. I was traveling on a gurney now, holding Jack's hand, as he filled a graying, bearlike man in on what was happening, babbling in a most uncoplike manner all of his fears of what was happening and his hope that the baby could be saved. Standing in for Andre. Being his best man. Except that it was my pain and fear, my loss, I might have been a spectator. Occasionally, the doctor asked me a question. I suppose I answered them, since he gave what sounded like satisfied grunts. I was draped in sheets and poked and probed. Then he raised his head and looked at me.

He had a big head with maniac tufts of graying hair, a jowly, worn-out face. He shook his head sadly. "I'm sorry."

Jack's hand tightened around mine and he made a sound that was suspiciously like a sob. "I'm sorry," the doctor said again. "There's nothing I can do. We're going to take you into the operating room and do a D and C. Theoretically, you could go home and let the process finish naturally, but there are so many risks involved." He mumbled a litany of risks and patted my arm. "Listen, it's not your fault. These things happen. Miscarriages are much more common than most people think."

Then, as if he wasn't sure I understood, he stopped patting and gripped my arm, gently but firmly, leaning in to make eye contact. "Doing too much aerobics, or working too hard, or taking a long bike ride, even getting the living daylights scared out of you—they don't cause miscarriages. It's not something you did. You have to believe that. Don't beat up on yourself . . ."

I wasn't crying. I wasn't going to cry. It was only that my eyes had sprung some leaks. I wanted Andre here. The hurt was bigger than I was, expanding and filling me, pressing on my heart and my lungs, filling me with a terrible ache. Closing my throat. Would I always lose everything I loved?

His fingers slackened. He lifted his hand and stepped away. "You'll be fine. And don't worry. You'll be pregnant again in no time."

By whom? I thought. *Oh, dear God, by whom?* I meant to be brave. Strong and stoic and self-contained. I meant to be a model patient. I meant to keep my shattered heart and hopes to myself until I was alone when I could sob into my pillow and wing my abject apologies to Andre, wherever he was. But the doctor's words severed the fragile bonds which held me together. As Mason or Oliver or Claudine, our son or daughter, our first child fought to make a painful escape from my body, my tears escaped as well, followed by sobs almost as wrenching as the pain.

The doctor took Jack by the arm and moved him away from me for a conference. I didn't see why they moved away. He didn't bother to lower his voice. "Your wife's having a hard time with this. Some women do. She's going to be fine. Just fine. But I suggest we start her on some Valium right away. It'll make things easier and it helps them forget . . ."

Helps them forget? Them? He might look like a worn old teddy bear, he might have tried to be kind and reassuring, but deep down, he was a pig. A know-nothing. He could give me a whole lakeful of Valium and I'd never forget one grim, ugly minute of the last week. Besides, since when did Jack Leonard start making my decisions for me? Right now, apparently, since the nurse, at his nod, swabbed my arm and stabbed me with a needle without asking or explaining.

Yessirree, I loved the way cops could take over when I was incapacitated. Only I didn't think I was. Or I hadn't been. But it was too late now. The Valium flowed in, pacifying me and stunning me, turning me into a human vegetable. Inert. Indifferent. Shattered but too tranquilized to pick up the pieces, sitting numbly beside myself, watching the action with bemused detachment. People came and went, shifting me here and there. Stuff was done. The situation was "handled." The baby that wasn't to be made its escape.

Somewhere in the night, one prisoner lay dreaming of his lost child. Another, in a jail cell, stared at a picture drawn with markers and fell asleep dreaming of his wounded child. In Merchantville, a small blond boy clutched a stuffed rabbit and dreamed of fishing with his father. A small soul winged its way to heaven. Safe within my chest, the pieces of my broken heart shifted and jostled and longed to be rejoined.

CHAPTER *19*

I WENT HOME wearing a set of surgical scrubs, a sickly green
that matched my complexion, a cluster of drugs in my purse, a
list of possible complications to watch out for on file in my
worn-out brain, with hard copy for backup. When I announced
I was going back to Merchantville, I expected a fight I didn't
have the energy for. I was going back only to work breakfast, so
as not to leave Theresa in the lurch, and then quit and pack my
stuff. I can be weird about follow-through sometimes. Jack
didn't argue at all. If anything, he was more visibly upset than
I. He drove me most of the way, pulling over just outside of
town. He patted me awkwardly on the shoulder, got into Roland's car, and they faded back into the darkness.

I drove the rest of the way alone, feeling disembodied and
surreal as I crept down Main Street into the silent town. Nothing about the world looked benign anymore. The shrubs were
black and menacing, the shadows outside the circle of street-
lights sinister and unfriendly. I was back only because I was such
a slave of duty, and because, in my drugged and weary state, my
brain's only working synapse had closed on the idea of conti-
nuity. Besides, it was a bed and it was close, and boy did I need
a bed. In my exhausted state, I couldn't formulate any alternative
scenario.

I had traveled a long way since my feisty and determined start this morning. Then I had been going to shake up the world. Now I had no plan. Not to sleep or to cry. Not where I would go with my pathetic little undercover investigation. Not even how I'd eventually get upstairs. Too many things had gone wrong. There had been too much death and disappointment, too many ugly things, too many losses, and none of it had brought me any closer to Andre. Maybe I was just a ridiculous romantic, but without him or the baby, nothing mattered.

By the time I got to Theresa's, I recognized the folly of my situation. I was dead on my feet, or rather, since I was sitting not standing, dead on my whatnot. I parked behind the restaurant, next to my faithful Dumpster, and lay down on the seat. The prospect of climbing stairs was daunting. I was too tired to get out of the car and walk the twenty feet or so to my bed and too depressed to think about anything beyond falling over. I'd been reamed physically and spiritually and left raw and bleeding. I would lie down and close my eyes and I didn't much care what happened after that. Someone else could type "the end" at the bottom of this page of my life.

It wouldn't be the first time I'd slept in a car. With its wide bench seat, it was almost as comfortable as the bed upstairs, and it was cooler down here. There was an actual breeze coming in the windows. My watch said I was supposed to be going to work in about three hours. I didn't see how.

When I heard the crunch of footsteps on gravel, I was reminded of other nights' nocturnal visitors. This alley was the rural Maine equivalent of Grand Central Station. People coming and going at all hours. Bad people. Without sitting up, I teased the gun out of my bag and stuffed it beneath the seat along with the list of names matching the license numbers I'd copied down in the church parking lot, which Roland had kindly left in the car for me. I was thankful for Dom's little storage compartment. I didn't dare be caught with either of those. Dora's fear of her dangerous husband might explain away the gun—doubtful now that the Reverend Hannon thought I was a cop—but there would be no explaining the list.

A shadow appeared in the driver's window, with a comment from the darkness. "You're out late." A rough, harsh voice. Unfamiliar. Not the unchristian Reverend. "Where'd you go to-night?"

"Yeah. Where did you go?" The second voice I knew. Roy Belcher, my faithful nemesis.

I formulated an answer, but between my brain and my body, there was a loose connection. When I tried to speak, no words came and when I tried to sit up, nothing happened. I just lay there, inert, too exhausted to care. Let them go pick on someone else for a change.

"Hey!" the stranger barked, his voice exploding. "Hey, girlie. I asked you a question. Where'd you go tonight?" Another time, another me, I would have told them both where to get off. Tonight I was too tired for anger. I had nothing left with which to feel resentment. I would have answered out of fear—I knew how awful these people could be—but I was utterly done in. I'd reached that stage of exhaustion where even thinking seemed too hard.

The door opened, bathing me in a sudden rude shower of light. I closed my eyes and put an arm over my face. "Go away. Leave me alone. I'm sick," I said.

"You been drinking?" the voice demanded as the speaker leaned in for a closer look. I smelled sweat and Old Woodsman's Fly Dope and some kind of oil. Gun oil, maybe? His volume was excruciatingly loud in the confines of a car. I cringed against the seat.

"Hey, you know I think she is sick," Roy Belcher said. "Really. She doesn't look good. I mean, she usually looks a lot better than this . . ."

Knowing that for most of these people, their default mode was irrational bullying, I made an effort to be coherent and interactive. Hard because, between my pathetic physical state and the Valium, capturing thoughts was like trying to scoop up egg whites. One sentence. A monumental effort. "Who's that with you, Roy?" I asked. My voice was little and light as air.

"What?" he demanded, and then he seemed to get it. Maybe

the words traveled more slowly because they were weightless. "Hey, Jimmy," he said, "meet your mother's new girl." There was a rustling in the darkness. "Dora, why don't you take that arm off your face and sit up, so you can meet Jimmy properly." People around here were so crazy. Matching totally uncivilized behavior with the most civilized conventions.

Not that my response mattered. Before I could move, Jimmy grabbed my arm and hauled me up, dragging me across the seat and out of the car. He was a massive man with long black hair, a full mustache, and a bushy black beard, sort of a halo for the dark side. I was sure I'd never seen him before so someone else must have been using his truck. I hadn't seen him at the church last night, either, but he could have been there. I hadn't had a view of the whole room.

"Dora, this is Jimmy." Roy spoke from behind the giant. I couldn't see him at all. There was so much deference in his voice, he might as well as have said, "This is God."

Jimmy McGrath didn't bother with civilities. He didn't offer to shake hands or mutter an acknowledgment. He held me there against the car, his huge hands like twin vises on my shoulders, and glared down at me. Illuminated by the light from the car, his face was scary. Scarred, pockmarked with the craters of bad acne, with narrowed, glittering eyes. Mean eyes. Evidently, personal hygiene wasn't high on his list. His skin and hair had a greasy sheen and when I looked down at the pinioning fingers, the nails were black. "Seein' as you're not feelin' well, I'll give you one more chance. Where'd you go tonight?"

I rested my head against the car, blinking in a desperate effort to keep my eyes open. The full trauma of the evening was finally catching up with me. I think I'm invincible. It always surprises me when my body lets me down. But it was letting me down now. I was pathetically weak and helpless. If he released me, I'd fall down. That would probably surprise them. Normally, having someone bully me and push me around gets my dander up and makes me more determined to resist. Tonight I had no dander. I could only stare at him.

"Where I go is none of your business." I didn't plan it, the words just popped out. Stupid answer to give these people. They thought everyone's business was their business. I was incapable of thinking of another. His fingers dug deeper.

"Now, Dora," Roy said, "people don't talk to Jimmy that way." He sounded like a prissy schoolmarm. Like a smarmy suck-up.

Jimmy was a ridiculously inappropriate name for this great thug. Jimmy was a cute little boy's name. This creature ought to be called Beowulf or Gargantua. Grendel's dam. Except that was Theresa. This was Grendel. "His mother doesn't own me. I just work for her." I didn't mean to say it; like the last wrong thing, it had just popped out. It was that damned disconnect again. I was thinking placating thoughts.

"This isn't about that," Jimmy said. "It's about whether people are with us or against us." He wanted to hit me. I could see it in his eyes.

"I'm neutral," I said. "I just do my job and try to mind my own business."

"Ain't no place around here for neutrality."

"Give her a break, Jimmy," Roy urged. "She's not from around here."

Jimmy grunted and shook me, the force of it sending my pain level to code red. I hung there, breathless with shock, limp and boneless as a rag doll in his hands. "It's pretty strange, you ask me, the way she showed up just about the time the trouble started." He shook me again and I gritted my teeth and tried not to scream. I thought I might simply fall apart. Burst open and spill all over the ground. That would surprise him. "Where?" He yelled it right into my face, his bushy countenance so close I could almost feel his whiskers; did feel hot flecks of spit.

It seemed like someone else was answering, but it was my voice that said, "I went to hell." A small sentence, sorrowful and confused, that summed it all up. His hands released me and I sagged against the car, sliding down until I was sitting on the gravel, a Raggedy Ann doll, held up only by my stuffing. The ground through my thin pants felt cool and damp and stones dug into me. "Excuse me." I looked sadly at the distance from where I sat to the stairs I had to climb. "I've got to go to bed. I have to be at work in three hours."

Jimmy McGrath loomed over me, shaking his massive head. "You aren't going anywhere until you answer my question."

I looked up at him. I didn't know whether he'd taken Andre or not but I knew that he was an evil man. I'm not a believer in auras but he had one so black it darkened an already black night. I wondered whether he was the child his mother had referred to as a "useless sack of shit." He raised one fist menacingly. In the odd illumination from the car light, it looked like a lumpy white softball thinly covered with coarse dark hair. "Where the hell did you go?"

I should have been cowering in fear—I didn't doubt that Jimmy McGrath was dangerous—but felt strangely indifferent. I was too tired to care about what was happening here. Nothing he could do could match what fate had already done. I put my arm down on the dirt and slid slowly sideways until my head rested on it. I closed my eyes and pulled my knees up toward my chest. It eased the pain a little. "I was at the hospital."

"Hospital?" He sounded surprised. "What for?"

"Hospital business."

A black-booted foot lifted from the ground beside my head and nudged my chin. "I didn't come here to play twenty questions, lady. What hospital business?"

I didn't want to answer but I didn't want to get stomped and I knew he'd do it. I've lived too long among the bad guys to be naïve about human behavior. "I was pregnant. Now I'm not."

His fist thudded against the car, thunderously loud in the quiet night. "Abortion. All these bitches . . ." he said. "Goddamn uppity women won't carry a man's child these days, they can't wait to rip it out . . ."

Shut up, I thought. *Shut up. Shut up. Shut up.* All that came out was a faint little whispered, "No."

He waited, but that was all I said. I was acting crazy but couldn't seem to stop myself. I'd used up all my emotions, including fear, common sense, and self-protection. What did I have to protect, anyway? I can get crazy sometimes, but tonight I wasn't me. I was like some wounded animal, too hurt to defend itself any longer, only biding its time, waiting for a chance to crawl away and either heal or die in peace. Scary as he was, Jimmy McGrath was just an obstacle in my path. I didn't want him to hurt me but I didn't have much energy to protect myself, either.

He grabbed my arm and hauled me up. I sagged in his grip. "You don't want me to hurt you, honey. Believe me, you don't . . ."

He was right. I didn't want him to hurt me. I didn't want anyone to hurt me. I'd already been hurt enough. Enough for a lifetime. It was a crappy choice—preserve my small remnants of privacy or share my sorrow with this violent bully. But I believed him when he said he would hurt me. This man would dispense pain with no more compunction than he'd have swatting a mosquito. I jerked my arm out of his grip and crossed my hands protectively across myself. There was no baby to protect anymore, but I felt incredibly, terrifyingly fragile, as if any blow might shatter me.

My legs were unreliable. I leaned against the car for support, feeling myself sliding, very slowly, down the slippery paint. Tried to brace my legs against the slide. "I was pregnant," I said, hating him for making me say it. The word "was" reverberated through me, echoes of "was pregnant, was pregnant" sending out shock waves of pain. "I started to bleed. It didn't stop. I got scared. I went to the hospital. They couldn't save it. I lost the baby. End of story. Okay?" A small surge of anger. "Is that all right with you, Mr. McGrath? Is it all right with you that I've just had the worst night of my life? Is it really necessary for me to stand around here discussing the most intimate details of my personal life with a complete stranger? Is that how you do things here in Merchantville? Corner people on their doorsteps when they're sad and sick and cross-examine them about it?"

I swallowed. "I came here to be safe. I came here to get away from being hurt and scared and threatened all the time. I came here to put my life back together . . . to find a place where I could live and work and have my baby. It's no better, Mr. McGrath. Just different people hounding me and threatening me. Just different bad things happening."

"Fuck." He turned on his heel. Was he leaving? Maybe I could make it upstairs if I crawled. Then he turned back. "If I call the hospital, they'll confirm that you were there?"

He must think I was a hell of an actress if he believed I was faking this. If he called the hospital, he might learn I was there. He might also hear that I was there with a bunch of state cops. I tried to sound indifferent. "I don't know what they'll do. Hospitals are weird sometimes. But where do you suppose I got these?" I plucked at the green shirt and pants. Fished in my bag and pulled out the prescriptions. "And these?" Waved my sheets of aftercare instructions in his face. "And these?"

From the shadows, Roy said, "Jeez, Dora. Are you okay?"

Fat lot of help he was. Worrying about whether I was okay when his good buddy Jimmy was shaking me like a rattle and threatening to kick me, punch me, or stomp me. He couldn't really be this simple, could he? These guys were too mean and impatient to keep a moron as a sidekick. So there was more—or, on a humanity scale, less—to Roy than met the eye. "Farthest thing from it," I said. "They wanted to keep me overnight—the hospital—but I said I had to get back here. Had to go to work. So please, can I go now? Get a little rest?"

"Hold on."

Such a fine choice of words. I was barely holding on and the way I felt tonight, it didn't seem like something I could do at will or on command. Right now I either had to sit down or fall down. I edged my way to the open car door and lowered myself slowly onto the seat, my whole body trembling with exhaustion.

"I think you're a cop. Sent here to spy on us. Another one of those useless new female cops, like the one shot one of my boys the other night. Goddamned uppity lesbo bitches with no notion of husband and family, no idea of a woman's proper place. Go out and take jobs that otherwise a man could have, let him hold his head up, support his family. God never meant it to be this way. He made the man the head and the woman to be the helper. It says so in the Bible."

This guy McGrath sure was a deep thinker, wasn't he? He hated the cops, they represented the government that needed to be destroyed because its actions were unconstitutional, and yet he was complaining that they let women be cops because it was taking jobs away from the men who really deserved them. And didn't his mother run her own business? But I was just as crazy. Even when I was collapsed in a helpless heap, I was still a knee-jerk feminist. There were things I might have said, but they'd only get me in trouble. Worse trouble. Clearly this was already trouble.

"I think you go out at night to meet other cops and give them your reports . . . I think that cop who got shot was coming back from meeting you. I think that's where you went tonight."

"You're crazy," I said, my guts dancing like frenzied snakes.

"Am I?" he said. "Ma would never think of it. She's way too trusting. But look who sent you here. Rosie. And what does her husband do? He's a fuckin' cop. Let's see who you really are." He grabbed my bag, pulled out my wallet, held it low so he could use the light from the car door, and went through it, grunting in disappointment as it revealed that I was indeed Dora McKusick. Dom had done it well, and just in time, too. I had my license. I had my credit card. I had my gas card. And I had my library card. All scattered on the ground at my feet. Too far away to retrieve. Jimmy McGrath slammed a fist against the car again. It seemed to be his way of punctuating his words. Poor rustmobile. But better it than me.

"Okay . . ." He tossed my wallet and my purse on the ground, scattering things everywhere. "Explain this to me. A truck was following you tonight. If you were really on your way to the hospital, if it was some big-deal emergency, why did you try to get away?"

We were playing twenty questions, but it was always his turn. I searched through the hollow shells of my mind and spirit for a plausible answer. I was so far out of gas I was running on fumes, and given his suspicions, what I said was important. "You ever been chased by two crazies in a pickup truck?" He grunted. I knew what he was thinking. People didn't chase Jimmy McGrath. He chased them.

"Mr. McGrath, I told you. I've got a husband who's sworn to kill me. Someone appears on my tail, following me close like that, and when I slow down where he could pass, he doesn't, what am I going to think? I thought it was him. I was running for my life."

"See, Jimmy. I told you . . ." Roy began.

He punched my car again. "Looks like you've got an answer for everything, honey, doesn't it? Well, we'll see." He waved his hand at my scattered belongings. "Roy, pick up this shit and help her up the stairs, will you?" A gentleman to the last, the malevolent Jimmy McGrath turned and disappeared into the darkness.

I was done in before my encounter with Jimmy McGrath. Afterward, I felt like I'd been put through a shredder. My knight in shining armor, Roy Belcher, scooped all the stuff, along with a generous helping of gravel, back into my purse, pulled me carefully to my feet, perhaps as afraid as I was that I'd break, and as much carried as escorted me to my door and up the stairs. He stood there awkwardly. "You want me to come in?" he asked. "You really ought to have someone with you. You look . . . excuse me for saying this . . . but you look like hell."

I'd been to hell. Was it so surprising that I should have brought some of it back with me? "A chat with your friend Jimmy will do that," I said, choking back hysterical tears. "I'll be okay. The doctor said I was supposed to take it easy. I just need some rest." I was afraid he was going to insist on staying, but Jimmy was waiting for him. He left.

I stumbled across the room, dropped my bag on the floor, and collapsed on the bed. The pain was bad but I couldn't get up again to take some pills. If I could have run, I would have run, but my body had given up. I lay in the dark, shivering with the aftermath of shock and the grim remnants of fear, not exactly crying, but with tears running down my face until the pillow was wet. My brain wasn't working well enough to figure anything out but I was certain that Jimmy McGrath was at the core of things. I just wasn't sure I was brave enough to find out how.

CHAPTER 20

WHEN MY ALARM went off at six, I could barely lift my arm to turn it off. It was sheer willpower that got me off the bed and into the bathroom, but then, I have more willpower than a roomful of probate lawyers. The woman in the mirror was a distant relative. Me in ten years. A gaunt-looking person with a grayish pallor and bruised-looking eyes. She had a beaten-down, defeated look and a lost, waif-like quality. Someone too often disappointed by life. Someone who needed to be rescued. I felt sorry for her. Would have rescued her if I could. I washed her face and brushed her teeth and crammed her hair into a barrette, too tired to bother to comb it for her. Then I dressed her, fed her some medicine for the unrelenting pain, and dragged her down the stairs.

I entered the kitchen with a very simple agenda: serve breakfast, quit job, pack, leave town. Theresa was rushing around like a dervish, her face tight and pinched. When she paused nearby, I opened my mouth to deliver my news, but before I could speak, she gathered up a handful of plates, snapped, "You're late," and headed into the dining room.

Mechanically, I tied on my apron and checked my pockets for my pad and a pencil. Crossed the kitchen to check the bins, stumbling twice over feet too heavy to move. Everything was full. Clyde glanced up from his cooking to ask what I wanted to eat. "I'm not hungry," I said. I didn't think I had the strength to chew and anyway, I wasn't interested. I went into the dining room to get away from his curious gaze, knowing that soon he'd be too busy to bother with me. Today I was the disembodied waitress. Or perhaps headless. Whatever it was, I was unlike myself, robotic, running on borrowed energy, and without a brain. I expected at any moment to simply fall over and lie there, unable to get up, like a turtle tipped on its back.

The dining room was full of staring eyes. By the time the breakfast rush was over, more than a dozen people had asked me what was wrong, and I had given a dozen versions of an unconvincing "nothing." People seemed to find my answer unsatisfying. About the only person who didn't ask was Theresa, which kind of surprised me, given how observant she was. But we were both so busy there wasn't time to notice much. Kalyn was off and Cathy hadn't shown up.

The four fishermen came in, sat in my section, and were eager as the rest of the crowd to pump me for information until Bump Peters, my geriatric hero, told them all to shut up and leave me alone. Roy Belcher came in. He wasn't in my section, but he stared at me until he must have memorized every grim wrinkle on my face. His excess of tender concern took the form of the words, "You're looking better today," hollered across the crowded room. Better than what, I wondered? The Reverend Stuart Hannon came in and sat with Belcher. They watched me and talked in low voices but neither one spoke to me. Joe Parker came in with his buddies, and they sat down across from Roy and Hannon.

It was a regular old-home week for militia members. It made the hair stand up on the back of my neck. I couldn't help thinking they were discussing Jimmy McGrath's theory that I was an undercover cop. It wasn't paranoid of me to think they were there as a warning. All I managed to pick up was a general restlessness that Jed Harding still hadn't been released and a desire to take some more dramatic action and to take it soon. I still wondered why Jed Harding's release was so important to them. Was it, as his mother had suggested, that Jed might have been involved in what had happened to his wife? Ex-wife. Was I just being foolishly naïve because I liked him? Maybe, knowing these guys, it was just a power thing. If they couldn't get him out, they lost face. But that didn't explain why Harding wanted to stay in, did it?

The most discouraging thing, out of all the discouraging things, was my deepened understanding of how evil and violent these men really were. I'd read it. Jack had warned me. But I'd had to see for myself. Kozak reinvents the wheel. And now that I had seen, I wanted to run home and cower there. This morning, in the cold, or rather, hot, light of day, coming back here at all seemed insanely foolish. But I'd been too stubborn to run. Even now, with my mind made up and despite the block of fear that filled my body, I was torn. I knew, instinctively, that I was close.

Okay. What was close? That I'd stirred up a lot of stuff, gotten some names. Gotten them looking at me too closely. What was that? And even if I was close, what was the likelihood that could I possibly get close enough in time? What if their dramatic something involved Andre? It was some comfort—but only a small some—that he'd been alive two days ago. Two days to this bunch, with their collective impulse disorder, was nothing. At any time, they could decide to kill him in a fit of rage, or just start chopping off bits of him and sending them to Augusta. That last thought sent me dashing into the bathroom. I emerged greener than ever and went on serving breakfast, even though the sight and smell of food was sickening.

It scared me that there were so many strangers in the place who didn't look like summer people. For every couple tables with families in shorts and T-shirts with restless kids babbling about fishing, swimming, and boat rides, there was one with MOM caps or Randy Weaver T-shirts and suspicious eyes. I wondered if the tourists noticed and if it made them nervous, too. Maybe these militia guys were invisible to the uninitiated.

I might as well have stayed in bed where I belonged. I picked up no clues, theories, or interesting pieces of gossip. Spying took attention and I needed all mine just to stay upright and keep my feet moving. Kalyn wasn't there, so I couldn't try to find out Mindy's whereabouts. Last night, despite my dazed state, I had described how to find the site of Paulette's murder to Jack, and told him about Kalyn, but I'd begged him not to do anything yet. Cops swarming all over the place right after Kalyn took me there would be a dead giveaway. For all I knew, he'd disregarded my request and the whole town was swarming with cops. Or might be at any moment. It was, after all, a murder, and a crime scene. I didn't even know if they could sit on their hands.

I wished Kalyn were here. Even if I didn't get a chance to ask her my questions, her helpful vitality would have been a nice antidote to Theresa's pinched coldness. About ten-thirty, after four hours without a break, I came into the kitchen carrying a heavy tray, tripped on a perfectly smooth floor, and broke a plate. Clyde took the tray away from me, set it down, and steered me into a chair. "You must rest," he announced. "And you must eat."

It sounded foreign, but it was just Clyde. I tried to argue, my ritual protest. "I'm not . . ." And we were still too busy for me to stop now.

"You must eat," he repeated, firmly. "You're not well, anyone can see that. I will fix whatever you like." Cathy still hadn't shown up, and every time the back door opened or closed, he looked at it hopefully. Stupid girl. If she wanted him, all she had to do was give up her dumb game-playing and open her arms. What she was doing was cruel.

I wondered what he knew. He was one of them, after all, but I didn't know how much they communicated, how fast news traveled, or where he stood in the hierarchy. I was counting the minutes until I could tell Theresa I was out of here. Besides, right now, kindness threatened my self-control. I had thought I needed to stay here and tough things out until I got something useful, but now every synapse in my body wanted to run for safety. I wanted to put my head down on my arms and bawl. I felt like such a phenomenal failure on all fronts. I didn't want to be waited on. I wanted to be shot.

"Don't be nice to me, Clyde," I said. "You'll only make me feel worse."

It was a good time to leave. In my current state, I was useless to Jack Leonard and equally useless to Theresa. There was no longer any need to knit baby blankets, but at least I could set up my new office and begin to sort things out there. Start staffing up. Stave off hysteria and despair by keeping busy. There was always plenty of work. I'd done it before and it was comfortingly mindless. I need both—comfort and mindlessness. Being here was like being tied to a stake and forced to watch a Neo-Nazi parade. The bad energy in the dining room worried me. I was afraid they were about to do something stupid. Something I couldn't do anything about.

Clyde shook his head. "I can see with my own two eyes, Dora. You couldn't feel worse. I will fix you . . ." He considered. "French toast. You like French toast? It's easy to eat."

"French toast would be great." I struggled for enthusiasm to repay his kindness, but my affect was flat. "I thought Cathy was working today."

"I thought she'd be here by now." He shrugged. "She's got to leave mid-afternoon. Theresa called Kalyn, but she didn't get any answer. So it all falls on you."

The thought that Kalyn wasn't answering gave me a chill. Had something I'd done—talking with her, going to that trailer—put her in danger? I was getting enough chills lately that I might be suffering from malaria. Emotional malaria. Today I was ready to believe that anything that went wrong in the world was my fault.

Natty and the other boy had arrived and were working on the food for lunch. Theresa was rushing about like an automaton, glaring at me from time to time. Cathy finally came in, tied on an apron, and began to work. She moved slowly, casual. Indifferent. I sat in the midst of it, knowing I should get up and help, and lacking the will. Feeling strangely removed, as though I wasn't really in the room, not a part of this scene anymore.

A week ago, Suzanne had been helping me into my gown and pinning on my veil, cursing as she hooked each tiny hook.

A week ago, I'd been a happy bride, watching through the window as my guests arrived, about to marry the man I loved and pregnant with his child. Now the man I loved had vanished and I'd lost the child. I couldn't rescue Andre and I hadn't been able to save my child. It was hopeless. I was hopeless. A colossal failure at everything. I couldn't do traditional womanly things and I couldn't do newfangled tough woman things. The fact that Kalyn wasn't answering was just one more thing to worry about. I sighed and, like a dog circling to flatten the grass before lying down, I circled through the gray fog in my soul, made a space, and settled into the midst of it, wrapped in despair.

Theresa cruised past my chair, sighed loudly, and went into the storeroom, banging the door meaningfully behind her. I started to get up but Clyde put a hand on my shoulder and said, "She and Cathy can manage. Stay." He set a steaming plate before me. "Eat."

Mechanically, I picked up my fork and did as instructed. I was just chewing my third bite when Theresa come over, pulled out another chair, scraping the legs loudly across the floor, and sat down with another sigh. "If you're going to work here," she said, "you've got to be willing to work. This is not some cream-puff job. I've got a business to run, not a charity. You've got to come to work on time, and when you're working, you've got to hustle . . . something you can't do if you're out until all hours of the night . . ."

I set down my fork, not hungry anymore, coming slowly back from the fog as I tried to make sense of this attack. I had been hustling for hours. I had been sitting maybe three minutes. "Theresa . . . Mrs. McGrath . . . I'm trying. I really am. It's just that I'm not feeling very well today." I did not want to share my personal business with her. I'd planned to wait until the mid-morning lull and then tell her I was leaving. But there had been no lull. Her sudden attack caught me off guard.

She peered at me with narrowed eyes. "Because you're not getting enough rest. You look like death warmed over, Dora. All the customers have noticed. What time did you get in, anyway?"

"It was pretty late," I admitted. "Look, Theresa, I . . . I appreciate all you've done for me, but . . ."

Theresa wasn't listening. She slapped her palms down on the table, exasperated. "I can't believe you've found another man already, Dora, but even if you have . . . you can't let that interfere with your work. Not if you want to stay . . . I'm not running some home for loose women here . . ."

I felt like I had as a teenager, getting the third degree from my mother. I was always a pretty good kid, and her suspicion about what I might be doing made me angry. I'd gotten up this morning after only a tiny bit of sleep, and against all medical and practical advice, come to work because I believed in doing my job, even if it was a job I hated. And because I knew breakfast was the busiest time of the day and it hadn't seemed fair to leave her stranded then. But I'd been trying to quit for hours—to give her some warning—and she hadn't let me.

I was too strung out by now to have any finesse. "I got to bed around three," I said, my temper flaring. I tried to rein it in and act like the docile Dora. "Do you want to know why?"

She shrugged indifferently. I didn't feel like explaining in detail, but her reaction made me angry enough that I did plunge into my personal business. Now that I was sitting and had relaxed some of my desperate control, I felt like I was having tiny fainting spells, consciousness coming and going like it was a camera lens and someone was trying to get the focus right. I'd been running too long on stamina alone, now I was running down.

"I was at the hospital having a miscarriage," I said. "When I finally got back, your son Jimmy was waiting out there. He dragged me out of my car, dumped out my purse, threatened to beat me up, and cross-examined me about where I'd been."

Theresa looked stricken, but all she said was, "Oh, really? You never mentioned you were pregnant. And as for my son, why would he do that? Jimmy doesn't even know you."

That last, at least, was right. Otherwise, it was as if she hadn't heard a word I said. Perhaps, during the night, Theresa had suffered a sea change into something smaller and meaner. She'd always seemed tough but fair; now she just seemed tough. Despite being a mother herself, she didn't show even a glimpse of compassion. Suddenly I couldn't stand this place another minute. I shoved back my chair and stood up. Standing made me realize I was worse off than I thought. I had to hold the back of the chair for support.

"Look, Theresa, I hurt and I'm bleeding and I'm supposed to be spending the day in bed. I've only had three hours sleep and I'm here at work trying to do my job because I know you need the help. I don't know how much more seriously a person can take things. I thought I might be safe here, but the people are even crazier than where I came from. I don't need to go from a husband who wants to knock me around to your crazy son who wants to do the same thing. Better the devil I know than the devil I don't . . ."

Everyone in the room was staring at me. I was icy cold and shivering. With shaking hands, I pulled my tip money out of my apron and crammed it into my shorts pockets. Then I dropped the apron on the table. "I quit." I wasn't getting anywhere anyway. Wearing myself out and pounding myself into the ground for no purpose didn't help Andre.

"Look," Theresa said, standing up herself and looking around the kitchen as if for confirmation and support. "You don't have to be so gosh-darned dramatic. Nor make a martyr of yourself, either. If you'd told me you were . . . uh . . . unwell . . . we could have managed and you could have stayed in bed. But I'm no mind reader . . ." She waved a bony hand at the rest of the crew, who were still staring. ". . . None of us are. But that doesn't mean we don't care . . . that we're not decent human beings. Finish your breakfast and then go on upstairs and get yourself some rest. We can talk about this later . . ."

I looked down at my plate of congealing French toast and shook my head. It wouldn't get any better. I couldn't cope with her practical kindness any more than I could cope with her coldness and indifference. I knew what it was like to run a business and worry about the bottom line. I did it myself. There was something missing in Theresa. Everyone talked about how she was hard but fair. Fair to herself, mostly. And I'd had enough. "No," I said. "I'll be going. It will be better for both of us."

Bravado. I couldn't go anywhere right now. If I didn't get out of this room and into bed in the next minute, I was going to humiliate myself by falling on my face in front of all of them. I wanted to rush upstairs, pack my bag, and go, but it wasn't in the cards. Not rush. Not stairs. Not pack. Not go. Crawl, stagger, stumble, creep. I made it to the door, defying their staring eyes, but even clinging to the railing, I couldn't manage the stairs. I huddled on the bottom step, watching the wall go from dark gray to light gray and fade into darkness again, until Clyde came, put an arm around me, and hauled me up. He left me sitting on the edge of my bed and went out, shutting the door softly behind him, never saying a word, as much an enigma as ever.

If I lived a dozen lifetimes, I'd never understand these people. Yesterday they had turned their backs and let Hannon's minions terrorize me. Today they were willing to let me fall on my face, and then, just as suddenly, they were kind. A matter-of-fact form of kindness. I was like a stray dog. Sometimes they fed me; sometimes they kicked me. I could go or stay and it wouldn't matter to them. The only person my presence here really mattered to was myself. Myself and Andre.

I should have been thinking about what to do next, but before I could, I tipped slowly sideways and tumbled into dreamless sleep.

CHAPTER *21*

I WOKE AROUND two in the afternoon because my room was like a sauna. It was so hot it felt like my blood was going to boil but I didn't have the strength to turn on the fan. I didn't think it was blood loss or delayed shock, it was simply exhaustion. I was always tired. The weeks leading up to the wedding I'd been working serious overtime, and I'd been running on borrowed energy all week—not only the energy to keep going at work, but the energy it took to keep from falling apart. It took a lot of energy to be tamped down, to maintain a low profile, and to keep from pounding on every door in town, asking if they'd seen Andre.

I was terribly thirsty and needed to take some pills, use the bathroom, do some stuff. I tried to get up but it was a repeat of last night. I sat up okay, but when I tried to stand, I slipped slowly off the edge of the bed and ended up sprawled on the floor, staring at the dust balls that had formed since my one attempt at housekeeping. At least this time there was no hulking brute like Jimmy McGrath to observe my humiliating weakness. I looked back in amazement at my morning, wondering how on earth I'd worked all those hours without collapsing. Well, I had collapsed, hadn't I? And just as soon as I got uncollapsed, I was packing my car, climbing behind the wheel, and getting myself out of here, making Jack Leonard a happier man. That didn't look to be happening anytime soon.

Being helpless increased my misery. I didn't need a horde of villains to entrap me and render me helpless. My own body had done it. It had betrayed me at a time when I needed to be at the peak of my form. More than ever in my life, I needed my wits about me and I needed to be able to depend on my strength and resilience. Needed to and couldn't. Strength and resilience, as much as a quick and orderly mind, had been the mainstays of my adult life. Now everything conspired to make me feel useless.

I was done here at Mother Theresa's, but there were still things I wanted to follow up. Lots of things. There were the forms from the shelter census to be gone over more carefully and compared with the names of the militia members on the list Roland Proffit had given me. There might be a connection between the two lists, a name that I recognized. Now that I knew what had happened to Jed Harding's wife, there were questions I wanted to ask his mother. Mary Harding might be fragile and weary but she was a good person, a moral person. I didn't think she would condone a horrendous murder, not even to protect her son or out of fear of his compatriots. Before I left town, we were going to talk.

Then there was Jimmy McGrath. Who the hell was he and why had he wanted to borrow his mother's truck when he had one of his own? Because it was bigger? And what did he want it for? Where was he taking it? Another time, a bold and headstrong Thea Kozak probably would have followed the truck or found out where the camp he was staying at was and checked it out. But this was the new, risk-averse me. I didn't take life-threatening chances. Or at least, I tried not to. Not when someone like Jimmy McGrath was involved, a bully who frankly scared me witless.

And I had to face the reality of my situation. I couldn't do it if I tried. The best I could do was get an address or a location for the camp. Tell Jack and his men to be on the lookout for the truck. I was lying on a dusty floor, sweaty and sticky, my brain the only part of me that still seemed to be working. It was intolerable. I put my palms down and pushed myself up so I was sitting. That was as far as it went. I had to rest before my next move. As I rested, I contemplated my situation.

I couldn't believe the mess I'd made of my life. I'd been left with only one task when Andre was taken—hold down the fort and take care of his child. Sure the doctor had told me that losing the baby wasn't my fault but I didn't for a second believe that. It must have been something I did. I was the mistress of my own fate, wasn't I?

I had survived up to this point, and fairly successfully, I thought, by a split-personality combination of being unusually optimistic, and by having big chips on both my shoulders that drove me and fueled my ambition. The first chip came from my parents: part of it from resentment that despite all my successes and efforts to please my father, he always took my mother's side, even when she was dead wrong; and part from the fact that no matter how hard I tried and no matter what I did, I could never please my mother. The second chip came from having grown up with a big chest and a pretty face, which, in high school, had made it difficult to be taken seriously or respected for my mind. I was still, these many years later, edgy and resentful about anything I perceived to be a slight because I was female, or a failure on anybody's part to take me seriously.

I had spent the years since my husband David's death restoring my balance and learning about compromise and perspective. It had been scary to take a chance on another relationship and it had been scary to take a chance on becoming Suzanne's partner instead of her employee. I'd worked hard on it. Hard enough so that when Andre proposed, I was willing to risk saying yes. And this was where I'd ended up. Just steps from the top, I'd tumbled down life's emotional staircase and broken my spirit. I was afraid that without bold acts and daring chances, Andre couldn't be saved. But I was afraid of Stuart Hannon and I was afraid of Jimmy McGrath. I was afraid of being hurt more, afraid of taking any more chances, even though I despised the pathetic, wimpy person I was becoming.

A fat, annoying fly circled my head, buzzing my nose, and after a few tentative waves of my arm, I gave up, too weary to chase it away. It seemed an appropriate companion, somehow, for my rotten life. The air in the room hung heavy. It had the breathless stillness of anticipation, as though the smoldering passions of this angry town had gathered within these walls.

Someone banged on my door, then entered without waiting for a response. Cathy McGrath, with a set and peevish face that she might have borrowed from her mother. She came in carrying a tray which she set on the bedside stand and then knelt down beside me, staring into my face and feeling my forehead. There were food stains on her clothes and her hair had straggled out its confines and curled wildly around her face. She looked weary, but flushed and pretty. The color that heat and effort had put in her cheeks suited her. Too bad she looked so cross.

"Clyde sent me," she said shortly. "I can't stay. It's a madhouse down there. They're like a bunch of baby birds. A whole roomful of baby birds with mouths open, peeping continually until you feed them. And Ma's down there, charging around like an enraged bull, won't explain what's going on or what's happened to you, snappish as hell. I really didn't have time for this, but Clyde insisted . . . He's such a Goddammed worry wart . . ."

She sat back on her heels. "I don't want to offend your independence or anything, but would you like me to help you up off the floor?"

I had to like someone with the guts to ask a question like that. "Just this once," I said. She grabbed my hands and pulled me up. Like her mother, she was surprisingly strong for someone so slight. It hurt to move and I lay down on the bed, ignoring the lumpy covers, and groaned. "There are some pills in the bathroom . . . if you wouldn't mind . . ."

She looked like she did mind, but waiting on people was second nature to her. "Hold on." She headed for the bathroom, then changed her mind. She dragged my chair over, set the fan on it, and turned it so that the air poured over me. I closed my eyes, relishing the cool, and wondered if maybe I wasn't going to die of misery after all. "Okay. Pills in the bathroom." I heard the snap of childproof covers. Water ran. And then nothing happened.

I had an awful premonition of what was happening in there. Awful enough to get me off the bed, across the room, and to the bathroom door. Sure enough. She was holding the pill container over the toilet, about to dump them in.

"Oh, Jesus, Cathy. Don't!"

She stopped, startled, and stared at me, the pink in her face deepening to scarlet. "What's wrong with you, anyhow?" she demanded. "You look awful."

But I was still focused on the pills. "Please," I said. "I need those . . ."

"What for?"

"Pain," I said. "Infection." I guess I shouldn't have been surprised that she didn't know. She hadn't been in the kitchen then. Her mother wasn't much of an explainer and Clyde was too shy to describe something so personal. I reached out and took the container from her hand. Shook out a pill and put it in my mouth. Got one from the second container. Snapped the lids back on and stuffed them in my pocket, away from her malicious hands. Away from a mean-spirited impulse to "get back" at me because she'd had to carry up a tray when she was busy. I grabbed the water glass and drank, the glass shaking in my hand and rattling against my teeth. I gulped it down, refilled the glass, and drank some more.

"Hey now. Take it easy . . ." She looked nervous and I wanted to whack some sense into her, some consistency. Either she cared or she didn't, right? One minute she's trying to dump my pills down the toilet and the next she's fretting over me.

What was going to happen to me if I drank too much water, something might hurt? It was a little late for that. Besides, taking it easy had never been in my vocabulary. I had walked early. Talked early. Climbed anything that crossed my path. I had always flung myself vigorously at life. I finished the rest of the water and set the empty glass on the sink. Then I closed my eyes and rested, leaning against the wall for support, hating the fact that I needed rest. I folded my hands over my abdomen where my baby had been. I couldn't believe that it was gone. How could it just come and go like that, like I was a transient hotel and it was just a passing traveler, when I had wanted so much to know her? Or him. It was just so damned sad.

"Hey." She sounded irritated. I opened my eyes and looked down at her. She shifted uncomfortably. "Look, I'm sorry about the pills. I just . . . I didn't know . . . I was mad, okay? I can't find out what the hell's going on around here. Not only with you. With everything. The whole town is going to hell and everyone is acting like it's normal . . . and then I've got to wait on you along with the rest of them."

"Look. I didn't ask you to come . . ." Awkward, talking around the lump in my throat, when I desperately wanted her to go away because I needed to throw my head back and howl with grief. Despite the names Andre had picked out, it should have been Noel or Holly. A Christmas baby. Long and strong with a curious nature and Andre's wonderful brown eyes. Gone with neither a bang nor a whimper, leaving me with nothing but a searing ache in my body and soul.

She put her hands on her hips and backed out of the bathroom, tossing her hair defiantly. "No. *You* didn't. Clyde sent me."

And then I understood about the green-eyed monster and why Cathy, who usually wasn't this bad, was being such a jerk. "He's a nice man, Clyde. Kind. Not how you'd expect a militia member to be."

"Yeah." She wanted to argue with me but I'd given her nothing to argue against.

"And he's crazy about you. Anyone can see that. And, except for the militia stuff, you like him, right?" Like we were two girls in the bathroom, chatting. Like the world wasn't going to hell around us.

"Yeah."

"Then what's your problem?"

She dragged the edge of her shoe along the floor, watching it with great concentration. "He seems awfully concerned about you."

Oh hell. She wasn't really this dumb, was she? Were we doing 1950's-style romance here? "You think a man who likes one woman can't be nice to someone else?"

"I didn't say that."

Oh please. I needed food and rest. I needed vision and clarity and wisdom. I needed my own personal cavalry to perform a daring rescue. This was no time to be hanging out my shingle and practicing marriage counseling. "Isn't one reason you like him because he's good to people? Because he's kind?"

"Yeah."

"So why does it bother you that he's kind to me?"

"I didn't say that."

No wonder their romance didn't seem to be getting anywhere. You couldn't talk to this woman. I took a deep breath. I wanted to scream in her face or grab her and shake her until some sense dropped into the slot and rolled somewhere it might do some good. "Oh, spare me, Cathy. You're sulking like a two-year-old because Clyde asked you to come up and check on me."

Underneath I thought there was a nice person, but Cathy's veneer had been laid on by her mother. It was self-centered, narrow-minded, and suspicious. "I've got to go," she said, turning and heading for the door. "Got customers waiting."

"Wait," I said. "Your brother Jimmy. What's the story with him?"

She looked nervously toward the door. "I can't talk about Jimmy," she said. "Ma would kill me. Jimmy's just bad, that's all. He hates everybody. You see him coming, Dora, walk the other way."

"Well, thanks for coming. I appreciate it." I decided not to mention the pills.

"Clyde . . ." she paused for emphasis ". . . will be glad to hear that."

"Then tell him thanks, too. And give yourself come credit, Cathy. A good man cares about you. That means something." I ought to know. A good man cared about me, too. I closed my eyes against the tears. I didn't want to start, afraid that if I did,

I'd never stop. It was only a metaphor, but I could imagine crying my heart out. I felt that sad.

The door shut and then feet pounded away down the stairs. I thought about eating, wondering what Clyde had put on my tray, but it took too much energy. I wasn't hungry at all but people are supposed to eat. I thought about walking back to the bed. That seemed daunting but if I could get there, I'd have the fan. I attended to necessities, and then, lurching like a drunken sailor, I crossed the room to the bed. I just lay and let the fan blow over me, waiting for the pills to work, waiting for my energy to be restored enough so that I could get out of here. It was taking too damned long.

Half an hour later, I'd gone from hurting and enervated to drugged and enervated and didn't think it was much of an improvement. It was then that the idea came to me. In preparation for this ridiculous undercover operation, Jack, in an effort to discourage me, had made me read a stack of stuff about the militia. Also, being Jack, he'd quizzed me and he'd lectured me and he'd brought in an ATF guy to do the same. The ATF guy's job had been to scare the pants off me. That's a lot harder than most people think, especially now that I've been through some awfully scary times. We'd talked about that, and then he'd suggested that even compared to what I'd experienced, these people were particularly bad.

"Fanatics," he'd said, "are almost more dangerous than we can imagine, because they're not deterred by the normal rules. It may seem odd for me to use the word 'normal' here, but most bad guys think maybe it's okay for you to die, but not for them. Lot of these militia types, they're different. When they're willing to die for their convictions, it isn't so hard to imagine taking other people with them. Same when they see themselves as soldiers. Soldiers are supposed to fight for their cause. And in wars, people die. The opposition dies. Traitors die. It's not a very big leap to think that anyone who isn't with you is against you, and thus the opposition, and it's okay to do bad things to them. Wars and armies. It's all about the end justifying the means, isn't it?"

He'd shaken a Camel out of his pack, lighted it, and blown

out a long column of smoke. "If I was you, young lady, I'd think twice about this crazy scheme of yours. They won't care if you're young and pretty, or that you're a woman. In fact, for a lot of these guys, the very idea that a woman might try to do something against them is worse than a man trying. See, according to their rules, you're supposed to be at home, tending the fire and the kids, maybe cleaning the rifles and making a few neat little homemade bombs, but even though you might be expected to shoot to protect the homestead, mostly you're supposed to be barefoot and pregnant. It's all about God and property and patriotism and their own twisted version of the Constitution."

His name, honest to God, was Jim Ferret. He was quick and smart. He smoked like a chimney, and he had a sweet, charming, avuncular way about him that instead of scaring me, made me feel safe. Even when he talked about the militia, men with guns, and death. I must be a real twisted sister. Now, knocked on my ass and sweating miserably here in my ugly little room, I remembered something else Jim had told me. Something very important.

"The way they've got things organized, it's hard to break in. Even the guys involved don't necessarily know the chain of command. Don't know who's calling the shots. Only way you penetrate an organization like that is to turn someone. These guys, see, a lot of 'em are pretty simple people. Life has screwed them, and then someone comes along and sympathizes with that and tells them that they can get back in control. It's very appealing, especially to someone who feels helpless against the system. They're comfortable with it because they've been convinced that they're the good guys. What you have to do . . . what we have to do . . . is convince them that they're wrong. Or that what the people they're following are doing is wrong. Get 'em to see the light. And then get 'em to talk."

"But Jim . . . how . . ."

He wasn't done. "Not too many of these ordinary guys who joined 'cuz they've got a beef with the government . . . guys like Harding . . . are real comfortable with the idea of blowing a daycare center full of kids to bits. They love their kids, their families. Love their country, too. Just that they've let someone twist their minds around . . ."

It sounded good to me, but Jim shook his head, lit another cigarette, and inhaled deeply. "Sounds easy, but it isn't. Not easy at all. People don't like to feel like fools. Don't like to give up beliefs that make them feel safe. And most of all, don't like to rat out their buddies." There was actually a twinkle in his eye when he said, "It's a guy thing."

But Clyde was in the militia and Clyde was a decent and gentle man. There had to be a way to reach him. Didn't there? That was the last thought on my mind before I fell asleep again. This time it wasn't dreamless. In my lifetime of hideous dreams, these were among the worst. I was being pursued through a forest at night, chased by a camouflage-clad army of gigantic babies. When they opened their mouths, their gums were toothless. They were bald and clutched their rifles in chubby fists. They spoke no language but communicated by strange cries, like the body snatchers. Just as I thought they were about to catch me, I burst out into a clearing lit by a huge bonfire.

In the center of the clearing, Andre lay on the ground, bound with so much rope around his arms and legs he looked like a mummy. Over him stood Jimmy McGrath, gigantic and menacing in the firelight, an ax in his hand. As I approached, Andre turned toward me, his eyes pleading with me for help. I hurried forward but I was surrounded by babies who babbled and clutched at me and held me there so that I couldn't help. Jimmy McGrath, with a malevolent grin, raised the ax and swung it at Andre's head. In my dreams, I can't close my eyes.

I was screaming. Screaming. Screaming. I didn't know how long I'd been screaming but my throat was raw and sore and I was soaked with sweat. Someone touched my back, feather-light and gentle, and made a soothing sound. Before Andre, I had never slept well. Having him there comforted me. The hand settled firmly on my shoulder. I murmured "Andre" and reached for it. "Andre. Thank God!" Clasped the fingers with mine. And knew it was not Andre's hand.

Clyde jumped back in surprise as I sat up and swung my legs over the edge of the bed, all the panic rushing back. In the hand that hadn't been comforting me, he still held a spatula.

"What the hell! I thought you were being murdered in your bed . . ." he began.

"Only in my mind. Sorry. Excuse me. Sick." I headed on trembling legs for the bathroom, not sure I'd make it, Clyde trailing after me with the absurd spatula still outstretched before him. My knight with shining cutlery.

I've probably thrown up, with all the drama and noise attendant thereto, before more strangers than anyone else in America, except perhaps that poor president who did it for TV cameras and got to be broadcast all over the world. It's one of those things that do not improve with experience. Throughout my performance, Clyde stood in the doorway, looking miserable, maintaining a white-knuckled grip on his kitchen tool as though it were a magic talisman which would protect him from the evil enchantments of a witch like me.

I tried to reassure him. Between bouts of puking my guts out, I repeatedly told him I was fine, but while he couldn't quite bring himself to help me, he couldn't bring himself to leave, either. Finally, when I was finished and stood leaning against the wall, my face buried in a towel, he found his voice. "You want me to call a doctor?"

"Just shoot me."

He was silent, perhaps actually considering my request, then he said, "You want me to get Cathy?"

"What for? Cathy hates me."

"Cathy doesn't hate you, she's just jealous."

I dropped my towel and stared at him incredulously. "Jealous? Please. If she wants my life, she's welcome to it." He didn't answer, only filled the water glass and handed it to me. I took a sip, wanting to gulp down the whole thing, knowing that moderation was the wisest course. Knowing that in my nature, despite years of imposing severe self-discipline, moderation wasn't always there.

And now that my death was no longer imminent, he turned to what he'd just heard. "Andre?" he said, suspicion warring with compassion on his wide face. "Andre?"

Always move from a position of strength, I thought. Right. I, who could barely get out of bed. Shaking all over, I took a deep breath and went for the gold. "Clyde, I'm not who you think I am."

CHAPTER 22

I watched Clyde's normally benign face change to something fierce and menacing. Watched him take a step toward me, one step and then another until he was towering over me and I was cringing against the wall, holding the towel out in front of me like a shield. It was like watching a friendly dog suddenly turn and snarl, unexpected and therefore more frightening. "Andre," he repeated. "Who's Andre? I thought your husband's name was Michael?"

"Andre Lemieux. The state trooper who's being held hostage. He's my . . ."

That was as far as I got before the spatula clattered to the floor and he grabbed me by the arms and hauled me to my feet. He held me there in an agonizing grasp, managing to squeeze all the places McGrath had bruised last night. My feet barely touched the floor, and he did it with as much ease as if I were a pixie. "Jesus H . . . so McGrath was right. You are a cop . . ." His voice was full of fury but his eyes were confused, flickering up and down me like he was searching for answers to a question he hadn't asked.

His grip tightened and I bit my lip to keep from crying out, unhappily aware that if I hadn't fallen asleep, I would be long gone. My life sure wasn't the stuff of fairy tales. He was no

Prince Charming. I had awakened not to the prince's kiss and the magic clearing away of the brambles, but to another round of violence and menace. In my new risk-averse avatar, I was no more free of pain and danger than before.

In the back of my mind, I wondered if she who had hesitated was lost. "No, Clyde. Listen. I'm not a cop . . ." Fear made my voice faint as a whisper.

That seemed to make him angrier. Before I could finish, he gave me a shake that made my head rock on my neck and made my senses spin. "Who the hell are you, then?" The words exploded in my face, so close we could almost have kissed. So close I could see the spots he'd missed when he shaved, his wrinkles, his fillings, and the pores of his nose. Sometimes violence is as intimate as love. "Who? And what the hell are you doing here?" He shook me again. My head spun dizzily and my stomach lurched and danced.

"Please, Clyde. Please. Don't shake me again. I already feel so sick. I'm afraid I'll . . ."

Like most men, he didn't deal with sickness well, so the plea had legs. He held me out at arm's length, ungentle, but steady, and glared down at me. "You'll talk?" he demanded. "No funny stuff?"

Funny stuff? My gun was downstairs in the car, energy and strength farther away than that. This was a case of as ye sow, so also shall ye reap. I had played Superwoman so long that finally, someone believed me. Another time, I might have laughed. It was comical, really, to have this big raging man perceive me as a threat. I was a dangerous woman. So dangerous that when he abruptly dropped his hands and let me go, I fell flat on my ass and could only sit there, stunned by the awful pain that the sudden jarring awoke. I pulled my knees into my chest, waiting for the worst to pass.

He loomed over me, the spatula back in his fist like a cudgel, and for an insane moment I imagined the headlines: EDUCATIONAL CONSULTANT KILLED BY SPATULA-WIELDING TERRORIST. Like I always say, people whose eyes glaze over when I say I'm a consultant have no idea.

"Get up," he ordered. "We need to talk."

"You think I'm doing this because I want to?" Tears were running down my face. I grabbed the fallen towel and dabbed at them with shaking hands. My whole body was trembling, as traitorous lately as these militia thugs. Willpower, Thea. Expecting that he was going to grab me again, and knowing that assistance from these people was proving far worse than doing it myself, I rolled over onto all fours, then onto my knees, and rose slowly to my feet. "We'll talk," I agreed. "Just let me take a pill and then we'll talk." I fumbled the pills out of my pocket, struggled with the cap, gave up, and handed it to Clyde. "Here. You do it." Anything childproof is well beyond the ability of an incapacitated adult.

He read the labels on both bottles before he opened them and set them on the sink. Did he think I was some latter-day Mata Hari, sucking down cyanide now that I'd been discovered? I tried to shake one out, but with my unsteady hands, they came out like salt from a shaker, sprinkling all over the sink and onto the floor. I stared at them, wanting to rescue them, paralyzed into inaction by choice. I could take one pill or save many. I glanced at the mirror, as if the woman in there might have an answer for me. No way. She was not someone I knew. A ghastly countenance with grayish-green skin, snaky coils of unwashed hair, and glittering red-and-green eyes. Someone from a science-fiction movie had invaded my body.

The smell of cooking rising from Clyde's clothes made my stomach do flip-flops. Hard to recall, at this moment, that I'd come here to rescue somebody. I couldn't even get a pill into my own mouth. Suddenly he reached past me, grabbed the glass, filled it with water, and shoved it into my hand. "Here. Take the Goddamned pills and let's get on with this."

Clyde, don't swear, I thought. *It doesn't suit you.* Mechanically, I picked up a pill, put it in my mouth, and drank. Maybe all I needed were orders. That was it. I needed a keeper. Andre and I had often joked about that. He thought I needed someone to supervise my life and make sure I had fun, got exercise. Ate. Took care of myself. It looked like he was right. While I drank,

Clyde picked up the spilled pills and put them back in the bottle. Good thing, because when I finished drinking, the glass fell out of my hand and smashed against the sink.

In the midst of all this awfulness, I was beginning to see things more clearly. Not about me and Clyde, or me and the rest of the militia, but some of the bigger picture. It was the moment to spring into action. To try and do something, if it wasn't too late. But though I felt better after a long sleep—at least, had felt better until Clyde shook me up and knocked me down—I was still far from being able to spring or leap.

I stepped past him, crossed the room, and lay down on my bed. I closed my eyes, and groaned. Today I couldn't even fool myself. I was not Superwoman. The springs sagged as he sat down beside me, and I tensed in anticipation of more grabbing and shaking. "So if you're not a cop, who the hell are you?"

"His fiancée."

"What?"

"Is it still Saturday?"

"Huh? Oh. No. It's Sunday. What does that have to do with anything? You a different person every day of the week?"

Poor Clyde. Who would have expected he had a sense of humor? "Explaining. Last Saturday I was supposed to marry Andre Lemieux. He never showed up. You guys took him. I came to get him back."

"That's a good one," he said. "You came up here, all by yourself, thinking you were going to get him back?"

"Yes," I said, and then, "Please don't laugh at me. I feel bad enough already."

"I'm supposed to believe this?"

"Why not? It's true."

"So who are you really?"

"My name is Thea Kozak. Theadora."

"Got anything to prove that?"

"You're kidding. Right now I may seem impossibly dumb to you, Clyde, but I was trying to do it right. I may have blown it here, but I tried. I tried to be Dora McKusick. You go look in my purse and you'll see that I've got all the right ID. I know what it's like to be pushed around, threatened, scared, deliberately hurt . . . this week, God knows, there's been plenty of that . . ." That one hit home. He blinked and looked away. "I even tried to be a good waitress . . ."

Grudgingly, he said, "You're not bad . . . So, if you're not a cop, what are you? ATF? FBI?"

"Educational consultant." Even now, sick as a dog, my own sense of humor kept popping up. I wished that I had a copy of this conversation on tape to listen to again someday. If there ever was a someday. No sane person would believe it.

Clyde didn't believe it, either. "Educational consultant! And I was born yesterday. Look, Dora, or Thea, or whatever your name is, you're in serious trouble here. I think it's time you started telling the truth."

I stared at him with my glittering red-and-green eyes. During my time in the restaurant, I'd rarely seen Clyde anything but serene. Now he was almost as overwrought as I was, his face red, his eyes confused, his hands knotted together in a menacing coil. Somewhere along the way, he'd lost the spatula again.

"You know how hard it is to prove a negative, Clyde?" He just stared and blinked. "Sorry. I mean, how am I supposed to prove that I'm telling the truth? Which I am. You want me to tell you about Andre? How I met him? He was the detective assigned when my sister, Carrie, was murdered. I hated his guts; he hated mine. Turned out we were made for each other. The night he proposed? I was coming back from a conference in Hawaii, a real bummer experience. He picked me up at the airport. Stopped in the breakdown lane. Knelt down right there beside the traffic and . . ."

I sat up and stared right into his face, talking louder and faster now. Not knowing what to say and unable to stop talking. How dare he think I wasn't me? That I wasn't here for love? Why else would anyone do this? This was exhausting and ugly and terrifying and it hurt. What could I say that might reach him? Touch him? Where was our point of overlap? What mattered to me that also mattered to Clyde? "You want to know what my wedding dress looked like? Like a giant satin and lace and pearl marshmallow, little scallops of lace here"—my hand fluttered lightly across my chest—"and on the sleeves. For half an hour I was the most beautiful woman in the world. How excited he was about the baby? The baby I lost? He had names picked out, Goddammit! Names."

Damn! Here he was, something soft coming into his face, and my throat was closing. I forced words past the lump, let the tears fall. "He was making a cradle out of tiger maple. Sanding it until it was smooth as glass." I had a flash of Andre's intent face, bent over the wood, a faint smile instead of his usually serious expression, running an exacting hand over the curve of a rocker. Saw him look up and see me, beckon me over, his smile broadening as he ran that same exacting hand over me, stopping where our child rested, a small sound of pleasure, or possession, or anticipation, escaping. I was here because of Andre. Because he had quietly, firmly, and with incredible persistence worn me down and burrowed his way into my heart.

Words I hadn't meant to say tumbled out. "I've never seen a man more excited about having a baby. Now I've lost them both. Everything I love, I lose, so why don't you just go ahead and shoot me?"

Hold on, I thought. I'm supposed to be trying to turn Clyde, not descending into another wallow of maudlin self-pity. But if I couldn't have the baby and I couldn't have Andre, then why bother? I didn't think I could go through this again, ever, this dangerous, painful business of falling in love. So what did it matter what Hannon and his band of murdering assholes did to me, anyway? What did it really matter?

"You're a hell of an actress, even for a cop," he said.

I slapped him as hard as I could across the face, and, as he sat there, trying to sort out whether to be surprised or angry, I screamed at him, "I wish I were a cop, Clyde. Then I could arrest you all. You and your buddies Stuart Hannon and Jimmy McGrath for kidnapping, assault and battery, to say nothing about the murder of that pathetic woman who was Jed Harding's wife . . . Paulette . . . And don't try to tell me that Paulette left town, because I wasn't born yesterday and I've seen that trailer. Have you?"

I gulped some air, then rushed on before he could speak. "I can see what makes them tick, Clyde. Power and intimidation. Chance to be big shots. But I don't understand about you. You're a decent guy . . . a good person. You're hardworking and kind. Gentle. In love with a pretty woman who, if she ever got her head unwedged, would see she loves you back. So I don't understand . . ."

I had to breathe again. He opened his mouth, and I blurted out, ". . . why you're mixed up with a bunch of murderers. Why you're willing to stand by and let them kidnap and kill people. Why you've let them brainwash you into thinking it's all for the cause, that you have to go along because it's militia business, when that's not what this is about at all, Clyde. Do you know why they really want Jed Harding set free? Do you? And I'll give you a clue. It's not because he's one of you . . ."

He stared at me. Opened his mouth, then closed it again, and stared. "Why don't you tell me," he said.

"They want Jed Harding out so they can kill him, Clyde. Because Jed Harding, for all his wild and crazy acts, is a good man like you, deep down. And he knows too much about what happened to his wife. He's the weak link. A person who might actually tell the cops what happened to her, or at least all he knows. The man who knows too much and someday might feel compelled to tell it. About Paulette. About Gary Pelletier. And probably, once he's talking, about other things they've done or plan to do . . ."

Suddenly my brain was coming alive. Buzzing like a chain saw, cutting through the jam of logs that had kept my thoughts dammed up. Suddenly I saw it all. Saw too much. Even as my words were pouring out to Clyde, I was looking ahead, and I saw more terrible stuff. "Taking Andre wasn't a random act, you know. They didn't just happen to kidnap him because he was the first cop who came by. They took him because he was the investigating detective on the Pelletier shooting, which led him to Harding's wife's murder. And because he was getting too close."

He was staring at me like I'd grown a second head, instead of merely finally getting a second wind. "This is a lot of bullshit," he said. "You're just trying to confuse me."

"Do you really think so? Do you know what happened to that woman? Does everybody know and nobody cares? Do you honestly believe that it's okay, if you're in the militia, to execute cops and cut women up with chain saws?"

"You're just trying to mess with my head," he said. "That's what they told us you cops will do."

"I'm just trying to straighten out your head. And I'm no cop." It was happening so quickly it was as if a mental defroster was clearing the fog out of my mind. I understood why Jed Harding had gone after the guy at the VA. Because he wanted to get locked up. He had counted on their honor, or sense of brotherhood—the militia code—to protect his family. That and the fact that it was a small town. They might look the other way if it was a dumb bimbo from away, like Paulette, who had cheated on her husband, but not if the victim was a grandmother or a small child. But Jed Harding had overestimated their virtue, or misunderstood their level of self-interest.

Clyde was shaking his head. Shaking me off. Starting to re-peat the stuff they'd told him. Trying to shore up his doubts with their wall of oh so credible propaganda. I could see it hap-pening, written all over his big, open face. I didn't have time to stay and convince him, either, because I could see something else. Something more terrible and immediate. Not about Andre, either. I could see what was going to happen next. Unless it had already happened.

He started to rise from the bed. "I think we'd better go see Hannon," he said.

There was one thing I knew Clyde cared about—those smaller and weaker than himself. Something I understood well. I put a hand on his arm. "Wait, Clyde," I said. "Listen. If I'm right . . . if their goal is to get Harding out so they can shut him up—and taking the cop didn't work—you know what they'll do next?"

He stared at me warily, his dark brows coming together over his eyes like storm clouds, his mouth folding up in a thoughtful knot. I started to speak but he held up his hand. "Wait a minute, will you? Let me think."

I let him think, sitting in the hot room listening to my heart pound. It was as though some manipulating god had fiddled with all my tuning dials. Suddenly the colors were more intense, my focus sharper, and I could almost sense our loud and angry words hanging in the air around us, too important to retreat until we were finished with them. Everywhere I looked they hung there, sharp, bright, intensely black words. My last challenging phrase, "You know what they'll do next," seemed to pulsate in the air like an LCD clock that needed to be reset.

I wasn't sure whether anything I'd said had penetrated, or whether my words had rolled right off and he was going to turn to me and ask me again if I was a cop. It could be that he'd simply seize me by the arm and drag me off for another tête à tête with the Reverend Stuart Hannon. If he did that, I had no more tricks in my bag. I'd bared my soul. I'd told him the truth.

I could hear the minutes ticking off on my clock. More than a few. It took an effort to hold my tongue, and I made it. I sat and held the downside possibilities at bay. I knew they would not deal kindly with me. The ticking of the clock. The pounding of my heart. The hovering words. The waiting. It was so surreal. But life at the edge of exhaustion is surreal, as is life lived on the cusp of danger. I'd been there before. Probably Clyde had, too. So I waited. He pondered. Both sweating as we breathed in the thick, oxygenless air. Finally he turned to me, his face no longer knotted or suspicious, but only terribly, grimly sad. "If they can't get Jed Harding out, and they're afraid he's going to break down and talk, there's only one other way to be sure that he won't."

A chorus of angels leaped up inside me and sang Hallelujah. "Right." I nodded. "They take the boy."

CHAPTER 23

THE BOY?" HEAVILY and reluctantly, though his mind had already been heading this way.

"That's right." I was sickened by the thought, yet chillingly sure.

There was something of a force of nature about Clyde. Once he'd made up his mind, there was no hesitation or pause to ponder the options. It isn't always the brightest bulbs that get things done. He was halfway to the door before I'd fully perceived that we were in agreement. He did pause then, but only to say, "Come on. We'd better get over there, see if the kid's all right and warn his grandmother. No time to waste."

The scorched scents of fear and tension hung in the air like ozone. I was dirty, unhealthy, and weak. No way did I constitute a suitable companion on Clyde's rescue mission. But I, too, needed to know what was happening. Nor did I wonder about whether this made sense. He was one of them, and yet he was doing this. Obediently, I bent to put on my shoes. As I did, I checked my watch. It was only nine. "What about the restaurant? Aren't you supposed to be down there cooking?"

He shrugged. "My cousin can do it. It'll be good practice for him. He relies on me too much. 'Course, Theresa will have a fit . . ." He watched me fumble with a shoelace, something I was managing with all the grace and adroitness of a four-year-old. "You want help with that?"

At four, I would have said a loud and defiant "No." At thirty-one, I just nodded. It's a slow process, but I'm learning to share and I'm learning to take. He knelt by my feet, wiggled them into the shoes, and carefully tied the laces in double knots. Here, I thought, was a man who should have children. And that thought put the lump back in my throat and the tears in my eyes.

I didn't bother to comb my hair, brush my teeth, or do any of the things a civilized woman in my situation would do. I had temporarily regained some momentum and I didn't want to lose it. I didn't know whether it was experience or an excess of caution, but I asked Clyde to wait for me outside while I dressed for battle, including trading my shorts for jeans and pulling on a bulky sweatshirt. I even made a detour through the bathroom to tuck my pills and other necessities into my purse. I expected to be coming back here to pack, but life had a way of changing my plans. Then I followed Clyde down the stairs, moving with aggravating slowness. Clyde didn't seem to notice.

I waited outside while he stuck his head into the kitchen and told his cousin he was leaving. He stayed in the doorway having some sort of discourse but I couldn't tell whether it was dealing with his cousin's timidity, Theresa's complaints, or a fond good-bye to Cathy. I leaned against the railing and thought upright thoughts. It was interesting that once we'd come to our joint conclusion, neither of us questioned the urgency of the matter. When he came out, he said, "Mind if we take your car?" and held out his hand for the keys.

I relinquished them without argument. He was clearly in better shape to drive. He opened the passenger door for me, waited until I was in, and closed it carefully behind me. I sometimes thought the world broke down into two types of men: those who held doors and those who didn't. Give me the door holders any day. Empirical evidence has shown me that this kind of courteous attention has a high correlation with decency. Still, as he was walking around the car, I released the drawer, took out my Barbie special, and slid it into my purse. Right now, Clyde and I were allegedly on the same side, but he was still one of "them." Just minutes ago, he'd been ready to strangle me or deliver me into the tender hands of Stuart Hannon. If I couldn't always be risk-averse, at least I could try to be careful.

It was a summer night, the last of the day's blue sky fading toward black. It was just at my favorite shade—the color that's called "Midnight Blue" in the Crayola box—with bright white stars beginning to peek through. Most of the cars were parked around Theresa's. A few people sat on benches, otherwise the main street was deserted. We cruised along it with the windows down, bringing in the warm scent of dust and freshly cut grass. In the distance, a mower hummed, a boat engine throbbed, loud music drifted up from the beach.

We turned at the church and rolled to a stop before Mary Harding's house. No one answered our knock at first. Fueled by what I'd seen at Mindy's trailer, I was entertaining visions of awful scenes on the other side of that shabby white wood when it finally opened and Mary Harding stood there, her faded flowered housecoat clutched together with one hand, peering anxiously up at us. She stared out, then retreated for a moment, turned on the porch light, and came back. "Pardon me," she said. "I couldn't see you before. Eyes aren't what they used to be. Is something wrong?"

"May we come in, Mrs. Harding? There's something we need to speak with you about." Suddenly I was seeing a different Clyde. A Clyde who made me wonder who he really was.

The mystery was enhanced when she said, "Of course, Mr. Davis, of course. I'm forgetting my manners. Come on in. Did Theresa send you?"

I'd never thought of Clyde having a last name before. It showed what a snob I was. How indifferent I could be, how uncurious about other people. But this was not the time for deep reflection or constructive self-criticism. We were here for a reason.

She led us into the kitchen, turning on lights as she went. Evidently, Mary Harding had been asleep and we had woken her. I felt badly, knowing how much she needed her rest. She looked wearily from us to the kettle to the sink. "Would you like some coffee? I've got instant."

Clyde looked down at his big feet. Poor guy. This was not an easy subject. "No coffee. No. Thanks, Mrs. Harding. We don't mean to take up too much of your time. We came because we were concerned about the boy."

She looked confused. "About Lyle? But why? He hasn't been up to any mischief. He hasn't been out of the house all day . . ." She had started to sit down but then she bobbed up again, a look of panic of her face. She reached out and grabbed my arm. "You don't mean *my* boy . . . Jed isn't . . . I mean . . . nothing has happened to my son, has it? It that why you're here?"

Clyde gave me a pleading look. I sat in the chair across from her and tried to keep my voice calm. "Mrs. Harding. Earlier this evening, Clyde . . . Mr. Davis . . . and I were talking about this business with the kidnapped policeman, and Paulette, and your son, Jed . . ."

"Jed's all right?" she interrupted. "Nothing's happened to him?"

"As far as we know."

Her head shifted, lifting her chin defiantly. "My son was not responsible for that . . . that kidnapping," she said. "Jed would never condone something like that. Besides, he couldn't have done it. He was in jail, as you well know."

"I know . . . that's why we came to see you. You see, Clyde and I are afraid that the same men who took that policeman, trying to force your son's release . . . might get desperate and . . ." This was harder than I thought. Upstairs in my room, it had seemed so clear. It was anything but clear when I tried to explain it to Mary Harding. But why should it be easy to tell a frail old woman that the ruthless men who had kidnapped a state trooper had done so because they wanted to free her son so they could kill him? Why should it be easy to talk about people who had committed a horrific murder by hacking a woman to death? Why should it be easy to tell her that her beloved grandson might be next? Even though I thought she already knew or suspected much of this.

"Mrs. Harding, we're afraid they may target Lyle . . ."

That was as far as I got before she put her hand over her mouth, her eyes horror-struck, her stiff little birdlike body bobbing with agitation. "No. No. No." She shook her head vehemently. "That's not possible. They'd never . . . What kind of a person are you to come around here at this time of night, waking me up and peddling such frightful stuff?"

"Mrs. Harding," Clyde interrupted. "We're nobody who is a threat to you. We just came because we're worried about the boy."

"Lyle's fine," she said. "He's fine. He's sleeping."

"I don't doubt that that's so, but we'd both rest a lot easier if you'd go check," he said.

Mary Harding might look fragile, but the same will that kept her going in the face of great adversity also supported a tenacious stubbornness, a stubbornness and a suspicion of strangers which I, at least, certainly was. She shook her head. "It's hard enough to get him to sleep," she said. "I'm not about to wake him just to prove to you that he's at home. Now, I appreciate your concern for me . . . for us . . . and all you've done . . . but everything's fine. I think you both should go."

I looked at Clyde but he didn't seem to have any suggestions. What more could we do? We'd tried. We could tell her the truth, as far as we knew it. I gave it one more try. "Look, Mrs. Harding, I don't know how much you know about what's going on around here . . ."

Mary Harding turned on me and suddenly she didn't look like a fragile old woman. She looked like a very cold, angry old woman. "I probably know a whole lot more than you do, young lady, seeing as you've been with us about a week and I've been around here for almost eighty years. And yes, I know why Jed's afraid to get out of jail and I know something happened to that worthless wife of his. But they've got their rule. They'd never lay a hand on the boy and you've no call to come around here, scaring me, and claiming that they would. Seems to me you've got a lot of nerve, a woman who can't even be bothered to comb her hair or wash her face, waking people up in the nighttime to scare them out of their wits with some crazy theory about my son's friends kidnapping his little boy. You don't know anything about us."

"Mrs. Harding . . . please . . . we just came to warn you . . ."

"I don't need to be warned about my own neighbors, missy." She rose in a clear act of dismissal.

There wasn't anything more I could do. And maybe she was right. I do have a habit of being very sure of myself but no one is always right. I got up, slowly and carefully, the way I had to remind myself to do things for a while, and turned toward the door. Behind me, Clyde tried one more time. "I wish you'd just consider . . ." then altered it to, "I'm sorry we bothered you, Mrs. Harding," and came after me.

She stood with her arms folded across her chest, watching us leave. Obviously her rules about seeing guests out didn't apply here, because she didn't walk us to the door. Clyde shut it behind us with a gravity and finality that signaled his discouragement better than words and walked, without speaking, down the steps. We were almost to the car when the screen door flew open and a distraught Mary Harding hurried out. "Oh, Lord help me," she cried. "Lord help me. You were right. They've taken the boy. They've taken my little boy. They've taken Lyle."

Clyde wheeled around and hurried back, bending down solicitously. "Come back inside," he said, with a nervous glance at the church. "We'll call the police."

Mary Harding shook her head. "What good can the police do?" she moaned. "They couldn't even get one of their own back." She covered her face with her hands. "I can't believe it. I can't believe it. The poor little thing. They won't know how to take care of him."

I followed them back inside, looking around for a box of tissues. I found one and handed it to Mary. She murmured a muffled "thank you" behind her hands and a moment later, looked up. "I can't believe it," she repeated. "They swore an oath . . . Jed told me . . . to protect each other's families . . . that was one of the most important things. Me and Lyle, we're all the family Jed's got."

But if she knew what they were willing to do to people—if she knew what had happened to her daughter-in-law—why did this surprise her? Because Paulette had been an outsider? Because she had sinned and so deserved what she got? No one deserved what she got. I bit my lip. This was not the time to ask that question.

"When did you last see him?" Clyde asked.

"When I put him to bed around seven-thirty. He was tired. Cranky. I hoped it was the heat but I was afraid he was coming down with something. And then I went to bed myself."

"So you have no idea how long he's been gone?" Not that it mattered much. There was so much wilderness around here that in ten minutes they could have disappeared in any direction.

Mary Harding drew a tremulous breath. "Not long. Maybe an hour."

"You didn't hear anything?" Clyde asked.

She shook her head. "I'm upstairs and he's down. And I had the fan on. I know. I shouldn't have. Sometimes he calls out in the night. But I was so hot, and if I don't sleep, then I'm useless to both of us . . ." She sighed. "When Jed's home, he takes care of the boy, nights. Since he's been gone . . ." She didn't have the energy to explain. Nor did she need to. We all understood. I also understood that this sudden shock was doing harmful things to Mary Harding, not just emotionally but physically. Her already pallid skin had gone beyond that to a deadly white.

"We have to call the police," I said.

"Why bother?" Mary Harding sighed, but she didn't argue. "Better to talk with Theresa."

I wanted to ask "Why Theresa," but instead I picked up the phone. All I heard was silence. No dial tone. I looked over at Clyde. "Line's dead."

"We'd better go back to the restaurant, then," he said. "We can use the phone there."

"I'm ready," she said, standing up. She was such a proper

woman that I was surprised she was willing to go without dressing first, but she didn't seem to care. Together we handed her carefully down the front steps and into the car. In the minutes since she'd discovered her grandson gone, she appeared to have aged many years. I sat in the back as we whooshed down the silent street and onto the dirt road behind the restaurant. One of us supported either elbow as we slowly climbed the few stairs and went into the kitchen.

Without a word, Theresa pulled out a chair and we helped Mary Harding into it. "Watch her," Clyde ordered, for Mary Harding looked like she might topple off her chair. Her skin had taken on an ashen hue and her breathing was labored,. "I'm calling an ambulance."

"You'd better call the police, too," I said.

"Mary doesn't want . . ."

"Call them! It's time to stop protecting men who hack people to bits, steal small children, and terrorize elderly ladies . . ." But arguing would only delay things and Mary Harding needed my attention. She was slipping off her chair, her hand clasped to her chest, her eyes half shut. I eased her down onto the floor, trying to remember my lifeguarding first-aid course. Loosened her robe and bent low enough so that I could hear her breathe. Except that I couldn't hear anything. Grabbed a piece of my hair and held it over her mouth. It didn't move.

"Help! She's not breathing. Who knows CPR?"

Theresa stared for a moment, frozen, then said, "I'll check the dining room. Maybe someone out there . . ."

Kalyn said, "Me, too," and hurried out after her. That left me and Cathy and Natty and Clyde in the kitchen.

I looked at him. "Natty?" He shook his head. "Cathy?" Another shake. At least she looked like she wanted to help. She just didn't know how. It was up to me to recall what I'd learned almost sixteen years ago. I checked her airways to be sure they were clear, took a breath, and went to work. Reviving someone is hard enough when you're fit and sixteen. When you're on the verge of collapse yourself, it becomes a grueling task. I kept at it, repeating the steps I'd memorized, until finally Mary Harding began to breathe on her own. I sat back on my heels, the room swimming, staring at the ring of blurry faces. "She's breathing again," I said. Around me, people who had been holding their own breaths sighed and started to breathe again, too.

As the whirling stopped and things settled down, I saw with a sharp stab of fear that one of the people who had been watching was the Reverend Hannon. Kendall Barker was with him, as was the silent Timmy, and some others I didn't know. He jerked his chin toward me. "Okay, the girl's done her job. Now take her."

CHAPTER 24

I LOOKED UP at his cold, ugly face, hoping that the surge of panic I was feeling might energize my brain and lead me to some plan or strategy or give me some magic words that would persuade him to leave me alone. Normally, being bullied and threatened doesn't make me fuzzy with fear, but I wasn't myself. I was barely up to the challenges of breathing and mobility and I was in a situation that called for a level of skill and adroitness few people other than professional negotiators possessed.

"Why do you want me and where are you taking me?" I asked, rising slowly to my feet.

He didn't answer, only signaled for his men to move closer. Then he pulled a photograph out of his pocket and slapped it down on the table. I didn't have to look. It was what I'd been dreading—a newspaper photo of me, looking like death warmed over, coming out of an emergency room, leaning on Andre's arm. Beside it, he placed another—me in my underwear and spiffy red high tops, standing in a bleak, wet field. Of course, the picture was black and white, so only I knew the shoes were red, that my lips had been blue, that other parts of me were both black and blue. And that then, too, I had been battered by life, faced terrible odds, and was struggling to go on. Only I knew that in the house behind me, a gunman stood with a high-powered rifle trained on me; that I was trying to save two hostages. Everyone who saw it knew just about everything else about me. Thank goodness for sturdy cotton underwear.

I've never been one of those people who crave fifteen minutes of fame. No reasonable person would want either of these photos of herself emblazoned across the papers for the whole world to see. And now they were coming back around to bite me on the ass, the ass that was so nearly displayed in the second photo. As Hannon's companions leaned in for a closer look, Clyde reached past me, picked up the second one, and studied it silently. "Nice," he said, setting it back down, and gave me a sweet smile. Absurd, yes, but the circumstances were absurd. At least no one suggested that if I wanted to waitress, I should have worked at Hooters.

Roy Belcher, whom I hadn't noticed earlier, snatched up the same picture, bent over it with a loose grin, and snorted. "Honey," he said, "you sure do live an interesting life." His eyes roved over me like dirty hands. "You wouldn't be half bad if you bothered to fix yourself up." If I thought fixing myself up would attract the likes of him, I'd learn how to fix myself down. But this wasn't the audience for that observation. I lowered my eyes and remained silent. I wanted to go on living my interesting life, or even a much less interesting life—these things always look more glamorous from the outside—but surrounded by all this menace, I wasn't feeling optimistic.

If nothing happened to prevent it, soon I would leave this room in the company of some very violent men—men who hacked the women they didn't approve of to pieces. Despite the heat in the room, even though I was wearing a sweatshirt, I shivered, wrapping my arms around myself to keep them from noticing. Across the room Kalyn was watching me and I could tell she wished she could do something. Instead, she hung her apron on a hook and headed for the door. "Night, all," she said, like this was a normal situation. Except that she stopped and gave me a quick hug, which wasn't normal at all, and whispered something I didn't quite catch.

Go home and call the cops, Kalyn, I thought. I didn't have much hope that she would, though, and even less hope that the cops would know where to look for me.

In the movies, this would be the moment when the good guys were racing against time to save me, or massing just outside the door, ready to rush in, guns blazing. Involuntarily, I glanced at the door. It was too dark to see anything, but I didn't get the feeling they were out there. The good guys didn't know what was going on here. From the dining room, someone hollered, "Hey, can we get some service out here?" I took a step toward the door and remembered. I didn't work here anymore. No one else moved to offer service, either. A few seconds later the door swung open, a man looked in, and then the door closed again. It was Clyde who picked up an order pad and went to see what he wanted.

"Okay," Hannon said. "Let's go."

I shook my head. It was risky to defy him but I had no choice. "Not yet," I said, nodding toward Mary Harding. "I can't leave her until the ambulance comes. She might stop breathing again."

He shrugged, looking down at her and then dismissing the poor woman on the floor as though he wasn't responsible for her condition, as though the fate of a fellow human being didn't matter. Probably, for him, it didn't. "She'll be fine. Let's go."

I searched the circle of faces until I found Theresa. In the past, at least, she'd seemed to have some clout with these people when she was willing to use it. "Theresa, are you going to let this happen? You know what these people are like."

Theresa shrugged, as indifferent as the rest of them. "Nobody made you come here, you know. You brought this on yourself." She looked around at the others. "I've got a business to run. I can't afford to make enemies around here . . ."

You lily-livered, two-faced, self-centered greedy old witch, I thought. *You have worshiped at the altar of the almighty buck until it has drained away your soul. If they can do it to Harding's wife and they can do it to me, they can do it to you. Unless your vicious son*

Jimmy, the useless sack of shit, protects you. Aloud, I said, "Theresa, I only meant I should stay with Mrs. Harding until . . . until help comes."

She looked at Mary Harding, and a flicker of something crossed her face. Compassion. Or gas. Or maybe sciatica. Something that pained her. She folded her arms resolutely across her chest. "She's right, you know, Stuart. She should stay with Mary until the fire department arrives, just in case . . ."

Oh thank you, Saint Theresa, you mercenary bitch, for small favors.

He shook his head vehemently, cutting her off with an abrupt, "Sorry, Theresa, no. I think the fewer witnesses to this the better, don't you?" He nodded to his minions, then took a step toward me and reached for my arm, but I'd had quite enough jerking around at his behest.

"Keep your hands off me," I said, stepping back. There was no way I was leaving Mary Harding. I'd saved her life once, and that made her my responsibility until I could hand her over to someone who knew CPR. Mary had trusted these people, which maybe made some of this her fault, but it was a mistake anyone could make. She had also tried to be a good person. She'd sacrificed the comforts of her old age to care for a child. She'd remained loving and loyal to her son. And these were her friends and neighbors. Even knowing what she knew, it had seemed reasonable to trust them. Most of them.

"Girl, you are forgetting something. You aren't in charge here." Hannon took another step toward me, anger at my defiance clouding his face. I was breaking his rules and I was doing it in front of people. A double-dipper sin.

The trouble with his thinking, the trouble with what was going on here, was that while the alleged underpinning of their actions was the preservation of democracy—at least as they defined it—they'd lost sight of what fundamental democracy was all about. In my book, it was about two things: preservation of the right of the individual voice to speak, even if it was a voice I didn't agree with; and acceptance of a common body of rules we'd all agreed upon, but which each of us individually then carried the responsibility to observe. I didn't think, though, that he was interested in my views on liberty. He only wanted obedience.

I didn't care. I drew myself up until I was looking him straight in the eye. "Not until the ambulance comes, you miserable excuse for a man. What if she stops breathing again? Why don't you try picking on someone your own size for a change, instead of helpless women and children?" As a delaying tactic, it wasn't very sensible—I knew he was mean and violent and that he could jerk me out the door anytime he wanted—but I wasn't in my right mind anyway. Besides, I suffer from a pathological inability to let bullies pick on people weaker and more helpless than myself. I looked down at Mary Harding. No one could look more helpless—a frail, ashen-faced woman with tiny, birdlike bones, lying in her faded cotton housecoat on a worn linoleum floor, fighting for breath.

His response was entirely predictable in a man whose notion of Christian charity was being good to himself, who managed life by belligerence and counseled that violence was acceptable, especially one who didn't like uppity women. He hit me. I was expecting it, so I managed to dodge the worst of it, but it was still enough to hurt and get my nose bleeding again. My poor nose, which I do my best to protect. It had been broken once and I'd sworn I'd never let that happen again. I'd sworn never to let a lot of things happen but they kept happening. Maybe that's why I never make New Year's resolutions.

I covered my face with my hands, feeling my nose gingerly, as the sting hovered there, sending out rays of pain that brought tears to my eyes. It didn't feel broken but the bleeding was quite spectacular. It gushed down over my mouth, between my fingers, along my arms, down my neck, and onto the front of my shirt. Gushed until I was choking on blood. I felt like I was drowning.

Cathy, who had come out of the storeroom with her arms full, stood there, frozen, staring at me in horror. Why was she surprised? Didn't she know what they were like? Had she been living in an ivory tower, or what?

Hannon stood and watched with satisfaction, looking around at his circle of sycophants to garner their admiration. Silly ass. As though hitting a woman in my condition was some sort of accomplishment. I worked at keeping my temper and not making a dive for his throat. It would only have made things worse for me, but I wanted to do it so badly.

"Here! Use this." Clyde shoved a clean kitchen towel into my hand. "I'll walk you to the bathroom." Bathroom. That's what Kalyn had said. I wondered why. Maybe she'd left me a note. Still holding the towel to my face, I got up and reached for my purse, which was on the table, but Belcher grabbed it and held it out of my reach like a taunting boy.

"What do you need this for if you're just going to wash your face?"

If he was trying to humiliate me, he'd have to try harder. I guess the newspaper photo hadn't registered. I would do a lot for love. "Thought I'd prepare for the trip. I don't need the purse," I mumbled through the towel, "if you'll just reach in and hand me one of those pads . . ."

He stared into the bag and his face reddened. There are men in the world who are perfectly comfortable with all the aspects of a women's sexuality, including stuff like sanitary pads, and then there are those who consider all that to be a part of our evil power and mystery. It's something we do to aggravate them and give us a reason to say, "not tonight, dear." Send one of those guys to the store to buy a box of Kotex and he'll come back four hours later, slightly tipsy, with another six-pack, chips, and both clam and onion dip, batteries, a jar of pickles, and no pads. Big surprise. He gave me the purse.

"Roy," Hannon said, "you go with her and check the room . . ."

"She can't go anywhere," Clyde said. "There's no window."

"All right. Then Roy, you stay outside the door."

"I'll be right back," I said. "Call me if Mary stops breathing." Gargled through blood, it didn't sound much like English. I'd had nosebleeds before but this one was a geyser. My arms were red to the elbow and my shirtfront was drenched. At least if I was going to bleed to death, it would be nice to do it in privacy, rather than expiring in a pool of gore in front of a group of staring thugs. On the other hand, I didn't want to linger too long, in case Mary needed me. I couldn't count on them to pay attention. I walked into the little room, flicked on the light, and locked the door behind me.

Alone at last, sort of, I checked the obvious places but I found no note. Oh well. It had been silly of me to hope. Or is hope ever silly? I set down my purse and faced the mirror, slowly lowering the towel, forcing myself to face the damage. No wonder Roy the romantic thought I ought to fix myself up. I was someone's worst nightmare. Christmas in July. Red and green eyes, green skin, and now I was daubed with garish red streaks. Two bright channels of red flowed from my nose. A surrealist's dream girl. A member of some obscure tribe, painted in anticipation of being sacrificed.

I froze there, bracing my hands on the sink so I wouldn't fall over. It wasn't because of how awful I looked, but because suddenly I was swept with fear of what was to come. I closed my eyes. This wasn't something I could plan for. I would just have to ride it out. But for now, for this terrible minute, I saw Paulette's trailer. The terrible destruction, the brutal crime that had taken place there. I looked at my fingers, at my hands, at my arms, and my feet, and knew how desperately I wanted to keep them. For the first time ever, my courage failed me utterly. I wanted to run out there, throw myself at Hannon's feet, and beg for mercy.

My peripheral vision caught movement behind me. As I watched in the mirror, frozen with terror, a hand snaked its way out of the shower where the cleaning tools were stored, and slowly began to draw back the curtain.

CHAPTER 25

THE HAND DREW the curtain back, and a man stepped out, holding a finger to his lips. I caught my breath, about to scream. It had been a day of too many surprises. Then I recognized him. Pressing my towel against my nose, I turned to look at Jim Ferret. He didn't look much like a knight in shining armor; he looked like a middle-aged man in a polo shirt and track pants, with thinning hair and a pleasant face. But he was here. And his glasses hid sharp eyes while his face hid a sharp mind.

"Turn on the water," he whispered, adroitly stepping over the mop bucket and brooms. He pulled the curtain shut behind him. "God, you look like hell. You don't know the meaning of 'take it easy,' do you?" He lowered the toilet lid, put two warm hands on my shoulders, and ordered me to sit. Gentle hands, which was a good thing, since Jimmy's hands had left my shoulders bruised and Clyde's hadn't helped matters any. I sat, limp and passive, while he wet some paper towels and gently washed my face and hands. Tipping my chin up like I was a little girl again. A girl with a sticky face.

"Tip your head back and pinch the bridge of your nose," he instructed. I did as I was told. My hand was trembling so with the aftermath of fear that I could barely hold it there.

"You're right to be scared," he said, "dealing with ruthless morons like these, but stay as cool as you can. They're losing it, you know. You can see it."

"How does that help me?"

"I don't know that it does. I suppose it means you're better informed."

"What are you doing here?"

"Well," he said, not exactly reassuringly, "I didn't expect to walk into this." He turned the faucets so the water got louder. "A certain waitress named Dora McKusick reported a gun theft? Guy lost a lot of firepower? Well, that's ATF, all the way. And there's a rumor going around about an armory robbery, possibly scheduled for this weekend?"

"Maybe that's why Jimmy wanted the truck."

"Jimmy who?"

"McGrath."

He nodded grimly, the first such reaction I'd gotten to McGrath's name, so I assumed that he knew something about Jimmy. "What truck?"

"Theresa's truck. The one she uses to get supplies for the restaurant."

"Big truck?"

"Pretty big. I don't know anything about trucks."

"Good girl," he whispered, nodding with satisfaction as if this confirmed what he already knew.

Roy Belcher pounded on the door. "You okay in there?"

"Still bleeding," I called back. That ought to fix him.

Jim put his finger to his lips and pulled a pad and pencil out of his pocket. "Who's out there?" he wrote.

"The Reverend Stuart Hannon, who seems to be in charge. Roy Belcher. Kendall Barker. A guy called Timmy, I don't know his last name. Clyde the cook and his cousin. Natty. A bunch of others. And Jed Harding's mother."

He wrote something again. "Know what they're driving?"

I shook my head. He held out his hand and dropped something into mine. "Tracking device," he said. "Put it in your purse or in your pocket. Someplace they won't look. And if you have to, lose it. It's not foolproof by any means, it's hard to track in country like this, but it may let us follow you. Meanwhile, your job is to stay alive. Don't take any chances . . . you know what these guys are like. We'll do our best to rescue you . . . if we get lucky, to rescue both of you . . ."

"All three of us. They've taken the boy, too, Jim. Jed Harding's little boy."

He nodded grimly. "Scum like this, they don't care who they hurt."

He certainly wasn't trying to be reassuring, was he? Why had he come here without an army? But that was unfair. He didn't have an army. And no one, as Theresa kept reminding me, had asked me to come. I was the one who wanted to play Lone Ranger. I just sometimes wished I had a Tonto or two. I reached for the pad and wrote, "In my car. Under the passenger seat. Lists of their license numbers. Lists of shelters. Survivalist's shelters. That might be where they're taking me. There or Theresa McGrath's camp."

I wrote the names of anyone I knew was involved, including the guys in the kitchen. "Any of these . . ."

He wrote, "Under the seat?"

"In a compartment. The button is underneath the rug, by the seat belt." I closed my eyes. It seemed like every part of my body ached, despite the pills I'd taken. I needed IV morphine and a long, long rest. "You'll let Jack know about the boy?" He nodded. "He's going to be so mad at me."

"Could hardly get madder at you than he is at himself, Thea. He'll never forgive himself if anything happens to you." He patted me on the shoulder. "You okay?"

I nodded. "Scared," I whispered. I thought the noise of the water was enough and writing took too long. I handed the tracking thing back. "I can't take this. If they find it . . ." I drew a hand in a slash across my throat.

"I'll see if I can stick it somewhere . . ." He took it and put it in his pocket. "You'd be a fool not to be scared."

"And my nose hurts."

"How's the bleeding?"

"Slowing down. Something else. Kalyn, the red-haired waitress . . . the one who tried to tell me you were in here? She knows stuff. And she might be ready to talk." I told him where she lived. But, though I wanted to stay in here forever, it was time to move on. Much longer and they'd beat down the door. Then they'd get Jim, too. I stood up, a little unsteady on my feet, and caught his worried gaze.

"What's wrong?" he asked. "Did they hurt you?"

I was going to shake my head but that didn't seem prudent. Not when I was just getting this bleeding to slow down. I just shrugged, unable to bring myself to tell him about the baby. Thinking about it made me want to cry, and things were bad enough already. "I've got to go . . ."

I could see that he wanted to lecture me; he probably had about a million "I told you so's" stored up. Instead he did what I'd been wanting someone to do ever since it happened. He put his arms around me and gave me the gentlest of hugs. Then he said, "I'll do my best, Thea. For both of you." I loved him for that. For giving me what hope he could. And for believing that Andre was still alive. Unfortunately, the hug made me want more comfort and I was in a comfort-free zone right now. He looked down at me, his expression curious. "What?"

"I want my mother." Which was odd because much of the time, I didn't even like my mother. But miscarriage was something my mother understood.

"If I were in your situation, I'd want my mother, too. My mother and a bunch of navy SEALS. Thea, not to put too fine a point on it . . . you're crazy . . . and you're brave . . . and I understand completely why you got yourself into this. But I'm scared for you."

He looked grim as he said it. Very grim. "I see from your face that you're hoping I'm going to rescue you and frankly, I've been in some pretty tough situations and I've never seen anyone who needed rescuing more. Trouble is—I can't. There are lots of them and just one of me. And maybe you didn't notice, sweet innocent girl that you are, but these guys are each armed to the teeth."

"Armed?" Dumb question. This was a militia, after all.

"You bet." He sighed, a sad, frustrated sound, and looked at me like a pet owner taking a beloved pet to be put to sleep. "I tried to tell you . . ." He stopped. It was too late for this to do any good. "Those dramatic rescues, complete with shoot-outs and explosions, where the heroes always escape unscathed? That's the movies," he said. "Real life's just as dangerous . . ." He took my hands in his, a firm grip meant to convey whatever strength and encouragement he could, and looked down into my face. "You don't know how much I want to fix this. I . . . life's not . . . Jesus, Thea . . . it doesn't get much worse than this!"

Belcher banged on the door. "Hurry it up in there," he said, "or I'm coming in!"

"Not much I can tell you at this point," Jim whispered. "Keep your head. Don't be provocative, no matter how much you want to be. Just stay cool and try to stay alive. No heroics. No defiance. Give them no reason to be angry at you. Any angrier than they already are. Whatever they want to dish out, keep your mouth shut and take it. However painful or degrading. This isn't about winning or losing, about honor or virtue. It's only about survival. Can you do that, do you think?"

"Been doing it all week." I said it bravely, but my heart was racing and I'd gone cold all over.

"And your nosebleed came from what? Running into a door?"

I shrugged. "Extreme provocation."

He shook his head. "Headstrong. That's what Jack said. I think." He frowned. "You've got to do better than that. Whatever the provocation. And we'll try our damnedest to get to you in time."

As reassurance went, it wasn't much but I had no right to expect more. "Someone has to get to Jed Harding," I said. "Make him realize how much harm his silence is causing. They've not only taken Andre, but his boy, and nearly killed his mother. He's been keeping his end of the deal; they haven't. He's got to be made to see that his loyalty is misplaced, if it was loyalty, and if his silence was to protect his family, it hasn't done much good, has it?"

He nodded, but I saw in his eyes what I thought myself. That it was a long shot. That Harding had more, not less, reason to keep silent now that they had his son. That he'd had the power to prevent this all along and hadn't used it. Why should he change now? Because he was fundamentally a good man? This town was full of people who, in theory, were good. When push came to shove, though, they scattered like frightened ducks, bobbing their heads and quacking and pretending to be real interested in bugs in the grass. This sort of thing couldn't happen, couldn't get out of hand like this, unless people kept their heads down and ignored it and let it have its way.

"Hell of a long shot," I agreed, "only what else have we got but long shots?" He nodded grimly.

I realized that there was no way he could leave, and I really did need to use this facility. "Can you turn your back for a moment? I've got to . . . uh . . ."

"I thought unisex bathrooms were the coming thing?" His smile was warm and brief. "I'll just go back where I came from and cover my ears." He disappeared back into the shower, drew the curtain, and left me to attend to business.

When I came out, Roy Belcher was waiting with an expression on his face so like a peevish husband that under other circumstances, I would have been amused. Right now, my face hurt too much to smile. My knees were knocking. I was nearly catatonic with fear. "Took you long enough," he said.

I lowered my eyes toward the floor, wiped a tendril of blood off my face, and placed my palm across my abdomen. "Sorry. I had to . . . uh . . . you know. And then wash the blood off my face and . . . Sorry. Is Mrs. Harding all right, do you think? Have they come yet?"

"Come along. You're keeping people waiting." He gestured with his hand and I realized, with a tremor of shock, that he was holding a gun.

Well, Kozak, I told myself. *It's like Theresa said. No one asked you to come. You wanted this, and by damn, you've got it. Or it's got you.* As he shepherded me into the kitchen, my head stayed bent. Not only because I wanted to appear submissive, but because the weight of fear and anticipation was bowing me down. As we entered, two men were gently lifting Mrs. Harding onto a stretcher. One arm slipped off and stayed off, waving a grotesque farewell as they began to wheel her out the door.

"Wait!" I called.

"Careful." Roy's voice growled in my ear as I felt the gun press against my side.

"You should know," I called. "She stopped breathing a few minutes ago. I had to give her CPR."

The men nodded and wheeled her out. As I watched the door close behind them, I felt as if my own fate was being sealed. In the opposite direction from hers. As Mary Harding rolled one way toward life and safety and care, I was going to roll another way toward danger, neglect, and, quite possibly, toward death.

CHAPTER 26

WHEN HANNON PULLED out a chair and ordered me into it, I was glad to sit. I'd started the day debilitated and now fear had finished the job. The term "weak-kneed" fit me perfectly. My legs, on the brief journey across the room to the chair, seemed to have melted and become boneless and rubbery. I wavered, stumbled, and finally had to grab Roy Belcher's arm for support, which pleased him immensely. These guys would have been dysfunctional in pioneer times. Nothing satisfied them more than weak women. I sank onto the seat and closed my eyes, wishing fervently that someone would beam me up, or that the cavalry would arrive, as I sorted through the ragbag of my character, looking for some strength or courage to see me through this.

I didn't want them to know how scared I was. I hate being vulnerable and weak. I'm used to being pretty tough—but that's in my own world—a world that may be challenging, demanding, and deceptive, but one that generally plays by society's rules. This was another world, one I had a hard time understanding. How do you argue that you're not someone's enemy when they've devised a particular code that says you are? How do you declare to ruthless people who are bent on kidnapping you that kidnapping is against the law, when they think they've opted out of all the laws? I suppose, looked at that way, these guys weren't so different from a lot of bad guys, were they? Most of the bad guys I'd encountered had argued themselves into a pretty good rationale for why their crimes weren't really crimes when committed by them.

There was no sense in looking around for help, either. Theresa had placed the almighty buck ahead of personal or civic responsibility. Cathy didn't seem to have formed any convictions. Clyde and Natty were both part of the movement. Kalyn was gone, and while I pinned some hope on her, it was like trying to put the tail on the donkey with a blindfold on. I didn't know where those hopes would end up. That left me with no one except Jim. He'd do his best, but by the time his backup got here, I'd be long gone, physically and perhaps temporally as well.

There was the thud of something being set on the table, and then Hannon's voice. "Okay, honey. I want you to drink this."

I opened my eyes on a room that suddenly seemed too bright. Light glinting off the cutlery, off the stacks of plates and glasses, off the gleaming teeth of my predatory audience. A glass of something that looked like milk hovered at eye level. I blinked and closed my eyes again. "What is it?"

"Something to make your journey more comfortable," he said. His words were so innocent. His tone was ironic and condescending but there was a hard edge of menace behind it. His face was no more reassuring. He stared down at me with cold eyes and his mouth was a thin, fixed line. I wanted to refuse but it was likely that if I didn't drink it on my own, I would be drinking it with their help, and besides, Jim's words echoed in my ear. Cooperate. Don't provoke. My stomach knotted. What if it was poison?

I reached out with unsteady hands and took the glass. Raised it to my lips. And froze there for a second, unable to go on. "Drink it!" he snapped. And I drank. It tasted like slightly gritty milk. I had no idea what was in it. And then, with a sense of time suspended, I waited. Did this cloud have a silver lining?

That come what would, I might see Andre again? And was that enough?

"Hold out your hands. Wrists together." I did as I was told. There are people who dream of being the center of attention, even if it is negative attention. Any and all were welcome to change places with me now. They bound my hands together with some kind of super-strong packing tape. Roughly. Tightly. With an economy that suggested they'd done this sort of thing before. Did the same thing with my ankles. As he pulled off a strip to put over my mouth, Hannon said, in a pompous, formal voice, "It is my duty to inform you that you are accused of spying against the Katahdin Constitutional Militia. If you are found guilty, the penalty is death." I had the proverbial snowball's chance of being found innocent.

He moved forward to stick the tape over my mouth. "Wait," I said. "I'm no spy. I'm not in the employ of any federal, state, or local government. I'm just a woman trying to find the man she's going to marry . . ."

"You'll have an opportunity to present your side of things," he sneered, "when the time comes." The question bubbled to my lips, "Did you do this to Harding's wife before you chopped her up?" but he slapped the strip of tape over my mouth before it got out. So much for Jim's advice. Given the chance, I would have been incorrigible. I would have pissed him off even more than he already was. He tore off another strip and wrapped it around my head. All tied up and ready for the UPS to come and take me away.

My ears were ringing and my face felt hot and flushed. Lights and sounds and faces assumed a distorted reality. Something certainly was coming to take me away. My own consciousness. I struggled to stay present and focused but some will other than my own was turning the knobs. The room turned into a bright loud blurry cacophony of sounds and senses and then faded toward fuzzy gray. Fuzzy gray men picked me up with fuzzy gray hands and carried me out into darkness. I could feel their hands on my body but the body felt disconnected from me. They dumped me in the trunk of a car, slammed it shut, and the gray became black. Since there wasn't anything else I could do, I decided it was a good time for a nap.

I woke because something was tickling my nose. Woke into a dense blackness and a profound silence. There were none of the electronic hums, whirs, or ticks of household appliances. No meters or pumps or clocks. Nothing mechanical spoke to itself here. I tried to bring my hand up to my face to scratch and got two. Two cold, numb things at the ends of my arms that rose up together and clubbed me in the nose, reminding me, as unpleasant sensations reverberated through my face, of the time immediately preceding my departure for this place. Wherever this place was. Whatever it was.

I let my senses inform me. I was lying on a dirt floor that had a damp, smooth slickness to it and a deep, earthy smell. There was a current of air moving through the room that stirred tendrils of hair and blew them across my face. There was no light, though, not even a glimmer. The room was the same with my eyes open or closed. I rolled over onto my back and listened. I wasn't entirely alone and it wasn't completely quiet after all. Somewhere in the room, I heard the faint sound of someone breathing. Supposedly, people deprived of one sense develop the others more highly. I didn't need to be blind to recognize this breathing, though. Sleep beside someone long enough and the cadence of their breathing becomes part of the background of your life, something that perhaps your mind doesn't know you know, but your body does. I knew who else was in the room.

Suddenly, the desperateness of my plight didn't matter so much, even if I was the helpless prisoner of a savage band of self-styled patriots, even if I knew what their savagery could lead them to. It was irrelevant that I was bound and battered and deeply chilled and lying on a hard, slimy floor. What mattered was that I was back in the same room with Andre. And he was breathing!

I rolled across the floor until I bumped up against something hard and then paused to listen. He was very close now. Sitting up, I explored the space in front of me with my hands. A hard wooden ledge with something padded on it. Padded and nylon. Probably a sleeping bag. Reaching further, I touched a back, then a shoulder. Rising awkwardly to my feet, I sat on the edge of the boards, then swung my feet up and lay down beside him. He slept on, soundless and still, as I stretched out beside him and fitted my body to the contours of his. Drugged, probably, or totally exhausted. Andre Lemieux had never been indifferent or unresponsive.

I nuzzled my chin into his neck and sniffed him, like a dog reunited with its master after a long absence. The stubble of his beard grated across my forehead and caught at my hair. He was dirty—the dirt of days without washing and the scent of sweat from struggle and fear. I loved him soap-scented and fresh from the shower but I loved this more. It was the scent of alive, of real. Beneath it all, the laundry scents of hot irons and starch lingered in his once crisp shirt. I snuggled closer and thought I felt a slight relaxing toward me. I wanted to whisper a million things to him but I couldn't. My mouth was sealed.

Until now, I had never admitted to myself how much I feared this moment would never come, how likely it was that Andre was already dead. I had kept those dark thoughts exiled to the edge of my consciousness. They had lurked there, peeking and flirting and begging to be let in, darting in whenever they had a chance, sneaking in when I tried to sleep. It had taken a lot of energy to keep them out. Now, curled up beside him, feeling the rise and fall of his breathing with my own chest, I experienced a powerful explosion of relief and release. I rested my head on his shoulder and let my tears fall.

I suppose I fell asleep, lulled by the rhythm of his breath, the warmth of his body, relief at finally letting down, the remnants of the drug. What woke me was a dazed muttering, faint at first, and then growing louder and more frantic as he emerged from sleep, simultaneously trying to orient himself and girding to do battle. Even in a debilitated state, Andre always woke like a cop. Kind of like a clock radio. One minute asleep; the next fully awake. His body suddenly flipped away from me as he turned, rigid, and barked, "Who?" then "What the . . . ???" and then, softly, wonderingly, "Thea?" And all I could do was make noises. His hands came up, with a metallic clink. Handcuffs? His slow fingers prowled anxiously over my face and then began tugging weakly at the tape.

"Stuff's a bitch," he said. "Going to hurt. So I guess this means they got you, too, huh?" and then, the fingers fumbling at the tape paused, and he said, "I thought you might come." Pause. "I didn't want you to and I hoped you would." Pause. "It's not professional, what I've been thinking. That I didn't want to die without seeing you again." Pause. "You're a crazy idiot and I love you."

That much talking exhausted him. His hands dropped away from my face. "Sorry. Not much. Good. For anything."

"Did they hurt you? What's wrong?" My mind formed the words but nothing happened. There was still tape over my mouth and I couldn't speak. It was just a jumble of sounds.

"They aren't gentle," he sighed, as if he'd read my mind. "But it's what they haven't done. Fed me. Let me . . . rest a little . . . then we'll work on that tape a bit more." He lay back down and I curved my body around his again. He sighed. "Sorry."

Don't worry about it, I thought. *Don't worry about anything. I'm not expecting performance right now. I'm marveling at existence.* We were a fine pair—the halt and the lame. But whether the cavalry made it in time or not, we'd been reunited. We lay on the lumpy sleeping bag on the hard, hard planks and breathed together. It was as intimate as anything we'd ever done. I thought he'd fallen asleep again until he startled me by whispering, "Will you marry me?" What was he asking? Whether, under the circumstances, I might want to change mind? Fat chance, I'd agreed to sign on for better or for worse. Worst, in this case. "Mumphf" wasn't much of an answer but at least it was heartfelt.

We drifted back into a kind of sleep. I didn't know whether it was day or night or how long I'd been here. It didn't matter. I couldn't do anything about anything anyway. If all I could do was just be, I might as well use the time to rest, just in case later on I was called on to do something more. What woke me were voices. Not Andre's. Kendall Barker and Roy Belcher.

"Sweet, isn't it, the way these lovebirds found each other," Belcher said.

Shut up, I thought. *Take your filthy mind and your filthy tongue and your ugly words and go away.* I kept my eyes determinedly closed.

"Pity to wake them," he said, grabbing my shoulder and shaking me. "Rise and shine, sweetheart." I pressed myself against Andre, not wanting to leave. This might be the last time. He gave me another shake. I rolled toward him, swung my feet over the edge, and sat up, stalling for time. Wherever he wanted me to go, nothing good waited. I planted my elbows on my knees and dropped my head into my hands.

Barker grabbed my wrists and jerked me to my feet, nearly dislocating both shoulders in the process. "On your feet, honey."

They had brought a lantern with them, one of those propane camping things that reeked of sharp blue light and hissed like a snake. The too-bright light accentuated Andre's pallor. He opened his eyes and stared at me dully. "Come on," Barker ordered. "Your boyfriend's not going to miss you. He's a little under the weather today."

I looked down at my feet and then back at them. Were they really such morons that they didn't realize I couldn't walk? I decided maybe they needed a visual aid, so I gave a little, awkward hop toward the door and stopped. Barker grunted. "Oh. Yeah." He pulled a wicked-looking knife off his belt, bent down, and slashed carelessly at the tape on my ankles. It was a miracle that I didn't end up with one less foot but I emerged intact. He pointed the knife toward me and used it to gesture toward the door. I had a run-in with a knife once and that was more than enough. Just looking at it, I could feel my blood gushing out.

I glanced quickly back at Andre. It was cruel of them to make me leave him now but then, these guys were walking, talking models of cruelty. I wondered, desperately and crazily, whether, in the style of *African Queen*, they might be persuaded to marry us before they killed us. Hannon was a minister, after all. But with tape over my mouth, I couldn't even ask. And, hopeful to the end, I was still dreaming that we'd be rescued. I swallowed hard and began walking toward the door.

CHAPTER 27

IT WAS STILL dark, which amazed me, the longest night in the history of the world, and it had been filled with life and death, peril and terror, love and reconciliation. With one of them in front of me and the other behind, they marched me like a prisoner under guard across an open field, up a slight rise, and up the front steps of a house. As we stepped into the front hall, Barker grabbed me by the shoulders, turned me toward a doorway, and said, "Kid's in there. See if you can figure out what he wants." He slipped his knife beneath the tape at the edge of my mouth, slashed, and jerked it free, spinning me halfway around and tearing out a handful of hair. Then he slashed the tape around my wrists and gave me a shove that propelled me into the room. Heeding Jim Ferret's words, I kept all my expletives to myself.

Except for the assortment of guns leaning against the wall, the unshaded bulb that hung from the ceiling showed a room that looked more like a college dorm than a militia stronghold. Pizza boxes, beer cans, empty chip and pretzel bags, and Styrofoam cups littered the floor and the few available surfaces. Lyle Harding was sitting on a tattered brown-plaid sofa that was spouting eruptions of crumbling foam through its many holes, his hands folded meekly across his lap. He looked small and lost, like a fairy child accidentally left in the wrong place. My precipitous entrance scared him and he drew back with a small cry, then gave me a tentative smile as he recognized me. "Dora. Have you come to take me home?"

Go ahead, I thought, *break my heart again. It's not hard to do right now. The poor thing's only held together with a few bent staples and some tattered hopes.* I swept a pizza box and some newspapers off the seat beside him and sat down, putting my arm around his shoulders and pulling him close. He trembled against me, his skin damp and chilly. The night had finally cooled and he was wearing only a pair of jersey shorts. I glared at Barker, watching in the doorway. "Did you think to bring him some clothes?"

His answer, not atypical of this group, was to launch a colorful backpack at my head. I snagged it out of the air and opened it, searching for a T-shirt. I didn't care if it would have been more womanly to let it hit me. I used to be a pretty good ball player. I found a shirt and slipped it over Lyle's head. "There," I said, trying to sound reassuring, "that should help warm you up. Want another layer?" He didn't answer, just nodded, his little head bobbing against my side. I dug around again, this time coming up with a hooded sweatshirt. Together we threaded his arms into the sleeves and I zipped it up.

"Dora, did you come to bring me home?" he asked again.

What was I supposed to say? I looked over at Barker but other than a frown, his face told me nothing. "Oh, Lyle, I can't take you home right now. They had to take your grandma to the hospital . . ."

He nodded solemnly. "Sometimes she gets sick. I used to go and stay with Mrs. Peters but she died, and Mr. Peters and my dad were always too busy. They had stuff they had to do together. That was after my mom left. So am I going to stay with you?"

I shrugged. "I guess you are."

He looked around sadly. After his grandmother's place, it didn't look inviting. "And is this your place?"

I might not be the world's best housekeeper but things had

never descended to this level of squalor. I shook my head, then jerked my chin toward the man in the doorway. "It's his, I guess. Hey . . . Lyle . . . that man over there said that you were upset but he couldn't figure out why. Is there something I can do for you? Something I can help you with?" I didn't mention that he'd been crying. He was a proud little boy, after all.

"I need . . ." He sniffed, then cuffed at his nose with the back of his hand. ". . . the bathroom. And I didn't want to ask him . . ." The word "him" shimmered in the air, full of fear and distaste. "He scares me."

"He scares me, too. Do you mind if I help you?"

"Of course not. You're my friend."

I looked at Barker. "The bathroom?" I had no illusions about what I'd probably find, but it should be okay for a little boy and if not, I could do a little hoeing out.

He jerked his head toward another part of the house. "This way."

I scooped Lyle up, balancing him gently on my hip and trying not to bounce him too much. I didn't know how long he'd been waiting and much as I liked him, I didn't want him peeing on me. We passed through a darkened room and waited while Barker opened the door and turned on a light. He stepped back and I held my breath as I went around him and peered in. It would never win any Betty Crocker Future Homemaker awards but it could be entered without earthmoving equipment and I didn't have to use one hand to hold my nose.

Lyle, on the other hand, looked around and said, "Phew! It stinks in here." But then, he was used to his grandmother's impeccable housekeeping and too young to understand that the same men who can shoulder rifles and march off to change the world balk at the sight of toilet brushes and cleaning products. I perched him on the edge of the tub, buffed things up a little, and, following his directions, perched him on the toilet and left him to fend for himself, with instructions that he would call when he needed me.

Standing outside the door, leaning wearily against the wall, I realized that I needed the facilities myself, and wondered if my purse had made the journey with me. It was sort of a double-edged sword, though. I could have used the supplies that were in it, but if my new friends had found the gun tucked neatly in the secret compartment—useful, according to the tag, for hiding keys or money—then they were likely to be even rougher than before. Spies got shot. Spies who tried to smuggle in guns probably got tortured and then shot. I decided not to think about it but at that moment, as if he'd read my mind, Roy Belcher came in with my purse and handed it to me.

"Thought you might need this."

He puzzled me, he truly did. I knew he was a vicious man but sometimes he acted so much like a bashful, dumbly sweet swain from the fifties that I wondered if he had a split personality. Or if it was all an act. Then again, this whole business made no sense. If you're trying to keep the cops from finding out your dirty little secrets, then stealing a cop and holding him hostage isn't all that smart. Unless what Jed Harding knew was even more damaging? Was there even more to this than brutal killings? Was murder only the tip of the iceberg? Then, if he was a weak link as well as one of the insiders "in the know," their eagerness to retrieve him made sense. And they never intended the cop to be found.

But what about the rest? What about kidnapping more people, including a woman and a child? Taking Lyle made sense if it ensured Harding's silence, but they couldn't be planning to keep the child forever. Maybe they weren't too bright. Maybe fanaticism had dimmed their brains. Or maybe I was just being dumb, thinking any of this had to make sense. Maybe they never stopped to analyze the consequences of their actions, or they didn't care, since according to the rules they played by, whatever they wanted to do was okay. Maybe they counted on everyone who had witnessed my abduction to have short memories about what they'd seen and long memories about what had happened to Paulette Harding. But didn't children count?

I managed a weak smile for Belcher. "Thanks."

"Boy seems to like you," he said.

"It's just that he knows me . . . a little, anyhow. He's a nice kid."

"Yeah, well. Paulette had some of that same sweetness. Not a brain in her head, though. She never did figure out that having an affair with another guy right under her husband's nose wasn't very smart."

"And then she ran away?" He nodded. "With the other guy?"

He shrugged. Appeared to ponder my question, then said, "Let's just say they both learned their lesson and won't be fooling around anymore." Maybe he really thought I didn't know.

My mind flashed back to that kitchen. Had there been signs of two bodies? I didn't think so. Whatever happened to Paulette's lover hadn't taken place in that kitchen. Funny how no one ever mentioned him but only her. Consistent, though, with the kind of double standard that allows men to have affairs but doesn't accord the same rights to women. Good married men can have affairs with bad married women and the taint doesn't seem to rub off. It was all Eve's fault. If she hadn't made poor Adam eat that fruit, none of this would ever have happened. But hadn't the serpent been a "he"? I didn't share any of that with Roy Belcher.

"Dora! Dora, I'm done." I tucked the purse under my arm and went to tend to Lyle. As I was carrying him back to the couch, he announced that he was hungry and I promised to fix him something to eat just as soon as I was done in the bathroom myself. I hoped there was some food in the house. They'd been starving Andre but I assumed that was political. I knew they were evil but couldn't imagine them not feeding a child. Part of my own magical thinking, I suppose. Why couldn't I imagine it, when I knew how bad they were? Because it helped me stay upright. Because, rational or not, assigning them some basic humanity made it easier for me to breathe.

Alone in the bathroom, I quickly tended to necessities and then, with a nervous glance at the door, which didn't seem to lock, I opened the bottom compartment of my purse. The gun was still there. My sweet little Barbie special. Still loaded. They couldn't really have missed it, could they? I couldn't believe it. It had to be some kind of a trick. They'd substituted blanks or something. How would I know if they had? To me, one bullet looked just like another. I tucked it away and went to ask about feeding Lyle.

Roy Belcher was waiting just outside, this time with a gun in his hand. He used it to gesture toward the door. "Kendall's in the kitchen. He wants to talk with you." Nothing in his tone or his manner was reassuring.

"I was hoping you might have something I could feed the boy. He says he's hungry."

"Lyle will have to wait." His tone was ominous.

"He's only a little boy, Roy. He's not part of this."

He grunted. "He's Harding's boy and that makes him part of this. You coming?" The gun moved away from the door and pointed at me. He didn't touch me but I could feel the cold metal, feel the tightening and puckering as my skin produced a Braille message of fear.

I knew the bully side of him wanted me abject and I gave him what he wanted. Without taking my eyes off the gun, I said, "What's going to happen to me?" I didn't have to fake the quiver in my voice.

He shrugged. "They don't explain themselves to me. Guess you'll have to see for yourself."

"I'm scared, Roy."

"Oughta be."

"Roy, I know what happened to . . . Paulette Harding. Is he going to do that . . ." I couldn't seem to get the words past my throat. I swallowed hard and forced them out. ". . . to me?"

All he said was, "Kendall and them, they didn't do that," and then, even more strangely, "but it had to be done. As a warning . . ."

"A warning to whom?"

He shrugged. "Women who . . . people who get out of line. Those who betray us . . . it's like the Reverend says. You're either with us or against us . . ."

"If Jimmy didn't do it, who did?" I don't know why I asked. I really didn't want to know.

He smiled, a sick, twisted grin that revealed, once and for all, the total corruption of his nature. "I did." He might as well have added, "And I can tell you this, honey, because you aren't getting out of here alive."

The horror of it zapped through me like an electric shock. How could anyone do something that savage and speak about it matter-of-factly? I saw in a flash who Roy was—the pathetic suck-up who will do anything to be liked. Anything. And while I'd felt stupid and foolhardy many times since embarking on this thing, I'd never felt like such a fool. This was the end. I was in the lion's den. And the lions were about to eat me.

I never should have come here. I should have stayed home and set up my new office. I should have waited patiently for Jack Leonard to do his clever policeman's things, defeat these bad guys, and bring Andre home to me. But no. It had been a whole week, and they hadn't found him. I'd found Andre, hadn't I? The hard way, true, but I'd found him. Touched him. Held him. Slept by his side. Had that many more hours with him. Hours I might otherwise have spent pacing the floor through restless days and sleepless nights.

He prodded me with the gun. "Come on, will ya. Don't make me use this." Obediently I went into the kitchen. It might be growing dimmer, but as long as I had life, I had hope.

Three men were sitting at the kitchen table. Kendall Barker, the Reverend Stuart Hannon, and Clyde. Clyde. Sweet, caring Clyde, the man I'd chosen to reveal myself to. One of the butchers of Merchantville. There was a fourth chair. Empty. Waiting. For Jimmy McGrath, I thought. Across the room, against the wall, was a single chair, also empty, waiting for me. Streaks of what looked like dried blood on the wall suggested that I wasn't the first person to enjoy such an inquisition. So did the bullet holes in the plaster.

Roy gestured toward the chair. "Sit," he ordered. I crossed the room and sat, my weariness suddenly back with me again, weighing me down like armor. Then we all waited, as heavy footsteps announced the arrival of the owner of that fourth chair.

Even before he appeared, I knew who had those heavy footsteps, knew what face would come through the door. And it wasn't Jimmy McGrath, though until now I would have bet the ranch that he was head of the whole shebang. I couldn't believe it. Magical thinking again. Judging a book by its cover. People who seem nice and kindly don't suddenly morph into villains and fiends. It was clear why I wasn't a cop. Despite my advancing age and plenty of negative experience, I was still far too naïve and trusting.

Bump Peters came in, nodded to the others, and sat down in the fourth chair. I sat and stared from Bump Peters to Clyde and back again. Over and over. I didn't know which surprised me more. Clyde, whom I had assumed was a very minor functionary in the movement, one who might be turned, who had seemed, earlier this same night, to have a conscience, or Bump Peters. I had taken him for a good-natured old duffer. If there was a lesson here, it was to be more careful making assumptions about people. I probably wasn't going to live long enough for the lesson to be useful.

Roy picked up a roll of tape from the counter and walked toward me, beginning to unroll a long strip. Oh rats. I wasn't vain but I really didn't want to lose any more hair. I wanted to look good in my coffin. But given what these guys did, hair was the least of my worries. I also wanted to be buried with all my body parts connected.

From the other room, Lyle's voice called, "Dora! Dora! Are you ever coming back?" It wasn't the words but the tone that got to me. All his fear and helplessness.

I looked at Bump Peters, who had risen and was holding a piece of paper that looked official. My indictment, perhaps. He no longer looked pleasant or benign. He looked serious, formal, and displeased. What I had taken for dignity was rigidity. Had I also mistaken condescension for kindness? I was too tired for this, for any of this. Too tired for terrorists. Too tired for small, sad children. I wanted to topple off my chair onto the dirty kitchen floor and sleep. Only fear kept me upright.

The past week had been a progression of kitchens. From my mother's impeccable kitchen, bustling with wedding preparations to the sticky discomfort and intensity of Theresa's kitchen. From Mary Harding's threadbare, well-scrubbed kitchen to the wrecked, blood-smeared horror of the trailer kitchen. Now it was all ending here, in yet another dirty, violence-filled kitchen. These guys didn't understand about kitchens, did they? Kitchens were for feeding and nurturing people, not for torture and killing. Too late for me, of course, but it only confirmed what I sometimes thought—it was time for women to start running the world. Far fewer women committed murder and mayhem in their kitchens.

"Dora!" The voice was a small, pathetic wail. "Please. It's dark in here and I'm scared. Aren't you ever coming back?"

I pulled myself together and looked at Bump Peters. "Mr. Peters, please. He's scared and hungry and he's only a little boy. Can I just fix him something to eat . . . some cereal or something . . . and see if I can get him to sleep before you . . . before you . . ." *Oh hell. Why not just say the words?* "Before you kill me?"

He shook his head, seeming surprised at my forthrightness. "Honey, no one said anything about . . ."

"Of course they didn't, Mr. Peters. Let's be honest with each other for once. You're a man who will break all the rules for your cause, and I'm a woman who'll break them for mine . . ."

"Dora? Dora, why don't you come?" There were tears in the voice now.

Peters sighed. "Go see to the boy. There's cereal in the cupboard and milk in the refrigerator . . . and a reasonably clean bedroom at the top of the stairs." I stood up but before I took a step, he waved toward me with his gun. "Your shoes," he said.

I sat back down and bent to take them off. It was a long way down and bending made me feel light-headed. This time, I noticed, Clyde didn't help. I wasn't surprised. Like with all the others, nothing about Clyde made sense.

"Hold on, Lyle," I called. "I'm bringing you some cereal." As a reprieve, it wasn't much. I was still dangling off a cliff face with nothing holding me in place but a small boy. I had a gun. They had an arsenal. And they had shoes. Trying to keep my teeth from chattering, I got up, fixed the cereal, and carried it into the living room.

CHAPTER 28

I PULLED THE covers up to his chin and bent and kissed Lyle Harding on the forehead. If life had gone differently, someday I might have been doing this for my own child. Might still, though it seemed unlikely. My child was lost and I might be lost, too. "Close your eyes," I said, hearing my own mother saying that to me. "Close your eyes and I'll tell you a story."

Obediently, he closed his eyes. "I love stories," he whispered. "Love them." A little smile lifted his mouth and once again I thought of a fairy child. He looked like something from the cover of a book I'd loved when I was little. My mother read me stories and my father told stories. She always said she didn't have the imagination to make up stories. I hoped I did. I'd never really tried before.

"Once upon a time there were three bears . . ." I said.

"I know this one."

"No, you don't. Now listen. Three bears who had run away from the circus and set up housekeeping in a hollow tree deep in the middle of a very large forest. One of the bears was a very good dancer, one of the bears was an excellent juggler, and the third bear could walk on his front paws. Unfortunately, none of the bears could cook, or clean, or knew the first thing about laundry, so their tree was a terrible mess. One day, the juggling bear looked around and sighed and said, 'We have got to do something about this mess!' "

Lyle giggled. "He sounds like my grandma." He yawned and nestled deeper into the pillow.

Outside, there were heavy footsteps on the stairs and Bump Peters appeared in the doorway. I put my finger to my lips. He nodded, but stayed where he was. What did he think, that I was going to jump out a second-story window, evade four armed men, and run off into the woods? I suppose that's why they'd taken my shoes. They couldn't do anything about the pregnant part but barefoot they could manage. Having him standing there made me incredibly nervous. There's something more upsetting about evil when it has a friendly face. I swallowed and tried to go on with my story.

"The bear declared that he was going out that very day to try and find them all a housekeeper. He set off through the woods and he hadn't gone very far before he heard sobbing noises coming from a clearing. There sat a kangaroo, sobbing as if her heart would break. The bear, thinking he would comfort her, burst out of the bushes and rushed toward her. It was the wrong thing to do. He'd forgotten that he wasn't in the circus anymore, but deep in a forest, where a charging bear was a scary thing.

"In an instant, the kangaroo was on her feet, and with just a few enormous hops, she was gone, leaving her luggage behind. Curious, the bear lumbered forward to see what she had left. He stared and shook his big, shaggy head. All she had for luggage was a bucket full of rags, several brushes, a crisp yellow corn broom, and a large purple feather duster."

I thought about Andre, who, like my dad, would have been our family storyteller. Andre with his deep, rumbly voice, kind of like one of the bears in my story. Andre, lying helpless somewhere underground, waiting for me to come and rescue him, while I waited in vain for the cavalry. They would have been here by now. If I closed my eyes, I could feel the warmth of his body, the shape of it, hear the sound of his breathing. Silent tears were running down my face.

"Dora? Dora? Why are you crying?"

Because we're all going to die and none of us want to, Lyle, I thought. Aloud I said, "I got something in my eye, sweetie. Shall I go on with the story?"

"Please."

" 'Aha!' thought the bear to himself. 'This kangaroo must be just what I'm looking for. Who but a housekeeper would have luggage like this?' He set off after the kangaroo but though a normal bear can travel long distances, he'd grown lazy and fat since leaving the circus and after a few miles, he had to give up. She was much too fast for him. 'It's that tail,' he growled. 'It's just like having a pogo stick.' He went back to the clearing, picked up the cleaning supplies, and went back home to tell the other bears what had happened.

" 'Oh, you're just a clumsy oaf,' the dancing bear said. 'I shall go out myself, find that kangaroo, and persuade her to come and work for us.' He stumped away through the forest, but though he walked all day and late into the night, he didn't find the kangaroo anywhere. Everywhere he went, he asked the animals he met if they had seen the kangaroo. All of them said yes, and pointed out the way she had gone, but no matter where he went, when he got there, the kangaroo was gone. He came home, tired, grouchy, and footsore, ate all the honey in the honey jar, and went to bed."

I stopped and listened. Lyle's breathing was soft and regular. I waited. He didn't complain or ask me to go on. He was asleep. I sat listening to him breathe, savoring what might be my last good moment on this planet. Then I wiped my eyes, got up, and followed Bump Peters down the stairs and back into the kitchen. He dumped himself back into his chair and gestured for me to resume mine.

As I lowered myself down onto the scarred white paint, I was overwhelmed with weariness. My shoulders sagged. My neck felt too fragile to hold up my head. My hair, what they hadn't torn out, was too heavy. I propped my elbows on my knees, holding up my wobbling head, and stared down at my bare feet. They looked so naked and vulnerable against the dirty linoleum, the toenails still a soft, shining pink from the pre-wedding pedicure.

Bump Peters cleared his throat. "Dora McKusick," he said, "you stand accused of being a spy . . ."

"Theadora Kozak," I interrupted. "My name is Thea Kozak."

"It doesn't matter. You stand accused of being a spy against the Katahdin Constitutional Militia . . ."

"It matters," I said. "Dora McKusick can't be a spy, She doesn't exist."

"All right. Thea Kozak, then. How do you plead?"

"For whom am I alleged to have been spying?" I may not have gone to law school myself but I am forever my father's daughter. Bump blinked and looked down at the paper he was holding.

"Aw, shit, Bump," Roy Belcher said. "Why don't you just skip the formalities and shoot the bitch?"

"Is this my trial?" I asked. I had no more idea what had come over me than they did. It felt like some impossibly bratty imp was speaking through me. An imp that wanted to defy any and all advice that Jim Ferret had given me. An imp I was too exhausted to control. And then, this looked so much like the end that Jim's voice didn't matter much anymore. The cavalry had had their chance and what had they done with it? No one was rushing in to save me. I might as well at least go out as myself. Speaking with my own voice. They might not answer my questions, but as long as I had breath, I would ask them.

"Is it?" the imp demanded.

"Yes," Peters said.

"I don't get to have counsel?"

"No."

"To speak in my own defense?"

"No."

"Do I get to ask questions?"

"No."

"Then it isn't a trial, is it?"

"No. It's a formality."

"Mr. Peters, I can see that you are a military man. The claim of right upon which your organization rests is the Second Amendment, correct, that a well-regulated militia is necessary to the security of a free state?" Where were these words coming from? I couldn't recall ever before in my life referring to the Second Amendment. An encyclopedic mind driven by hysteria? Wouldn't Jack have been proud of me, seeing how well I remembered what he'd made me read? When St. Peter asked me about my life on earth, I could tell him about going to Jack Leonard's summer school, and how much I'd learned there.

Bump Peters nodded solemnly. "Every able-bodied man between the ages of seventeen and forty-five."

Outside, I thought I heard something. Probably just more of the bad guys, but a girl could hope. To distract them, the imp went on talking. "Even if this is a court martial, and not a trial, I should be afforded some due process rights, shouldn't I? You can't claim your rights under the Second Amendment and deny me mine under the Fifth, can you?"

"In time of war," he said, "certain rights are suspended."

Can you have a war, I wondered, if the other side won't play? The militia and their imaginary friends—or, in this case, enemies. "How did you ever get to be so careless about human life, Bump?"

"Roy's right," Reverend Hannon said. "You should just shoot her."

The imp turned on him. "Exactly what kind of god do you think you're serving, anyhow, that lets you talk that way?"

"A god who ordained that man should be the master and woman his helper," Hannon said. "A god of vengeance and wrath."

Outside, I heard an engine shut off and a door slam. The men looked expectantly toward to door. "Sounds like Jimmy's back," Clyde said. It was the first time he'd spoken.

But Stuart Hannon wasn't finished with me. "If you'd kept your place, if you'd stayed at home and done your duty, you wouldn't be in this mess now . . ."

"What about 'wither thou goest I will go; and where thou

lodgest, I will lodge'?" I asked. "I *was* doing my duty. Was I supposed to stay home and dust when my beloved was in such danger?"

"Don't waste your time, Stuart," Peters said. "She'll talk you around in circles. This girl's got an education. She thinks she's real smart. But we haven't got time for chatting and game-playing. We've got a truckload of guns to move and plans to make. They're letting Harding go tomorrow." Meaning they didn't need Andre anymore. Or me. As if he'd read my mind, he raised his gun and pointed it at me.

I stood up. I don't know why. To flee? To fling myself at Bump Peters' feet and beg for mercy? To get away from the merciless imp in my head who kept making things worse? Because getting executed was a formal occasion requiring a formal response? Who knows? I stood as he fired and the shot, which was meant for my head, hit me in the center of my chest, knocking me off my chair. I slammed into the wall, my head snapped back, blood was pouring out of my nose and running everywhere as I collapsed on the floor like a rag doll, consumed by the enormous pain in my chest. Blood pooled, warm and sticky, under my face. I closed my eyes and waited for death to stop the pain.

Footsteps thundered across the floor as Jimmy McGrath burst into the kitchen. "We've got to move!" he yelled. "Move! Look at this. Someone stuck a Goddamned tracking device on the truck."

CHAPTER 29

I DIDN'T DIE. It was one of those times when, ironically, I wished I could, but I didn't. I had taken Jack Leonard's advice. I had worn the stupid vest. It was a flat-out miracle and an example of their stupidity that they hadn't discovered it when they were hauling me around, but they hadn't. Maybe they'd just thought it was some strange undergarment. Maybe all their significant others still wore corsets. And so it had saved my life. I felt like I'd run full tilt into an oncoming two-by-four but I was alive. It hurt so much I felt faint and dizzy with the awfulness of it. I wanted to hunch my shoulders and bend my body to cup the pain and cushion it. I wanted to thrash and scream and let the agony out. Except that I couldn't move. I had to lie there and play dead and hope that they wouldn't be any more careful about my life or death than they had been about my vest and my gun.

While they all clustered around Jimmy McGrath, deciding what to do, I practiced being dead. Being limp. Not breathing. It was Clyde who knelt down and checked my pulse. I smelled the residual cooking smells on his clothes and recognized the gentle flutter of his fingers on my neck, looking for a pulse. The fingers fluttered and rested, snugging up exactly where I checked my heart rate myself. He couldn't have missed it. I could be limp and boneless. I could keep my respirations shallow. But I couldn't stop my heart. His fingers rested there for a long time—an eternity for me, playing possum there and waiting to be found out. Then he sighed and said, "She's gone." All my questions about Clyde and who he really was rushed back. There was no one to ask.

Besides. I was dead on the dirty floor in a pool of my own blood. The dead don't have questions. The dead have Andre Lemieux, the homicide detective, to ask their questions for them—like who killed Paulette Harding. Only I knew the answer to that. The thought of Andre set my pulse racing. How on earth was I going to get from here to there without someone noticing that I wasn't dead?

Another set of feet came toward us. Maybe to double check? *Please don't*, I thought. *Don't come any closer. I might have some awful disease. Get my blood on you and, like Lady Macbeth, you'll bear the taint forever.* The feet stopped. "It's this Goddamned bitch who's responsible. She sicced the cops on us. You can bet on it." Jimmy McGrath's voice. "I told you she was a spy." I wanted to open my eyes. Didn't. Felt the silence like a tangible thing.

I felt Clyde move away. There was another silence. I wanted desperately to know what was going on. It took effort to restrain my curiosity. It would have taken more to move. I lay and worked hard at being dead.

"You think she planted the tracking device?" Clyde asked.

"It doesn't matter. She's the one who put 'em onto us." The feet came closer. He roared "Bitch" and kicked me. It rolled me over and slammed me up against the wall. If I hadn't been dead, I would have screamed. I thought of Paulette and fervently hoped I wasn't about to be kicked to death.

"Give it a rest," Clyde said. "You'll get blood all over your shoes. We haven't got time for this anyway. Not if we're about to have company. You see anyone following you?"

"Nah."

"We haven't got long," Bump said suddenly. "It's time we were out of here. You didn't unload the truck, I hope?"

"Found it after we'd unloaded," Jimmy said glumly.

"And you didn't immediately start loading again?"

"Fuck," Jimmy said. "Of course I did. I'll go tell 'em to hurry."

"Hold on," Hannon said. "I agree. We've gotta go. But what do we do with the cop and the kid?"

"Shoot 'em," Bump said. I hated him for his lack of hesitation. A pleasant-faced, grandfatherly old man who didn't have to think twice about killing a child. I wanted to get up, grab my gun, and go after him. I forced my arms to be still. My breathing to be shallow. My body not to twitch. "Shoot the kid, then burn the house. You, Clyde. Do the kid. Roy, go take care of the cop. Jimmy and Stuart will come with me. We gotta get the rest of the stuff packed up. Can't leave it here. Not after tonight."

Feet hit the floor. Doors slammed. I heard Clyde pounding up the stairs. Pounding back down. No gunshot, but even though he'd declared me dead, I didn't trust him. Didn't trust any of them. All he'd have to do with a little kid like that was put a pillow over Lyle's face. He fiddled with the woodstove. I heard the clank of lids and dampers. I heard newspaper and kindling and the scratch of a match. *Hurry up, Clyde. Hurry up. He's going to kill Andre.* I smelled smoke. The lid clanked down. The door slammed behind him.

I used the chair to help myself up. It hurt like hell but it didn't matter. What was a little discomfort in the face of life and death? My purse was still on the floor by the chair. I bent down as slowly as a geriatric doing plies. I got the gun out, made sure it was ready to fire, and headed out, lurching like the hunchback from a Mel Brooks movie. It hurt to breathe. My bones ached. My sternum felt like it was only held together by the surrounding muscles and skin. I tumbled out the door and down the steps, and looked around, trying to remember which way I'd come.

It was dark, but a black that was softening as the first gray light of dawn pushed its way over the horizon. The ground was cold and wet with dew. Sharp things and hard things stabbed at my bare feet. I crossed the lawn, slipped down the slope, and began walking across the big field. I'd remembered it as open but now I saw there were occasional trees. Ahead of me was Roy Belcher's dark figure striding purposefully forward. Coming toward us, barely discernable in the darkness, a trio of men, two of whom seemed to be carrying the third. Not a hell of a lot of cavalry under the circumstances.

Belcher was probably carrying something that could blow the three of them off the face of the earth in seconds flat and his hand was moving up. Getting ready. The rotten little bully lived for moments like this. What had I heard somewhere once? That bad guys are just like the rest of us 95 percent of the time. In his other 5 percent, Belcher just slipped the bonds of humanity.

The men coming toward us would have to drop Andre before they could shoot, by which time, Belcher would have blown them all to smithereens. Cops are required to give warnings before they shoot, but I was no cop. The last time I tangled with bad guys, I did it feeling a powerful and righteous anger and an endorphin-powered confidence in myself. This time, I had no confidence and no endorphins. It was instinctive. I took some quick steps forward, raised my gun, supporting it in two hands as I'd been taught, and fired. I kept it pointed toward Belcher and kept on firing until the gun was empty. Fired at his back. Fired at his side, fired as he turned to face me. Fired as he took a step forward and brought his gun the rest of the way up. I fired until he fell onto the ground and lay still. If I'd had more ammunition, I would have gone right on firing.

I sat down then, a surprised collapse, the sudden boneless fall of a baby just learning to walk. Still holding the gun, I brought my knees into my chest, and rested my head on them.

If I'd been a movie heroine, I would have run, lithe and girlish, across the stubbly field and thrown myself into Andre's arms. The makeup people would have touched up my face and hair so that the masses of sticky blood that coated my face and neck were vestigial and insouciant, so that my blood-stiffened hair bounced free. But this was no movie. Real women don't pump gas, they run out of it. I sat there in my collapsed and wretched heap and waited for them to come up to me. This time there were no endorphins. No sense of triumph. No heady glee at beating the bad guys. Outwitting was one thing. I lived by my wits. Killing was quite another.

Behind me, shots and shouts told me that more of the cavalry had arrived. That the fortress was under siege. And then I thought about Lyle and pushed myself to my feet just as Roland Proffit came up. "Roland. Upstairs In the house. Bedroom at the top of the stairs. Lyle Harding. The little boy. If he's still alive. They were going to set the house on fire . . ."

He pressed a button and spoke quickly and briefly into his shoulder mike, passing the information along, then described our location and asked for some medical assistance. I wasn't really paying attention. I took a step toward Andre, he took one toward me, and we kind of collapsed in a heap at their feet. Andre on top, half crushing my chest, one arm flung over me, and one leg over mine. "Don't mind us, guys," I choked out. "We're always like this when we've been apart a few days." I closed my eyes and let everything go, feeling nothing but the nearness of his body, his breath on my neck, his precious weight pinning me down.

I had been running, staggering, lurching, limping, crawling toward this moment ever since Dom had come up the stairs a week ago and given me the bad news. My mother called me stubborn. My pediatrician called me determined and resolute. Jack Leonard used the word "headstrong." It was my favorite. It made me feel brainy and brawny. If being stubborn, determined, resolute, and headstrong were what it had taken to get to this moment, then I was deeply grateful for being all of them. I was, quite simply, deeply grateful just for being here.

They let us stay together in the emergency room. Hard not to, when we had everyone including the governor on our side. Most of them modestly left when the nurses took off my shirt, but not Roland Proffit and not Jack Leonard. It wasn't anything they hadn't seen before. A nice, serviceable navy-blue bulletproof vest, blood-soaked and a little the worse for wear. Jack beamed like a proud father. Even with the vest, the bullet had left me black and blue and bloody. The doctors and nurses fretted and clucked and sent me off for X rays of my chest and ribs. Fretted and clucked and stuck me with needles. Soothed and clucked as they patched me with bandages and shot me full of delicious, lassitude-inducing drugs. Poor Andre didn't get such good drugs. They mistook him for a pincushion, stuck him full of needles, and began pumping him full of fluids.

Finally, when medical science had done all it could to alleviate our suffering, they wheeled us into a double room, tucked us into beds, and left us alone. Two minutes later, I'd made the perilous journey from my bed to his, planted myself at his side, and fallen asleep, held firmly in place by the weight of his arm.

CHAPTER 30

I WAS AWAKENED by some rude people who were talking loudly quite close to my bed.

"It's a match made in heaven, if you ask me."

"I don't know about heaven . . . but you're right. They're perfect for each other."

"If it weren't for the chaos that they cause, I'd use 'em on every case. Look how many things we cleared up last night . . . armory break-ins, thefts from private gun collectors, murder, more murder, kidnapping. More kidnapping. Attempted murder."

"I don't know, Jack. I'm not sure you can call shooting Thea attempted murder . . ."

"Juggernauticide?" Jim Ferret suggested. "And temporary insanity isn't a crime. It's a defense."

"Can you two please shut up," I said. "Some of us are trying to sleep."

"Sorry, Princess . . ." This was a new voice. "We wanted you to enjoy your breakfast while it was hot."

"Dominic Florio, hospital food and enjoy don't belong in the same sentence. And what are you doing here? This isn't even your state, never mind jurisdiction."

"But you, dear lady, are my personal responsibility. After all,

I'm the one who helped get you into this mess."

I looked over at Andre, filthy, unshaven, and still deeply asleep, nestled into the contours of my body, and felt a surge of something. Amazement. Gratitude. Love. It did more to restore me than any medical treatment could have. I lowered my voice and said something polite and welcoming. "It's always great to see you guys, but if you wake him up, I'll kill you."

"I told you," Dom said. "First thing in the morning, she's always a charmer."

"Put a sock in it, Florio," I said sweetly. I tried to sit up but the day after an injury is always the worst. That's when things that don't hurt in the midst of an adrenaline rush begin to scream and complain and carry on. I got as far as lifting my head and gave up. "Can someone ask this bed to sit up please?" Dom raised the bed a little and Andre didn't even stir. He was sleeping through all of this. Or was it sleep? I put my hand on his chest, felt the warmth and the rise and fall, and told my heartbeat to settle down. He was right here and he was alive.

I wanted to talk with them, to have them fill in the pieces, but I wanted to let Andre sleep. I wanted to let Andre sleep and I didn't want to leave him. Not even to go as far as the next bed. It was a quandary I wasn't sufficiently restored to sort out yet.

I stared at the trio of them helplessly. Jack Leonard still hadn't slept. That was obvious. The skin beneath his eyes was puffy and blue, he hadn't shaved, his arms hung limply from his slouched shoulders like burdens too heavy to lift. He looked asleep on his feet, as though, if I poked him, he'd fall into the nearest chair and begin to snore without preamble. But it was a peaceful exhaustion. The incredible tension which had hummed around him the other night was gone. He smiled wanly at my scrutiny and ran a hand over his military short hair. "I might sit down, if you don't mind?" He dropped into a chair and sighed. A big sigh. Gratitude at being freed of the burden of staying on his feet.

Jim Ferret looked like he'd gotten a piece of the action. There was a bandage on his forehead, scratches and bruises on his face, and blood on his shirt. One arm was in a sling. Like Jack, he looked worn-out. But he was still smiling, a mischievous look that was very different from the serious demeanor he'd worn when he sent me out to meet my dreadful fate with only a faint hope of rescue. "Who would have thought," he said, "that beneath that girlish exterior lurked an Annie Oakley?"

"Calamity Jane is more like it," I suggested. "Are you okay?"

"Hey," he shrugged. "I'm a hero. Who could ask for anything more?"

The more we could ask was that this hadn't happened at all. Maybe they had better coping mechanisms than I. Cop School 101:Dealing with the awfulness. I was hunkered down on a tiny island in the midst of a great dismal swamp. If I moved a fraction in any direction, I'd fall into a great black wallow of despair.

Beside me, Andre snuffled loudly, muttered something, and flopped over onto his stomach, snaking an arm around me and pulling me close. They all leaned forward eagerly. Their chat with me was mere politeness. What they'd all come for was a male-bonding experience. Well, all except Dom. I knew he was here for me. "Patience, guys," I said. "He needs his beauty sleep."

"Yeah," Jim said. "And given how he looks now, it's gonna take a lot of sleep. Besides, poor guy's still got a wedding to go through. Nothing's harder on a man than that."

If it hadn't hurt to move, and if I'd had anything handy that was light enough to lift, I would have thrown something at him. "Why don't you guys come back later, when he's awake?"

"Hey!" Dom protested. "You can't send me away. I came to feed you breakfast. I'm here to cut your toast." Truth was, I didn't want him to go. Dom was my lifeline to balance and sanity. Jack and Jim were both good men, but they'd been through this with me. They were both tainted with memories. The best man of all snored softly at my side, but he'd been there, too. He came with his own baggage. In the end, it was Florio who would hear my confession.

"And I'm here to assist," Jim said. Over in the chair, Jack's head had slumped back. He was sound asleep.

"Poor guy," I said. "We've got a spare bed . . ." I said it lightly, though there was nothing that moved me like a brave and tired man. The one beside me. The ones in this room. All the good men who'd worked around the clock this week. We were all speaking lightly. It was too soon to get into the stuff we really needed to talk about. Everyone was too weary. Too bruised. But there was one thing I had to know. "The little boy. Lyle. Is he all right?"

"He's fine," Jim said. "A little shaken up, but fine. Clyde Davis got him out of there as soon as he could . . ."

But I needed more reassurance. "He's fine? You're sure?" Jim nodded. "Where is he staying?"

"He's with his father."

"Oh."

"It's a mess," Jim agreed. "Harding was staying in jail because that's where he thought he'd be safest. And he only cared about being safe because of his family. Because of Lyle. He thought there was a deal—an agreement to protect each other's families. As long as he stayed in jail, he was safe, and his family was always safe. He saw the militia as another military organization, and that meant playing by the rules. Once they snatched his kid . . . it had exactly the opposite effect from what they expected. It was supposed to ensure his silence and make him eager to get out. Instead, it made him talk. Almost too late. I think you saved the boy's life."

"Clyde Davis saved the boy's life. I couldn't even save my own life. That was just a fluke, really."

Jim and Dom both looked at me like a pair of indulgent uncles regarding a feeble-minded but much-loved niece and shook their heads. "You wore the vest," Dom said. "It saved your life."

I lay there for a moment, silently contemplating the enormous pain where the bullet had struck. Today it felt like I'd been impaled on a mortar shell. I couldn't breathe or move without pain. But I should have been lying in a morgue with a bullet through my head. They could talk till the cows came home and I'd never feel heroic. Lucky, maybe. Profoundly disenchanted with human nature. And confused, but not heroic.

"Clyde Davis. There's a story there, right, Jim?" He nodded. "You remember what you said to me, about trying to turn one of them? Well, I picked Clyde. It didn't look like it had worked, but then so many odd things happened. He was kind, he acted like one of them, he seemed to be on my side, and then he was back with them again. I didn't know what to think, not that there was much chance for clear thinking. I thought he might be one of yours and was afraid he'd blow his cover."

"A good man who didn't know which way to turn. We were working on him. Looks like you finished the job . . ."

I closed my eyes and was back in that farmhouse kitchen, sitting in my chair, staring at the four of them around the table, doing my provocative lunatic act—the one I hadn't been able to control. Roy Belcher saying "Just shoot the bitch." Bump raising his gun. Clyde's hand coming out too late. Me jumping up. The sudden, enormous punch to my chest that had lifted me right off my feet.

"He tried to keep them from shooting me but he was too late. It all happened so fast. If he'd succeeded, they might have shot him." I put my hand on the bandage. It probably would hurt for weeks. More ugly pictures for the inside of my head. I ought to see a shrink. It was time. Too many bad things had happened, too many black memories piled up like soot in my brain. I wished I could just take my head to a car wash and have the whole inside scrubbed out with those big, goofy brushes, dried with warm blowers, waxed to a brilliant shine, and buffed, so that I came out all fresh and new. Restored and optimistic. I was afraid that if these guys left, if I was ever left alone again, I wouldn't be able to fight off the black despair. I had lost my baby. I had shot a man. I would never be the same woman I was a week ago.

"Don't bottle it up inside," Jim said. "You need to talk about it."

"After breakfast," Dom said. "Come on, Princess. Time to eat."

I knew Dom was reading my mind. He may not have been

there to change my diapers or beam at my first steps, but he's been there to watch me learn to walk like a grown-up. He's watched some of my brave, faltering steps toward wisdom and courage. Watched me obsess about love and commitment, about fear and honor and truth and loyalty. He's seen me struggle through hurt and abandonment, through lies and betrayal, through the terrifying realization that someone wanted me dead and was willing to take the necessary steps to make that happen. He's watched me pull myself together, recover, and go on. He probably knew what I needed better than I did.

"Dom, I . . ."

He bent and kissed my forehead. "I know, Thea. Black thoughts. Jim's right. You've got to talk about what happened, but not now. Keep 'em away as long as you can. Until you've rested. Till you can talk with Rosie and we can get you back home to your mother . . ."

Rosie I understood, but my mother? "My mother?" It seemed like an odd idea, since my mother and I are seldom on the same wavelength and since my mother's specialty is criticism of everything I do, especially the dangerous situations I get into.

"Who knows more about losing babies?"

"I feel like such a failure."

"Your standards are too high," he said. "You've already done more good things than most people do in a lifetime. Over and over, you manage to come through. You're an incredible woman and you always think you've failed. Open wide."

I opened wide and he sailed in a delicious forkful of poached eggs and buttery toast, and it wasn't even cold. I chewed and swallowed. "This is not hospital food."

"Of course not. What do you take me for? Am I not the one and only Dominic Florio? Rescuer of maidens in distress? Purveyor of fine breakfasts, lunches, and dinners for those incarcerated in hospital-type institutions?"

"Don't! Do not make me laugh. I cannot . . . could not . . . stand the pain."

"Sorry. Open wide."

We got through more of the food, and, because he knew me

well, there was plenty of it—with a minimum of pain and laughter. Jim Ferret hovered nearby, a bit jealously. Finally he said, "Hey, how come he gets to have all the fun?"

"Fun?" Dom muttered. "You think this is fun? I'm a working man, you know. A working cop who keeps having to take time off from work to come and bail this woman out. I've lived a long time and I've never known anyone who can get into so much trouble." He touched his temple. "Believe it or not, when I met her, my hair was black. I thought we finally had her cured, you know. Last weekend I was even willing to put on an uncomfortable suit and a sober tie to go watch her get married. Settled down. Barefoot and pregnant. And now look where I am."

He cleared his throat with a mock harrumph. "I mean, look at this. It can't be sex, right? She's grimy and disheveled, desperately in need of a bath, and even that rewarding peek at cleavage I might otherwise get is covered with bandages. Besides which, she's in bed with another man." He waved a fork in my face. "Open wide, Princess."

Andre stirred beside me and opened his eyes. Saw the forkful of egg and opened his own mouth. Without batting an eye— cops, after all, are so cool—Dom fed him instead. Forkful after forkful, while I just lay there and watched. "You two!" Dom muttered. "I feel like a bird with chicks."

"I'm no chick," Andre growled.

"Shut up and eat," Dom and I said together. Obediently, Andre opened his mouth. Finally, the food was gone and Dom put down the fork.

"You got coffee?" I asked.

"Loaded with cream and sugar, just the way you like it. Black for him."

"She can't have coffee," Andre said. His voice was weak and weary still, but it was blissful to hear it. "She's pregnant."

This is it, I thought. *Once again I get to deliver intensely personal news with an audience.* My adventures were giving me a great deal of sympathy for people like queens and presidents who were always surrounded. But when I opened my mouth to explain, the words wouldn't come. The best I could do was take his hand, place it where it had rested so many times while he talked to the baby, and whisper, "Gone."

"No." A single word, so loaded with pain it seemed to have been torn from him.

Now I had to explain. "The doctor said it wasn't anything I did. That these things happen often, especially with first babies. That fear, and anxiety and hard work and too much exercise, none of those things cause miscarriages. They just happen . . . because there's something wrong with the baby." It didn't sound comforting to me. It just sounded like an excuse. I couldn't make it sound any better because there was nothing better about it. Because there's no way for someone, even a wordsmith like me, to put a good spin on something that's only sad and tragic. No silver lining. It's not a silver lining to parents who've lost a baby that it might have been defective. It's only a reason.

"It was what kept me going," he said. "You and the baby."

"It was what kept me going, too. You and the baby."

"Was it . . ." He swallowed. "Was it awful . . . for you?"

"Jack did his best. But yes. It was awful for me. I wanted you. I needed you there so badly. It was so heartbreaking and I felt so out of control. I still feel . . . I don't know. Hollow. Failed. Less than a woman somehow. That I can't do the important things right, like get married and have children."

He fumbled until he found my hands, and took them both in his. "We'll just have to try again. Think about how . . ." His voice tripped on the barrier of his sadness, and for a moment, he couldn't speak. "I guess we're just the kind of people who weren't meant to have it easy. I was going to say think about how much fun we'll have trying again."

He kissed me then, a kiss full of promise that reminded me of our very first kiss, in my kitchen, the night my partner Suzanne dropped by unexpectedly to announce her engagement, and Andre dropped by to ask me some questions. Everything was a fluke, really. I felt terribly unlucky just now, because of Claudine, or Oliver, or Mason, and all that had happened. But looked at another way, we were lucky. We were still here. We still had our future before us.

"I can't believe you found me."

"The bungee cord, remember?"

"I hoped. Thinking about you is what kept me from losing my head. I knew I had to be careful."

"Me, too."

"You weren't careful enough," he said. "They shot you."

"You weren't careful enough," I said. "They got you."

"I think," he said thoughtfully, "that we'd better hurry up and get married before anything else happens."

"Not until you shower."

"Not until you wash your hair."

"For better, but not for worse?"

"This is pretty damned close to worst," he suggested. "We have to pull ourselves up a little or there's nowhere to descend to."

"You've got a point."

"Coffee's getting cold," Dom interrupted. We'd forgotten anyone else was in the room.

"Dom, didn't Rosie come with you?"

"Ah," he said, "we're not good enough for you, is that it?" He spoke to an imaginary audience. "Come, let us away. The princess wants her women about her. What about it, Detective? You want a hand getting to the shower?"

"Sure." Dom and Jim went around the bed to help Andre. I watched him slowly swing his legs over the edge of the bed and had to fight an impulse to grab him back, afraid to let him go, even for a second. Because I needed to be touching him. Because I didn't want to be alone.

"Hey," I said. "But what about me?"

"You want us to help you into the shower?" Dom asked with a mock leer.

"The princess wants her women about her."

He checked his watch. "They should be along any minute. There was something about a robe and nightie and suitable undergarments. Shampoo, lotion, a toothbrush, and a hairbrush. You know. Women's things."

"They?"

"Rosie and Suzanne. Oh, were you feeling neglected?"

"Take my prince away," I commanded, waving a few fingers. The lovely, airy full-arm wave that the words required was completely beyond me. "Take him away and bathe him. Or boil him. Or whatever is necessary."

Andre stood beside the bed, as elegant as I in his limp cotton hospital gown. Exhaustion still lay heavily on him. His shoulders were bowed and his face was drawn, but he grinned at me. "You ain't so fresh yourself, honey," he said. As he limped away, leaning heavily on the two of them, he said, "Did you hear what that woman said? Boil him? Was ever a man so fortune-favored in his choice of wives?"

"Right," Jim Ferret observed. "Better she should have stayed at home and knitted blankets." I still had nothing to throw at him. Luckily, at that moment, the door opened and Rosie and Suzanne came in. They brought tears and hugs and love and clothes. They had come to fuss, debrief, nurture and console. The princess had her women about her.

CHAPTER *31*

P EOPLE, EXCEPT MAYBE in Vegas, don't normally have weddings on Wednesdays, but we did. My mother, perhaps more prescient, unless it was hopeful, than I, had insisted that they leave the tent up. The beautiful arbor that my father had built for me was still decorated. The rest of it, chairs, piano, food, linens, flowers, band, and guests, had to be reassembled. But Andre insisted that he didn't want to wait until the weekend. Andre, who at first had been rather like a deflated balloon, worn down by hunger and dehydration after a week of deprivation, had perked up quickly as they pumped in the fluids and nutrients. As soon as the doctors had given clearance, he'd been carried off and debriefed and shown to a clamoring press, clean, but not pressed. Trimmed but unshaven. Ravaged, yet handsome and heroic.

Allegedly, the press had been clamoring for me, too, but Jack didn't make me go. No, the truth was, Jack wouldn't let me go. He'd come to the room, given Suzanne and Rosie one of his cool looks, and said, "Could I have a minute alone?" Then, after they'd left, he stood at the foot of the bed, and said, "Just so you'll know. The press wants to talk to you. I'm not letting them near you. I hope you don't mind."

He let me get as far as, "Jack, I don't know . . ." before he shook his head, slowly and with a gravity and authority he seldom used with me. Mostly he yelled at me.

He surrendered his distance and came and sat on the edge of my bed. "You don't want to do this, Thea. Maybe you think that there are things which need to be said . . ."

I must have a very transparent face, because he smiled, gently, and shook his head. "Yes. I know. There *are* things that need to be said, about law and order and evil, about whether people matter, about whether children matter. About who has the courage to act. But that's not what will happen today. They're not looking for a speech, they're looking for sound bites. They'll swarm all over you, asking how it felt to be shot. Were you scared? Did it hurt? Why you were wearing the vest. Where you got the gun. How you learned to shoot. How it feels to have killed a man. Questions you don't want to answer in public. Things you don't want to revisit in front of strangers."

"I know, Jack, but I . . ."

"I've tried to stay out of your way, Thea, haven't I? I let you go up there . . . Goddammit, Thea, I gave you the vest and the gun!" I nodded. The truth was that, for all my bravado about how no one controls me, he probably could have shut me up in Rapunzel's tower, especially since he knew what I was getting into, when I didn't. And while it might have seemed to both of us like the right thing to do, sending a civilian into a lethal situation, and giving her government property—the vest and a gun—wouldn't look particularly good in the press, for either of us. Besides, he wasn't barking at me and he wasn't giving orders. He wasn't trying to intimidate me; he was trying to explain.

"Look, I know you. I know you'll think about this, that these are questions you'll ponder in privacy, by yourself. Discuss with Andre. Maybe with some of us, if you think it will help. I'd like you to talk with our psychiatrist . . ." He broke off. This was something he thought was important but it was not where he wanted to go right now. "You've done enough. Endured enough. Been hurt and scrutinized enough. You wouldn't let me do it before, but please, Thea, let me protect you now."

"I'm such a lousy judge of character," I said. "I thought Bump Peters was just a sweet old man."

"So did everyone else, Thea. That's how it works. People aren't supposed to suspect those in charge."

"And Roy Belcher. I never got a handle on him. He seemed so evil and yet he seemed like such an idiot. He killed Paulette Harding, you know."

Jack's eyes narrowed. "I know that, but how do you know that?"

"He told me. Matter-of-factly. Said it had to be done. But he didn't tell me why."

"Penance, probably. To make up to the others for having had an affair with her. That's how she learned about the armory job, and when she and Roy had a fight, she called us to rat him out . . ."

"Which is how Pelletier got killed." I still couldn't believe what I'd just heard. "He killed . . . hacked up . . . chopped into pieces a woman he was having a relationship with? I always wondered what happened to the man who was involved."

But Jack wasn't finished. "He killed her to show Jimmy McGrath that he was tough and worthy. That he was willing to do violent acts. He was desperate to have McGrath's approval. It was like sixth-grade playground stuff . . . with a human sacrifice."

"None of it was necessary," I said. "A whole town with its collective head in the sand, letting this stuff happen . . ."

"Your little red-haired waitress friend didn't sit on her hands . . ."

"Kalyn?"

"She called us after they took you, begged us to help. And she put us in touch with another woman who used to work at the restaurant. Paulette's roommate. Mindy . . . she'd been hiding her, since the night Paulette was killed. The strain must have been terrible . . . hiding out . . . knowing what had happened . . . doing nothing about it. But you were the tipping point."

"But now she's talked about it? Mindy, I mean?" He nodded.

My mind was veering toward that black place again. "Belcher killed Paulette. And I killed him."

"It's not the same, Thea. Not even close. You shot Belcher to save three lives. Maybe more."

"I shot him."

"I'm being an idiot," he said. "You need to talk with someone. I wouldn't let one of my men go any time at all without counseling after something like this, and I've left you twisting in the wind. I'm sorry, Thea. I'm sorry."

He turned away from me and I lay there, staring at his bent shoulders, thinking that Jack did command and control so well it was easy to forget he was human. This was hard on him, too. Awfully hard. "I'm all right, Jack. I don't need special attention. I just need Dom and Rosie and Suzanne and Andre. The people who love me. Who keep me balanced."

He stood up. Squared his shoulders and looked down at me. Not Jack Leonard, Andre's friend, nor Jack Leonard, Andre's boss, not even the Jack Leonard who moments ago had been trying to take care of me. This was Jack Leonard, my boss. The man whose life involved responsibility for putting other people's lives on the line. "You always think you know, Thea, but you're not always right. You need to talk to somebody. I'll take care of it," he said, and left the room.

No sooner was he released by the press, than Andre was back in our hospital room, where I lay surrounded by my maidens, asking, "When are we getting married?"

By that time, having been without him for a few hours, I'd fallen deep into a black funk. He lay down beside me, threw an arm across me, and yawned. "When?" he repeated.

"Wednesday."

"I have to wait that long?"

"I have a low-cut dress, dahling," I said. "Right now, my chest looks like an enormous purple plum exploded underneath my skin. My nose is swollen. I have two slightly blackened eyes, in case you hadn't noticed."

"I hadn't noticed," he interrupted. "You look incredibly beautiful to me."

Go ahead, I thought. *Take my breath away. Wrap me in your love and make me gorgeous. I'm still waiting until Wednesday.* "Everything hurts when I move," I said. "Call it vanity if you will, but I want to walk, not limp or stagger, down the aisle. I want to be able to take that deep breath when I first spot you in all your penguin splendor without spreading agony. My mother is still going to want all the trappings, and even on an expedited schedule, trappings take time. We marry on Wednesday. However . . ."

I paused for dramatic effect. "I am not letting you out of my sight between now and then."

He muttered something in French.

"What?"

"Very intimate," he said. "We eat, sleep, shower, and get dressed together? None of this bride-and-groom-can't-see-each-other-before-the-wedding hooey?"

"No hooey," I agreed. "We should have done this last time."

"Hold still," Suzanne said. "You may be thinner but this dress is still just as slippery."

Across the room, Andre lounged against the bureau, fiddling with his cuff links. "Can I help?" he asked.

"You!" Suzanne snapped. "You should get out of here. Don't you want this to be a surprise? You're supposed to wait until she comes down the aisle to see how drop-dead gorgeous she looks. Why don't you go downstairs and make sure everything else is ready? Go tweak boutonnieres and straighten lapels or something. Nip into the back room and have a bracing bit of Scotch."

With most people, he would have argued, but for Suzanne, he went as quietly as a lamb. Accepting just a little bit of hooey for the sake of surprise. A minute later, she straightened up. "You're done. And this time, we didn't forget the shoes. Ready for your veil?" She picked it up off the dresser and handed it to me. I pinned it into place and glanced in the mirror. Hot damn! Despite my slightly swollen nose, my bruised cleavage, and the lingering circles under my eyes, it had happened again. I was a beautiful bride.

Despite my resistance to all this wedding hooey, the months of shopping and picking and choosing and decision-making had worn me down. I was observing all the traditions. Something old—the beautiful gold-and-pearl earrings Suzanne had given me. Something new, my incredible gaudy marshmallow of a dress. Something borrowed—my mother's last pair of off-white panty hose, since mine had sprung a run right out of the box. Something blue—a silly garter of white lace and blue velvet Rosie Florio had made. I carried a bouquet rich with white scented lilies, trailing ribbons that matched my bridesmaids' dresses.

My mother knocked on the door and burst in without waiting. I think she was afraid something would go wrong again and we'd never have this wedding. She stopped halfway across the room as I turned from the mirror to face her. I saw tears spring into her eyes. She closed the distance between us and hugged me. Very, very carefully. I was still fragile. "I'm sorry," she said. "Oh, Thea. I'm sorry. For so many things . . . for so many wrong . . . so many unfair judgments . . . the awful things I've said . . . for the many, many times when I should have said this before and was too stubborn to do it. Mothers . . . as you will learn for yourself . . . aren't perfect. All we really have going for us is love."

Now there were two of us with tears in our eyes. For years I'd imagined this moment. Longed for it. Now, when it came, I was speechless. Blindly, I swept past her and down the stairs, my beautiful, shiny dress floating around me like a cloud.

My father waited at the bottom, handsome and distinguished and he, too, had tears in his eyes. Wasn't this supposed to be a happy occasion? My bridesmaids lined up in front of me in their lovely, luminous dresses the colors of Caribbean water. Jack and Andre and the minister were waiting. Michael came and gave my mother his arm. It was time.

Maybe all brides cry. I don't know. This was my first real wedding, once removed. The walk down the aisle, the music, the people standing, their faces alight with love and tears, it all passed by in a blur. I relinquished my father's arm, and took

Andre's. We stepped forward and stood before the minister and the cadence of the words flowed over us. Jonetta Williamson got up in all her glory and sang a breathtaking version of "Take My Hand, Precious Lord." As she sang the words, "I am tired, I am weak, I am worn . . ." Andre reached down and took my hand, and a rumble of approval went through the guests. *You see*, I thought. *Now you see why I did it. How could I not?*

I felt blessed. I felt awed. I felt staggered by reality. We were really and truly and finally here. At last the minister got to the heart of the matter. "Theadora McKusick Kozak, do you take Andre Joseph Lemieux to be your lawful wedded husband, to have and to hold from this day forward, to love and to cherish, for richer, for poorer, in sickness and in health, so long as you both shall live?"

I was dizzy with the power of those words. I felt the mantle of responsibility fall on my shoulders like a warm and welcome cloak. It seemed as if the world was holding its collective breath, waiting for my answer. I had traveled long and hard to arrive at this moment. I looked into his face, the one I wanted to see on the pillow beside me for the next fifty years, the one I'd come so close to losing. Better get this over with before something else happened.

"I do," I said.